SINS OF THE
FATHERS

By J. A. Jance

J. P. Beaumont Mysteries

UNTIL PROVEN GUILTY • INJUSTICE FOR ALL
TRIAL BY FURY • TAKING THE FIFTH
IMPROBABLE CAUSE • A MORE PERFECT UNION
DISMISSED WITH PREJUDICE • MINOR IN POSSESSION
PAYMENT IN KIND • WITHOUT DUE PROCESS
FAILURE TO APPEAR • LYING IN WAIT
NAME WITHHELD • BREACH OF DUTY
BIRDS OF PREY • PARTNER IN CRIME
LONG TIME GONE • JUSTICE DENIED
FIRE AND ICE • BETRAYAL OF TRUST
RING IN THE DEAD (NOVELLA) • SECOND WATCH
STAND DOWN (NOVELLA) • PROOF OF LIFE
STILL DEAD (NOVELLA) • SINS OF THE FATHERS

Joanna Brady Mysteries

DESERT HEAT • TOMBSTONE COURAGE
SHOOT/DON'T SHOOT • DEAD TO RIGHTS
SKELETON CANYON • RATTLESNAKE CROSSING
OUTLAW MOUNTAIN • DEVIL'S CLAW
PARADISE LOST • PARTNER IN CRIME
EXIT WOUNDS • DEAD WRONG
DAMAGE CONTROL • FIRE AND ICE
JUDGMENT CALL • THE OLD BLUE LINE (NOVELLA)
REMAINS OF INNOCENCE
RANDOM ACTS: A JOANNA BRADY
AND ALI REYNOLDS NOVELLA
DOWNFALL • FIELD OF BONES

Walker Family Novels

HOUR OF THE HUNTER • KISS OF THE BEES
DAY OF THE DEAD • QUEEN OF THE NIGHT
DANCE OF THE BONES: A J.P. BEAUMONT
AND BRANDON WALKER NOVEL

J. A. JANCE

SINS OF THE FATHERS

A J. P. BEAUMONT NOVEL

wm

WILLIAM MORROW

An Imprint of HarperCollins*Publishers*

Excerpt from *Missing and Endangered* copyright © 2020 by J. A. Jance.

First William Morrow premium printing: May 2020
First William Morrow international trade paperback:
September 2019
First William Morrow hardcover printing: September 2019

Print Edition ISBN: 978-0-06-285344-8
Digital Edition ISBN: 978-0-06-285345-5

Cover design by Richard L. Aquan
Cover photograph © David Gn Photography/Getty Images

20 21 22 23 24   QGM   10 9 8 7 6 5 4 3 2 1

*For Dan, a go-to-the-mat grandpa,
and in memory of Stormy Girl.*

SINS OF THE FATHERS

PROLOGUE

My name is Beaumont, J. P. Beaumont. J. P. is short for Jonas Piedmont, but that's a long story. Recently I've learned that sometimes when life hands you the unexpected, you just have to run with it. For instance, I never expected to retire from police work. Far too many of my fellow cops tend to die while still in harness but not necessarily in the line of duty, unless stress-related illnesses—like too much booze, high blood pressure, early-onset heart ailments, and suicides—fall into that category.

I spent most of my career working in the Homicide Unit at Seattle PD and was happy to do so until all of a sudden I wasn't. Why? Because the brass upstairs decided to promote a brown-nosing pile of crap and my least favorite partner ever, a fellow by the name of Paul Kramer, to be my boss. That was it. I was done. I pulled the plug and walked.

But what is it they say about one door closing and another opening? About the time I quit Seattle PD, Ross Alan Connors, who was the Washington State

2 J. A. Jance

attorney general at the time, came calling and asked me to go to work for him on his Special Homicide Investigation Team, fondly referred to by those of us fortunate enough to work there as "the SHIT squad." There was something wonderfully ironic about being able to tell people with a perfectly straight face that "I work for SHIT." What made it even better was that my direct supervisor on that job was a cantankerous SOB named Harry Ignatius Ball, who to this day prefers to be addressed by his full name, as in Harry I. Ball. Try telling someone that you work for SHIT and your boss's name is Harry I. Ball. See how far that gets you!

But the thing is, working for Special Homicide was a good deal for me. I got to keep working. I met and married a wonderful gal named Melissa Soames (Mel for short), and I gave my pension a healthy boost in the right direction. Then one winter's day, it all came to a crashing halt—literally. Ross Connors died and Harry was gravely injured in a car wreck at the base of Seattle's iconic Space Needle while they were on their way to a Christmas party. (Ross, as politically incorrect and cantankerous as Harry, refused to call it a holiday party. As far as he was concerned, it was a Christmas party, like it or lump it!)

As soon as Ross's successor came on board, SHIT was shuttered and we were all given our walking papers. Mel landed on her feet with a gig as the new police chief in Bellingham, Washington, ninety miles north of Seattle. As for me? Suddenly I found myself in the odd position of being an unwillingly unemployed househusband, a position for which I am not exactly well suited.

For starters, I'm a lousy cook. So is Mel for that matter. Our answer to the question of what's for dinner is generally carryout. Mel's office is in downtown Bellingham. Our home is several miles south of downtown proper, on a street called Bayside in an area called Edgemoor in what's known as Bellingham's Fairhaven district. When possible, I join her for lunch downtown, so we often have our main meal of the day both out and together. On this particular Monday early in March, lunch together was a no-go due to Mel's being the guest speaker at a local Rotary Club meeting.

Months earlier I'd been drafted into helping solve the homicide of a longtime acquaintance, a former *Seattle Post-Intelligencer* reporter by the name of Maxwell Cole, and being caught up in the complexities of that case gave me a whole new lease on life. As a result, Mel had encouraged me to fill out the paperwork and apply to become a licensed private investigator in the state of Washington. That process was now complete. I had my license, but I hadn't exactly been out pounding the pavement looking for cases to work. I'd done a couple of background checks and had been involved in research on a couple of cold cases for a volunteer organization called the Last Chance, but nothing about any of those had really grabbed me. For one thing I was enjoying spending time with the new love of my life, a ninety-pound coal-black Irish wolfhound named Lucy.

Lucy had come to Mel and me under what was supposedly a temporary fostering arrangement after a domestic-violence incident. I believe the term "temporary fostering" is actually an oxymoron, because once a dog worms its way into your heart, you're pretty much stuck.

The DV incident, complete with an officer-involved shooting, had occurred in Bellingham, Mel's bailiwick. A local women's shelter had taken in the battered victim and her two kids. I understand that there are shelters that also accept animals under those circumstances, but that particular one in Bellingham didn't. There was simply no room at the inn for the dog.

Having never owned a dog in my life, I wasn't the one who stepped to the head of the line and volunteered to bring this one home, especially one named Rambo, as she was known back then. Nope, Mel did that all on her own without so much as a by-your-leave from me. In case I haven't mentioned it before, Mel is a strong-minded woman—and strong-willed, too. When she showed up with that humungous Irish wolfhound in tow, I did what any reasonable, right-thinking husband would do under the circumstances—I overcame my profound but unspoken misgivings and went with the flow.

After opening our door to the dog and even after learning that her original name was Lucy, I wasn't necessarily prepared to open my heart. That changed, however, when the domestic-violence perpetrator, let out on bail, came looking for Mel, knife in hand. The incident had taken place in a churchyard across the street from Belltown Terrace, our Seattle-area condo building. In the course of the ensuing fight, Lucy literally took a serious stab wound rather than a bullet for my wife, most likely saving

Mel's life. From that moment on, I'm proud to confess aloud to one and all that "I love Lucy!"

There was, however, and continues to be, a period of adjustment. For one thing, when we brought Lucy home after her lifesaving surgery at an emergency veterinary hospital in Seattle, she was still one very sick puppy and required round-the-clock nursing attention, which was willingly, if not always cheerfully, provided by none other than yours truly. Incidentally, I've never been especially adept when it comes to caring for the sick or injured.

I was still in college when my mother died of breast cancer. Back then there wasn't a whole lot of discussion urging women to have yearly mammograms, so the kind of "early detection" that is far more common now just wasn't happening. By the time my mother's tumor was discovered, it had severely metastasized, and it was already too late. The doctors did what they could. For me, sitting helplessly on the sidelines, it seemed like the treatments and possible cures they prescribed and inflicted on her were worse than the disease itself. It's still hard to admit this, but I was relieved when she breathed her last, because that meant her suffering was finally over. That's a hell of a burden for a college-age kid to have to carry around, and so many decades later some of that guilt still lingers.

Decades after that, Karen, my first wife, also died of breast cancer. We had been divorced for years, and her second husband, Dave Livingston, was the one who performed those incredibly tough, day-to-day sickbed duties. Come to think of it, that's probably one of the things that he and I have in common—walking through cancer-patient/ caregiver hell. These days there are kids, stepkids, and grandkids all involved, and when it comes to sharing holidays and birthdays, Dave and I are almost always on the same page. We probably won't ever be the best of pals, but we know how quickly everything can be snatched from your grasp, and we're both determined to savor every moment.

But I digress. Dealing with Lucy when she first came home called for real hands-on nursing care. She was unable to walk on her own. In order to get her to do her business, she had to be half carried in a kind of sling. (By the way, if any of the rest of you are faced with an ill or aging dog, one of those firewood-carrying canvas or leather slings will fill the bill nicely.) But with a ninety-pound dog, it wasn't easy for either Lucy or me. The first time she was able to go in and out by herself was a huge relief for both of us.

The vet told us that her injuries were serious enough that it might take months for her to fully recover, if she ever did. We were advised that she needed to take it very easy. In other words, I was supposed to keep her from overexerting herself—no running, no jumping, no becoming too excited. Good luck with that, because Lucy somehow failed to get the memo.

My first wife, Karen, was someone who never minced her words. When it came to disciplining the kids, she said I was as useless as . . . well, as certain items of female anatomy applied to a male boar. I sometimes resent the way political correctness has robbed us of some of the English language's most colorful expressions. But then again I digress. I'm seventy-two years old, so I'm entitled to digress. I'm also entitled to tell the same stories over and over if I choose to do so.

The real upshot is this: If I was useless when it came to disciplining the kids, you can bet I'm not much better when it comes to disciplining dogs. Our half-acre lot is on a bluff overlooking Bellingham Bay. The house is located at the front of the lot, with a long stretch of grassy lawn leading down to the property line. Out of concern for grandkids' safety, that whole stretch of property (regularly mowed by someone who isn't me) is surrounded by a six-foot-tall wooden fence. Because of the difference in elevation, the fence doesn't interfere with our view of the bay from either the house or the deck, but it does keep unwary little kids from tumbling down the bluff. It's also tall enough to keep Lucy inside.

For a while during her recuperation, Lucy was content to walk sedately on a leash at my side, both inside the yard and out. But a month into her recovery, on a day when I inadvertently left the slider open and let her out into the yard unaccompanied, she took off like a shot—racing down that long stretch of grass and back up to me as though I'd just given her the best present ever. She seemed to suffer no ill effects from her excursion, but I didn't exactly come straight out and mention it to Mel. Free-range running became Lucy's and my dirty little secret.

Mel is a cop. She's up, dressed, and away from of the house early in the morning. Sometimes I rise and shine in time to have coffee with her, but more often than not she's long gone before I poke my head out of the bedroom. So Lucy and I often have the mornings to ourselves. I make coffee, feed the dog, and then settle in by the gas-log fireplace to work my collection of online crossword puzzles, something that is evidently not an Irish wolfhound–approved activity. Each morning, at the stroke of ten, Lucy lets herself out through the doggy door. She finds her wet Frisbee wherever it might have been left out in the yard, brings it inside, and drops it on my bare toe. Subtle she's not. She's giving me a clear message that it's time to go play.

And so we do. Her doggy DNA hails from Ireland. That means she's totally oblivious to wind or rain. I bundle up in sweaters and jackets, sometimes topped off by a hooded slicker. All Lucy requires is for me to stand on the deck and fling the Frisbee as far as I can so she can go speeding down the hill, catch it in midair, gallop back up the hill, and drop it at my feet. She would be happy doing this for hours on end. I have a somewhat more limited attention and energy span, but that's what we were doing that morning when Lucy abruptly dropped the Frisbee and hurried over to the side gate, standing on her hind legs at full alert and peering over the fence at someone who had just driven down our driveway.

The house is one of those view homes where visitors have no real access to the front door without being let in through the side gate, which—because of Lucy—we keep latched and locked. That means guests are let in through the back door, where they can be ushered into the great room via a short hallway next to the kitchen.

It's been my experience that most arriving guests

don't want to come face-to-face with a soaking-wet almost-hundred-pound dog with a head the size of Godzilla's, so even before I heard a car door open and close, I ordered Lucy into the house and put her in a "stay on your rug" command at the far end of the living room. By the time the doorbell rang, I was already on my way to answer it.

I spent years as a cop. Mel is a cop. We've both made enemies here and there along the way—the kinds of enemies who aren't especially good at forgetting or forgiving. Security peepholes are fine as far as they go, I guess, but if someone carrying a weapon shows up on your doorstep intent on plugging you full of holes, the last place you want to be is standing in front of a door with your eye plastered against a peephole. Our system is different. There's a security camera mounted over the outside door with a feed to a monitor located on a wall inside the kitchen. That way we're able to know who's at the door without our being anywhere near it.

I checked the monitor as I went and could see a man as he stepped up onto the porch. He wasn't anyone I recognized right off. He appeared to be in his sixties, maybe, balding and rail thin. I was pretty sure he wasn't a Jehovah's Witness, because instead of carrying a fistful of religious tracts he was holding an infant carrier in his right hand and had what looked like a bright pink diaper bag strapped over his left shoulder.

When the doorbell rang, Lucy made her presence known with a low-throated woof from her spot in the living room, but a quick check behind me told me she hadn't strayed from her spot on the rug.

Her obedience training at the Academy of Canine Behavior in Bothell, Washington, was top-drawer.

I opened the door. "Yes," I said. "May I help you?"

"Detective Beaumont?" my visitor asked uncertainly.

He was indeed rail thin—to the point of being gaunt—and had dark circles under his eyes, as though he were suffering from a severe lack of food as well as a lack of sleep.

"I used to be Detective Beaumont, but I haven't been that for a very long time," I told him. "Sorry, but are you someone I should know?"

"You probably don't remember me. My name's Alan Dale. Way back I used to be head carpenter with a traveling show company. I was with Jasmine Day when she played the 5th Avenue Theatre down in Seattle years ago. This is my granddaughter, Athena," he added, gesturing toward the infant, whose face was completely obscured by a pink receiving blanket. "May we come in?"

Thirty years flashed by in an instant. Jasmine Day had been a former rock singer who seemed destined for real stardom until her career was derailed by drug and alcohol abuse, not unlike what happened to Janis Joplin. The difference between the two is that Janis Joplin died very young, while Jasmine went through treatment and got well. Once out of rehab, she had reinvented herself as a jazz singer. Jasmine had been in Seattle playing a two-night gig at the 5th Avenue when the investigation into the death of a local stagehand had placed her directly in my path and blown her comeback tour to smithereens. For the last two songs of her final set, she had ditched the glam by peeling off her long blond wig. Standing alone onstage in heartbreaking simplicity, she had reverted to the old gospel music she'd sung in church as a child back home in Jasper, Texas. Gospel singing had been there at the start of her career, and that night at the 5th Avenue she returned to her roots in a concert-ending performance that garnered thunderous applause.

The last I'd seen of Jasmine Day, she and Alan, the touring company's former head carpenter, were headed back to her hometown in Texas together. As they were leaving, they had asked if I'd consent to being best man a few months down the road at their wedding. I had agreed, of course, but my participation never came to pass. Later that year they sent me a Christmas card saying that they'd ended up tying the knot in a spur-of-the-moment ceremony in Vegas. That long-ago card was pretty much the last I'd heard from either of them—until now.

"Alan Dale, well, I'll be damned!" I exclaimed, reaching out to shake his free hand. "Long time no see. How the hell are you?"

"Not well," he said. "I'm afraid I need your help. I'm looking for a private eye, and somebody at Seattle PD told me that's what you're doing these days."

I hate it when Mel is right. That was exactly how she had goaded me into shaping up and getting my private investigator's license—by saying that someday there would be people out there in the world who'd desperately need my help and that I'd be better able to help them with a license than without. And now here was Alan Dale, standing on my doorstep big as life and requesting my assistance.

"That's what I am these days," I acknowledged, "a private eye, so come on in and get out of the cold. Let's talk about it. Can I get you some coffee?"

"Please."

"Cream and sugar?"

"Black," Alan replied. "Black and strong. I need all the help I can get." That's when he caught sight of Lucy, lying flat on her rug, studying him intently from across the room with her very unsettling black-eyed stare.

"What about the dog?" Alan asked warily, lifting the baby carrier chest-high, although if Lucy'd had a mind to go after the baby, that wouldn't have been nearly high enough to keep Athena out of reach.

"Have a seat, and don't worry about the dog," I assured him, turning the bean setting on my De-Longhi Magnifica to full strength and pushing the brew button. "Lucy may look fierce, but she loves kids. Not only that, I told her to stay on her rug, and she will."

"You're sure?"

"Count on it."

As I stood in the kitchen, watching the brewing coffee dribble out through the spouts into the cup below, I couldn't help wondering what was coming. One thing that seemed pretty certain—it probably wasn't going to be good. Nonetheless, whatever it was, I was also pretty sure I'd run with it all the same, just like Lucy and her damned Frisbee!

There was one important thing about Alan Dale's proposed case that I didn't see coming, and it's this: No matter how fast you run, you can't outrun your past.

CHAPTER 1

BY THE TIME I brought coffee into the living room, Alan had removed the baby's outer layer of pink blankets. I took a look inside the carrier as I set the cup down on a side table. I don't know much about babies at the moment. I'm sure I'll know a lot more three months from now when my new grandson is expected to arrive on the scene. In the meantime it occurred to me that the baby in my living room appeared to be very new. So what was Alan Dale doing driving solo up and down the I-5 corridor with a newborn infant in tow?

"What's her name again?" I asked as I sat down. "And how old is she?"

"Athena," he answered, "Athena Marie, and she's six weeks old—six weeks tomorrow. She just got out of Children's Hospital yesterday."

The natural follow-up question would have been "Where's her mommy?" but something—some newfound restraint that never used to be part of my conversational makeup—kept me from going there.

"How's Jasmine these days?" I asked instead.

He shook his head miserably, looking as distraught as anyone I'd ever seen. "I lost her," he said simply.

The word "lost," used in that context, generally means one of two things. Either Jasmine had done Alan wrong and had taken off on him or else she had died. The utter defeat and desolation in his demeanor hinted at the latter.

"What happened?" I asked.

"Hep C," he said bleakly.

And that said it all. Hepatitis C, an often-fatal liver infection, can be contracted any number of ways, including by reusing dirty needles, but it can also come about due to serious drinking. I've been sober for years now, but there was plenty of serious drinking in my past. When they started advertising that new hep C treatment on TV a couple of years ago, I went to see my doc and got tested—"an ounce of prevention," as Mel had called it. When I came up clear, we both felt as though we'd dodged a bullet. I knew that Jasmine Day had been deep into drugs back in the late seventies, a time when things like HIV and hep C weren't even a blip on the radar for most people. I hadn't a doubt in the world that she'd been an IV drug user back then and that hep C had been lying in wait, ready to spring on her, years and years after she quit using.

"When?" I asked.

"A little over ten years ago," he said.

"There are medications for that now," I offered.

He nodded. "I know. They were coming then, too, but by the time Jasmine tried to get in to one of the human trials, it was already too late for her. She was sick for a long time, in and out of the hospital. No insurance, of course, so we ended up losing pretty much everything, including the house. If it hadn't been for Jasmine's mom, I would have been up shit creek."

"I'm so sorry to hear about this," I said. "But what's the deal here, Alan? Why do you need a PI?"

"It's about my daughter," he told me, "Jasmine's and my daughter. Her name is Naomi—Naomi Louise Dale."

Knowing that hep C can be transmitted from mother to child, I hated asking the next question, but I did it anyway. "What about Naomi?" I asked. "Does she have hep C, too?"

Alan shrugged and slumped in his chair. "Maybe," he said darkly, and then, after a pause, he added, "Make that probably. She might have inherited it from her mother, but she's also been into drugs big time for years, so she could very well have contracted it on her own. At the time Jasmine was diagnosed, we tried to encourage Naomi to get tested, but by then she wasn't listening to a word we said. I doubt she took our advice."

"I take it Naomi is Athena's mother?"

Alan nodded, and his reply made me wonder, if that was the case, why was baby Athena riding all over hell and gone with Alan rather than with her mother? And if Naomi had come down with hepatitis C . . .

"If Naomi has hep C," I asked, "what about Athena?"

"I worried about that, too," Alan admitted.

"Given the family history, I asked Athena's doc at Children's to test her. He says she's clear."

"Thank God for that," I murmured. "So what's the story, then, Alan? Why exactly did you come looking for me?"

"Naomi's gone missing," he answered. "I'm hoping you can find her."

"She went missing somewhere around here?"

"Yes," he said. "She disappeared in Seattle."

"Tell me what happened."

"When Naomi was admitted to Harborview in late January to have the baby, she listed her grandmother, Helen Gibbons, as her next of kin."

"Helen is Jasmine's mother?"

Alan nodded. "Yes," he said. "Helen is my mother-in-law. After Naomi disappeared, the hospital called Helen, and she called me."

"You're saying Naomi disappeared from the hospital?"

"Yes, right after giving birth, she got dressed and walked out before anyone realized she was gone."

"And left Athena behind?"

"Abandoned her at the hospital," Alan corrected. "At the time Naomi took off, Athena was locked up in Harborview Medical Center's neonatal unit because she was both premature and underweight. She was also addicted to methadone. As I said, the hospital called Helen, and she called me. I quit my job—I was working a bus-and-truck show in Cincinnati at the time—and caught the next plane out. By the time I got here, Harborview had already transferred Athena over to Children's. I've been with her ever since."

"On your own?"

"Yes, on my own," he said with a hopeless shrug. "Who else is there? Helen has health issues that make it no longer feasible for her to fly. I've had a room at the Silver Cloud in Seattle's University District for over a month now, but I haven't spent much time there. It's expensive as all hell, and I wouldn't be able to cover it if Helen weren't willing to help. But it's close to the hospital. While Athena was an inpatient, I generally stopped by the hotel just long enough to grab a shower and eat some breakfast. Most nights I spent in the nursery at the hospital—holding her, rocking her. She was hooked on methadone at birth and had to go through withdrawal." He shuddered, remembering. "It was horrible," he managed at last, choking on the words as he spoke. "How a mother could do that to her own baby—feed her that kind of poison—is more than I can understand!"

Alan broke off then. I sat there in the silence trying to figure out where I fit into this unfolding family drama. Was he searching for his missing daughter in hopes of affecting some kind of reconciliation with her, or was he concerned that Naomi had landed in hot water, and he was here hoping to bail her out of it?

"Methadone is what they use to help get addicts off drugs," I said at last. "Maybe Naomi was trying to get clean."

"I doubt it," Alan said. "The thing is, now that Athena has been released from the hospital, I'll have to locate someplace less expensive for us to stay until we get things sorted out."

"What things?" I asked.

"If I hadn't shown up, Athena would have gone straight from the hospital into foster care," Alan explained. "I'm petitioning to be appointed her legal guardian, but that takes time. I've been appointed her temporary guardian for the next thirty days, but achieving legal-guardian status can take up to a year. I'm not even allowed to leave town with her until all of that is settled, and that's why I have to find Naomi now. The only way to shortcut the process is for Naomi to go before a judge and voluntarily relinquish her parental rights. I won't be able to take Athena home to Jasper with me until that happens."

Legal guardianship? Whoa! Here was a widowed guy in his sixties signing on to take full responsibility for a newborn baby? That takes guts—lots of them. My respect for Mr. Alan Dale shot up about ten-thousandfold.

The baby stirred in her carrier and made a tiny bleating noise. Alan immediately dug in the diaper bag and produced one of those foil-covered containers that are advertised on TV for keeping hot things hot and cold things cold. After removing a baby bottle, Alan leaned over and lifted Athena out of her carrier. That's when I noticed that while we'd been talking, Lucy had silently oozed her way across the hardwood floor until her nose was resting on her front paws less than two feet away from the baby carrier. She had somehow managed to drag the rug along with her. It was still under her rump—barely. That meant she hadn't officially broken my stay-on-the-rug command, but she was pushing the boundaries.

"Lucy," I said reprovingly, "what do you think you're doing?"

Without raising her head, she thumped her long tail at me in acknowledgment, but her intent black eyes remained focused totally on the baby.

Alan settled Athena in the crook of his arm and offered her the bottle. As she began to pull on the nipple, Alan sent a wary glance in Lucy's direction.

"What the hell kind of plug-ugly-looking dog is that anyway?" he asked.

Since it seemed like a change of subject was in order, I told him the Rambo/Lucy story, about how the dog had been brought into the picture and trained precisely to help protect a woman and her two small children from a guy who loved to rule the roost with iron fists. On the day when push really had come to shove, and for his own protection, the jerk had made sure that the dog was locked in the bathroom before he'd launched what turned out to be his last-ever attack on his wife.

"My understanding is that Lucy almost tore the bathroom to pieces trying to get out so she could take him on."

"But she didn't hurt the kids?"

"Far from it. She protected them."

"So if she started out being named Rambo," Alan asked, "how did she turn into Lucy?"

"The asshole wife-beater was the one who gave her the Rambo handle. Later, when I met her trainer, I discovered that the dog's original name was Lucy, and that's what Mel and I call her—Lucy. The DV incident happened here in Bellingham, where my wife, Mel, happens to be chief of police. After the attack, she was able to place the woman and her kids in a shelter, but they couldn't take the dog along with them. That's how she ended up here with us. Originally we were supposed to foster the dog until her family got into some kind of permanent housing. About that time, though, the bad guy was cut loose from the slammer and came gunning for Mel. When he showed up, Lucy got in the middle of the fight and ended up being stabbed, thus saving Mel's life. It cost a bundle in vet bills to patch her up, but it was worth every penny. And when her family ultimately decided against taking her back, there was no way I was willing to part with her."

Athena had evidently drunk her fill. After putting the bottle away, Alan threw a cloth pad over his shoulder. He placed the baby on that and then patted her on the back until she burped.

"She's probably ready for a diaper change," he said. "Where should I do that?"

I directed him to the guest bedroom. While he took care of business, I made both of us another cup of coffee. I was back in my chair in the living room by the time they returned.

"I wrapped up the diaper in a plastic bag and left it in the bathroom trash," he said. "I hope that's okay."

"Don't worry," I said. "I'll take care of it." Cleaning up after Lucy has made me a whole lot tougher in those messy regards than I ever used to be.

After being fed and changed, Athena seemed perfectly content to go back into her carrier. While Alan was carefully tending to that, I studied his appearance. I couldn't imagine being his age and staying up night after night with the daunting task of tending to a newborn baby 24/7, especially a drug-addicted preemie infant. No wonder the poor guy had dark circles under his eyes. He was probably completely exhausted.

Alan didn't notice the new cup of coffee until after he had resettled himself in the chair. "Thanks for the refill," he said. "I appreciate it."

I glanced at my watch and realized it was already half past noon and well into lunchtime. "What about some food?" I offered. "Have you had anything to eat?"

"Breakfast back at the hotel is all," he answered.

In my experience those "breakfast included" breakfasts don't amount to much.

"I'm not exactly a gourmet cook," I told him, "but I'm capable of making a killer ham sandwich when called upon to do so. How about one of those?"

"Sure," Alan agreed. "That would be great."

I left him there and went to the kitchen. When I returned a few minutes later carrying two ham sandwiches on separate plates, I found him fast asleep in the chair. I didn't wake him. Lucy, having abandoned all pretense of staying on the rug, had curled herself into a surprisingly small ball and positioned herself between Alan's feet and the baby carrier. I let her be, too. She had yet to decide if Alan posed a threat to the little one, and she obviously wanted to place herself between the baby and him, just in case. Given her unfortunate history, I didn't blame her a bit.

Without disturbing any of the three, I placed Alan's sandwich on the table next to his cup before retreating to my own chair and my own thoughts, which under the circumstances turned out to be more than slightly problematic. Naturally my mind wandered back to the night before Jasmine Day's final performance at the 5th Avenue Theatre. I couldn't come up with an exact date, but I estimated it must have been somewhere in the late eighties—1988 or so. And there are plenty of reasons my thought process about those times and places is somewhat fuzzy.

Let's just say that the eighties weren't especially good for me. For one thing I was still drinking at the time—drinking a lot. When Karen divorced me, I did what every drunk in the world always does—I blamed her for everything. The fact that our marriage had ended was all her fault. It had nothing whatsoever to do with me or with any of my actions. And trust me, my actions back then were pretty far out there.

And then a miracle happened, A spark of light—a beautiful lifeline, I thought—named Anne Corley appeared on the scene. She was like a brilliant shooting star blazing through my universe. One moment she was there, and the next, just as suddenly, she was gone. She left me with money—a fortune, in fact—but she also left me with a broken heart, and after she died at the base of Snoqualmie Falls, I was in far worse shape than ever, and so was my drinking.

People don't just happen to drop in on their local neighborhood AA meeting for no reason at all, without having done some pretty scuzzy things that finally bring them to the realization that they're in deep trouble. At the time I was an unmarried heterosexual male—both divorced and widowed. I was also oversexed and underfed, which means I was out on the prowl and looking for action way more often than was good for me or for anybody else. Thank God that was long before the #MeToo movement arrived on the scene—otherwise I would have been run out of town on a rail.

By the late eighties, the sexual revolution was a couple of decades old. The pill was readily available, and hookups and one-night stands were pretty much the order of the day. Unfortunately, one of my one-night stands happened to have been with Jasmine Day. It had been a put-up deal. I'd been called to the theater to investigate the death of that murdered stagehand. Eventually it turned out that the traveling show company had been using the tour as cover for transporting illicit drugs back and forth across the country.

When I turned up at the theater asking awkward questions, the stage manager had been anxious to keep a lid on the investigation, at least until after Jasmine's gig was over. With that in mind, he'd comped me to a front-row ticket. What I didn't realize at the time but what Jasmine understood full well was that whoever ended up in that comped seat on any given night also got to have Jasmine Day's "companionship" that evening after the show. It was one of those standing pay-to-play arrangements. Jasmine had wanted a comeback tour, and playing escort to the producer's "honored guests" was the price of admission. What she hadn't known was that most of those comped-seat introductions placed her in the presence of known drug dealers, thus steering suspicion away from the real bad guys and onto Jasmine herself. I didn't exactly tell her right off that I was a cop working a case, and it turned out I was doing "undercover" work in more ways than one.

After a dinner with way too much booze under our belts and not nearly enough food, Jasmine's and my trip to the bedroom and everything that happened therein had been consensual on both sides. I seem to remember that she'd ended up driving us back to my place from the restaurant, something I seldom let happen. But our so-called affair was what it was—a one-night stand with no strings attached. Two days later, the morning after the whole drug-transportation conspiracy had exploded into two more homicides, Alan Dale and I had both been waiting outside the King County jail when they released Jasmine from custody on the homicide charge. She came through the door and immediately broke into sobs, walking past me without a glance and seeking solace in Alan Dale's comforting arms.

As soon as I saw the two of them together, I understood that their relationship was the real deal and I backed off completely. I don't know if Alan had any knowledge about the reality of Jasmine's comped-seat arrangement. He might have known, or then again he might not. He sure as hell didn't know that the bus-and-truck company was really nothing more than camouflage for a drug-smuggling outfit, and neither did Jasmine. The investigation into that concluded weeks later without either one of them ever being charged with a crime.

And now, all these years later, here was Alan, asking for my help. Obviously Jasmine must not have told him about what had happened between the two of us. If she had, it seemed unlikely that he would have come to me looking for help concerning his errant daughter. And if Jasmine had never told him about it, I sure as hell wasn't going to be the one to fess up.

Alan let out a soft snore, startling himself awake. "Sorry," he said, sitting up straight. "I didn't mean to drop off like that."

"Not to worry," I told him. "I suspect you needed that nap way more than you need either food or coffee."

"Probably," he agreed, picking up his sandwich. "So where were we?"

"I believe you were going to tell me about Naomi," I told him. "Maybe we should start there."

CHAPTER 2

I waited until Alan's sandwich was gone before moving forward. "All right," I said, pulling out my iPad. "If I'm going to help you on this, I need to know the details of what I'm up against."

In the old days, my tools of choice would have been a ragged little notebook and a stubby pencil, but those seem to have gone the way of the buggy whip. Now I'm iPad all the way.

Alan leaned back in his chair, looked across at me, and said, "What do you need to know?"

"Everything," I said, "starting with what you've been doing in the thirty years or so since I last laid eyes on you."

"Jasmine and I went home," he said simply, "home to Jasmine's folks' place in Jasper, Texas. Her dad was still alive back then. Jasper is north of Beaumont."

Since Beaumont, Texas, my father's hometown, is the real origin of my last name, I happen to be well versed in the location of that particular city.

"I'm from Oakridge, Oregon, originally," Alan continued. "Jasmine and I grew up in small towns, and when we bailed on Seattle, we were ready to be away from big cities and off the road. We both figured that Jasmine's career was over, but I was pretty sure that with my carpentry skills I could find enough work to keep body and soul together no matter where we lived. We found a house—Jasmine's folks helped us with that—and we moved in together. We were planning to get married eventually, but when Jasmine turned up pregnant unexpectedly, we moved up the wedding date."

"And got married in Vegas," I put in.

"Exactly," he said.

"And then what happened?"

"Jasper's a small town. Everybody there knew that Jasmine had been a big star once, and in their eyes she still was. She started singing again, only at church to begin with, but people paid attention. When Helen asked Jasmine to come to perform at a statewide Christian women's conference, something totally unexpected happened. She was a huge hit, and it was the beginning of Jasmine's next chapter, as it were. She had started out singing gospel music. She had gone from there to rock, rock to jazz, and finally from jazz back to gospel."

"Full circle, in other words," I commented.

"Right," Alan said. "She picked up several paying gigs just from that first conference alone. She did mostly church-sponsored events where she told her story and sang gospel songs. Everyplace she went, her program was a hit. There aren't huge amounts of money to be made in the Christian-music business—at least there wasn't back then—but by the time Naomi was three, Jasmine was making almost as much from her appearances as I was bringing in from working construction.

"And that's when we decided to turn it into a business. She recorded a couple of albums, and then we bought a van and took our show back on the road. I went from being a head carpenter to being a tour manager. I set up the gigs, drove the van, sold the merchandise, did the billing and bookkeeping. When Naomi was little, she went along with us. When it was time for her to go to school and we needed to be gone for a couple of weeks at a time, she stayed with Helen and Gabe."

"Jasmine's father?" I asked.

Alan nodded. "Gabe Gibbons was the world's best grandpa, and Naomi loved him to pieces."

When it came to gold-star grandpas, it seemed to me as though I was currently in the presence of one of those, but I didn't try voicing that opinion to Alan. He wasn't in a place where he'd be able to hear a compliment, much less accept one.

"You said, 'was,'" I interjected. "What happened to him?"

"Grandpa Gabe died in a car wreck when Naomi was thirteen, and she took it real hard. It was as though the bottom had fallen out of her world. She lost interest in everything. Her grades dropped. By the time she got into high school, she was a mess. She started hanging around with a bad crowd, got herself into some serious trouble, and ended up being expelled. Once she got kicked out of school, she never went back. I'm sure you know the drill."

The truth is, I knew that drill all too well. When my daughter, Kelly, dropped out of school and ran off with a wannabe actor/musician, I was sure she was a goner, too, but I was wrong. It turns out she wasn't then and still isn't a goner. Eventually Kelly got her GED and enrolled in college, where she ended up earning not only a bachelor's degree but a master's degree as well. She runs a chain of early-childhood-development centers in southern Oregon. As for that supposedly worthless wannabe actor/musician? Jeremy, my son-in-law, is now a well-respected band director and drama teacher at the high school in their southern Oregon town.

"So Naomi ran away from home?" I asked.

Alan nodded. "Jasmine could see where Naomi was headed better than I could, because she'd already been down that road. Naomi left home and dropped out of our lives completely. For a while she stayed in touch with her grandmother, with Helen, but the last time she stopped by to visit, she stole money out of Helen's purse. That was the last straw as far as Grandma Gibbons was concerned. It was also the last time we heard anything about her or from her until that phone call from Harborview Medical Center."

"She didn't come home to visit when her mother was sick and dying?" I asked.

"No," Alan said, somberly looking off into the far distance, "and she didn't come home for the funeral either."

"So when did she leave?" I asked, picking up the iPad and getting ready to drill down for details.

"When did she leave Jasper or when did she leave now?"

"Now."

"January twenty-fourth," Alan answered, "a couple of hours after Athena was born. She stayed around long enough to fill out the birth certificate and name the baby—Athena Marie Dale. She's listed as the mother. The father is listed as 'unknown.'"

"So whoever the father is, she probably didn't marry him or take his name."

"I guess," Alan replied.

"What about an address? Did she give one of those?"

"On the form it's listed as NKA. They told me at the hospital that translates to 'no known address.'"

"So she was homeless, then?"

"Evidently."

I looked over at Athena, wrapped snugly in blankets and sleeping peacefully in her carrier with what looked like a smile on her tiny lips. She had no idea how lucky she was, but I did. In the Pacific Northwest, it's not nearly as frigid in early March as it is in January or February, but it's still wet and plenty cold. Six weeks earlier at the end of January would have been a terrible time to take a newborn baby—especially a frail premature one—from a hospital nursery to a tent in some homeless encampment with no heat, plumbing, or sanitation. If that had been Naomi's only post-hospital option, maybe leaving Athena in the nursery was the best possible decision she could have made for either one of them, but that wasn't an opinion I could voice aloud to Alan Dale—certainly not right then.

"Did Naomi have any known associates?" I asked.

Alan shook his head. "When she ran away from home originally, she took off with a boyfriend named Brad Walters. I tried looking him up when Jasmine was so sick. Turns out he was already dead—he died of an overdose. After that the trail went cold."

"So why would Naomi come to Seattle?" I asked.

"I have no idea," Alan told me.

"No friends or relations in the area?"

"Not as far as I know."

"Do you have a photo of her?"

Alan reached into his wallet. "This is all I have. It was taken her sophomore year in high school, just before she got kicked out and went on the lam."

He handed me a dog-eared, well-thumbed color photo, one that he'd obviously been carrying around in his pocket for all those intervening years. It was a headshot, the kind used in school yearbooks everywhere. The dark-haired teenage girl in the picture looked decidedly unhappy, but there was something disturbingly familiar about her, and it took a moment for me to figure it out. She looked just like Kelly—just like my daughter, who also looks a bit like me.

Holy crap! I thought as a hard knot formed in my gut. *Did Jasmine ever notice? Did Alan?*

"She was what age when this was taken, fifteen or so?" I asked quickly, trying to conceal my discomfort.

Alan nodded. "About that, I guess."

"You don't have any more recent photos?"

"Nope."

I used my iPad to copy the photo and then handed it back to Alan, hoping he didn't notice how much my hand shook as I did so.

"You're sure you don't need this?" he asked before returning it to his wallet.

"For the time being, no," I told him, "but I reserve the right to change my mind."

I know for a fact that Harborview has all kinds of security cameras. They cover the entrances and exits, the waiting rooms, the hallways, and the lobby areas. There might even be video footage showing exactly when Naomi left the hospital and how. That would be one of the first things I did. If you're not a cop working a case, laying hands on security-camera footage isn't easy, but it can be done.

"Have you reported her missing?"

Alan shook his head. "Obviously Naomi's heavy into drugs," he said. "She may have gotten herself into all kinds of trouble trying to feed her habit. For all I know, there might be a trail of arrest warrants out there waiting for her from Jasper to here. I need to find her long enough to have her sign-off on the paperwork. I don't want to land her in even more trouble."

At that point I didn't want Naomi Dale in more hot water either, but there was also a new reason for concern. There might be a much more current photo of Naomi Dale to be found in Seattle PD's collection of mug shots. Again, those would all be readily available to cops but not necessarily to former cops turned PIs. And there was another possibility as well, a far grimmer one at that. Athena was born addicted to methadone. As I'd mentioned to Alan, it's a drug that is often used when addicts are trying to get clean. The problem is, once you go off hard drugs for a time, if you happen to suffer a relapse, what might have been a safe dosage prior to treatment may well prove fatal after someone has been clean for a while. It occurred to me that there was a good chance Naomi's body was lying unclaimed and unidentified in the King County M.E.'s Office.

As soon as that idea crossed my mind, I dismissed it. If Naomi had been living rough on the streets and doing drugs for a decade and a half, she was bound to have had more than one run-in with the law. Had the M.E. entered her prints into AFIS, they would have led straight back to her family in Jasper, Texas—to her father, to Alan Dale. No, if Naomi was dead, Alan Dale most certainly would have heard the news by now.

This was yet another piece of information that I couldn't share with my new client, and I couldn't help but wonder if he was holding back as much as I was. I doubted it. I was the real liar here, make no mistake about it.

"All right," I said finally, setting my iPad aside. "When it comes to finding her, you haven't given me much to go on, but I'll do my best."

"How expensive is this going to be?" Alan asked.

Having seen the family resemblance in that photo, there was no way in hell I was going to charge him a penny. "Sorry, pal," I said. "There are some things friends can't buy. Besides, I don't need the money nearly as much as I need the work. Once a cop, always a cop, and I miss the job like crazy."

"Wait," he objected. "You can't do that. I'll be glad to pay."

"No you won't," I told him. "Your hands are more than full right now. My son and daughter-in-law are expecting a baby of their own in a couple of months. I've been helping Scott get the nursery ready. By now they've spent a small fortune accumulating necessary baby gear, and you'll need to do the same. So spend whatever you would have paid me on outfitting Athena's nursery. If she ever asks, you can tell her the decor came from one of her grandmother's old friends."

"Really?" he managed, choking out the word. "I don't know how to thank you."

"You don't need to thank me," I told him, "and here's another thing. Do you remember where I lived back then?"

"Vaguely," he answered. "It was a penthouse in some fancy condo building downtown. Why?"

I doubted he remembered the exact address of Belltown Terrace, but since he and Jasmine had stayed there with me for a week or two while the homicide and drug-dealing investigations had been winding down, he had the general idea.

"Mel and I still own it," I told him. "We go there sometimes for weekend getaways, but most of the time it sits empty. You and Athena are welcome to stay there for as long as you need."

"For free?" he asked.

"For free," I repeated.

I'd like to think that I'm the kind of person who would have offered him shelter under any circumstances, but in view of the fact that the infant in his care might turn out to be my own biological granddaughter, it was mandatory, especially since the cheapest digs in town—and his only viable alternative—would have been one of those by-the-hour motels on Highway 99.

"But that's too kind," he objected. "I couldn't possibly take advantage of you like that."

"You can and you will," I told him, handing him my card. "When you get back to your hotel, send a text to my cell-phone number. That way I'll be able to get a hold of you. Go ahead and stay there tonight. That'll give me time enough to sort out some arrangements. Tomorrow I'll come to town to start looking for Naomi. I'll also help you and Athena get settled into your new digs."

"Are you sure?"

"Yes, I'm sure."

"Okay," he agreed reluctantly, slipping the card into his pocket.

And that was all it took. From there on out, it was a done deal.

CHAPTER 3

ALAN AND ATHENA packed up and left a short time later. It was far enough into the afternoon that I expected they'd be caught up in Boeing traffic leaving Everett and heading south into Seattle, but I didn't need to burden the poor man with any more bad news. When he caught up with the traffic mess, he'd be able to deal with it without having agonized about it in advance.

The morning chill and rain had given way to sunshine, so I leashed Lucy and the two of us went out for our customary walk down to the village center and back. Fairhaven had been a boomtown back in the late 1880s. In those days it was a busy harbor serving both fishing fleets and timber companies. Now all that remains of its once-healthy shipping industry is the fact that it serves as the terminus of the Alaska Marine Highway Ferry. That's the official name, but around here most people refer to it as the "Alaskan Ferry."

One of Fairhaven's earliest and most colorful settlers, the guy who gave the village its name, was a canny wheeler-dealer and storyteller named Dirty Dan Harris. Eventually he was swindled out of both his wealth and his properties by a pair of low-down schemers, a physician and wife—Dr. A. S. and Mattie Shorb. These days the only remaining trace of Dirty Dan in town is a restaurant bearing his name. It's a steak-and-chop kind of joint and one of Mel's and my perennial favorites.

When Lucy and I returned from our walk, I took the first tentative steps in my search for Naomi Dale by placing a call to my son. Following in his father's footsteps, Scotty works for Seattle PD these days in what's known as the TEU—the Tactical Electronics Unit. It's his dream job, one that combines his lifelong ambition of becoming a cop with the engineering and high-tech skills he developed and honed while earning a degree in electrical engineering.

"Hey, Pop," he said when he answered. "What can I do you for?"

"I'm working a missing-persons case," I told him. "I was wondering if you could run a name for me. I need to know if she has any outstanding warrants and if there's something I should be worried about if and when I find her."

I'm sure Internal Affairs wouldn't have approved, but between Scotty and me no further conversation was needed. "Who are we looking for?" my son asked.

I gave him Naomi Dale's name and listened as he typed it into a keyboard. Compared to me, he's a lightning-fast typist. I'm still strictly a hunt-

and-peck sort of guy. While Scotty was doing the
search, I held my breath. If he did turn up a mug
shot, would he notice the striking resemblance between Naomi Dale and his own sister?

"Sounds like you've got yourself a real winner,"
he told me, finally. "If you're looking for violations, take your pick. We've got driving under the
influence, driving without a valid license, driving
without valid insurance, disturbing the peace, shoplifting (twice), as well as a drunk and disorderly.
She's been arrested numerous times, but she's served
surprisingly little jail time. On each of the traffic
violations, she was given fines, which she paid. On
the shoplifting charges, she was given suspended
sentences. For disturbing the peace, she was given a
ten-day jail sentence, which she served. The drunk-
and-disorderly case was dismissed because the cop
in question didn't show up in court."

"In other words, she's likely to be a handful."

"Yes," Scott agreed, "and should probably be
handled with care. I can send you a mug shot if you
like."

"Please," I said. "And do you happen to have an
address?"

"I don't know how good it is, but the one that's
listed here is from that last shoplifting charge, and
it's over in West Seattle. Still, that address is from
more than a year ago, so it may be out of date." He
rattled it off, and I jotted it down.

"Do you need anything else?"

"Nope," I said, "that's all."

"Got it," Scotty replied, "I'm sending now."

A second later I heard the distinctive chime of arriving messages.

"Watch yourself out there," he warned.

"Will do," I told him. "And thank you. You've been a huge help. How's Cherisse by the way, and how are things going for you?"

"Are pregnant women always cranky?"

Obviously the answer to my question should have been, "Not so good." And I'm pretty sure my reply to his query wasn't at all what he wanted to hear either.

"In my experience they are," I told my son. "They're mad as hell about anything and everything most of the time, and the closer it comes to delivery, the worse it gets."

"Terrific," Scotty muttered, "that's just great!"

"When are we going to get cracking on putting that crib together?" I asked.

"My day off is Wednesday," he said. "Want to drop by then?"

"Sure thing," I told him. "Text me and let me know when I should show up."

I enlarged Naomi's mug shot to full screen and spent some time studying it. This more recent image showed Naomi Dale to be even more of a dead ringer for my daughter, Kelly, than the school photo had been. Mel maintains that men are far too literal-minded. They tend to see what they expect to see and nothing else. That was evidently true here. Clearly Naomi's resemblance to his sister had gone completely over Scotty's head, but my call to him had at least put one worry to rest. Naomi had a record. Her prints were on file. If she was stowed in a morgue someplace, someone would have noticed.

My next step was to go looking for a glimpse of Naomi around the time she left Harborview. It would have helped to know exactly when she arrived and when she was admitted, but I knew better than to tackle the hospital directly asking for patient information—HIPAA rules and all that. What I needed instead was a work-around. Since I'd recently added the name of Sergeant Albert Thorne of the Arson/Bomb Squad to my contacts list, I dialed his number next. The ABS is part of Seattle PD, but because of Al's regular interactions with the Seattle Fire Department, I thought he might be my best bet.

"Hey, Beau," he said once I identified myself. "How's it hanging?"

Al's telephone persona hasn't changed in decades.

"What's up?" he added. "You interested in bluffing your way into another arson investigation anytime soon?"

With Al's help I'd gained unauthorized access to the scene of an arson/homicide investigation. We'd both broken several rules in the course of that little escapade, and we were lucky not to have been caught—luckier for him than for me. He could have lost his job. I'm retired. So I owe him one, big time.

"No thank you," I said. "I believe I'll pass on that score, but I do need some help."

"What kind of help, legal or not?"

As noted above, his question wasn't exactly out of line.

"I'm working a missing-persons case," I told him.

"The woman in question, one Naomi Louise Dale, was born in Jasper, Texas, February twenty-first, 1989. She disappeared from Harborview sometime during the day of January twenty-fourth of this year. She was transported to the hospital by ambulance at an unknown time from an unknown location on either the twenty-third or the twenty-fourth—I don't know which. On the twenty-fourth, she gave birth to a daughter. A few hours later, she left the baby in the neonatal unit and abandoned ship."

"Walked off and left her baby there, just like that?" The moral outrage in Al Thorne's voice palpable.

"Just like that," I agreed.

"Is she nuts or what? Why else would a woman pull a boneheaded stunt like that?"

My experience in AA made it problematic for me to discuss anyone else's addiction issues with outsiders. In this instance that included any discussion of baby Athena's addiction issues as well, so I left that part of the equation out of the story. It didn't matter, though, because I'd had Al hooked the moment he heard that Naomi had bailed on her newborn.

"Anyone who would do something like that has to have 'mental issues,'" Al grumbled. "It sounds like she never should have had kids in the first place."

"I agree with you there," I told him. "Obviously Naomi is one troubled individual. Her father flew into town as soon as he heard what happened. He's the one who's been taking care of the baby in Naomi's absence. He's trying to be appointed the child's legal guardian so he can take her back home to Texas. In order to do that, he needs to find his daughter and get her to relinquish her parental rights."

"So what do you want from me?" Al asked. "Time she was transported? Where they picked her up? Names of the EMTs involved? That sort of thing?"

"Yes," I agreed, "all of those and anything else that strikes your fancy."

"It's late in the day," Al said. "I don't know how much I can accomplish right off the bat, but I'll go to work on it and let you know."

"Thanks, Al," I told him.

Mel walked in just then. It was her night to cook, so she'd come home bearing gifts—a bag of take-out that smelled suspiciously like teriyaki chicken. Putting the food on the counter, she bent down to greet Lucy, who is also known to have an appreciation for the occasional bite of teriyaki chicken delivered surreptitiously under the table.

"Who was that on the phone?"

"Al Thorne."

She frowned. "Al Thorne," she repeated. "Isn't he the guy who helped you with the fire-inspector incident at Maxwell Cole's house?"

I nodded.

"What's up with him?"

"It turns out I caught a case."

"Really," Mel said. "What kind?"

I knew in advance this was going to be a very long story. When Mel and I first connected, we both had a lot of miles on our respective odometers. We'd agreed from the get-go that whatever happened before we met was off the table—as in "no harm, no foul." And even had we done an exercise in full disclosure, I doubt Jasmine Day's name would have turned up. What happened between Jasmine and me was a "night." It wasn't a "thing." It didn't come close to rising to the level of a romance, much less a relationship or an affair. But that photo—the one of Naomi that looked so much like Kelly—was going to be a showstopper. I knew I had to tell Mel what had happened sooner rather than later, chicken teriyaki notwithstanding.

"It's a missing-persons case," I said. "You need to hear all about it, but first you should see this."

With that I reached for my iPad, located my copy of Naomi Dale's school headshot, and passed the device over to Mel.

After studying the screen for a moment, she shrugged and handed it back. "What's the big deal? It's a picture of Kelly acting like a surly teenager. Aren't all teenagers surly?"

"*That's* the problem," I told her. "This girl isn't Kelly. Her name is Naomi Dale. She's the missing person in question, and what makes it a big deal is this: Twenty-nine years ago, I had a one-night stand with Naomi Dale's mother, a woman named Jasmine Day."

Mel Soames is cool and collected most of the time, but that was more than she could handle. She staggered slightly and then dropped heavily onto one of the stools at the kitchen island.

"If she's the missing person, then who's your client?"

"A guy by the name of Alan Dale, Naomi's father—the man who raised her from day one."

"What does he want? Is this some kind of blackmail scheme?"

"It's no scheme," I assured her. "As far as I can tell, Alan's a hell of a nice guy."

"Does he know he's not her real father?"

"I don't know."

"Does he have any idea that you might be Naomi's biological father?"

"Most likely not," I answered. "If he did, it seems like I'd be the last person he'd be asking for help in locating her. As for Naomi? She's gone missing, and he needs me to find her."

"He *needs* to find her or *wants* to find her?" Mel asked.

"Needs," I answered. "Naomi walked away from Harborview within hours of giving birth to a baby girl."

Mel actually gasped. "Walked away and left her baby behind?"

"Not just a baby—a premature, underweight baby who was born with a full-blown addiction to methadone."

"That's awful," Mel murmured.

"Yes, it is," I agreed. "The baby's name is Athena. Alan has spent the last six weeks seeing her through the worst of drug withdrawal, all the while commuting back and forth between the neonatal unit at Children's Hospital and the local Silver Cloud Hotel."

"He's been looking after her on his own?"

"On his own," I confirmed. "Alan's a widower. He's trying to get the state to appoint him to be Athena's legal guardian on a permanent basis. In order to do that and be able to take Athena back home to Texas with him, he needs to find Naomi and get her to relinquish her parental rights. He's stuck here until he can make that happen."

"Sounds like a hot mess," Mel breathed.

"It is," I acknowledged. "And just so you know, I told him he and Athena are welcome to stay at Bell-town Terrace until such time as they're able to go home, however long that takes."

"Which could be a while," Mel said.

"That, too," I agreed. "I'm planning on driving into town tomorrow so I can sort out keys and garage-door openers and anything else that needs to be handled. Once I get them settled in, I expect to hang around for a couple of days to see if I can get a line on where Naomi's gone off to."

I stopped talking then and waited to see what would happen next. I didn't have long to wait, and what did Mel do? She got up from the stool where she was sitting, walked over to me, and gave me a long, heartfelt hug.

"You're a good man, Mr. J. P. Beaumont," she told me, "a very good man. Take it from me, under the circumstances I think you got it just about right. Now, what can I do to help?"

CHAPTER 4

MEL AND I ate dinner where we often do—sitting side by side at the kitchen island. Mel had a glass of merlot. I had a non-alcoholic O'Doul's. There are plenty of AA hardliners who give me grief about that from time to time, but I've been sober and drinking the occasional NA O'Doul's for more than twenty years now. I have yet to go off the wagon on an O'Doul's-fueled bender or awakened with an O'Doul's-induced hangover, so let's just leave it at that.

While we ate, I told Mel the story—the whole thing—starting with that long-ago 5th Avenue Theatre case that had turned into a double-homicide investigation. The initial victim, a local stagehand who turned out to be working undercover for the DEA, had been plugged full of holes by someone wielding a cobalt-blue stiletto shoe and then pushed off a cliff. Shortly after the shoe guy's death, someone administered a fatal overdose to his sick and dying roommate.

This version of the story included the background on the comped-ticket arrangement that had been designed to cast Jasmine Day as the drug smuggler's fall guy. I also told Mel about the resulting tryst between Jasmine and me. I related the details behind Naomi Dale's initial running away from home along with her more recent disappearance from the hospital. The long tale ended with my telling Mel about Alan Dale's six-week round of caring for his tiny, drug-addicted granddaughter, who, as it happened, was most likely also *my* tiny drug-addicted granddaughter. Yikes! But Mel took it all in stride. When I finally stopped talking, she sat studying me intently with her chin resting in the palm of her hand.

"How old did you say Alan is?" she asked.

"Mid-sixties most likely."

"So a senior citizen and a widower besides?"

I nodded.

"And he'll be doing this all on his own?"

"Jasmine's mother, his mother-in-law, is evidently still alive and willing to help out, but she's an even more senior senior citizen with some ongoing health issues, so I don't know how much she'll be able to do."

"Well, then," Mel concluded, "there's really no choice, is there? Obviously we have to help." She fell quiet for a moment. When Mel Soames drifts into one of her thoughtful pauses, I've learned to use an old and extremely valuable interrogation technique. I shut up and wait to see what she's going to say next.

"What kind of formula does Alan Dale use?" she asked finally.

I never saw that one coming. "Formula?" I asked stupidly. "I have no idea."

"And what kind of diapers?"

When it came to diapers, I was completely out of my depth. "Beats me," I said.

"You know as well as I do that the cupboard in the condo is bare."

We go there only a couple of weekends a month, and on those occasions we generally eat out. Other than a few sodas in the fridge, we don't keep many supplies on hand.

"True," I agreed.

"You also know that grocery stores—real supermarket kinds of grocery stores—are pretty thin on the ground in Belltown these days. Text Alan and find out what his formula and diaper preferences are. Then I'll go online and order those, along with some other groceries—the basics—and have them delivered to Belltown Terrace first thing tomorrow morning. The doorman can put the cold stuff in the fridge. I'll have him leave the rest on the counter so Alan can put it away himself. That way he'll have some idea of what he has and where to find it."

"Good thinking," I said.

"While you're at it, why don't you give Marge Herndon a call?"

Marge Herndon was the Nurse Ratched–style RN who had looked after me and put me through the rigors of PT when I came home after my bilateral knee replacement. Think of her as your basic human buzz saw. She's tough. She smokes like a chimney. She issues orders and expects them to be obeyed without delay and without question—a drill sergeant, in other words.

"Check with Marge and see if we can give Alan her number. While Athena was an inpatient, Alan might have spent hours at the hospital every day, but he wasn't completely on his own. He had round-the-clock nursing staff to take up the slack. Now it's all on him. Without some respite help and the ability to get a good night's sleep occasionally, he'll wear himself out completely. And if something happens to him, what will become of Athena?"

Remembering the dark circles under Alan's eyes, I knew that Mel was on the money, and I couldn't help but applaud her calm and practical approach to the problem. My only issue here is this: A little bit of Marge Herndon goes a very long way. I'd been relieved once I was well enough to bid her a fond farewell, but then the accident happened—the one that had killed Ross Connors and left my SHIT-squad supervisor, Harry I. Ball, a double amputee. When it was finally time for him to be released from rehab and he was in need of nursing assistance, I'd swallowed my misgivings and recommended Marge for the job. I had expected Marge and Harry to be at loggerheads from the moment they met. Nope. How wrong could I be? It wasn't a matter of opposites attracting, because the two of them are so much alike it's spooky—including the fact that they're both chain-smokers. What I never saw coming was that they would fall in love and get married—which they had.

So yes, Mel was correct. Marge was exactly the

right person to provide the respite care that Alan needed, but I looked forward to calling her with about the same amount of enthusiasm I would have mustered in anticipation of an upcoming root canal.

I put the ordeal off as long as possible by texting back and forth with Alan about the shopping-list situation. Finally, though, it was time to take the plunge. When I dialed Marge's number, she must have had her hand on the phone, because she answered after only one ring.

"Hey, Beau," she said when she answered. "If you're looking for Stubs, I'll have to go get him. The rain quit and the sun came out, so he's having his last smoke of the day out on the deck. After all those weeks in the hospital and rehab, I'm afraid he's turned into one of those no-smoking-in-the-house Nazis."

Marge had just called Harry "Stubs"? Are you kidding? Two things here. Most honeymooners have pet names for each other—sweetie pie, honeybun, babe, sweetheart, and darling all come to mind. It takes a particularly dark sense of humor to refer to your fairly new husband who also happens to be a double amputee as "Stubs"! And Harry was now enforcing a no-smoking rule inside the house he shares with Marge? The guy has more guts than I ever gave him credit for.

"Actually, I was calling to speak to you," I said.

"How come?" she wanted to know. "Has one of your hips given out on you now? Getting old is hell."

"Nothing like that," I told her quickly, before

launching into a brief overview of Alan Dale's situation.

"Sure," Marge said when I finished. "Sounds like the poor guy has a whole lot on his plate. Feel free to give him my number and tell him to call if he needs help. I have to drive Harry to PT in the mornings three days a week, but other than that I'm pretty much free and easy."

"Not free, presumably," I told her. "Keep track of your hours and bill me accordingly—for both your hours and your parking expenses."

These days parking spaces around here are scarce as hens' teeth, as my mother would have said. They also cost an arm and a leg.

"Fair enough," Marge said. "Glad to help out."

By the time I got off the phone with Marge, Mel had her nose buried in her laptop's screen. "What time do you plan on being there in the morning?" she asked.

"Midmorning, I suppose." I answered. "No sense in driving into town through rush-hour traffic."

"Okay, I'll ask for the groceries to be delivered around eleven. That way they should get to Belltown Terrace about the same time you do."

"What do we do about Lucy?" I asked.

"Wherever you go, she goes."

Mel's response was delivered in her customary no-nonsense, last-word fashion, one implying that the subject was no longer up for discussion. I gave it a shot all the same.

"I'm going to be working a case," I argued. "I can't be dragging Lucy with me everywhere I go."

"Yes you can," she replied. "From what you've told me, Naomi may be living on the street or in one of those homeless encampments. That means you'll be searching in some pretty sketchy places. You know better than to venture into something like that with no backup. It's a big no-no. Not only is Lucy uniquely qualified to perform backup duty, she has the scars to prove it."

No argument there—about the scars, I mean, and ditto for Mel's very valid concerns about my going into potentially dangerous situations without proper backup—that's Police Academy 101.

"Yes, ma'am," I conceded. "Wherever I go, Lucy goes."

"Thanks," she said with a smile. "You're a very gracious loser."

After that we set about sorting out keys and garage-door openers so Alan would be able to come and go as needed. Once the kitchen was cleaned up, it was late enough to call it a night. We were actually lying in bed before I finally got around to asking Mel about her day.

"It was fine," she said, snuggling close. "The people at the Rotary luncheon loved me. Compared to what you were up against today, my day was a walk in the park."

CHAPTER 5

LUCY AND I were up, out, and on our way south shortly before nine the next morning.

Soon after coming to live with us, the dog had decided, on her own, that when traveling by car her preferred seating arrangement was in the backseat, positioned directly behind me, preferably with her chin resting on my left shoulder so she could keep an eye on traffic out the front windshield.

For those of you unfamiliar with the relative size of Irish wolfhounds, let me say this: Lucy is a big dog. Her head is large, and her massive coat of flyaway black hair makes it even larger—enough so that when we're in the car, as far as people looking in from the outside world are concerned, her head completely obscures mine. To the people we meet in other vehicles—oncoming ones on two-lane roads and passing ones on four-lane highways, it looks as though the dog is at the wheel of my Mercedes.

Some people see the humor in the situation,

honking or laughing or giving us a thumbs-up. A few drivers have been so astonished that they've come close to losing control of their own vehicles. I suppose I could put Lucy on a lie-down command and keep her completely out of sight. No doubt she'd do as she was told, but as I may have mentioned earlier, I've never been very good when it comes to maintaining discipline with children or dogs. Besides, I like the idea that we're offering folks a little lighthearted cheer as we travel Washington's highways and byways.

I had told Alan that we'd be at the Silver Cloud by ten thirty, and we were. When I called to let him know we were out front in the parking lot, he sounded completely frazzled. "I'm having some trouble getting packed up. Athena is in constant meltdown mode, and I'm at my wits' end. Would you mind coming up and holding her for a few minutes while I finish pulling things together?"

"No, problem," I said. "I'll be right up. What room?"

"Three-sixteen," he told me.

After taking Lucy for a brief but necessary pee walk, I left her in the car and headed upstairs. The Silver Cloud evidently didn't have a bellman on duty. On the third floor, I found a partially loaded rolling luggage cart parked outside Room 316. The door was ajar, and the earsplitting wails of a squalling infant flowed out of the room and echoed up and down the hallway.

I tapped on the door. Alan opened it the rest of the way with a bawling Athena cradled in one arm. Her little face was screwed up in anguish, and her tiny clenched fists were flailing as though she were a boxer prepared to take on all comers. I found it astonishing that something so small could make that much noise. As for Alan? The poor guy looked completely done in. His eyes were bloodshot, and the dark circles under them were more pronounced than they'd been the day before. It was the morning-after look of someone who'd really tied one on, but I was quite sure he hadn't.

"How are things?" I asked.

He shook his head. "I don't know what's the matter with her. She was up most of the night, and so was I. We're probably driving the other poor guests on this floor nuts. As for getting packed? I've been trying, but with her like this I haven't been able to get my act together."

"Hand her over," I said, bravely holding out my arms. "I'll take Athena downstairs with me and get her out of your hair. That way you'll have a moment to yourself."

"Where will you take her?"

"Down to my car. It's parked right out front."

"All right, and thank you," Alan said gratefully. "I'll be down as soon as I can."

Self-conscious about the racket we were making, I carried that tiny, wiggling, and very noisy bundle back down the hallway. When I needed to operate the elevator buttons, I put Athena up on my shoulder and balanced her there one-handed. By the time we made it back down to the lobby, she had managed to produce a very unladylike burp, which left a distinctively white, telltale stain dribbling down the front shoulder of my newly dry-cleaned sport jacket. My mother always insisted that I never leave home without a freshly washed and ironed hankie in my pocket. Thankfully, that advice remained one of the guiding principles of my life, and the hankie I had with me that day came in very, very handy. Handy, yes. Altogether successful? Not really, and as I cleaned up the mess, I couldn't help but remember that old song from the fifties—"The Naughty Lady of Shady Lane."

Still, the burp itself must have done the trick, because whatever was bothering Athena suddenly disappeared. By the time I finished mopping off the jacket to the best of my ability, she had quieted down. As we exited the front lobby, Athena was already asleep in my arms. Once I opened the car door and started to get inside, Lucy saw the baby and promptly went nuts. If Athena and I were going to be in the front seat, Lucy wanted to be there, too—all ninety-plus pounds of her. She was half over the passenger seat before I managed to summon my official dog-command voice.

"Sit," I ordered firmly. "Sit and stay." Lucy did both, but she didn't like it, and she whimpered softly from time to time, letting me know that she wasn't the least bit happy.

Alan had already told me he'd been up all night. It was one thing to give him Marge's number and expect him to initiate contact with her in case he needed help. It seemed unlikely, however, that he'd pick up the phone, dial a complete stranger, and ask her to come over to give him a hand with his precious granddaughter. Realizing that was never going to happen without some kind of intervention on my part, I took the bull by the horns and called Marge myself.

"I'm just now meeting up with Alan and Athena at the hotel," I told Marge when she came on the line. "I expect we'll be at Belltown Terrace in the next forty-five minutes or so, getting them settled in. How about if you just happen to stop by about then, too? That way you and Alan can be properly introduced, and if he does need your help, he won't have to feel like he's leaving Athena in the care of a complete stranger."

"Sounds good to me," Marge said.

"He also just told me that he and Athena were up all night long. The poor guy looks like death warmed over. If you could maybe put in a couple of hours this afternoon so he could get some rest . . ."

"No problem," Marge said.

"And one more thing . . ."

"What's that?"

"As far as Alan's concerned, you're a friend of the family who's stepping in and lending a hand out of the kindness of your heart."

It killed me to do so, but I managed to utter those words with a totally straight face.

"Mr. Dale is not to know that you're paying the bill?"

"Correct."

"Okeydokey," Marge said. "Whatever floats your boat."

As we ended the call, it occurred to me that this was the most amiable Marge Herndon had ever been. Maybe marriage was actually starting to agree with her and mellowing her out.

For the next fifteen minutes or so, I sat in the car holding Athena and trying to come to grips with the idea that this tiny human being, now sleeping peacefully in my arms was, unknowingly and through no fault of her own, sowing all kinds of chaos and complications wherever she went. She wasn't just disrupting Alan Dale's life, she was throwing my life into disorder as well, because by then I was pretty sure Athena Dale really was my own granddaughter. What in the hell was I going to do about that?

Alan appeared a few minutes later, wheeling the fully loaded luggage cart out to a rented Honda Accord parked three spaces from my Mercedes. With Athena in hand, I exited the S550 and went to join him. The first item he unloaded from the luggage cart was the infant seat, which he placed in the backseat on the Honda's passenger side.

"Go ahead and put Athena in that while I load everything else," he said.

It turns out my task assignment was easier said than done. It took me several false starts to finally manage to belt Athena into her infant seat, but when it came time to secure that with the vehicle's seat belts, I found that complex operation to be far above my pay grade. After filling the trunk, half the front seat, and half the backseat with accumulated stuff, Alan at last stepped forward to take charge of the seat-belt issue while I returned the cart to the hotel's front lobby.

When I came back, I handed Alan a Mapquest printout of how to get from hither to yon. He studied it for a moment.

"This doesn't look too hard," he said, "I think I can manage."

"Be advised," I warned him. "The map in your hand is for backup purposes only. What Mapquest doesn't understand is that due to the rapid expansion of the Amazon campus, the whole south Lake Union area is now one huge building project. Several of the streets they suggest you use to get from I-5 to Belltown Terrace are currently blocked for construction. I think we should take 45th over to I-5 and head south. We'll exit at Stewart, turn right onto Denny, take that all the way over to Second, and turn left on that. Belltown Terrace is a couple blocks down Second on the right. This route takes us a little out of the way, but it'll be better in terms of traffic."

"So I should just follow you?"

"Yes," I told him. "If we do get separated, once you're on Denny keep going until you hit Second. The garage entrance is off Clay one block beyond the light at Second and Broad. I'll wait for you inside the garage on the P-1 level and guide you down to our assigned parking places."

"I can't tell you how much I appreciate this," Alan said. There was a tear in his eye as he said the words—a tear I pretended was invisible.

"Not to worry," I said, clapping him on the shoulder. "I'm happy to help. If our situations were reversed, I'm sure you'd do the same. Are you all checked out?" He nodded. "Okay then, let's roll."

It was after eleven when we finally left the hotel and headed downtown. Fortunately, traffic was as reasonable as it ever gets around here. Most of the

University of Washington commuters were either at their desks or in class by then, so traffic through the University District wasn't all that bad. We made it down I-5 and onto Denny with no problem, but once we turned onto Denny, a bus pulled out of the bus lane directly behind me, slowing Alan down and blocking his view. Luckily, the last-minute directions I'd given him paid off. He caught up with me a minute or so after I pulled in to the P-1 level of Belltown Terrace's garage.

Mel's and my parking spaces are on level P-4. Once Alan arrived, I put the Mercedes in gear and led the way down to P-4, where I directed him into Mel's customary spot, the one nearest the elevator. After exiting the car, I handed him Mel's garage-door clicker to put on his window visor and gave him her set of keys.

"Belltown Terrace is a secure building," I explained. "When the garage door is closed, the remote will let you into the garage and give you access to the lower parking levels. This key lets you into the building's front entrance and into the garage-level elevator lobbies. Once inside the elevator, you'll also need to use the same key to operate the elevator from the garage levels. The other key lets you into the unit."

Alan clicked open the trunk on his rental. It was full, as was every inch of available space inside the car. "How the hell am I going to get all this crap upstairs?" he asked despairingly.

"Don't worry," I said. "I'll take Lucy and Athena with me. There's a grocery cart parked right there in the elevator lobby. Load as much as you can onto that. It'll most likely take more than one trip. Just remember to keep the elevator key with you at all times."

I held the lobby door open long enough for Alan to retrieve the P-4 grocery cart. Once he headed back to the car, I used my key to activate the penthouse button so Lucy, Athena, and I could head upstairs. The elevator stopped at the main lobby. When the door slid open, who should be standing there but Marge Herndon herself.

Spotting Bob, the doorman, over Marge's shoulder, I gave him a wave. I had called him during the drive into town to warn him that Mel and I were about to have guests staying over for the foreseeable future, so he was already in the know even before Marge showed up. Bob was on the phone, but he greeted me with an answering wave. It was, in fact, due to Bob's wife's long-term friendship with Marge that she had come into our lives in the first place.

"You're a little late, aren't you?" Marge grumbled, glancing reprovingly at her watch as she stepped into the elevator. "I thought you told me you'd be here by eleven."

"Sorry," I said. "That was the plan, but there were a few unavoidable delays."

"And I can't believe they let you bring that monster of a dog in here," she continued. "You're sure it'll be all right riding in the elevator?"

At that very moment, Lucy, was sitting quietly at my feet, behaving perfectly and minding her own business. In other words, Marge Herndon hadn't changed her stripes very much after all.

"Lucy will be fine," I assured Marge before deftly changing the subject. "How did you know we were here?"

"Bob saw you drive into the garage on one of his security monitors," Marge answered.

The door slid shut. "Presumably this is the little bundle of joy?" she asked, lifting a corner of the blanket and peering inside.

"Yes she is," I answered. "Meet Athena. I have it on good authority that she kept her grandpa up most of the night."

"All right, then." Marge sniffed, squaring her shoulders. "It sounds to me like I showed up just in the nick of time."

CHAPTER 6

UNSURPRISINGLY, MARGE MET up with Alan Dale and immediately took charge of the situation. She marched back down to the garage with him and returned a few minutes later with the P-3 grocery cart as well as the one from P-4, thus turning what would have taken three trips into two. Since I was staying over, I maintained possession of the master bedroom and moved the new arrivals into the guest room. When Mel and I don't have company, that room is mostly her private domain—a combination study/dressing room. When the room is needed for actual visitors, Mel and I share the master suite and we bring the guest room's Murphy bed into play.

In my experience most work crews function better if there's one person in charge and calling the shots. My efforts to assist Marge in the operation of the Murphy bed were (a) not appreciated and (b) unhelpful. Since I now had an actual clue to follow up on—the West Seattle address for Naomi Dale that Scotty had given me—Lucy and I bailed on the furniture-rearranging and grocery-stowing process in favor of going to work. Besides, why hang around where you're not wanted? Instead, after collecting my car from P-4, my partner and I headed for West Seattle.

I grew up in Ballard, a Seattle neighborhood that's located north of downtown proper and on the far side of the Ship Canal. Back when I was a kid, Ballard was mostly a Scandinavian enclave. Scotty and Cherisse's new house is only a few blocks from the location of the now-demolished apartment building where I grew up. In the intervening years, Ballard has become something of a melting pot, with far more of an international flair than when I lived there.

West Seattle is a mostly working-class neighborhood of the city, located west and a little to the south of downtown, on the far side of Harbor Island and Elliott Bay. So although both Ballard and West Seattle are part of Seattle proper, when I was growing up, West Seattle might just as well have been on the far side of the moon. I might have ventured across the Duwamish River a time or two for high-school basketball or football games, but for me and my pals West Seattle wasn't a place we visited of our own accord. There was plenty for us to do and plenty of mischief for us to get into much closer to home.

Later on, when I became a cop and even later a homicide detective, I was never assigned to the West Seattle Precinct, although I dealt with several cases that took me over there. As a result, to this day West Seattle remains pretty much terra incognita as far as I'm concerned. Consequently, that early afternoon, before ever leaving the garage at Belltown Terrace, I keyed the address on 24th Avenue SW into my GPS.

I set off with a hopeful heart, heading south on Second Avenue on my way to the West Seattle Bridge. A few years ago, on the occasion of my knee-replacement surgery, Second Avenue still functioned as a relatively fast and convenient route for traversing the downtown area. Sadly, that is no longer the case. Construction projects abound. The proliferation of bike paths that give bikers the right of way and slow down everybody else has turned Second Avenue into a gridlock nightmare morning, noon, and night. Traffic was heavy enough that it made me think about how slow progress must have been for Seattle's founding fathers when Arthur Denny and the rest of his crew crossed the country by wagon train close to a century and a half ago.

Most of the people who made the long and arduous trek with him had come west looking for suitable farmland. Once they made it as far as Portland, the majority of the group took one look at the Willamette Valley and decided to stay put. Denny, on the other hand, saw himself as a businessman rather than a farmer. He, along with his family and a small group of like-minded pals, wanted something different—they were intent on locating a place where they could establish a new city. They boarded a ship, the schooner *Exact*, and sailed north along the coast. (I have no idea why that shard of memory—the ship's name—has stuck with me through all the decades between now and the time

I took the required Washington Constitution class in eighth grade!)

At any rate, Denny's group came ashore at Alki Point in Duwamish Bay in the midst of a cold November only to discover that someone had screwed up. The cabin they'd planned to use for shelter during the winter months was not yet completed. They finished building it and moved in, but the months they spent there were cold, wet, and miserable. Not only did they have to deal with constant rain, they were also at the mercy of unpredictable tides and currents. When spring finally arrived the next year, they went looking for greener pastures, leaving Alki Point in the dust and settling on a site near Elliott Bay, which is where downtown Seattle is now located. Over time West Seattle developed into a mostly residential area filled with relatively inexpensive bungalows that provided affordable housing for the families of people who worked in the industrial areas that eventually grew up to the south of what is now downtown Seattle.

With the GPS guiding the way to 10100 SW 24th Avenue SW, Lucy and I crossed the West Seattle Bridge onto Fauntleroy and then south on 35th Avenue SW. The only big surprise along the way was my learning, by motoring past the location, that there's now an outpost of my favorite local barbecue joint—Pecos Pit Bar-B-Que—in West Seattle.

The drive down 35th seemed to take forever, but I have to say traffic there moved a hell of a lot better than it does on Second Avenue in downtown Seattle. I turned left onto Roxbury and then right on

24th. As soon as the GPS announced that we had arrived at our destination, I could see the problem. On the house in question, the windows and doors were all boarded up, with colorful bits of graffiti covering every available surface. An official-looking sign of some sort had been affixed to the chunk of plywood that stood in for a front door. Examining the derelict, I realized Scotty was right. This might have been Naomi Dale's address once, but that was no longer the case. The place was completely deserted.

Driving past, I noticed an oversize billboard in the weed-choked yard next door. The sign claimed that a subdivision called Mayfield Glen, a development containing eight homes with prices starting in the mid-$900,000s, would be coming soon to this location, compliments of Highline Development. The billboard was up, but there was no accompanying Environmental Impact Statement sign anywhere in sight. That meant that construction on this little McMansion project, all its houses with close to zero lot lines, wouldn't be starting anytime soon.

I parked at the base of the billboard. Then, with Lucy on a leash, the two of us set out on an exploratory stroll around the neighborhood. I had driven in rain coming south from Bellingham. Things had dried out somewhat during my wait at the Silver Cloud, but now as we exited the car, the drizzle started up again. To begin with, it was more of a cold mist than a real downpour—not enough to warrant bringing along either the umbrella or the rainproof jacket that I generally keep in the trunk.

The Mayfield Glen project's outer perimeter was fenced off with a cordon of orange netting. Inside I spotted four houses, which had at one time been small but identical wood-frame bungalows. Now all four were in various stages of decay. Three of them were boarded up and decked out with layers of competing graffiti. There was a gaping hole in the roof of one. On another the front porch had collapsed and fallen away from the remainder of the building. Two of the four, including the one where Naomi had lived and the one next door, seemed close to being habitable. At least their mossy roofs were still intact, and the front porches were still attached. It made me sad to realize that these humble little places had once been homes filled with proud working families, their lives and laughter. Now they were forlorn, abandoned ruins, awaiting the inevitable arrival of bulldozers and wrecking balls.

"Well," I said aloud to Lucy, "it looks to me like whoever runs Highline Development came here bargain shopping and is about to make a killing."

In the latest iteration of *Magnum, P.I.* on TV, the guy goes around wrecking his pal's Ferraris with astonishing regularity and discussing his exploits with a good-looking blonde who happens to be a retired secret agent. Scenes containing both characters are filled with plenty of flirting, complete with banter filled with all kinds of sexual innuendos. I, on the other hand, was reduced to discussing my cases with a dog. Was that a surprise? Not really. I admit I was a bit startled the first few times I found myself talking to Lucy, but I'm used to it now. I especially like the fact that she doesn't talk back, although she always appears to be interested in what I'm saying and maintains steady eye contact. Besides, she was here as my backup, and I felt it was important to keep the lines of communication between me and my partner up and running.

By the time Lucy and I finished our little walk, the mist had morphed into a drenching rain, and we were both soaked. I keep a canvas seat saver in the backseat of the S550. That way, if Lucy has wet or muddy paws when she climbs into the car, she doesn't get dirt all over the leather upholstery. After putting her into the backseat, I found myself wondering about the official-looking sign I'd seen plastered on that hunk of front-door plywood. Leaving Lucy in the car, I hiked a leg over the orange netting barrier and walked up to what had once been Naomi Dale's house.

Here the porch was still attached, but it was nonetheless very dicey. The wood surfaces were all coated with moss, and as soon as I started up the steps, I slipped and tumbled right back down. I wasn't hurt. I had landed in muddy grass that was forgiving enough that I didn't damage either of my fake knees, but by the time I got back on my feet, I discovered that an invisible nail on the step railing had taken a gouge out of my jacket sleeve, tearing the material, but without slicing into the skin of my forearm. The poor blazer, which had been fresh from the cleaners that morning, was now both dirty and done for.

Up close and personal, the posted sign was official and to the point: THIS PROPERTY CONDEMNED! The fine print declared that the residence had been red-flagged by the city building inspectors and was no longer fit for human habitation. The sign was dated December 23, 2016.

"Way to go, guys," I muttered under my breath, addressing any number of nameless and faceless city bureaucrats and building inspectors. Obviously the powers-that-be at city hall had nothing on Charles Dickens's good old Mr. Scrooge and had seen fit to throw a pregnant woman out onto the streets just in time for Christmas. Happy holidays indeed!

About that time Lucy started barking like mad. Hurrying toward the Mercedes, I saw a white-haired woman wearing a bright yellow slicker and using a walker standing near my car. As I headed in that direction, she hobbled away from the Mercedes with Lucy still inside and voicing her very strenuous objections. Spotting me, the woman stopped short and waited while I scrambled back over the netting.

Looking at her, I had no idea how old she might be, although I estimated her age to be somewhere in the neighborhood of upper eighties to low nineties. A prominent widow's hump was so severe that she had to look at me sideways as I approached, peering up at me through thick, Coke-bottle lenses.

"And just who might you be?" she demanded.

I learned a long time ago that a homicide investigator's best friend is often the nosy little old lady who lives next door. Eventually that might prove true in this case as well, but for right now she was regarding me with enough ferocity that I was afraid she was going to haul off and whack me over the head with her walker.

"My name is J. P. Beaumont," I told her. "I'm a private investigator. And you are?"

"Hilda," the old lady said. "Hilda Tanner, but most people call me Hildie."

I reached into the side pocket of my soaked jacket and dug out what was now a very soggy business card. The cards were newly printed and had come in a box with a little faux leather carrier, which I'd left behind that morning when I slipped several pristine cards into the pocket of my freshly dry-cleaned jacket. Now the cards were even worse for wear than the jacket, but that wasn't much of an issue, since Hilda dropped the card into the pocket of her slicker without giving it a glance.

"Investigating what?" my inquisitor wanted to know.

"A missing person," I said, "a young woman named Naomi Dale, who according to my records used to live here."

"I'm surprised you're smart enough to investigate anything, since you don't have enough good sense to come in out of the rain," Hilda Tanner sniffed. "And why on earth would anybody drive around in a fancy car like that with a ferocious wet dog locked in the backseat?"

I started to say that Lucy wasn't ferocious at all—that she was doing her job and defending my property, but taking a hint from Thumper's father, I kept my mouth shut.

"Naomi," Hilda mused then, with a faraway look in her rheumy eyes. "Yes, that was the name of Petey's girlfriend. The last time I saw her, she was PG—quite a ways along, in fact. I wondered if the kid was Petey's child or someone else's, but of course that was none of my business."

The term PG used as a synonym for pregnancy was something I hadn't heard in a long time. It was a word my mother had employed when one or another of her clients had come looking for wardrobe updates that would accommodate "being in a family way." Scott and Cherisse talked about having a "bun in the oven," but nobody talked about being PG anymore. And looking at Hilda Tanner, I suddenly realized that this spry but seemingly ancient woman and my mother had probably been contemporaries. As for the identity of the father of Naomi Dale's baby? That might have been none of Hilda Tanner's business, but it was certainly mine.

"Petey?" I ventured. "Can you tell me Petey's last name?"

"Mayfield," she answered at once. "His given name is really Peter, after his grandfather, but I've always known him as Petey. He was the apple of his grandmother's eye—until he went off the rails, that is. Even so, Agnes never gave up on him. Petey was in and out of jail and in and out of rehab—drugs, you see—but Agnes always let him come home, gave him and whatever riffraff he dragged home with him a place to stay and food to eat and never charged anybody a dime of rent either. Generous to a fault, poor Agnes was, may she rest in peace."

"Agnes died?" I asked.

Hilda nodded. "Several months ago, evidently, but I only just found out. Wasn't able to go to the funeral. In fact, I don't even know if there was one. It's a crying shame."

"Do you have any idea where Petey is now?" I asked.

"Beats me," she said. "He comes and goes like that. He took off last fall sometime and left that poor girl there all alone. Agnes had been carted off to a nursing home or some such several months earlier. I couldn't help but feel sorry for . . . What did you say her name was?"

"Naomi," I answered. "Her name is Naomi Dale."

"Well," Hilda resumed, "she stayed on until just before Christmas. That's when those guys from the city came by and threw her out. Last I saw of her, she was walking down the street pushing a grocery cart loaded with as many of her worldly goods as she could manage. They were covered with a blue tarp and stacked so high I'm surprised she could see over the pile."

Clearly Hilda Tanner was a font of knowledge when it came to things I needed to know. To that end I wanted to be on her good side.

"Is there somewhere we could go to talk?" I asked.

She glared at me. "You're not a serial killer, are you?" she demanded. "If so, you should be advised that I'm armed and dangerous. I never step out of the house these days without carrying my late husband's loaded .22 revolver—there's too much crime around here and too many gangs. If some young punk looks at me and thinks I'm a helpless little old lady, he has another think coming."

And so did I. When cops on the street encounter concealed weapons, someone yells "Gun!" and everyone dives for cover. When Mel had insisted

I bring Lucy along as backup—a backup who was currently locked away in the car, it's worth noting—I don't think she ever envisioned my being caught up in an armed confrontation with a gun-wielding octo- or nonagenarian. I hadn't envisioned it either. (By the way, if you're questioning my use of the term "nonagenarian," that kind of useless knowledge is what a lifetime of working crossword puzzles will do for you!)

"Definitely not a serial killer, ma'am," I said politely. "I spent more than twenty years with Seattle PD."

Hilda was not impressed. "Doing what?" she asked disparagingly. "Issuing parking tickets?"

"I was a homicide detective for most of that time."

"Well, then," she said. "In that case I suppose you must be reasonably trustworthy. We'd better go inside and get you out of that wet jacket before you catch your death of cold, but that dog of yours is definitely not welcome. I have cats, you see, and bringing a dog into the house simply wouldn't do."

CHAPTER 7

HILDA TANNER LED me to a house situated directly across the street from the mostly uninhabitable collection of tumbledown wrecks that had belonged to the late Agnes Mayfield. Hilda's house sported a relatively well-maintained roof and was set in a spick-and-span yard. Her lot, like the others on the street, was fairly deep, and I was pretty sure that if and when she got around to wanting to unload the property, some gung ho developer would be more than happy to add at least two more McMansions to this still-dowdy, working-class neighborhood. I followed Hilda as she made her way up the walk and then used a zigzagging wheelchair ramp to negotiate the six steep steps leading up to the deck of her front porch.

"They built the ramp for my late husband," Hilda explained, answering my unasked question. "Clyde died five years ago. Randy, my son, wanted to take the ramp out, but I told him to leave it be. After all, I was getting up in years, too, and I could see that one day it might come in handy for me as well. What do you know! Now it has, but I didn't start using it until I was damned good and ready." With that she opened the door and gestured me inside.

Hilda Tanner had mentioned she had cats, and given her obvious eccentricity, I should have realized that meant she had more than two. I counted seven at least, but there were likely more lurking in other rooms. The place reeked with the eye-watering odor of litter boxes that weren't emptied nearly often enough. The interior of the place wasn't just hot, it was boiling. If the thermostat was set at anything under eighty degrees, I'd be surprised.

Hilda stopped just inside the door long enough to whip off her rain slicker and hang it on a wooden hook. As soon as she did so, I saw the telltale bulge of that .22 revolver weighing down the right-hand pocket of the old-fashioned wraparound apron she wore underneath. I was relieved when she took the handgun out of her pocket and laid it on the kitchen counter. Then she pulled a chair away from the dining-room table and stationed it next to a heat register.

"You might want to hang your jacket here," she said. "It'll dry quicker if you're not wearing it." Intent on being a good guest, I was busy complying when she asked, "What can I get you—a cup of tea, maybe?"

I looked down at the immense black cat sprawled across the center of the dining-room table. He had raised his head at my approach and was regarding me with some suspicion. It seemed likely that any cup of tea would be served with a healthy dose of cat hair.

"Thanks, I'm good," I said. "I don't want to be any bother."

After divesting myself of the jacket, I retreated to the living-room space and settled into a butt-sprung easy chair while Hilda bustled around the kitchen preparing her own mug of tea. "Randy keeps telling me I should move into some form of assisted living, but none of those places allow pets, and I'm not leaving here without taking my precious kitties along. That means I won't be leaving here until they drag me out toes-up."

What would become of Hilda's "precious" kitties at that point was something it was best not to consider.

Hilda came back to the dining room with a steaming mug in hand and used one arm to brush the cat off the table and onto a chair before taking a seat. "Shoo, Rocky," she ordered as the offended animal hopped off the chair and sidled away, lashing his tail and leveling a reproachful look in her direction as he departed. "You know you're not supposed to be up here," she told him. "Now, where were we?"

I had left my iPad in the car. Wanting to have a record of our conversation, I hauled out my phone instead and then joined her at the dining table. "Do you mind if I record this interview?"

"Heavens no," Hilda said. "Go right ahead. What do you want to know?"

It took a moment to get my phone's recording app up and running. "What can you tell me about the Mayfields?"

"Pretty much everything," she told me. "We were neighbors and good friends for years and years. Peter Mayfield's people came here to West Seattle early on, you know," Hilda answered.

"What do you mean by 'early on'—as in pioneers?" I asked.

She nodded. "His great-grandfather, Harold Mayfield, didn't show up with the Dennys and all those other first-on-the-ground guys, but Harold's arrival wasn't all that much later. He laid claim to a chunk of land, cleared off the trees, and started a dairy farm. During the Roaring Twenties, when housing was in short supply, Pete's grandfather Richard, who inherited the property from Harold, cut what he thought was going to be a great deal with a local builder. They subdivided the farm and turned it into a slew of lots. Rather than giving Richard cash money for the land, they worked out an arrangement so each of his four sons would come away with his own lot, along with a brand-new house that was bought and paid for. Those were the first houses to be built. The contractor and Richard expected to split the proceeds from the sale of all the other houses. Three or four more houses, including this one, got built before the crash happened, and that was the end of that. After that, the whole project ground to a halt."

The crash in question was obviously the one in 1929. All of this was interesting, of course, but it was also ancient history. Still, it seemed best to let the old lady tell the story in her own rambling way. "The Mayfields lost everything?" I asked.

"Yup, every single thing except for those four newly built houses. Figuring he was going to make a fortune selling the other houses, the old man had mortgaged the original farmhouse to the hilt in order to pay building costs. He lost that, too, and ended up committing suicide. The family managed to hold on to the other four houses during the Depression, but only just barely.

"When World War II came along, all four brothers enlisted in the army. Pete, Agnes's husband, was at Normandy for D-day and fought in the Battle of the Bulge. Of the four boys, he was the only one who came home. Since none of the other brothers had kids or wives when they died, Peter inherited the other three houses and hung on to them as well, renting them out some of the time, paying the taxes, and thinking that one day they'd be worth a pretty penny. Peter and Agnes married right after the war, and the two of them looked after his widowed mother, which probably explains why they didn't have kids of their own until later in life. That woman was a handful. When Peter died, Agnes ended up with the whole shebang. She probably should have sold out a long time ago, but like a lot of people our age, she was set in her ways."

"So what did Peter do once he came back from overseas?" I asked.

"He went to work for that steel company over by the Duwamish. My husband, Clyde, worked there, too. That's where they met and became friends. Pete was the one who told us the house across the street from his—one of the few from that original project—was about to be sold. We managed to snap it up, and we've been here ever since." Then, after a pause, she corrected, "*I've* been here ever since. But Pete and Clyde carpooled back and forth to work for years, right up until Clyde got hurt. Pete passed away in the late seventies. I forget which year."

"But he and Agnes had kids?" I prodded.

Hilda nodded. "That's right—a boy and a girl, Lenora and Arthur. Lenora was whip-smart and pretty as all get-out, but mean, just like that grand-mother of hers. Lenora's married to some kind of Microsoft bigwig and lives over in Bellevue."

"Any idea what her last name is?"

"Nope." Hilda's answer was delivered in a manner that hinted there might be more to the story, and it turns out there was. "Lenora was always bright, but like I said, not only was she mean, she was also on the uppity side—thought she was better than anybody else. She went off to college, got her degree, and has been looking down on her West Seattle roots ever since. Although now that it's turned into something of a gold mine for her, she may have had a change in attitude if not a change of heart, at least as far as West Seattle is concerned."

"A gold mine?" I asked.

"According to what I heard, Lenora didn't bother waiting around until poor Agnes was in her grave before selling the properties right out from under her."

"You're saying Lenora is the one who arranged the Mayfield Glen deal with the developer?"

"That's my understanding," Hilda said. "There's

supposed to be an estate sale at Agnes's place next weekend—not this weekend but the one after this. Once that's over, all four of the houses will be bulldozed to smithereens, the trees will be clear-cut, and a whole batch of those ugly box houses will be going up. So long to my view, such as it is."

"And you don't remember her last name?" I asked.

"Nope," Hilda declared. "If I ever did know it, I blocked it out long ago. She got married at some fancy church over on the Eastside. Clyde and her father were the best of friends, but we weren't good enough to be invited to the wedding. Pete never would have stood for our being treated like that, but he was gone by then, and Lenora always ran roughshod over her mother. So Clyde and I didn't go, and I haven't had a single thing to do with Lenora ever since."

Obviously there was no love lost there, probably not on either side. I might be able to dredge the woman's name out of property records, but the most direct route would be to stop by the developer's office and ask. I paused long enough to write a reminder to myself to that effect.

"Anyway," Hilda continued, "I would have hated to be in Agnes's shoes with my end-of-life arrangements in the hands of that snot-nosed bitch, pardon my French! And once Agnes passed on, Lenora didn't even bother to let us know so her friends could attend her services. Can you imagine? Unforgivable, if you ask me."

Lenora No Last Name certainly sounded like a piece of work. "What about Lenora's brother?" I asked. "What became of him?"

"Poor Arthur," Hilda murmured sadly with a shake of her head. "Coming behind an older sister who was such an all-star would have been bad enough, but Arthur was, well . . . slow. He was a cute kid, skinny as a rail, but when it came to school, he was a real dunce. He got held back a couple of grades in grammar school and was always in the principal's office because he was too busy being the class clown to bother doing his schoolwork.

"Agnes was in her forties when she had Arthur," Hilda added, "and babies with older mothers sometimes have problems. I asked Agnes a couple of years ago if it was possible that Arthur was dyslexic. Nobody knew much about those kinds of things back in the old days. Arthur dropped out of school when he was a freshman in high school. Never was able to hold much of a job, drank too much, and turned into a loser through and through. I've always thought the same thing was true of Petey— that he was just a chip off the old block. I'm sure that's why Agnes always looked out for him the way she did, but then she mostly raised him, so what else would you expect?"

"She raised him?" I asked.

"Pretty much," Hilda replied. "Arthur was nineteen when he got his seventeen-year-old girlfriend pregnant. Sadie wanted to give the baby up for adoption. Agnes wouldn't hear of it. The kids got married in your basic shotgun-style wedding. Clyde and I were invited to that one, but the marriage didn't last. A couple of years later, Sadie ran off with someone else. She left Petey behind, ostensibly in the care of his dad and grandmother, but the truth was, he was mostly with Agnes. Arthur was in and out of Petey's life for a while, but he died in a car wreck when the boy was in his early teens."

So here we were with another generation of less-than-fit parents. I was hearing the sound of history repeating itself—of people making the same kinds of bad decisions and passing them down as a legacy from one generation to the next—from Arthur to Petey and now from Petey to Athena. Although I had to admit, when it came to making bad multi-generational decisions, I didn't have a hell of a lot of room to talk.

"What can you tell me about Petey?" I wondered. "How old is he?"

"Don't know exactly. Late twenties, I suppose, or maybe early thirties. He started acting out after his father died. Got into trouble his sophomore year of high school and ended up getting expelled. I don't think he ever even got a GED. He ended up in juvie first and then did a couple of stints in the King County Jail when he was older. Once he got into drugs, he was a lost cause. Whenever he got desperate enough or broke enough, he'd come home to Agnes. After she caught him stealing from her, she no longer let him stay at the house, but she did allow him to hang out in the house that had once belonged to Pete's brother—to Arthur's Uncle Warren. She let him bunk in there whenever he needed to, but he's been gone for a while now, too," Hilda added after a pause.

"Since last fall?" I asked.

She nodded. "Just before it started getting cold and wet. It wasn't all that unusual for him to be gone for months at a time before he'd turn back up again. The last time I caught sight of him wasn't very long before the power got shut off."

"The power to the place where Naomi and Petey were living?" I asked.

Hilda nodded again. "I'm guessing that once Lenora took charge of Agnes's affairs, she turned off the utilities."

"Did Lenora know that Naomi and Petey were staying in one of the houses?"

"I couldn't say," Hilda answered. "Maybe she did, maybe she didn't."

"So Petey took off, leaving Naomi alone with no heat or water?"

"I guess," Hilda replied. "I never saw anyone else over there with her."

"Did you ever talk to her?"

"I tried, but you know how people like that are—suspicious of everyone, skittish. I saw her sitting out on the porch from time to time—smoking. Once I went over to have a word with her, just to be polite, but she got up, turned her back on me, and went inside the house. Not very neighborly, if you ask me, and you'd think she'd know better than to smoke when she's expecting, but that's the way kids are these days."

It turned out that smoking cigarettes while pregnant was the least of Naomi's transgressions. Naomi Dale and Petey Mayfield were both way too old to qualify as kids. So much for that lame excuse!

"What about Agnes?" I asked. "Did she have any kind of relationship with Naomi?"

"Not so's you'd notice," Hilda told me. "By last

spring Agnes was starting to have memory lapses. Even if the two of them were best of friends, Agnes might not have remembered from one day to the next. We neighbors all took turns looking in on her and making sure she was all right. Then one day Lenora came riding in on her high horse—or should I say broom? She picked up her mother and carted her off without ever bothering to tell any of Agnes's friends that they were leaving or where she was going."

Yes, Lenora No Last Name really was a piece of work.

I glanced at my watch. Lucy was still locked up in the car, and it was far later than I expected. Even if we left right now, rush hour would be in full swing by the time we made it to the West Seattle Bridge.

"Thank you for all your help, Mrs. Tanner," I said, shutting off the recording app on the phone. "I should go. I've taken up too much of your time."

"But what about the girl?" Hilda asked. "You told me earlier that Naomi was missing. Are you going to be able to find her?"

"I hope so, but I don't know. These days there are lots of people in Seattle living out of grocery carts covered with blue tarps."

"Where did she come from originally?" Hilda asked.

"Texas, I believe."

"Well, I hope she's all right," Hilda added, "and the baby, too. She must have had it by now. Will you let me know if you find out anything? That baby would be Agnes's great-grandchild, you see, and I'd like to know if it's okay."

"The baby's fine," I said. "Her name is Athena, and she was born at the end of January. The one who's gone missing and may not be all right is Naomi."

"But you'll let me know when you find her?" Hilda insisted.

"Of course," I said, making a promise I wasn't at all sure I could make good on. "I'll try to keep you in the loop."

CHAPTER 8

I'D BEEN GONE for a long time, but unlike Hilda Tanner's Rocky, Lucy doesn't hold grudges. She greeted me with a thumping tail wag and immediately assumed her customary automotive position with her chin glued to my shoulder.

Walking to the car, I had noticed that although my jacket had mostly dried out, my shoes hadn't. But dry or not, the jacket was in exceptionally sorry shape. Earlier I'd made note of the developer listed on the coming-attractions sign located on Agnes Mayfield's property—Highline Development. A quick check on line told me that the Highline corporate office was only a mile or so away, right there in West Seattle. It would have been simple to stop by in passing, but then something my mother always used to say came to mind: "You never get a second chance to make a good first impression."

Right then my torn and mud-splattered jacket wasn't nearly up to "good first impression" standards. Between that and the reality of worsening afternoon traffic, I headed for Belltown Terrace instead, hoping there would be no unfortunate mishaps between hither and yon. One of Seattle's most spectacular traffic-jam events featured a semi loaded with frozen crab that had overturned near the West Seattle Bridge, turning hour-long commutes into six-hour nightmares. (If you think I'm kidding about that, you can always Google it and see for yourself!)

While my jacket might not have been fit for a drop-in visit to a real-estate developer's office, it was just fine for stopping by the Pecos Pit Bar-B-Que. As I said, the outlet in West Seattle was brand-new—at least it was new to me. For decades Pecos Pit operated out of a born-again gas station across from Sears on Seattle's First Avenue South. That's how people used to give directions to the place—it's right across from Sears. Now that Sears is going the way of the dodo bird, those directions no longer work. The building once occupied by Sears now functions as the headquarters for Starbucks. From what I understand, Safeco Field is about to be renamed for a cell-phone company, and the Kingdome is long gone, too. Clearly I'm turning into one of those cranky old codgers who pine for the way things used to be as opposed to appreciating how they are now. But I digress. Again!

At Pecos Pit I ordered up some carry-out dinner fixings—a quart each of beef brisket, baked beans, and coleslaw in foam containers along with a dozen sesame-seed-covered hamburger buns. For dinner that evening, I'd be serving barbecue-beef sandwiches, some assembly required.

I was standing at the counter waiting while the staff put together my to-go order when my phone rang, Al Thorne's name appearing in the caller ID. Clearly he was off work now and using his cell phone.

"How's it hanging?" he asked when I answered.

Al's standard bad-taste greeting never varies. His sense of humor is only one step up from fourth-grade-level knock-knock jokes, and he's a walking, talking catalog of clichés, but he's a good guy with a heart in the right place, so I try to overlook his linguistic shortcomings. Since he was calling me, I assumed that meant he had news.

"What have you got for me?" I asked.

"The Mount Baker Tunnel," he replied.

The Mount Baker Tunnel is on I-90 between the bridge across Lake Washington from Mercer Island and the Rainier Avenue interchange. When you're traveling westbound, that's the first freeway exit inside Seattle proper.

"What is this?" I asked. "An afternoon traffic report?"

"That's where the aid car picked up Naomi Dale, just to the west of the Mount Baker Tunnel," he told me. Somehow or other she made it over the Jersey barrier and was standing there on the shoulder of the interstate, trying to wave down a passing vehicle. A Metro bus driver called it in. She was staggering all over the place, and he said he missed hitting her by bare inches. The poor guy almost crapped his pants. If he *had* hit her, she would have been squashed flatter than a pancake—her and that unborn baby of hers, too. When a squad car showed up, the cops on the scene figured out she was in labor. They're the ones who summoned the ambulance. The EMT didn't know what she was on at the time, but he told me she was high as a kite. He said they dropped her off at Harborview at eleven forty-five the night of January twenty-third.

"And Athena was born a while after that," I concluded.

"Any luck getting a line on the missing mama?" Al asked.

"Not so far," I replied. "I found out where Naomi used to live and got a line on who the likely father might be, but I have no clue about what became of her after she left the hospital."

"How's the baby doing?" Al wanted to know.

"As far as I can tell, the baby's doing fine. It's her grandfather I'm worried about. The poor guy is in his sixties and has worn himself down to a nub looking after a newborn on his own. I'm letting them stay at my Seattle condo for the time being, until he can get the parental-rights thing handled. And I've hired someone to come in and take over some of the baby-tending duties so he can have a moment to himself—maybe even take a nap."

"I remember how that worked," Al said. "The wife and I had two kids under the age of three, and I don't think either Jan or I got more than an hour's worth of sleep at a time, and that was with two of us looking after them. I can't imagine surviving looking after a newborn all on my own, especially not as old as I am now. Let me know if there's anything more I can do to help."

"You already have helped," I told him. "Thanks for that."

My order came up. To spare Lucy any kind of temptation, I loaded the food in the trunk for what turned out to be an excruciatingly slow trip home. My first choice for getting back to Belltown Terrace from West Seattle has always been Highway 99 to the two-level roadway called the Alaskan Way Viaduct, where I exit at Columbia and then make my way northward to Belltown through downtown Seattle. The local traffic planners, an oxymoron if ever there was one, have decided in their infinite wisdom that the sixty-year-old viaduct has to go, and in a year or thereabouts it'll be torn down. So whenever I drive that way now, it's with an advanced case of separation anxiety. On this trip my sense of unease was exacerbated by my singular lack of progress on the case.

If anything, my afternoon chat with Hilda Tanner had elicited a lot of information, none of it helpful to my client. If anything, it had made things worse. Now instead of needing to locate one missing person, I needed to locate two—Alan's daughter, Naomi, and her AWOL boyfriend or maybe spouse, Petey Mayfield. I suspected him of being Athena's supposedly "unknown" father. Once he was located, and if a DNA match revealed him to be her biological father, then Alan would need both Naomi and Petey to relinquish their parental rights. Good luck with that! They sure as hell didn't seem to be taking much responsibility at the moment!

Driving north on Fourth Avenue, between Stewart and Bell, there's a point during that stretch of street when suddenly the futuristic centerpiece of the Seattle's World Fair, the Space Needle, materializes right there in front of you. It's one of those deals where, because of surrounding buildings, now you see it, now you don't. That day in the traffic barely inching northward, seeing the Space Needle suddenly appear sent me down a rabbit hole of memory.

I graduated from Ballard High School in 1962. Commercial fishing was a way of life in Ballard back then, and most of my friends spent their summers working with the fishing fleet on family boats—boats that belonged to their fathers or their uncles—and they made tons of money doing so. I tried fishing once and was sent home in disgrace with a nearly fatal case of seasickness. So that summer after graduation, when all my pals took to sea, I went to work at the World's Fair as a groundskeeper. I worked the late shift, and when the monorail cars finished their last runs of the evening, one of my jobs involved cleaning them.

The whole time I was growing up, I loved bubble gum. That one summer of cleaning those cars cured me of bubble gum for life.

Be that as it may, the other thing that summer did for me was turn me into a Space Needle junkie. My kids and grandkids have loved having dinners in the revolving restaurant at the top. It used to be that whenever the Space Needle came into sight in the Seattle skyline, either driving or flying, I always felt a profound sense of homecoming, but now everything has changed.

That appalling traffic accident, the one that cost Ross Connors his life and Harry I. Ball his legs, has colored my thinking about the Space Needle. At the time it happened, Seattle Center had been full of merrymakers celebrating the season and the Needle itself had been decked out like a Christmas tree. Having lives snuffed out or permanently changed against that backdrop of seasonal celebration had infused a dose of melancholy to my attitude toward the Space Needle. That afternoon driving home from West Seattle, rather than seeing it as welcoming, I felt something close to despair.

The parking garage was still open, so I left the bags of food from Pecos Pit with the parking attendant and took Lucy to the dog-walking area just across from the garage entrance.

Through the years what was once routinely referred to as the Denny Regrade has morphed into being called Belltown. When I first moved into my condo, the building across the street was a union hall. Over time, the union sold out and the building was occupied by one of those megachurches. The Congregation remodeled the interior but left behind a small patch of grass—the only one for blocks, as it turns out. As a public service, the church maintains that as a dog-walking area. Until Lucy came into my life, that part of the church's good-neighbor policy was entirely invisible to me.

Originally this was just a harmless piece of grassy lawn, but now, like the Space Needle, the churchyard, too, had taken on a darker meaning. This was the place where Ken Purcell had come looking for Mel, with the deadliest of intentions in his heart and a knife in hand. It's the place where I came close to losing both Mel and Lucy. The dog had deflected Purcell's attack on Mel, and he had stabbed Lucy instead. With Lucy out of commission, the only thing that had turned the tide of battle in our favor had been the timely intervention of a homeless guy named Sam Shelton and his trusty pit bull, Billy Bob. With Lucy down for the count, Sam and Billy Bob had sprung into action. Not only had Sam's dog disarmed the asshole, he'd done a credible job of mangling the guy's hand before Sam saw fit to call him off.

I had subsequently learned that Sam, an imposingly large and scary-looking black man, is also a Vietnam vet suffering from PTSD. Because he can't tolerate being in crowds or enclosed spaces, he remains unwaveringly homeless. A fire-escape alcove from the church basement is his residence of choice, and he and Billy Bob spend their nights there, summer and winter, sleeping under the collection of tarps and blankets that Sam rolls around in an overburdened grocery cart.

After that almost-fatal encounter, I'd gone looking for Mel's saviors. I had wanted to help them and even went so far as to locate a shelter where both man and beast would have been welcome. Sam's response had been, "Thanks, but no thanks. Let us be." So I'd backed off and minded my own business, but these days whenever I walked Lucy, I was sure to have a spare bag of kibble or a Milk Bone in my pocket for Billy Bob. This time was no exception, but since it was too early and they had not yet arrived on the scene, the kibble remained in my pocket.

Once Lucy finished up, we headed back inside. On the way through P-1, I noticed that Marge's Kia Sportage was still parked in one of the public parking stalls, but once we arrived upstairs, she was nowhere in sight and neither was anyone else. I put the food bags on the counter and was feeding Lucy when Alan Dale finally made his appearance. He came into the kitchen carrying a basket of freshly laundered baby clothes and set about folding them.

"Hey," I said, "how are things going?"

All afternoon I'd been wondering and worrying about how Alan and Marge would get along. His response surprised me.

"Where on earth did you find that wonderful woman?" he asked.

For me, as far as wonderful women are concerned, Mel Soames is the first name that comes to mind. "Which wonderful woman?" I asked.

"Marge," he answered. "She's a treasure. I got to sleep for three straight hours this afternoon and took a long, hot shower besides. By the time I woke up and came out of the bathroom, Marge had already done three loads of laundry."

I don't mind being wrong, but being wrong twice—first about Harry I. Ball and Marge and now about her and Alan Dale—was downright perturbing. The truth was, though, Alan looked far better than he had earlier that morning at the Silver Cloud. The dark shadows under his eyes were slightly less exaggerated, and I suspected that those three hours of sleep were more than he'd had at one time for as long as he'd been in Seattle.

Rather than comment on any of that, I focused on the food. "I picked up some takeout on the way home. Are you hungry?"

"Starving," he said.

So even though it was earlier than Mel's and my usual dinnertime, I heated the brisket and the baked beans. Alan and I were in the kitchen chowing down a few minutes later when Marge emerged from the guest room with baby Athena in hand. Marge deposited the baby in a little seat of some kind—a kind of slinglike thing that kept Athena at a gentle thirty-five-degree angle.

"Now that you're finally home," Marge said, giving me one of her disquieting looks, "I should probably head out soon."

It occurred to me that if Marge made it to age ninety, she'd be able to give Hilda Tanner a run for her money.

"I know Harry used to love food from Pecos Pit," I said. "Would you like me to bag up a to-go order for you both?"

"Probably a good idea," she agreed grudgingly. "I'll be getting home too late to cook."

By then Alan was well into his second brisket sandwich and eating like he was one of those starving children from China my mother always used to warn me about. I left my own sandwich resting on my plate long enough to box up food for Harry and Marge. Even so, when I finished, I could see there was still more than enough left over for another meal for Alan, Mel, and me.

"Thanks," Marge said as I handed her the to-go bag. "By the way, the rocker's from Mrs. Bailey down in 1703."

"What rocker?" I asked.

Marge gave me another stink eye. "If you're going to have a baby around, you need to have a rocking chair," she advised. "I asked Bob at the front door to track one down for us. It's on loan for the duration."

With that she flounced out, taking her food and her oversize purse with her.

"I can't believe it," Alan marveled after she left. "Marge is really terrific. She suggested that maybe I should try to grab a nap. While I was sleeping, she put away all the groceries, fed Athena, bathed her, and did a bunch of laundry. And once I woke up, being able to shower at leisure without worrying was amazing. Marge also said that she's willing to drop by and help out whenever I need her. In fact, she's coming back tomorrow so I can go talk with Athena's caseworker from Child Protective Services, to see if there's any way we can get provisional approval for me to take Athena home to Texas."

"That's Marge for you," I said. "She's all wool and a yard wide—with a heart of gold."

And happy to bill me for every minute, but Alan Dale didn't need to know any of those gory details. That arrangement was strictly between Marge and me, and I wanted to keep it that way.

CHAPTER 9

AFTER DINNER WAS over, I cleaned up while Alan went into the guest room to feed Athena. I heard him turn on the room's wall-mounted TV. In terms of space, I guess the amenities in our guest room weren't all that different from what he had become accustomed to in his suite at the Silver Cloud, except I'm pretty sure the hotel clerk wouldn't have tracked down a rocking chair for his convenience. He came out a few minutes later.

"She'll sleep for a couple of hours now," he said, "but I have to say that barbecue was amazing. I didn't know anybody outside of Texas could cook like that."

"I guess they call it Pecos Pit for a reason," I told him.

I offered him a beverage and was pleasantly surprised when he went for a glass of straight tonic. With that my new favorite drinking buddy and I settled into the living room to watch the sun set over Elliott Bay.

"Did you make any progress?" he asked.

It was time to come clean, more or less. I spent the next half hour giving him a detailed report of what I'd learned while sitting amid layers of cat hair in Hilda Tanner's humble abode.

"Tomorrow morning when I see that caseworker, do I need to tell her that we now suspect Petey Mayfield may be Athena's father?"

"I think you do," I advised him. "In cases like this, full disclosure is always the best strategy. Supposing we locate Naomi and get her to sign off, but then Petey shows up from somewhere out in left field and won't sign or tries to cause trouble. Even if he does, I doubt he'd have a leg to stand on, since he abandoned both Naomi and her unborn baby long before Naomi abandoned Athena, but still it's better to be up front about it."

"Neither of them should have any say in this," Alan muttered.

"That's how it looks to both you and me," I told him, "but I have a feeling Social Services may have a whole different take on the situation. In my experience they usually try to reunite families rather than break them apart."

Of course, some families are so screwed up that they need to be disbanded, but I didn't say that aloud to Alan Dale. He already had more than enough to worry about.

"So what's next?" he asked.

"Have you filed a missing-persons report on Naomi?"

"No," he responded. "Should I?"

"I think it's time."

"All right, then. If Marge can stay that long, I'll try to get that done after my appointment with Social Services. Where do I go to do it?"

"Where's your appointment?"

"Downtown somewhere—on Third Avenue, I believe, at Third and James."

"Seattle PD is just a block or two away from there, uphill at Fifth and Cherry. You can file the report there. They're likely to tell you that since Naomi's an adult, she has a right to disappear if she wants to. In this case, however, I'm hoping Athena's needs will take precedence."

"What are you going to do?"

"I'm going back over to West Seattle and have a chat with the developer who's planning on building all those McMansions on what was once Agnes Mayfield's property. If I can get their office to spring with a last name for Petey Mayfield's Aunt Lenora, maybe I can get her to file a missing-persons report on him."

"What are you going to tell the aunt?"

"The truth—that we believe her nephew to be Athena's father and that we need to locate him in order to request that he put Athena's future on track by relinquishing his parental rights."

There was another thought in my mind as well— that if Athena really was Agnes and Peter Mayfield's great-granddaughter, she might be in line for some kind of inheritance—from them, to say nothing of an inheritance from me. Those were parts of the story I had yet to disclose to anyone else, including not only Alan Dale but also my own kids, Scott and Kelly.

"Will she help us?" Alan asked.

"We'll have to wait and see."

Mel called about then so we could chat during her drive time home. Alan excused himself to go watch TV, but I think he really wanted to give us some privacy. I brought Mel up to date with my day's worth of exploits, although it's possible I neglected to mention that Hilda Tanner was walking around with a loaded handgun tucked away in her apron pocket. There are some things that are better left unsaid.

Once the call was over, leaving me to my own devices, I went into the family room, dropped into my favorite chair, and turned on my iPad. And then, just for the hell of it, I googled Highline Development. On their Web site I read the company's history, which, as it turned out, was also the story of a family who despite suffering terrible hardships had somehow succeeded in achieving the American dream.

In the early 1900s, a Japanese sailor named Takumi Nishikawa jumped ship in San Francisco and made his way north to Washington State, working as a farm laborer en route and doing the same work he'd done before leaving Japan. Eventually he brought his wife, Suki, to the United States, where they both became citizens. Along with their two sons, they built a thriving business raising and selling berries. That all went away in the aftermath of the attack on Pearl Harbor. While Takumi, Suki, their daughters-in-law and grandchildren waited out the war in Minidoka, their two adult sons served in the U.S. Army's legendary 442nd Regimental Combat Team.

When the war was over, only one son, Henry, came back home. Henry was the mastermind behind the creation of a start-up real-estate operation that more than seventy years later remained in business, having morphed into a still-family-owned enterprise called Highline Development. According to the Web site, the company's current CEO was listed as Suzanne Nishikawa, none other than Takumi and Suki's great-granddaughter. Another great-grandson, a guy named John Nishikawa, was listed as Highline's primary builder, so they were keeping the construction part of the business in the family as well. I came away from the Web site feeling as though I had just encountered a piece of Seattle history, one of which I'm sure Arthur Denny would have approved.

As I shut down the computer, I couldn't help but marvel at how much of Seattle's twentieth-century history was wrapped up in the stories of those two very different families—the Mayfields and the Nishikawas. Their separate experiences of World War II had been from two very different perspectives, but now, more than seventy years later, they were doing business together. And tomorrow, dressed in what I hoped would be somewhat more respectable attire, I planned on paying a call on Suzanne Nishikawa.

I'd heard what Hilda Tanner had to say about Lenora's real-estate transactions. Now I wanted to hear the story from Suzanne's point of view. I was hoping that somehow she'd be able to put me on the trail of Naomi Dale and Petey Mayfield. Barring that, at least she'd be able to point me in the direction of Lenora No Last Name.

It was almost nine by then and about time for Lucy's last walk of the evening. The Belltown area has become a lot more wild and wooly than it was when I first moved into the neighborhood. Late at night there's an unwelcome element out there making the streets less than safe, and I'm not just talking about the guy who targeted Mel and Lucy either. As a consequence I try to make our last walk of the evening early enough so all the tough guys are still ensconced on their designated stools in disreputable bars rather than out roaming the streets beating up innocent passersby.

Before I collected Lucy and her leash, though, I went to the kitchen and made up another Pecos Pit brisket sandwich, which I wrapped in plastic and stuck in the pocket of my dog-walking jacket along with kibble and a Milk Bone for Billy Bob.

Once outside and across Clay, Lucy and I had the dog-walking area to ourselves. I let her relieve herself, and then we went looking for Sam in the fire-escape alcove leading up from the church basement that is his private domain. The alcove is relatively sheltered from the elements by a generous overhang, When I saw Sam's cart parked at the top of the stairs, I knew he was there. I worried about waking him, but chilly as it was—mid-forties—I figured both Sam and the dog would sleep better on full stomachs than on empty ones.

"Knock, knock," I called down the stairs. "Anybody home? Sorry to wake you. It's J.P. and Lucy."

An unwieldy lump of something stirred at the bottom of the stairs. When you're sleeping outside in weather like that, it takes a whole mountain of blankets to hold in the heat.

"Hey, Beau," Sam said, emerging from his bundle. "What's up?"

Lucy and I were a known element. Rather than barking or growling at us, Billy Bob darted up the stairs for a dog-to-dog tail-wagging greeting.

"I know it's late, but I brought Billy Bob some treats and a sandwich for you."

Gradually Sam finished divesting himself of blankets and stood up, looking more like a hulking bear than a man.

"A sandwich?" he repeated, making his way up the stairs. "What kind of sandwich?"

"Pecos Pit Bar-B-Que beef brisket," I told him.

"Pecos Pit? No shit! That's mighty white of you."

And then we both laughed. We were friends. We didn't know each other during the Vietnam War, but we'd both been there and we knew what it meant. As a consequence we understand what's important and what's not important, and the current climate of poisonous political correctness strikes us both as stupid. In this case no offense was meant and none taken.

Sam lumbered up the stairs and then rummaged through the grocery cart until he located the tin dish that I knew belonged to Billy Bob. He held it out to me while I poured in the kibble, topped off with a Milk Bone for dessert. By the time we finished, Billy Bob was already there, seated at our feet, ready and waiting.

As the dog chowed down, I handed Sam his sandwich. "What are you doing in town?" he asked between bites. "You're usually only here on weekends."

"I caught a case," I told him. "I'm trying to locate a missing person."

Sam took a bite and chewed it for a time. "Man, oh, man," he said, "this stuff is pure heaven. Thank you."

"You're welcome," I said.

He took another bite and chewed that one. "So this is one of your PI gigs?" he asked.

"Yup."

"I told one of the guys down at the Gospel Mission that I have a friend who's a private investigator. He told me I was probably hallucinating, but this sandwich is no hallucination, and neither are you."

Lucy was tugging on the leash, so I let her lead me off and left Sam to finish his sandwich in peace, but those few steps away combined with the words "Gospel Mission" caused the proverbial lightbulb to go off in my head. Naomi Dale and Petey Mayfield were both homeless and had been for years. Inside the demographic that makes up Seattle's homeless population, Sam Shelton probably counted as an elder statesman. For a boots-on-the-ground confidential informant in this case, who could be better? However, homeless though he may be, Sam is a proud man. He was happy to accept a sandwich from a friend, but a monetary handout? No way!

So while Lucy did her second duty of the evening, and after I had deployed and disposed of the necessary bag, I went back over to Sam with an offer I hoped he couldn't refuse, even though I was making it up as I went along.

"It's actually two cases rather than one," I explained. "The missing persons are a relatively young couple, twenty-somethings, who've both been homeless for some time. Their names are Naomi Dale and Petey or Peter Mayfield, although they may be using different names."

"Married?" Sam asked.

"Not as far as I know."

"They're involved with drugs?"

"I don't know for sure, but probably. Petey disappeared from a home in West Seattle that was owned by his grandmother. He took off sometime last fall, leaving Naomi behind—alone and pregnant. Late in January someone dropped Naomi off on the shoulder of I-90 just this side of the Mount Baker Tunnel, where she almost got run over by a Metro bus. When the cops showed up, not only was she high on drugs, methadone most likely, she was also in labor. The baby was born at Harborview on January twenty-fourth. Naomi walked out of the hospital shortly after giving birth."

"Leaving the baby behind?"

"Yes."

Sam knew the drill, and he got straight to the heart of the matter. "She left the baby there because she was addicted?"

"Probably," I answered.

"How are you tied into all this?" Sam wanted to know.

"The baby's name is Athena. She's through withdrawal now and has just been released from

Children's Hospital. I'm working on behalf of her grandfather, a man named Alan Dale. He's Naomi's father, and he needs to locate both parents."

"So they can take care of the baby or sign away their parental rights?" Sam asked.

Once again Sam was on the money.

"The latter," I replied. "In order to take the baby back home to Texas, Alan needs to be appointed as Athena's permanent legal guardian. For that to happen, both parents have to sign off. By the way," I added, "the grandfather has authorized me to pay a reward—five hundred bucks—to anyone who can help us locate either one of them."

"So a thousand bucks total?"

"Yes," I said. I happened to have several copies of Naomi's mug shot in my pocket, and I handed one over to him.

He studied it for a moment before slipping it into his pocket. "Looks like Naomi's had some problems with cops," Sam noted.

"Yes, she has," I agreed.

"Let me ask around," Sam said. "I might be able to figure something out. If I do learn anything, should I tell Bob?"

If Sam had a cell phone, I'd never seen any sign of it. Bob, the Belltown Terrace doorman, was in charge of the unending supply of kibble and dog treats that a grateful Mel and I supplied to Billy Bob whenever we were out of town.

"Sure," I said. "That works."

"Thanks for the grub, Beau," Sam said. "I thank you, and so does Billy Bob."

As Lucy and I headed across Clay, they were already on their way back down the stairs. When I first met Sam, I felt sorry for him. Now I understand that how he lives is his choice, and he's not looking for sympathy. He's looking for live and let live.

We rode up in the elevator. I finished working my day's worth of neglected crossword puzzles and then set about getting ready for bed. Lucy usually hits the sack before I do. When it was time for lights-out, I looked at Lucy's bed, fully expecting to find her there, but she was nowhere in sight. I went through the whole apartment, hunting for her. Finally there was only one room left to search—the guest room. Alan had left his bedside table lamp lit, and the door was slightly ajar—a telltale Lucy-size width ajar. I eased it open wide enough to see inside, and there she was, curled up into a tight ball on the floor underneath Athena's bassinet-style travel crib.

Lucy's message was clear: Any bad guy with evil intentions who might try to get close to Athena Dale was in for a big surprise. Remembering that other fabled Irish wolfhound—the one from the poem "Beth Gelert," set in the North Wales town of Beddgelert—I knew that Lucy was living up to her ancient bloodlines and heritage by doing exactly what nature had always intended her to do—protect those most in need of protection.

So did I make her leave her self-imposed duty station and come to bed? I did not. I believe I've already told you that when it comes to disciplining kids or dogs, I'm hopeless.

CHAPTER 10

SOMETIME IN THE wee small hours of the morning, I was wishing my first wife, Karen Beaumont Livingston, was still around so I could have had the pleasure of telling her how very wrong she was. She had always insisted that I was stone deaf when it came to hearing babies cry overnight. Maybe years spent shooting on gun ranges have given me a kind of situational hearing loss that always used to block out the sounds made by our babies. Unfortunately, it doesn't seem to have the same effect on other people's babies.

That night, every time Athena let out the smallest cry, I came wide awake and wasn't able to fall back asleep afterward. The next morning, when Lucy cold-nosed me awake because it was time for her walk, I was short on shut-eye. It was all I could to do stumble out of bed and pull on my clothes. How Alan Dale had managed to live for close to six weeks on minimal amounts of sleep was more than I could imagine. Staggering out of the bedroom,

I found Lucy had her leash in her mouth and was waiting by the front door. Alan, with Athena tucked in the crook of his arm, was standing in front of the microwave warming a bottle filled with baby formula.

"Morning," he said. "Care for some coffee? Marge taught me how to use the machine."

"Thanks," I said. "Go ahead and press the buttons. I need to walk Lucy, but it won't take long. It'll be nice to have coffee ready and waiting by the time I get back."

We made quick work of it. Lucy and I were down to P-1, across the street, and back in the elevator in a flash. It would have been a lengthier excursion had Sam and Billy Bob been in residence, but his grocery cart had already broken camp. No doubt they were off in search of someplace that offered free breakfasts.

Once back in the unit, I fed Lucy before grabbing my coffee mug and joining Alan in the living room. He was seated sideways on the window seat, feeding Athena and staring out the window. "I'll bet you never get tired of this view," he said, nodding toward the water.

On this unexpectedly sunny day, the view was especially gorgeous, with the blue expanse of Elliott Bay fringed by the rugged snowcapped peaks of the Olympics in the distance.

"Not so far," I told him.

When Lucy finished eating, she came into the living room and walked past me without a glance, settling at Alan's feet and lying down with a heartfelt sigh. Alan had evidently passed some kind of doggy security test and was no longer viewed with as a potential threat.

"Did you know Lucy slept in our room last night?" Alan asked.

"I noticed," I said, realizing in that moment that I was also slightly jealous. My faithful companion had deserted me.

"The first time I got up to feed Athena, she was right there, sleeping under the crib," Alan continued. "She just looked at me when I came into the room with the bottle. When I picked Athena up and brought her over to the rocker, Lucy came over and settled down on the floor beside us. When I put Athena down again, Lucy went back under the crib. Pretty amazing."

He finished feeding the baby and then glanced at his watch. "My appointment is at nine thirty," he said. "Marge told me she'd be here around eight thirty. How long will it take me to get to Third and James?"

"Not long," I told him. "Just walk over to Third and catch a southbound bus."

"Wouldn't I be better off driving?" he asked.

"With the cost and scarcity of parking the way they are in Seattle right now, I'd say taking the bus might be a better bet."

"All right, then," Alan said, sounding dubious, "but would you mind holding Athena for a couple of minutes while I jump in the shower?"

"Not at all," I said, with more confidence than I felt.

He brought the baby to me, but before handing her over, he placed a piece of cloth the size of a large hankie on my shoulder. "You'll need to burp her," he advised.

My usual dog-walking attire consists of a comfy sweat suit that happens to be far more washable than the dry-clean-only jacket I'd been wearing the day before, but I was grateful for the gesture. "Thanks," I said. "Good to know."

Moments after Alan's back was turned, Athena delivered a very drippy burp that proved the protective cloth to be a necessity as opposed to an option. She was awake for the next little while, staring up at me with wondering eyes. Did she realize I was a stranger and not her grandpa—at least not the grandpa she was used to?

I spent the next several minutes examining her delicate features. Her eyes were a bright blue that reminded me of my granddaughter's Kayla's eyes when she was a newborn. So did the thin wisps of blond hair haloing her head. Her fingers were tiny beyond imaging, but when she grasped onto my index finger, she did so with a remarkably tight grip. I studied her with a combination of awe and amazement, as well as a growing sense of responsibility toward this child of a child I hadn't known I had.

Alan was still finishing his shower when Marge marched in, all hustle and bustle, barking orders left and right as the door closed behind her. Suddenly it seemed like an excellent idea for Lucy and me to make a timely exit as well. I handed Athena off to Marge and went to shower and dress myself. While I was in the closet, I examined yesterday's jacket. Even though it was one of Mel's favorites, knowing the damage was beyond repair, I tossed it into the trash.

Before leaving the room, I paused long enough to give Mel a call. "How's it going?" she asked.

"Bit of a full house around here," I admitted. "I didn't get much sleep because I woke up every time Athena uttered a peep."

"And," Mel added, "I suppose Marge is driving you crazy?"

"That, too," I agreed.

"I'm planning to come down after work tomorrow. That way I can pitch in with the baby while serving the dual purpose of giving you a break from Marge and Marge a break from you."

Mel understood the dynamics of Marge's and my prickly relationship all too well.

"Eat in or out?" I asked.

"That depends on what time I get away from the office and how much traffic there is between here and there," she told me. "We can decide tomorrow."

"Sounds good," I said.

"What's on your agenda today?" she asked.

"I'm going to pay a call on the folks at Highline Development and see if I can come away with a last name for Petey Mayfield's Aunt Lenora. If I do, I'll see whether she's willing to file a missing-persons report on him."

"Good luck, then," Mel said, "but I've gotta go. I have a meeting with the mayor in fifteen."

"Good luck to you, too," I replied.

"Not to worry," she said with a laugh. "Compared to the last mayor, this one is a piece of cake."

Out in the kitchen, I found Alan and Marge in a huddle, conferring over what needed to be done and when. "Hey, Alan," I said, picking up Lucy's leash, "Lucy and I are going to head out, too, so I can give you a ride there. I'll take Lucy out for one last walk and meet you on P-4."

It was clear outside, clear and sunny, but with the cloud cover gone it was also bitterly cold. The truth is, it was probably only in the mid-thirties. People from Chicago or Maine would be all over me about calling the mid-thirties "bitterly cold," but in case you haven't noticed, people who live in Seattle are well known for being weather wimps. That goes just as much for high temperatures as it does for low ones. We don't approve of weather extremes at either end of the spectrum.

I was grateful Lucy was quick about getting down to business. I had just loaded her into the backseat when Alan emerged from the elevator lobby. Because Third Avenue is closed to automobile traffic at certain times of the day, I dropped him at Second and James and pointed out how to get back up the hill to his Child Services appointment and then on up to Seattle PD at Fifth and Cherry to file Naomi's missing-persons report.

It seemed to me that nine fifteen was a bit early to show up at Highline Development, so I headed on down Fourth Avenue South and pulled in to the Denny's parking lot. Mel may have had an appointment with His Honor the mayor. I had a scheduled morning meeting with a Grand Slam.

Overnight, during the times when Athena had

awakened me, I'd had a chance to mull over some of the things Hilda Tanner had told me. One thing that struck me as odd was her mention of the upcoming estate sale. The orange netting designating Agnes's property as a construction site was already in place, but did the proposed estate sale mean that Agnes's goods were still inside her little frame house? Why would that be? In my experience sellers usually vacate and empty out their premises before a sale closes, especially if the structure involved is destined for the wrecking ball.

Guzzling coffee and waiting for my order, I opened my iPad and located Zillow. If you bring up the right page, you can see what's for sale as well as the sale prices on nearby properties that have recently changed hands. It took some scrolling around before I was able to zero in on Agnes Mayfield's West Seattle neighborhood. When I did so, I was in for a surprise.

All four of the Mayfield houses, including the one Agnes had recently occupied, had sold in the low $200,000s, well below the going rate, even for teardowns. Similar lots in the neighborhood had sold for or were listed for sale at amounts close to double that. JDLR is copspeak for "just doesn't look right," as in something seemed amiss here. Not only that, the closing date on those transactions had been in early October, months after Agnes, reportedly suffering from dementia issues, had been carted off to a care facility of some kind. So was this a variation on a theme of elder abuse? It wouldn't be the first time some underhanded relative or real-estate developer had taken advantage of an innocent pensioner, cheating him or her out of hearth and home.

My original plan had been to walk into Highline Development and ask for information straight up, hoping to come away with Lenora's last name. Now it seemed as though a bit of subterfuge might be necessary. I had yet to meet Lenora No Last Name, but if she was the kind of schemer I was beginning to suspect she was, I would need to find some other means of identifying her rather than showing my hand to the developer.

When I finished my part of the breakfast, I asked for a "doggie bag." Back at the car, Lucy was happy to polish off any and all uneaten pancakes. After that we headed back to West Seattle. With the GPS calling out the directions, I drove straight to the address I'd lifted from Highline's Web site. I found the office in a strip mall on 35th, tucked in between a nail salon and a chiropractor's office. Two doors away was a Subway sandwich shop. I drove into the parking lot and pulled up next to a sporty red Boxster S that was parked directly in front of the office designated as the home of Highline Development. There was nothing in the area that looked the least bit alarming, so once again I left Lucy, my backup dog, locked inside the S550.

When I walked into the office, I noted that the young woman at the receptionist's desk who greeted me was clearly of Asian descent. Dark eyes peered out at me from a perfectly formed face. Her glossy black hair was parted in the middle and fell straight to her shoulders. She was most likely a thirty-something, but that was just a guess. The Web site had said Suzanne Nishikawa was the company's CEO, but it seemed unlikely that a CEO would be seated at the reception desk.

"Would it be possible for me to speak to whoever is in charge?" I asked.

"Who might I say is calling?" she asked in return. "And do you have an appointment?"

I had no appointment, and I had already decided against handing over one of my business cards, which, after yesterday's disaster, I was carrying in the waterproof plastic wallet provided by the printer. I was here undercover, as it were. Considering the circumstances, revealing the fact that I was a private investigator seemed like a bad idea. In this case it struck me that a mixture of truth and fiction was probably in order. I've never been an especially capable liar, but since I was speaking to a complete stranger, I hoped my face wouldn't give me away.

"I'm interested in that housing development of yours down on 24th," I said.

"Are you intending to make a purchase?" she asked.

"Well, yes, I could be," I hedged. "My wife and I are on the verge of splitting up. I'm looking to buy another place, but I should probably be speaking to an agent about this."

At that and with her face breaking into a welcoming smile, the woman rose to her feet and came around the desk with her hand extended in greeting. "Actually, I am the one in charge," she told me. "My receptionist is out sick today. My name is Suzanne Nishikawa. And you are?"

"My name is Beaumont," I told her, "J. P. Beaumont."

I've met a few real-estate developers in my time. They've mostly been cigar-chomping, loudmouthed jerks. Suzanne Nishikawa appeared to be a white horse of an altogether different color. She wasn't just petite—she was tiny, but not as tiny as she would have been without the assistance of a pair of amazing four-inch heels.

Until Mel Soames, a true fashionista, came into my life, I never knew anything about highend female attire. She's my sherpa when it comes to women and the clothing they wear. Unless I missed my guess, the shoes currently on Suzanne Nishikawa's feet would clock in at right around four hundred bucks a pair. She wore a bright yellow suit with a skintight pencil skirt. The suit was made of some kind of shiny, satiny material that fastened around her slender waist with three bright gold buttons. In other words, she was a looker who believed in dressing to impress. Her designer duds, makeup, and nails were perfect, and the ring on her right hand sported a diamond solitaire that was downright eye-popping. Everything about her said she had money to burn and wasn't the least bit shy about showing it off.

She led me into an inner office. The walls were decorated with framed photos and two separate degrees from the UDub (as my alma mater, the University of Washington, is referred to around here). One was from the Department of Architecture and the other was an M.B.A. from the UDub's Foster School of Business. As for the photos? It looked as though Suzanne Nishikawa had been West Seattle High's version of the "it" girl for her graduating class. The framed pictures were all copied blowups of what must have been yearbook photos. According to the accompanying captions, during her senior year in high school Suzanne had not only been head cheerleader, homecoming queen, and student-body president, she had also been class valedictorian.

"Looks like you were a real all-star," I commented as I took a seat.

"Not good enough to get into Harvard," she said with a wry smile. "SBA, as we say around here—smart but Asian. I thought about joining that class-action lawsuit, but I decided screw it. Why bother? I've done all right without going to Harvard. I stayed home, went to the University of Washington, and earned three degrees in seven years flat. Since I sold real estate for my dad on the side, I graduated with zero student debt."

"Good for you," I said. "That probably explains why there's a shiny Boxster S parked just outside."

"Right," Suzanne agreed with a grin, but once the grin faded, she was all business. "I bought it a few months ago. Tell me a little about yourself, Mr. Beaumont," she added.

There could be no doubt that Suzanne was a crackerjack when it came to sales. She'd heard my name one time only and had made a mental note of it. You can always count on commissioned salespeople and politicians to remember people's names.

Now came the time for me to spin my bit of yarn. "My wife—my current wife, that is—and I live in a downtown condo in Belltown," I told her.

"We've been through a bit of a rough patch lately, and counseling isn't helping. If we do split up, I'll need to downsize. With traffic so jammed up in the downtown corridor these days, I thought a move to someplace in the burbs might be just what the doctor ordered."

"I'm sorry to hear that you're encountering marital difficulties," Suzanne said with an understanding smile, "but when life throws you those kinds of curves, it's always a good idea to have a backup plan."

There was a small conference table in one corner of the room, and that's where she directed me. On it was a stack of beautifully designed color brochures entitled *Homes at Mayfield Glen*.

"What's Mayfield?" I asked.

"The land we're building on was once part of a farm that was originally settled by one of West Seattle's earliest residents, a guy named Harold Mayfield. It was subdivided into lots in the twenties with plans to build single-family dwellings, but once the Great Depression came along, that never came to fruition—until now. Last fall several pieces of property came into the hands of an heir who was willing to sell, and here we are. It's taking more time than expected to get permits and approvals, so we're not ready to break ground just yet."

I thumbed through the brochure. "None of these are view properties?"

"Not really," Suzanne answered. "One has a peekaboo view of the downtown Seattle skyline from the upstairs master bedroom. Unfortunately, that one is already spoken for."

"You've sold one of the houses without even having broken ground?"

She smiled. "That's the reality when it comes to Seattle real estate these days. The nine-hundred-fifty-thousand-dollar price tag is for standard builder's-grade materials. As a pre-reconstruction buyer, you could have a bit of a discount off that. You could also choose to add in a number of upgrades in terms of customizing, appliances, and finishes."

"May I take one?" I asked, picking up a brochure.

"Of course," she said with a smile. "That's why they're here. In addition, our real-estate division represents many other properties if you're interested in something a little smaller."

I rose to my feet. "Thank you so much," I said. "Obviously, I'm not ready to make any kind of decision just yet, but I'm glad to have this in my back pocket as a possible option."

"When you *are* ready, Mr. Beaumont, please give me a call," she said, handing over a business card of her own that included a whole panoply of telephone numbers. "We'll be only too happy to be of service."

CHAPTER 11

BACK IN THE car without having learned much of anything, I used my iPad to locate a nearby park on Cloverdale and took Lucy for a quick but chilly walk. It turns out that time spent dog walking is also good for thinking. Once Lucy was finished, I knew where we were going next—the King County Recorder's Office in the courthouse on Fourth Avenue in downtown Seattle. The nearest parking garage with any availability was two blocks away at Second and Cherry. Walking there made me wonder how Alan was doing with his part of the operation.

Entering the fusty, marble-floored building that is the center of King County government felt very familiar. I had been there for countless courtroom proceedings, but this was my first time stopping by the Recorder's Office. It was high noon when I stepped into the main waiting room. I expected a crowd at the front desk, but there wasn't one. Evidently these days most people do their searches online rather than going straight to the horse's mouth.

I spent a lot of years in the world of old-school bureaucracy. In those days it was always the poor newbie—the employee with the least amount of seniority and the least experience—who was left manning or womaning the front counter during the preferred lunch hour. I was prepared to deal with a certain amount of incompetence, but I knew that even a novice in the office would be more adept at searching out records than I was.

Nonetheless, I was a little taken aback to see that the young woman standing behind the counter sported a pink-and-purple Mohawk. I came of age when women in the workforce wore two-piece suits or dresses along with heels and hose. In those days wearing pants was strictly forbidden. In fact, back in the late sixties I'm not sure pantsuits had even been invented. This woman wore faded jeans topped by a T-shirt that said BITE ME! Her arms were alive with countless tattoos, and her ears sported at least seven studs each. She also wore a nose ring.

"May I help you?" she asked. An ID lanyard hanging around her neck identified her as Linda Collins. She might have looked scary as hell, but her greeting was cordial enough.

"My name is Beaumont," I told her, "J. P. Beaumont." I produced one of my business cards and handed it over. "I'm working for a client whose great-grandmother recently passed away, and I'm wondering if you could locate the deeds for several parcels of property."

I was the one doing all the talking, but it wasn't clear if the Tattooed Lady on the far side of the counter was listening to a word I said. Instead she

stood there mutely staring down at my business
card.

"J. P. Beaumont," she murmured at last. "Didn't
you used to work for Seattle PD in homicide?"

That was unexpected. "Yes, I did," I admitted.

"My grandpa used to talk about you all the time,"
she replied. "He always said you were one of the
best—that you solved more cases roaring drunk
than most people could cold sober."

Talk about a backhanded compliment.

"And your grandfather is?"

"Conrad Collins," she answered, "but people at
the department used to call him Corky."

That was a name out of the past. Detective C.
Collins and I had the shared idiosyncrasy of using
our initials as opposed to our given names. At work
I was usually called J.P., but for reasons I never quite
fathomed, Detective Collins was dubbed Corky. In
fact, I believe that day in the county Recorder's
Office was only the second time I'd ever heard the
name Conrad. The first time had been at his retirement party. Corky was about ten years my senior,
and the moniker had been well established before
I ever came on the scene. In addition, the words
"solving cases drunk" could have applied to him
every bit as much as they did to me. Corky and I
had knocked back more than a few adult beverages
together back in our old Doghouse days.

"I'll be damned," I said. "How is Corky these
days? Be sure to tell him I said hello."

The expression on Linda's face darkened. "I
doubt it would do much good," she said. "Gran had
to put him in a memory-care facility up near where

they live in Phinney Ridge. These days when she goes to see him, he usually thinks she's his mother. I'll tell Gran about meeting you, though. It'll mean a lot to her that someone still remembers him. Now, what do you need?"

I opened my iPad to the Zillow page, told her what I was looking for, and passed the device across the counter to her. Looking down, she studied the screen while her fingers moved like lightning over her own keyboard.

"You need the current deeds?" she asked.

"And any previous ones."

In less than five minutes' time, Linda reached down and produced a stack of paper that had just shot out from a below-counter printer.

"Here you go," she said with a smile, slipping the pages into a file folder, which she handed to me. "We usually charge for printouts, but today only I'm giving you the friends-and-family discount."

"So what do I owe?" I asked.

"Not a thing," she said. "Any friend of Gramps is a friend of mine."

"Thank you," I said. "Thank you very much."

I took the file folder and left the office. Outside in the drafty lobby, I paused long enough to examine them. Currently the properties in question were held by Highline Development, purchased on October 1, 2016, from a seller named Lenora Elizabeth Harrison. The properties had all been quitclaimed over to Lenora by Agnes Mayfield on August 1 of the same year. At last Lenora No Last Name was nameless no longer—she had both a middle name and a last one as well.

Based on what Hilda Tanner had told me, that meant that the properties had come to Lenora from her mother for free shortly after she'd carted Agnes, the previous owner, off to an assisted-living facility of some kind. Had the quitclaim deeds been signed while Agnes was still in possession of her faculties or not? And what about that lowball purchase price subsequently paid by Highline Development?

Something about all this reminded me of the deal Lenora's great-grandfather had struck with a developer just before the stock-market crash of 1929. Based on that, I now had a pretty good idea of who it was who had already spoken for that one not-yet-built but no-longer-for-sale McMansion. It seemed all too plausible that Lenora had unloaded her mother's properties for a below-market price in exchange for having a ready-made house free for the taking.

And if Lenora was a cheat, what about the people at Highline Development? Had they known about Agnes Mayfield's mental-health issues at the time the quitclaim documents were signed? They might not have, but Lenora sure as hell did. Those realizations led me to one simple conclusion: All of Lenora's actions here pointed in the same direction—a deliberate attempt to swindle Petey Mayfield out of his rightful share of his grandmother's estate.

I could have sat down with the iPad and used my copy of LexisNexis to find out exactly what I needed to know, but in this case I decided to press the Easy Button. Heading back to the parking garage and knowing today was Scotty's day off, I dialed his cell.

"Hey, Pop," he said when he came on the line.

I like it that he calls me that. "Great minds. Want to come over later today? We can assemble the crib first and then go to dinner at Fishermen's Terminal."

"Sounds good," I said, "but first I need some help."

Yes, it's illegal for cops to use police resources to obtain private information, but it happens all the time. Don't ask me how I know.

"I need an address and anything else you may have on a woman named Lenora Elizabeth Harrison. I believe she lives somewhere on the Eastside."

"I'm at home today, but I can get it for you." Less than a minute later, as I walked into the parking garage, a text from Scotty came through, giving me an address on 12th Avenue NE in Medina, Washington.

Medina, just north of the city of Bellevue, is an incorporated entity in its own right. It's small enough that it should probably be referred to as a "burbette" rather than a suburb, but since Medina is also the location of Bill Gates's massive Lake Washington digs, housing there probably boasts the highest per-square-foot costs of anywhere in the state. And since Hilda Tanner had told me that Lenora Mayfield had hooked up with a Microsoft exec, it made sense that he'd be looking for a nesting spot in that exclusive enclave.

Back in the car, I fed the address into my GPS. From where I was in downtown Seattle, the fastest way to get to the Eastside was across Lake Washington on the Evergreen Floating Bridge on 520. Back in the good old days—I wish that phrase didn't come to mind so often—the 520 Bridge was free. It was also crowded. Now the structure has been rebuilt and reconfigured in a way that added lanes, but it's definitely not free. It's also not nearly as crowded. I suspect overpriced tolls have something to do with that. Mel and I have decals on our respective windshields that register the toll every time we cross the bridge, but whenever we have to refill our so-called Good To Go! account, it makes me want to grind my teeth. Drivers around here pay all kinds of gasoline taxes that are supposed to cover the costs of road construction and maintenance. Unfortunately, state governments aren't required to live within their means the way taxpayers have to.

Offended by learning about the extent of Lenora's sneaky scheming, I left downtown in a state of relative agitation. By the time I drove across the lake with Lucy's chin welded to my shoulder, I had calmed down. I've learned to keep a washcloth in the car. It functions a lot like Alan's burp rag for Athena. It keeps dog drool from dribbling down the inside of my shoulder.

The GPS sent us off 520 at 84th, the first exit after the bridge. We drove past a golf course and turned right at the end of it. At 12th Avenue NE there were a couple of those newer stacked-box-looking houses that seem to be sprouting up like weeds everywhere, but when I finally located the address Scotty had given me, the house was totally invisible from the street. Concealed behind the barrier of a twelve-foot-high laurel hedge, there was no need for a No Trespassing sign, because the hedge was totally impenetrable. The only means of egress was through an imposing ten-foot-tall gate made of sheets of rusted corten steel. There was a post holding an intercom situated on the left side of the driveway. I pulled up next to that, buzzed down my car window, and pressed the call button.

"May I help you?" asked a disembodied voice.

"I'm here to see Lenora Harrison."

"Do you have an appointment?"

"No."

"May I tell Mrs. Harrison your name and what this is about?"

"My name is J. P. Beaumont. I'm a private investigator looking into the disappearance of her nephew Peter, aka Petey, Mayfield."

Lucy and I sat there for the next five or so minutes, cooling our jets. Then finally, without another word from the intercom, the heavy gate rolled open. What was on the other side was breathtaking, and about as far from Lenora's humble beginnings in her parents' West Seattle home as can be imagined. Before me was a sprawling mansion, painted pastel yellow with dazzling white trim and shutters. The columns lining the front porch made the house look downright palatial. The house was surrounded by a spread of immaculately manicured lawns punctuated with blossoming cherry trees and tall weeping cedars. The circular driveway was made of redbrick pavers and widened into a courtyard directly in front of the house. Off to one side stood a four-car garage. Parked nearby on this clear spring day were three recently washed and waxed vehicles—a white

Tesla Model S, a black Porsche Carrera GT, and a bright red Ferrari California T with the top down. Talk about conspicuous consumption!

As I approached the house, one of the double front doors opened and a woman stepped out onto the porch. The first thing I noticed about Lenora Elizabeth Harrison was her flaming red hair. She was relatively tall and dressed in a long-sleeved, figure-hugging top worn over a pair of skintight designer jeans. The jeans came complete with a few of those ladderlike tears in both thighs that reveal the peekaboo flashes of bare flesh that are seemingly a high-fashion necessity these days.

I grew up dirt poor. If I ended up with a hole in the knees of my pants, my mother patched them. When the pants were no longer patchworthy— usually because I'd outgrown them and they were inches too short—they went into the trash. Seeing a rich babe wearing torn jeans and posing as poor is something that, like the toll on the 520 Bridge, makes me want to grind my teeth. And speaking of posing, she stood at the top of the steps leaning against a wooden column with her hands on her hips as if daring me to try coming inside. I remembered that particular stance from my old Fuller Brush–selling days. It meant, "Don't even bother."

"Okay," I said to Lucy as I unbuckled my seat belt. "You might as well stay in the car. It doesn't look as though the welcome mat is out."

"Good afternoon," I said, extending one of my cards as I approached the front porch.

"My name is Lenora Harrison, and you are?" she asked.

"As I told the person over the intercom, my name is J. P. Beaumont. I'm a private investigator looking into the disappearance of your nephew, Peter Mayfield."

Lenora took the proffered card and studied it for some time. While she examined the card, I examined her. According to Hilda Tanner, Lenora's younger brother had been born when Agnes was in her early forties. That would mean Agnes would have been in her late thirties or early forties when Lenora was born. Looking at the woman on the porch, it would have been easy to place Lenora Harrison somewhere in her fifties or maybe her early sixties. I had no doubt that "she'd had some work done" on her face, leaving behind one indelible giveaway—the vertical lines above her lips that told everyone who saw her that she'd once been a smoker.

At last, rather than keeping my business card, she simply handed it back to me. Not only was the message rude, it was also painfully clear. Whatever I was doing about Petey had nothing whatsoever to do with her, and she wasn't the least bit interested.

"If my nephew's gone missing, why is a private investigator looking for him rather than the police?"

"That's actually why I'm here," I explained. "In order to involve law enforcement, someone needs to file a missing-persons report. According to a neighbor, Hilda Tanner, you're Petey's nearest blood relation."

"Hilda Tanner," Lenora sniffed. "That old battle-ax? Why can't she ever mind her own business? As for Petey? He's just like his dad—never settled down, never had a decent job. How can he be missing from home when, as far as I know, once he left my mom's house he's never had a real home? As for my filing a missing-persons report? It's not gonna happen, so why don't you get back in your car, drive on out of here, and go back to wherever you came from?"

In other words, *Here's your hat, buddy, what's your hurry? And don't let the door slam you on the butt on your way out.* Make that the gate rather than the door. And when it comes to the critical issue of making a good first impression? Lenora Harrison had flunked that test fair and square. She was the kind of woman that Mel might well refer to as a "ringtailed bitch."

"Thanks for your help," I told her. "You've got a lovely place here."

"We like it," she allowed.

That was what she told me, but I couldn't help wondering. If this lavish and very upscale spot was Lenora's home base right now, what the hell was she doing buying up a not-yet-built place in West Seattle? The McMansions at Mayfield Glen would be a big step up from the place across the street where Lenora had grown up, but compared to this? Moving to Suzanne Nishikawa's West Seattle development would be a huge step down.

So what was the deal here? And what was my next move?

The imposing corten gate rolled open as I approached it from the inside. As it rumbled shut behind me, I had no idea where I was going to go or what I was going to do as a follow-up. Years of experience told me that missing-persons reports filed by nodding acquaintances are generally nonstarters. A report filed by me or by Alan Dale or even by Hilda Tanner would most likely produce a bored yawn followed by a raised-eyebrow question of, "What business is it of yours?"

There was certainly no love lost between Lenora Harrison or Hilda Tanner in either direction, but as I merged back onto I-5 from 520, I remembered something Hilda had said about an upcoming estate sale scheduled to take place at Agnes Mayfield's former residence. And then there was that other thing Hilda had mentioned—about when Agnes was beginning to have dementia issues, Hilda and some of the other neighbors had taken turns looking in on the ailing woman. Did that mean there was a chance Hilda Tanner might still have a key that would let me inside Agnes's abandoned house to have a look around? As a sworn police officer, I wouldn't have been allowed to enter a residence and search for evidence without having enough probable cause to obtain a search warrant. But when I became a private eye, those constraints went right out the window.

Over time I've learned a lot about the workings of DNA. Mitochondrial DNA flows from mother to child. Having a DNA profile of Agnes Mayfield would help us build a familial DNA connection to her grandson, Petey. That might not help us if Petey was still alive and kicking, but what if he wasn't? What if Petey was deceased and his unidentified remains were sitting unclaimed, filed away in the locked storage unit in some M.E.'s office? In that case a DNA profile from Agnes might be the key to discovering what had become of him.

By the time Lucy and I were traveling southbound on I-5, I had reached the conclusion that we were headed for West Seattle. As for Lucy? She was headed for West Seattle, too, but she clearly wasn't happy about it. Rather than sitting with her chin resting on my shoulder, she was curled up and moping in the backseat, most likely missing her morning Frisbee chase.

Working as a private investigator might be fine for human beings, but for dogs? Not so much.

CHAPTER 12

BY TWO O'CLOCK in the afternoon, traffic on I-5 was already bumper-to-bumper, and it didn't improve much once I turned off toward the West Seattle Bridge. Steam from the steel plant where Peter Mayfield and Clyde Tanner had toiled for decades rolled out of the smokestacks and into the air, creating a white puff of cloud against a still-blue sky. I felt a sudden kinship to those two old guys—men I'd never met—who had formed a lifelong friendship while laboring at backbreaking work in that challenging environment. In a way finding Petey would be a resolution for Peter Mayfield and Clyde Tanner as much as it would be for Alan Dale and Athena.

During the drive to Hilda's, and wanting to worm myself back into Lucy's good graces, I asked Siri to direct me to a dog park in West Seattle. It turned out that Westcrest Park wasn't all that far out of our way. I pulled in and parked. Then, with Lucy on a leash, I retrieved the spare Frisbee I've learned to keep in the trunk for occasions such as this. Once she relieved herself, we headed for the off-leash area and I let her rip. Lucy is such a big, gangly beast that people and most other dogs tend to give her a wide berth. In this case there was an obnoxious little dachshund who was determined to give chase. He ran after Lucy, nipping at her heels the whole time. Lucy, for her part, ignored the noisy little creature, but I was surprised that such a short-legged dog could run fast enough to keep up.

After half an hour of play and a drink from the community dog fountain, we got back into the car and headed for Hilda Tanner's place. When I knocked on her front door, I heard the walker thumping across the living room as she came to answer.

"Who's there?" she demanded from behind the closed door.

I appreciated the fact that she was cautious about opening the door to unidentified strangers, but I wondered if she was standing on the other side with that revolver of hers either in her hand or in her pocket.

"It's Beaumont again," I said, "J. P. Beaumont."

When she opened the door, Hilda was once again wearing her apron, and the telltale bulge in her apron pocket was there as well. Hilda truly was armed and dangerous.

"What are you up to now?" she asked as a television set tuned to full volume blared in the background.

"I'm here to ask a favor," I told her. "May I come in?"

"I suppose," she allowed.

As I entered the house, I saw the tails of several of her precious kitties streaking off for parts unknown.

"What kind of favor?" she wanted to know.

I had decided during the Frisbee-throwing exercise that my best bet for putting Hilda Tanner on my side was to turn Lenora Harrison into the opposition. I made my way to the sagging easy chair and took a seat while Hilda settled on an equally sagging couch and used the remote to mute the TV set. I noticed the program that was playing was *Forensic Files* on HLN.

"You like forensics?" I asked.

Hilda shrugged. "When Clyde was alive, we watched the news constantly, hour after hour. After he died, I quit the news completely. The local news is all traffic and weather. Since I don't drive anymore, the traffic is none of my business, and I find out what the weather report is as soon as I open my eyes in the morning. And I don't like those network shows with all those different characters coming and going. It's too confusing. So I watch this. What I like best about these shows is that the bad guys usually get caught."

"Actually, that's the reason I'm here today—forensics."

"What do you mean?"

"I went to see Lenora Harrison a little earlier in hopes I could get her to file a missing-persons report on her nephew."

"And?" Hilda asked.

"She refused."

"That figures."

"So that's why I came to see you."

"You want *me* to file a missing-persons report?"

"Not exactly," I replied. "I seem to remember your mentioning that there's going to be an estate sale at Agnes's house in the near future."

Hilda nodded. "Not this weekend but the following one—on Saturday and Sunday."

"Does that mean that Agnes's goods are still inside?"

"As far as I know."

I already knew Hilda was a fan of *Forensic Files*, but was she actually paying attention to the content? "What do you know about mitochondrial DNA?" I asked.

She gave me a dismissive shrug. "That's the DNA that passes from mother to child."

"Bingo," I replied with a grin. "And that's what I need—something containing Agnes Mayfield's DNA so we can establish a profile for her that might in turn lead us to her grandson, Petey."

"So you'd use Agnes's DNA to create a missing-persons report?"

"More or less," I hedged.

I didn't want to mention that as far as finding Petey was concerned, having his grandmother's DNA profile would most likely be effective only in identifying his remains. What was important for me and for the job Alan Dale had hired me to do was the hope that Agnes Mayfield's DNA profile would establish once and for all whether or not Petey was Athena's father.

"What do you need from me?" Hilda asked.

"You told me yesterday that when Agnes's mental and physical capacities began to fail her, you and other neighbors looked in on her from time to time. Is that correct?"

"Yes."

"Did any of you report Agnes's deteriorating condition to anyone—like Social Services, for example, or to Lenora?"

"Certainly not," Hilda said with a shake of her head, "and why would we? We were all in the same boat. Agnes wanted to live out her days in her own house on her own terms. That goes double for me."

"When you went to look in on her, how did you gain entry to her house?"

"How do you think?" Hilda asked in return. "With a key, of course. In case you haven't noticed, I'm not exactly built for climbing in and out of windows."

"Is it possible you still have access to that key?"

"Of course," Hilda replied. "If Lenora had asked for it back, I would have given it to her, but she never gave me the time of day, and I didn't see any reason to go chasing after her begging to return it. So that's what you're asking? You want me to let you into the house?"

"It would be a huge help," I said.

"But don't you need a search warrant?"

"Nope," I said with a smile. "I'm a private eye, not a cop. And we're not looking for evidence that will hold up in a court of law. Being allowed into the residence by someone who has access is good enough for my purposes."

"All right, then," Hilda said, rising to her feet.

"Let's do it now before it gets colder or darker. I'm pretty sure the power's turned off there, too."

Hilda retrieved a key ring from a kitchen drawer and then pulled on a heavy-duty sweater. Together we made our way down the wheelchair ramp and across the street to her old friend's house.

"I haven't been here since she left," Hilda murmured as she limped up the sidewalk to Agnes Mayfield's front door. "Makes me too sad to see the place going to rack and ruin."

And it was. There was grass growing up through cracks in the concrete walkway. Here and there shake shingles were missing from the roof. Dead leaves were piled up at one end of the front porch, and a slippery coating of moss made walking treacherous. Here there was no wheelchair ramp, so I half carried Hilda up the front steps before going back down to retrieve her walker. All the curtains were drawn, so it was impossible to see inside, but behind a flimsy screen a crack in the corner of one of the front windows revealed that they were single-paned ones that had most likely been installed when the house was built.

The front door, however, was anything but flimsy. It was solid-core mahogany, covered with a layer of faded and peeling varnish. There were two locks, one in the doorknob along with a separately installed dead bolt. The key Hilda produced unlocked both, and we stepped inside. The closed curtains also allowed very little light to penetrate the room. It was like walking into something that resembled a musty mausoleum. The place stank of mold and mildew, with just a hint that probably indicated the presence of a dead critter of some kind up in the attic. Agnes tried flipping on the light switch, but nothing happened. By then, however, our eyes had adjusted to the dimness.

"Bedroom?" I asked.

Since this house was a carbon copy of Hilda's, she led the way through the gloom without any hesitation. The bedroom was neat, with a properly made bed. Other than a pair of bedroom slippers on the carpet next to the bed, nothing was out of place.

"Wouldn't you know!" Hilda muttered.

"What?"

"Those were Agnes's favorite slippers. Why didn't Lenora let her take those along?"

Why not indeed?

The flowered bedspread was eerily familiar. It was the same pattern that had been on my grandparents' bed when I first reestablished a connection with them after a lifelong estrangement. Next to the bed on a dusty table was an arrangement of four small gold-framed photographs. I picked them up and examined them one by one. The first was a wedding photo. The World War II–vintage hairdos and clothing told me that Agnes and Peter were the smiling bride and groom. Next came what I recognized as a senior-class portrait of a much younger version of Lenora, followed by another of a boy who was presumably Lenora's younger brother, Arthur. The last one, and the only one in faded color, showed a gangly, grinning boy wearing a Little League uniform along with a catcher's mitt.

"That one's Petey," Hilda informed me. She was standing beside me as I scanned through the photos. "That was just before he got off on the wrong track—after he stopped playing baseball."

"May I take this?" I asked.

"I don't see why not," Hilda said with a shrug.

I slipped the framed photo into my pocket. On the chest of drawers where I had hoped to find a hairbrush or comb, there was nothing but a crocheted doily and an old-fashioned jewelry box complete with a windup ballerina on top.

"Where's the bathroom?" I asked.

Hilda gave a sigh. "This way," she said.

The bathroom was tiny and dated. I had a feeling there was asbestos in the antiquated tile on the floor. The basin, cracked and rusty, was of the two-faucet variety that went out of fashion years ago. The claw-footed bathtub, like the single-pane windows, had obviously been part of the original design. There was no shower. A drinking glass containing a lone toothbrush sat on one corner of the basin. As far as I was concerned, that toothbrush meant pay dirt. There was a medicine chest set in the wall over the basin. The mirror on that was mottled and desilvering around the edges, but when I opened the door, I found exactly what I wanted—a hairbrush and comb. Unfortunately, that's also when I realized that although I had come in search of evidence, I hadn't been fully prepared to find it.

"Crap!" I exclaimed.

"What's wrong?" Hilda wanted to know.

"These are what I need—the toothbrush and the brush and comb—but I didn't think to bring along any evidence bags."

"I'll get you one," Hilda told me. "I know where Agnes kept her Ziploc bags." She hobbled off and returned a few moments later carrying two gallon-size plastic bags. I put the toothbrush in one and the comb and brush in the other.

"Thanks," I told her. "That's perfect."

"Do you need anything else?"

"Not really," I said. "This is great."

"Well, there's something *I* need," she huffed under her breath. She banged her way out of the bathroom and back into the bedroom. When she emerged, she was carrying the wedding picture, which she slipped into her apron pocket right next to the revolver.

"Other than Petey, nobody else is going to want this picture, and if he shows up, I'll give it to him," she said. "But Peter and Agnes were good friends of ours. This will give me something to remember them by."

I nodded. "I can't imagine that they wouldn't want you to have it."

I was starting to worry about timing. If I didn't head home soon, I was going to miss my crib-assembling date with Scotty.

"We should probably go," I said, but Hilda seemed reluctant to leave. She stood still, surveying the room as though looking at it for one last time and saying her good-byes.

"Is anything missing?" I asked.

"What do you mean?" Hilda wanted to know.

"Does it look as though Lenora has gone through the place and taken anything?"

"I doubt it." Hilda said with a shrug. "Why would she? Agnes's stuff never would have been good enough for her snot-nosed daughter."

With that, Hilda and I turned and left that sad little house, closing and double-locking the door behind us. For me it felt like slamming the door on someone's life and throwing away the key. I didn't ask Hilda, but I'm pretty sure she must have felt the same.

I had planned on dropping Lucy off before going to Scotty's place, but in the interest of saving time she came along to Ballard with me. When Scotty and Cherisse bought their house, it had come with a room that they had intended to use as his "man cave." Once they knew a baby was coming, the man cave space had been repurposed into a nursery.

Scotty had removed each of the crib pieces from its individual packaging and had laid all of the items out on the floor. By following the instructions, we had the crib put together in no time. Cherisse's contribution to the project was to dress up the now-assembled crib with a mattress, a pad, and a teddy bear–decorated fitted sheet. Once the job was done, we headed out to dinner.

Cherisse's bout with early-pregnancy morning sickness had passed. She had transformed from a gray, pinched, and starving waif into a glowingly expectant mother. At dinner the conversation seldom strayed far from talking about the upcoming baby.

"We've decided on a name," she told me at last.

"You have?"

She smiled. "Jonas Pierre Beaumont," she said, "after his two grandfathers."

Cherisse Madrigal Beaumont came to the United States from France on a student visa. She and Scotty had met in school and had fallen in love. They'd made plans for a blow-out destination wedding, but those had been suddenly scaled back when her father, Pierre, had suffered a recurrence of prostate cancer. He passed away soon after their hurry-up wedding. So yes, their choosing his name made sense. Their choosing mine was a real honor.

"Hear, hear!" I exclaimed, raising my glass of lemonade to hers. "Sounds like there's going to be another J. P. Beaumont in the family."

But for me their apparent joy stood in stark contrast to Naomi's appalling situation, and the difference between the two was enough to break my heart. Needless to say, I didn't wreck the spell by bringing up the possible unintended consequences of my one-night stand with Jasmine Day.

It was neither the time nor the place, and I just flat couldn't.

CHAPTER 13

WHEN LUCY AND I stepped off the elevator at the penthouse level, my first thought was that we had exited at the wrong floor. Most of the time, the only food that ends up here is takeout, but now the undeniable aroma of cooking food—onions, garlic, basil, and beef—was all around us. When I opened the door to the unit and stepped inside, the utter deliciousness of it was almost overwhelming. Glancing into the kitchen, I spotted a large baking dish filled with lasagna cooling on the counter. Alan Dale and Athena were in the family room with the TV on. I didn't blame him. The TV in the guest bedroom is tiny compared to the one in the family room.

"I take it Marge cooked up a storm today?"

Alan nodded. "She says I'm nothing but skin and bones, and she's determined to fatten me up. Have you eaten?"

I felt a stab of guilt. When Mel isn't around, I'm used to coming and going without having to report to anyone. "I had dinner with my son and his wife," I said. "Sorry, I should have called to let you know."

"No problem," he said. "Now that it's cooled down some, I'll put the leftovers in the fridge."

"How's Athena?"

"She's been fussy today," he said, "a little colicky."

"How'd you fare today?" I asked. The baby might have been fussy, but Alan didn't look especially happy either.

He sighed. "The social worker says we're the ones who have to find Athena's father."

"DSHS won't help with that?"

Alan shook his head. "Unfortunately not, and without having Athena's father sign off they won't consider allowing me to take her out of state. The social worker's suggestion was that I give up, go home, and let the state place Athena in foster care somewhere up here while we wait for the fatherhood question to be sorted out. I told her that wasn't going to happen. I'm afraid the meeting didn't end on a very good note."

"You filed a missing-persons report on Naomi?"

Alan nodded. "And I tried to file one on Peter Mayfield, too, but the guy I talked to told me no dice. He said I didn't have enough information—no date of birth, place of birth, occupation, physical description, last known address, or even an approximate date when Petey disappeared. In other words, I got nowhere on that. So how about you?" he asked. "Did you make any progress?"

"Quite a bit, actually," I said. "With the help of one of Agnes's neighbors, I managed to collect a toothbrush and a comb and hairbrush from her house. If I can call in some markers, maybe I can get someone to create a DNA profile on her that will connect up to Athena's DNA."

Alan's face brightened. "So we'd know for sure that Petey was Athena's father, but we'd still need to find him. Anything else?"

"I spoke to Petey's aunt, Lenora, but she wasn't exactly helpful—and not especially concerned to hear that he's gone missing either. She strikes me as a not very nice woman. I think there's a good chance that she's deliberately trying to cheat Petey out of his share of his grandmother's estate."

"Really?"

"In talking to one of Agnes Mayfield's neighbors, I learned Agnes was suffering from some kind of worsening mental condition. At the time when she was supposedly transferring those West Seattle properties over to her daughter—properties that most likely made up the bulk of her estate—there's a good chance Agnes was in no condition to handle her own affairs, to say nothing of disposing of her property."

"What do we do next?" Alan asked.

"As I said before, I'm going to call in some markers and try to get DNA profiles on both Agnes and Athena. By proving they're related, we'll also be proving Petey is Athena's father. Depending on the provisions in Agnes's will, Petey might be in line to inherit something. And if Petey is really gone, his portion might be passed on to Athena, especially if we can prove that there was wrongdoing on Lenora's part."

"But that'll all take lawyers, money, and time," Alan groaned.

"It can't hurt to try," I said. "You look after Athena and leave the rest to me."

My cell phone rang in my pocket. I had missed my commute-time conversation with Mel, and I thought it would be her. However, caller ID said DOORMAN.

"Mr. Sam Shelton is here to see you," Bob said, "Mr. Shelton and Billy Bob."

"Thank you. I'll be right down."

I grabbed a Ziploc bag and a covered plastic storage container from the cabinet. I loaded the first with kibble and the second with a hefty helping of Marge's lasagna. Then, with those and some plastic silverware in hand, I headed down to the lobby. Sam and his dog were standing outside, under the awning.

"Come on in," I said, holding the door open. "I brought both of you some dinner. We can go on up to the sixth floor. There are undercover picnic tables out by the running track."

"Are you sure?" Sam asked dubiously.

"I'm sure."

I knew there were a few of the more hoity-toity residents of the building who would turn up their noses at finding a homeless man and his dog riding in the elevator, but too bad. Sam and Billy Bob were my guests. Fortunately, we made it on and off the elevator without anyone joining us. I led him outside on the sixth floor, and we settled in at one of the outdoor picnic tables.

In terms of amenities, having an outside recreational area at a downtown high-rise is supposed to be a big deal. And, I suppose, there are a few days in the dead of summer when it's actually nice. But what the architects somehow failed to take into consideration is the weather patterns created by nearby buildings, which means that most of the time the outdoor area on Belltown Terrace's sixth floor would work just fine as a Formula One wind tunnel. As Sam and Billy Bob dove into their food, they were totally unaffected by the cold, but then again they were used to living outside. I wasn't, and I was freezing. I was also dying to know what had prompted Sam to show up in the lobby, but I tried to maintain my role as a proper host and waited until he finished his meal and pushed his dish aside.

"That was wonderful," he said. "Thank you."

"You're welcome," I told him. "Now, what can I do for you?"

"I may have a lead on your missing mama," he said.

"Really?"

He nodded. "The people who live on the streets have an informal underground of sorts."

I already knew that. It was that very underground that had alerted us to the unwelcome presence of Ken Purcell lying in wait for Mel.

"What's it telling you?"

"Do you use I-90 much?" Sam asked.

"Hardly at all," I said. "For most of what I need, 520 works just fine. Why?"

"You told me that the cops picked Naomi up just west of the Mount Baker Tunnel. There's a homeless encampment just up the street on the embankment on the north side of the interstate."

This was hardly news from the front. There are homeless camps everywhere in Seattle these days—on sidewalks, under bridges, under the Alaskan Way Viaduct, wherever. And then, of course, there were Sam and Billy Bob, living under a mound of blankets and tarps in a fire-escape alcove in the churchyard right next door to where we were right now.

"So?" I asked, hoping he'd get to the point.

"It's for women only," he said. "No boys allowed."

"And?"

"I heard a rumor that a while back there was a woman there who was expecting a baby. And when it came time for her to have it, the women from the encampment helped boost her over the Jersey barrier in hopes someone would pick her up and take her to a hospital."

"Which is exactly what happened," I said.

Sam nodded. "I've also been told that a day or so later she turned back up at the camp. My source said she wasn't expecting anymore, but she didn't have the baby with her either."

"Did they say her name was Naomi?"

"Didn't give a name."

"Is she still there?"

"Hard to say," Sam said. "Maybe, maybe not."

"How's the best way to approach this?" I asked.

Sam gave me an appraising look. "As far as I can tell, you're definitely not a girl," he observed. "Didn't you hear what I said? That camp is strictly no boys allowed, and the woman who runs it is one tough cookie."

It goes without saying that the people who live on the street have to be tough. If they're not, and sometimes even if they are, they don't survive for long.

"What do you suggest?" I asked.

"If you go there, you'll need to bring a woman along with you, someone who can act as an interpreter or negotiator or ambassador, but don't think for a minute that you can bring along that missus of yours. Those women will spot her as a cop, and you won't get anywhere."

It was almost as though Sam had read my mind. As soon as he mentioned that I'd need to have a female escort to visit the all-girl encampment, Mel Soames was the only name that came to mind. Admittedly, she does look like a cop—a very attractive cop, from my point of view—but even when she's out of uniform, that law-enforcement presence is always front and center and there for all to see.

"Any suggestions?" I asked.

"Ever hear of the Pike Street Mission?" he asked.

I had to think about that for a minute, but then I remembered. The last I knew, it had been a tiny shelter operating in the repurposed basement of a defunct bar off a rat-infested alley near the Pike Place Market.

"Isn't that the one a lady named Reverend Laura Beardsley runs down by the market?"

"Reverend Laura passed away a couple of years ago," Sam informed me, letting me know that I'd been out of touch with my downtown Seattle roots for a while.

"Her shelter's still called the Pike Street Mission," Sam continued, "but they had to move. The building they used got torn down so someone could build an upscale hotel. They're down closer to Pioneer Square these days. And the reason I'm suggesting them is that now they mostly cater to women. The director from there might have some standing with the ladies out on I-90."

One of Belltown Terrace's heartier residents came out to do nighttime laps on the lit running track. The first time he jogged past where we were sitting, Billy Bob issued a low-throated growl. Sam stood up at once. "We'd best be going," he said. "It's past our bedtime. Thanks for the grub."

"I'll walk you down to the lobby," I told him. "But remember, if we find Naomi at that camp, the reward is yours."

"Fair enough," he said, "and just so you know, I'm still on the lookout for Petey."

My phone was ringing as I rode back up in the elevator. "Good evening," Mel said. "Sorry to call so late. I was stuck in a city-council meeting. How was your day?"

Letting myself back into our unit, I discovered that the leftover lasagna had been put away, the dishwasher was running, and Alan Dale and Athena were nowhere in sight. I took the phone into the family room and gave Mel as complete a rendition of the day's doings as I could manage, ending with my conversation with Sam Shelton.

"Her name's Rachel," Mel said. "Last name Seymour—at least that's the name I remember."

"Who is Rachel?" I asked.

"The person who took over running the show at the Pike Street Mission after Reverend Laura died," Mel replied. "She was a guest speaker at a YWCA luncheon I attended a few months ago. She's an unlikely-looking CEO, but she's also a pistol and very, very impressive."

"I guess I'll be meeting her in person tomorrow," I said.

"When you do," Mel advised, "here's a word to the wise. Rachel may belong to that group commonly referred to as little people, but the terminology she prefers, as clarified in her speech, is dwarf."

"Yes, ma'am," I replied. "I'll be sure to mind my verbal p's and q's."

I spent some time on my iPad making a to-do list for the following morning, and Rachel Seymour's name was on the top line. Next up was a visit to the County Clerk's Office to find out whether or not Agnes Mayfield's will had been probated. Third came a necessary visit to the King County Medical Examiner's Office for a bit of DNA-profiling advice. Once those items were handled, it remained to be seen if an attempted visit to that all-female homeless camp would be in order.

After I'd laid out a mental itinerary for the following day, I worked a few crosswords to let off steam. I had just plugged the iPad in to charge overnight when Lucy stood up, walked over to my chair, and gave me "the look" that meant it was time for her last walk of the evening.

"Okay, girl," I told her. "Let's go."

It was a quick in and out. When we came back, I finished getting ready for bed. By lights-out once again Lucy was nowhere to be seen. I didn't need to search the whole unit this time, because I knew exactly where she'd be—in the guest room, either next to the crib or under it. So I gathered up Lucy's bed and carried it from my room into the guest room for her, a variation on a theme of the mountain moving to Muhammad.

Sure enough, there she was, curled up under the crib. When I shoved the bed under the crib with her, she climbed onto it and favored me with a grateful thump of her tail. Most people would tell you dogs can't talk, but they're wrong. That tail thump was the equivalent of a verbal thank-you if ever there was one.

CHAPTER 14

ATHENA WOKE ME up a couple of times overnight, but both times I was able to go right back to sleep. Maybe I had adjusted to the new reality that there were other people—people who weren't Mel—on the premises. When I woke up at 7:30 A.M., it was to the familiar aroma of bacon, eggs, and toast coming from an unfamiliar location—our condo's kitchen. I donned my dog-walking duds before venturing out of the bedroom. Alan was standing at the stove wielding a spatula. When I reached for the dog leash, he stopped me.

"Don't bother," he said. "I already took Lucy out. Athena was asleep, and I figured the least I could do was make myself useful. The doorman showed us where we were supposed to go. I picked up after her and everything. I haven't fed her, though. I didn't know how much you give her. As for your eggs, how do you like them? I scrambled mine."

"Over easy," I told him, "if you don't mind, that is."

"Not at all."

I dished up Lucy's food and turned on the coffee machine. By the time my morning java had burbled into my cup, two more eggs were sizzling sunny-side up in the pan. When Alan flipped them gently with a flick of his wrist and without breaking either yolk, I was duly impressed.

"You're pretty handy when it comes to rattling those pots and pans," I commented as he expertly slid the eggs onto a waiting plate. "How'd you learn to do that? If I ever attempted that move, the eggs would end up either on the floor or the ceiling."

"My mom cooked in a diner most of the time I was growing up," Alan said. "She's the one who taught me."

"Is Marge coming over today?" I asked.

"Nope," Alan said, buttering the toast. "I told her I thought I could handle it. After a couple nights of sleep, I'm feeling half human again."

Alan added a piece of buttered toast and two perfectly done pieces of bacon alongside the eggs on our plates, and we settled in at the counter to eat.

"So what's your plan for the day?" I asked.

"Athena's due back over at Seattle Children's for a checkup later this morning," Alan told me. "Once that's over, we'll just hang out here, if that's all right."

"It's fine with me," I told him. "Do whatever you want."

"How about you?"

"I've got a list of places to go and people to see, none of them necessarily dog-friendly. Would you mind looking after Lucy?"

"Not at all," he said. "She's a great dog."

I remembered Alan's initial wariness when he'd first caught sight of Lucy a few days earlier. In the course of three short days, that long-legged hairy beast had won him over the same way she had me.

When we finished eating and were putting the kitchen to rights, I handed Alan an unused sandwich bag.

"What's this for?" he asked.

"I'm pretty sure Mel has cotton swabs in her medicine chest. I'd like you to use one of them to swab the inside of Athena's cheek. When you finish, put the used swab in this."

"For DNA?" he asked.

I nodded.

"Sure," Alan said, "will do. Back in a flash."

I went into the bedroom to change from dog-walker duds to something decent. While I was brushing my teeth and looking at my face in the mirror, I realized that another DNA profile was in order as well—my own. I left the house a few minutes later with a bag containing Athena's DNA sample in my left-hand pocket and the one holding mine in the other. One way or the other, we were going to find out the truth. Either Athena Dale was my granddaughter or she wasn't. As far as I was concerned, that was far more important than ascertaining whether or not Petey was her father. He was, according to his Aunt Lenora, a loser with very little to offer his daughter. On the other hand, what I could offer her was something else entirely.

A few minutes later, when I headed out the door, Lucy exhibited zero interest in riding along. I didn't blame her. She had spent most of the previous two days confined to the backseat of the S550. Even so, I confess to being slightly miffed. At the very least, she could have pretended to want to come with me.

As I drove down Second Avenue toward Pioneer Square, I told Siri to dial Rosemary Mellon's office number. Dr. Roz, as she prefers to be called, is a relatively new addition to Seattle's crime-fighting community. Tired of snow, she'd left Chicago behind and had hired on with the King County Medical Examiner's Office a number of years earlier. An uncompromising woman with a dark sense of humor, for a long time Dr. Roz had worked the morgue's night shift, but her profound sense of duty and her penchant for helping cops solve homicides—this retired cop included, by the way—had led to her inevitable promotion. She was now King County's chief medical examiner and permanently stuck working what she considered to be "the boring" day shift.

"Hey, Beau," she said when she picked up. "How's it going?"

"I need a favor and was hoping I could take you to lunch."

"Today?"

"Yes, today."

"Good luck with that. We've got no scheduled autopsies on tap, but I've got three groups of high-school STEM kids touring the morgue today, with exactly half an hour between them. As long as we eat in the cafeteria at Harborview, I could probably manage eleven thirty, if that's okay with you. It's not fancy, but it'll work. What kind of favor?"

"Let's talk about it when I get there."

"In other words, this sounds like something we maybe shouldn't discuss in my office?" she asked.

"Exactly."

"Okay," she finished. "Meet in the cafeteria at eleven thirty. If you're asking a favor, you're buying."

"Fair enough," I told her.

I managed to score an open slot in the Triangle Parking Garage at Second and James. It was conveniently located between my two intended destinations—across the street from the Pike Street Mission and a few short blocks away from the King County Courthouse.

Homeless shelters—legally established ones, that is—are divided into two separate categories. Some operate on a twenty-four-hour basis and people staying there are considered to be residents. The other kind is for transients and offers overnight shelter only. People come in out of the rain and cold in the evening and check out the next morning. The first version of Pike Street Mission, under the direction of Reverend Laura Beardsley, had been of the latter variety and had been limited to a total of six beds—cots, really. The new version, under the direction of Rachel Seymour, had risen to the level of residential and could accommodate up to twenty residents.

The shelter was located in what had long been restaurant space. It had gone through a number of iterations over the years, opening and shutting down with astonishing regularity as one owner after another disappeared into some kind of financial black hole. When I stepped inside, I saw that very little of the restaurant identity remained. Just to the left of the front entrance was a small chapel. To the right, where a maître d' might have stood in the past, was an office with the word DIRECTOR stenciled on the door. Part of the commercial kitchen had been redesigned to function as the source of food for a small communal dining hall where a few residents were still finishing breakfast. Adjoining that was a lobby area with a wall-mounted TV set surrounded by a collection of sofas and chairs. The remainder of the space had been carved up into a series of studio apartments, each containing a bedroom and a private bath.

I turned to the right and knocked on the door to the office.

"Come in."

The room was small. A well-used wooden desk took up most of the floor space, leaving room—barely—for two visitors' chairs. Directly in front of me, a large computer monitor sat facing the far side of the desk, with neat stacks of paper situated on either side. At first glance the room appeared to be empty, but then a tiny fist appeared on one side of the monitor, turning it slightly. The motion revealed a woman so small in stature that she'd been completely invisible behind the intervening screen.

"Yes," she said, "may I help you?"

Reverend Rachel Seymour sat bolt upright on a chair that had been raised high enough to make the surface of the desk workable for her. She was probably somewhere in her fifties. Her dark hair was pulled back in a bun. She wore a black blazer, complete with a white clergy collar showing at her throat, and she was all business.

"My name is J. P. Beaumont," I explained, handing her one of my cards. "I believe you might have met my wife a few months back at a YWCA luncheon. Her name is Mel Soames. She's the new chief of police in Bellingham."

"I remember her," Reverend Rachel Seymour said. "Mel and I managed to exchange a few words in the course of the luncheon. She's very impressive."

"She said the same about you, Reverend Seymour," I told her.

"Call me Rachel, please," she said. "Have a seat, Mr. Beaumont. To what do I owe the pleasure?"

In order to enlist Rachel's help, I needed to tell her the story, and over the course of the next half hour I did exactly that. Well, almost. I might have neglected to say that there was a good chance I was Naomi Dale's biological father. After all, that had not yet been confirmed. She listened quietly, nodding occasionally as I spoke.

"Your source is correct," Rachel said when I finished. "I'm familiar with that particular encampment, and it's definitely limited to women only. Many of the women who find themselves on the street these days are fleeing from domestic-violence situations or have been victimized while homeless. A surprisingly large number of them are suffering from PTSD, and that's why so many shelters, including this one, don't take in men, although God knows there are enough men out there who are also being victimized and are in need of help. So what are you asking?"

"I was hoping I could get you to agree to accompany me to the camp and intercede on my behalf in order to verify if Naomi is actually there. With any luck we may be able to persuade her to come speak to her father and perhaps even agree to relinquish her parental rights."

"And if she refuses?"

"I don't know," I said. "I suppose that puts us back at square one."

"Just to be clear," Rachel told me, "I won't accompany you to the camp."

My heart fell. So my pitch hadn't worked. It was a complete washout.

"Okay, then," I said, starting to get to my feet. "Sorry to have taken up so much of your morning. I'll be on my way."

"I didn't say I wouldn't help," Rachel said, motioning me back into my chair. "I said I wouldn't take you there. That would be a provocation. I know Dorothy, the woman who's in charge. We've had several previous dealings. If Naomi Dale is actually there and willing to come with me, fine, I'll bring her here. This might be a neutral place for Naomi and her father to meet with each other, but I won't do anything by force, Mr. Beaumont. She has to be willing to come."

"I understand," I said.

"But not to worry," Rachel added with a smile. "I may have a way to sweeten the deal. I learned just a few minutes ago that one of our residents will be vacating her room later on this afternoon. We have a waiting list, of course, but as the director I have some discretion in that regard. Considering everything Naomi has been through and with her child's well-being hanging in the balance, she may be amenable to coming along if I can offer her an alternative to sleeping in a tent."

I could barely believe my ears. "Thank you," I said. "Thank you so much."

"I think you and Mr. Dale have good cause for a hopeful outcome," Rachel continued. "According to what you've said, Naomi left her baby at a hospital where she could be properly cared for. She didn't give birth to Athena on the street and drop her into the nearest dumpster. And she gave the hospital her real name and her grandmother's phone number in Texas. She might have been desperate, but I think she wanted Athena to be found and given a chance."

I should have had brains enough to just keep quiet at that moment, but I didn't. "When do you think you'll be able to go?" I asked.

An amused Reverend Seymour smiled at me. "I've met people like you before, Mr. Beaumont. If somebody gives you an inch, you think you're a ruler."

"Exactly," I agreed with a grin. "You've got me dead to rights."

She shook her head, as if in exasperation, and then consulted her watch. "I have a noontime meeting. If I can make room for this to happen later on today, I will." She picked up my business card. "What's the best number to reach you?"

"My cell phone," I told her. "I'll be waiting to hear."

Feeling downright triumphant, I didn't exactly

skip when I walked out the front door of the Pike Street Mission which is no longer located on Pike Street. My two fake knees precluded skipping, but I came very close—as close to it as I've come in years—because, for the first time, I felt as though Alan Dale and I really were making progress.

CHAPTER 15

As I MADE my way from the mission to the courthouse, I was practically walking on air. I was tempted to stop long enough to call Alan and give him the news right then, but I didn't. What if Reverend Seymour wasn't the kind of miracle worker I hoped she was? What if Naomi refused to leave the encampment? Worst of all, what if I was dead wrong and she wasn't even there? Nope, it would be better to hold off on saying a word until I saw how things played out.

I'm afraid my dealings with Linda Collins in the County Recorder's Office the day before had left me with unrealistic expectations about how the world worked. In the County Clerk's Office, rather than a tattooed, studded, and pink-haired young lady, here I was dealing with a posted notice that told me to take a number and wait. Not a good sign. I watched the people working behind the counter, trying to estimate how long each set of transactions took and which of the several clerks was likely to be available when it was my turn. Naturally, I ended up with a sour-faced old biddy whose idea of customer service was somewhere south of what you find these days in your local branch of the Department of Licensing.

It was no surprise that I drew the woman I'd deemed to be the surliest of the bunch. Her name tag told me she was Katy Lamb. She might have been a "Lamb," but she wasn't exactly meek.

"What can I do for you?" she wanted to know. The question was asked with a snarl and in a tone reminiscent of someone asking, "Would you like a punch in the nose?"

"I'm here to find out if someone's will has been probated," I told her. "Can you help me?"

"Whose?"

"The name is Agnes Mayfield."

"Middle name?"

"I don't know."

"Date of birth?"

"I don't know."

"Date of death?"

"I don't know."

This was going sideways in a hurry, probably not unlike Alan's unsuccessful attempt at filing a missing-persons report on Petey the day before.

The woman behind the counter placed both hands on her hips and frowned up at me. "Exactly what *do* you know?" she demanded.

My being surly back wasn't going to make things better. I hauled out one of my business cards and passed it across the counter.

She looked at it. "So?" she asked.

"I'm working on behalf of a client," I said, "Mrs. Mayfield's great-granddaughter, Athena."

"Then I suggest you contact your client and have her provide some information on the deceased. It'll make both our jobs easier."

"Athena happens to be a six-week-old infant who was abandoned at birth by both her parents," I replied. "I have reason to believe that her great-aunt, Agnes's daughter Lenora, is trying to cheat my client out of her portion of the inheritance."

"Someone's trying to cheat a baby?"

I nodded.

Katy Lamb's transformation was instantaneous. "Why didn't you say that to begin with? Let me see if I can help. What do you know?"

I gave her the paltry details I had at my disposal. In the end and in a matter of minutes, working with nothing more than Agnes's first and last names as well as her address, Katy Lamb handed over a treasure trove of material. She provided me with death certificates for both Peter Arthur Mayfield and Agnes Matilda Mayfield. Agnes's date of death was listed as December 20, 2016. Cause of death was listed as complications of Alzheimer's. Manner of death was listed as natural. Agnes's will had not yet been probated, but Peter's had. It was simple and straightforward. He left everything he owned to his wife, Agnes. If she preceded him in death, his estate, after final expenses, was to be divided in equal shares between his two children, Lenora and Arthur, per stirpes.

I work crossword puzzles on a daily basis. I know

a lot of words, but the term "per stirpes" wasn't part of my repertoire. "Arthur died years ago, but what does this mean?" I asked Katy, pointing at the puzzling words.

"That means that if Peter's son, Arthur, died leaving behind living children of his own, those children would inherit whatever remains of his share, divided equally among them. The same would hold true for the next generation. How many kids did Arthur have?" Katy asked.

"One only," I replied. "Another Peter, aka Petey, who happens to have gone missing."

"And he's Athena's father?"

"That is correct," I affirmed, knowing full well that the word "presumably" wouldn't cut it with someone like Katy Lamb.

"Then Arthur's share would pass on to Athena through her father. Let me take another look at Mr. Mayfield's will," she said. I handed it over, and she studied it for some time. "This will is a cheapy—simple and to the point. It was signed and dated back in 1973. I'm guessing that Agnes had her own will drawn up at about the same time. Once a couple has gone to the trouble of hiring an attorney and drawing up wills, they generally take a 'set it and forget it' point of view. When the first spouse dies, if the surviving spouse doesn't remarry, he or she leaves things be. In other words, the second will remains valid and unchanged."

"You're saying that Agnes may have drawn up her own will at the same time with many of the same stipulations?"

"In my experience that's highly likely," Katy

answered. "And do you see the name of the firm here?" she asked, pointing

"Stockman and Dodge?" I read aloud. "What about it?"

"They're still in business, Mr. Beaumont," Katy told me with a smug smile. "Their offices are just a few blocks up the street from here at Third and Marion. If Agnes's original will is still valid or if a new one has been drawn up in the meantime, someone in their office might possibly know about it and be able to help you."

"And what if an heir is MIA at the time the will comes up for probate?" I asked.

"That's why I suggest you contact that law firm. Athena's guardian would be able to petition that the father's share be held in trust until he's either located or declared to be deceased. And if that's the case—if it turns out Petey is dead and if the terms in Agnes Mayfield's will are the same as those of her late husband's, Petey's share would automatically pass through him to his only surviving child—to Athena."

I felt like leaping over the counter and giving Katy Lamb a smooch on her brightly rouged cheek. I did not.

"Thank you," I said. "Thank you so much. You've been a huge help."

"Good luck to you, Mr. Beaumont. I'm glad someone is looking out for that poor little girl. It sounds as though she needs it."

By the time I was back out in the lobby, I felt like I was batting a thousand. But there, directly in front of me across the lobby, was that other office—

the County Recorder's Office. I checked my watch. I had at least twenty minutes before my meet-up with Dr. Roz. So, since one good turn deserves another, instead of heading straight for the elevator I went to the Recorder's Office. Linda Collins wasn't out front at the counter, but someone there went back to get her.

"How's it going, Mr. Beaumont?" she asked when she turned up a couple of minutes later. "What can I do for you?"

"I was wondering where Corky's staying these days," I told her. "Even if he doesn't know me, I thought it might be nice if I dropped by, just to pay my respects."

"He's at a place called Holman House up in Phinney Ridge," she told me. "It's only a few blocks from their house. That way Gran can walk over to see him whenever she wants without having to wait for someone to drive her."

"Great," I said, making a note. "I don't know when I'll get around to it, but I'll make it a point to do it soon. He was a big help to me when I was new in homicide. It's the least I can do."

"That's wonderful," Linda said. "And how's that other thing going?"

"Making progress," I told her. "In this business it doesn't get any better than that."

CHAPTER 16

HOSPITAL CAFETERIAS ARE not known for their fine dining, but if you need to eat and dash, they work. Dr. Roz was already at a table with a loaded tray in front of her by the time I arrived. I went through the line and grabbed a piece of pizza and a cup of coffee.

"Hey," I said, taking a seat. "I thought I was supposed to buy."

"You're late," she told me, pointing at her watch.

I had missed the target by only a couple of minutes, but she was right. "Sorry," I muttered.

"It's okay," she replied with a smile. "I'll catch you next time. What's the story?"

"I need to create a DNA profile," I said. "In actual fact I need three DNA profiles—in something of a hurry."

"Rumor has it you're a PI now," she said. "Are you working a case?"

"Yup."

"I just got promoted to be chief M.E.," she said. "There are a number of old-timers around here who aren't exactly thrilled at the idea."

"Congrats on that promotion, by the way, but what are you saying?" I asked.

"As of this minute, I'm operating under a microscope. If I tried doing something off the books and it got back to the powers-that-be in county government, I'd be up the proverbial shit creek. So what's going on?"

I told her. I had passed the story along often enough by now that I'd learned to boil it down to reasonable proportions. As per usual, in talking about Naomi and Athena's situation, I left my own possible parental involvement out of the discussion.

"So I've got two cheek swabs along with the hairbrush, comb, and toothbrush I removed from Agnes Mayfield's bathroom. With profiles on all of those in hand, I should be able to prove that Athena is Agnes's biological granddaughter. As such, she could be in line to receive a portion of Agnes's estate. So where can I go to get a deal on quick-and-dirty DNA profiling?"

"I might have an answer for you," Dr. Roz said. "How do you feel about making charitable contributions?"

"Depends on the charity," I said. "Why?"

"Have you ever heard of the Sholeetsa Project?"

That one stumped me. "The what?" I asked.

"You're from around here, right?" Dr. Roz asked. I nodded. "Seattle born and bred."

"So you know about Chief Sealth?"

"Of course, I know Chief Sealth, aka Chief Seattle—the city's Native American forefather. Why?"

"Sholeetsa was Chief Sealth's mother. I guess that makes her Seattle's foregrandmother."

"Presumably the project you mentioned is named after her, but what is it?"

"As a cop, you surely know that crimes against Native Americans in general and Native American women in particular are vastly underreported and often go unsolved. One of the primary reasons for that is a lack of DNA profiles inside the Native American population. Even with DNA found at crime scenes, both victims and perpetrators often end up going unidentified.

"The Sholeetsa Project is a nonprofit, headquartered here in Seattle, that is trying to rectify that situation, and not just here in the Pacific Northwest either. They're going nationwide. They have an up-to-the-minute lab, along with well-trained technicians, doing nothing else but creating DNA profiles in the Native American community. They're also in the process of launching an ambitious program to collect DNA samples from tribal members all over the country in hopes of vastly expanding the number of Native American profiles present in DNA databases. Not surprisingly, the Sholeetsa Project is strapped for cash."

"And looking for donations?"

"Indeed," Dr. Roz said. "Let's say some random Anglo guy just happened to wander in off the street looking for some help with creating DNA profiles. If said guy happened to be willing to add some dollars to the project's coffers, I'm pretty sure said profiles would be forthcoming."

In the world of law enforcement, that kind of wheeling and dealing would be called a bribe. In the private sector, it counts as a charitable donation. But under the current set of circumstances, if a donation would get the job done, I was all in.

On occasions like this, it's nice to be in a position to have money to burn, something for which I give thanks to my second wife, Anne Corley, every single day. When she flashed through my life, she left me a considerable fortune, along with some very canny money managers. Over time that fortune has grown. Mel's and my financial future is assured. My kids—the ones I knew about at least—are taken care of. As for the rest? I'm at a stage in my life where it's becoming all too clear to me that you can't take it with you. From time to time, on those occasions when I feel inclined to spend money like a drunken sailor, I'm free to do so.

"Once they create the profile," Dr. Roz continued, "they can pass it along to whatever law-enforcement agencies need to see it. As far as that missing father is concerned—Petey, you called him?"

"His name is Peter, but everyone calls him Petey."

"I suggest you create a file on Petey with NamUs. It's a nationwide missing-persons database. You can enter the details you know about him, including dental records if available. In this case you should also include his grandmother's DNA profile. That way if he's lying unidentified in a morgue someplace, his DNA and hers will show up as a familial match."

"NamUs?"

She spelled it out for me. "Anybody can use it—cops, families, M.E.s. Of course, if you get a hit on one of those, it's most likely not going to be good news."

"Understood."

Dr. Roz pulled out her phone, studied the screen, and then pressed a couple of buttons. A moment later my phone dinged. "I sent you a text with the Sholeetsa Project's Web site," she explained. "Their CEO is a friend of mine, a lady named Loretta Hawk. You'll like her."

"I'm sure I will."

Dr. Roz's phone buzzed, and she leaped to her feet. "Oops," she said. "I hate to eat and run, but the next batch of STEM kids is already waiting in my office."

Off she went, leaving me there staring at her text. The Sholeetsa Project hadn't been on my to-do list when I left home earlier that morning, but it was on it now—in a big way. I swallowed my last bite of pizza, finished my coffee, and headed out—in search of Chief Sealth's mother and ultimately my very own daughter.

CHAPTER 17

BACK IN THE car, I loaded the address for the Sholeetsa Project into the GPS and headed for Columbia City down by Boeing Field. It seemed ironic. Here I was using modern technology to search for even more modern technology, but I was using all that technology to do antiquated police work. You pick up one lead and follow that to the next one. Back in the old days, we called it "shoe leather." If there's a more current bit of jargon, I'm unaware of it.

Harborview Medical Center is on the edge of Capitol Hill, east of downtown Seattle. Columbia City is just south of downtown proper. I hopped on I-5 southbound, and ten minutes after waving good-bye to Dr. Roz, I was pulling in to the Sholeetsa Project's parking lot.

Columbia City, just north of Boeing Field, is mostly industrial these days. Relatively narrow streets are lined with old-fashioned redbrick buildings. I seemed to remember that once upon a time the building housing the Sholeetsa Project had been a paint store. The façade remained unchanged. With my collection of plastic bags in hand, I headed inside. As soon as I stepped through the front door, I felt as though I'd landed on a Federation starship. The place had been gutted. All trace of the space's humble retail origins had been stripped away, leaving behind an interior that was shiny, sleek, and modern. The well-lit lobby area was relatively small but not at all cramped. Beyond that, a thick glass wall allowed visitors a view into the working guts of the place—a scientific lab so up to date that it would have been the envy of a lot of universities. Inside the lab several white-coated technicians were hard at work. At the far end of the lobby a sliding door operated by a key card opened into the lab. A stern message had been stenciled onto the glass—NO UN-AUTHORIZED ADMITTANCE.

I approached the reception desk and handed my business card over to the young woman seated there. "I'm here to see Loretta Hawk," I told her.

The receptionist nodded. "I believe she's expecting you. Her office is just over there," she added, pointing behind me.

I was a little surprised at this casual approach. "I just let myself in?"

"As long as her door's open, people are welcome," the receptionist replied. "It looks open to me."

As soon as I appeared in the doorway, I spied a woman seated behind a desk covered with neat stacks of what were evidently well-organized files. Everything about Loretta Hawk spoke of her origins. She was Native American through and through. I estimated her age to be somewhere in her fifties. Her face was narrow, her nose aquiline. Her facial wrinkles weren't furrows so much as they were laugh lines. Her shoulder-length hair was smooth and straight. It was mostly black but with hints of gray—that natural kind of gray you earn by putting in your time on this planet. When she stood up and stepped around the desk to greet me, I saw she was wearing a pair of jeans (with no holes in the legs, by the way) and a western shirt as well as a pair of snakeskin boots. There was an eye-popping turquoise squash-blossom necklace at the base of her throat, and an assortment of showy turquoise rings adorned her hands.

"You must be white man with heap big wampum looking for DNA," she said with a welcoming smile.

That amazingly politically incorrect comment stunned me to momentary silence.

She grinned at me, her brown eyes twinkling. "That was a joke!" she explained. "I usually start out by telling my visitors if we'da sunk that *Mayflower* when it first showed up, we'd never have had any of this trouble. But Roz told me I might be able to wheedle some money out of you, so I decided to play nice. Have a seat, won't you?"

I sat, placing my collection of clear plastic bags on the part of her desk that was closest to my chair and next to an engraved brass nameplate that said LORETTA M. HAWK, PH.D.

"These are the three samples you want profiled?" Loretta asked.

I nodded. "The comb, hairbrush, and toothbrush are all from one individual. The cheek swabs are from two others."

"What's the story here?"

I gave her an abbreviated version. When I finished, there was a momentary pause. "So what do you know about me and about this?" Loretta asked, with an expansive wave that included the whole operation.

"Not much," I admitted, "other than the fact that you're trying to increase the Native American presence in national DNA databases."

"All right," she said, with the twinkle back in her dark eyes, "now that you've shown me yours, I'll show you mine."

It was another politically incorrect joke, a slightly off-color one. The woman behind the desk had a barbed sense of humor. No wonder Dr. Roz liked her. So did I.

"Understood," I said, smiling back to let her know I got it.

"There's nothing wrong with the term 'Native American,'" she added, drawing air quotes around the words, "but I consider myself to be an American, period. I grew up on the Rosebud Sioux. Back then I was called an Indian, and as far as I'm concerned, I still am. If people are offended by that, too bad. I'm also Lakota. What other people call me doesn't matter in the least. As long as the people throwing names around stay out of my way so I can get the job done, they can call me Grandma Moses for all I care."

"I'll bear that in mind," I told her.

"There were a lot of obstacles growing up on the reservation," she continued, "but I was a smart kid—a very smart kid—and my teachers noticed. When I said I wanted to be a doctor when I grew up, they didn't tell me it was impossible. No, they took me seriously. My home life might have been a disaster, but the people at school—the teachers, coaches, and counselors—encouraged me and kept me going. Once I was in high school, they helped me track down scholarships. I was in my first year of medical school in Grand Forks, North Dakota, when my mother was murdered back home. She died in an unlit parking lot behind a scuzzy bar just off the res."

"I'm sorry," I said.

Loretta nodded. "Thank you. It's more than thirty years since that happened. I was in my early twenties, but it still hurts. I had to drop out of school, go back home, and take care of my younger brothers and sisters. I got a job with the tribal police to make ends meet and wound up working as a dispatcher."

"Was your mother's case ever solved?" I asked.

"Not at the time," she said. "As I said, the murder happened off the reservation rather than on it. The case got tossed back and forth between the tribal police and the local authorities, and the cops who were eventually assigned to solve it showed very little interest. There are a few places in the Dakotas where the idea that 'the only good Indian is a dead Indian' still prevails. That was far more pervasive back then than it is now. My mother was an Indian. She was also a diabetic with a serious drinking problem. She never went anywhere without a purse filled with little booze bottles in case she woke up in the morning and the bars were closed.

"But then, a number of years ago, something changed. Suddenly there was a new sheriff in town, and he decided to create a cold-case unit. My mother's case was one of the first ones he ordered reopened. The murder happened in the seventies, so DNA identifications simply didn't exist back then. Amazingly enough, however, physical evidence from my mother's homicide had been preserved, and not just preserved but properly preserved. When it was examined in the state police lab, not only were they able to create a profile of the assailant, they also got a hit. The perpetrator, John Turpin, turned out to be a friend of my mother's—an old drinking buddy, really—who by the early two thousands was doing time in prison on multiple sexual-assault charges."

"His DNA must have turned up in the national criminal DNA database," I suggested.

"You got it."

"Is that why you started all this?"

Loretta nodded. "That was the original inspiration. Once my brothers and sisters were out of school and launched, I figured it was too late for me to go back to medical school—too much time had passed. Instead I got a Ph.D. in microbiology. And all the while, both back on the reservation and while I was in school, I kept seeing my family's history repeated over and over for other families. Horrible crimes would be committed and, likely as not, they went unsolved. Even before I got my Ph.D., the idea of doing something like this was niggling at the back of my mind. It's all I ever talked about, and then one day when I was here in Seattle on a job search, someone put me in touch with a guy named Bill Patton. Ever heard of him?"

"The name sounds vaguely familiar," I said.

"I'm not surprised. His younger brother, Robby, was murdered when they were both in their teens. Robby's homicide was never solved—until last year, by Seattle PD's Cold Case Unit. They used one of those open-source familial DNA databases to home in on a guy who had never been on law enforcement's radar for Robby's murder. Unfortunately, Bill didn't live long enough to see his brother's killer go to prison. But as soon as I talked with Bill Patton, he and I were on the same page. We had both lived with the same kinds of unsolved tragedies haunting our lives, and he was determined to try fixing that problem for others.

"Bill was a multimillionaire in his own right. When he died, he left me this building along with enough money to gut it, rehab it, build the lab, and purchase equipment. It was his idea that we use Chief Sealth's mother's name. He also left an ongoing trust fund to cover expenses, but it seems like there's usually a shortfall in that category, which is why we're always looking for money.

"Back when I was a kid, diabetes was one of the biggest concerns in the Native American community. As part of the research, I remember a team of people showing up at my elementary school and asking for all the kids to leave urine samples. Even though the adults were dead serious about it, we kids thought it was hilarious that we all had to pee in bottles. I don't think it's funny anymore, and we're using that diabetes research as a model. We're sending teams of people out to schools and churches on reservations, to tribal council meetings, dances, and rodeos, to collect as many cheek swabs as possible. Those samples are what we use to create profiles that we're adding to DNA databases across the country. And you know what? It's working. So far we've been instrumental in solving several long-cold cases. We've used familial DNA taken from kids who are currently attending grade school to locate perpetrators in homicides that happened decades before those kids were even born."

Damn. Loretta Hawk was a cagey woman all right, and she had just nailed me square in the sweet spot. When it comes to my personal hot button, tempting me with solving cold cases does the job.

"Where do I sign up?" I asked.

"Sign up?"

"You'll take my Amex, won't you, or do I need to write out a check?"

"Amex would work," Loretta said. "How much do you have in mind?"

"Ten for starters," I said.

"Ten dollars?" she asked with a disappointed frown.

"I meant ten thousand."

"Whoa," she said, brightening. "Heap big wampum indeed!"

I briefly considered cracking a joke about spending money like a drunken Indian, but I didn't. It was okay for Loretta to be politically incorrect, but

I doubted that was a two-way street. Instead I pulled out my Platinum Card and handed it over. It took a few minutes and a call to the Amex concierge desk to make sure all was in order. When we finished the transaction and I stood up to leave, Loretta reached across her desk and gathered my assortment of plastic bags.

"How soon would you like your profiles?" she asked.

"As soon as possible."

"It figures," she said. "Anglos are always in a rush. I don't suppose you've ever heard of Indian time."

"Never," I admitted.

"Don't worry," she said. "We'll do these on white-man time, and I'll call you as soon as they're ready."

CHAPTER 18

LEAVING COLUMBIA CITY that afternoon, I really was on a roll. There was enough good news out there that I was prepared to go straight back home and share some of it with Alan Dale. I hit northbound traffic just south of the I-90 interchange, and that's when my phone rang. The notice on my sound system's screen told me Mel was calling.

"Hey," I said, pushing the button that allowed me to answer hands-free. "Are you about to head out?"

"I wish," she said regretfully. "A couple of lame-brains staged an attempted bank robbery in downtown Bellingham this afternoon and then made a run for the Canadian border. In the process they wiped out several parked vehicles, hit a poor woman in a crosswalk—who may or may not make it—and then took out a dozen cars when the state patrol tried to stop them on northbound I-5."

"So we're talking multiple incidents with multiple responding agencies."

"You got it," she said. "My media-relations officer should be able to handle this, but the mayor wants me on hand in case there's any blowback. . . ."

"And whatever the mayor wants, he gets."

"Exactly," Mel replied.

I think both Mel and I had been surprised to learn how little of Mel's job as chief had to do with actual police work and how much of it had to do with politics.

"So I'm stuck here for the time being," she said. "I may be able to come down tomorrow morning, but then again maybe not. I'll have to let you know. How are things with you?"

She was in a spot where she needed some good news, and so I delivered. "White-man time?" Mel giggled when I finished telling her about my new and very politically incorrect, self-identified "Indian" friend. "Loretta Hawk sounds like a kick. I think I'd like to meet her."

"I think you two would hit it off, and based on our ability to make contributions I'm pretty sure that can be arranged."

"As in pay for play?" she asked.

Those precise words made me think of Jasmine Day, and it wasn't a comfortable feeling.

"It sounds like you're verging on wrapping this thing up," Mel said, helpfully changing the subject.

"Knock wood," I told her. "We'll have to see what, if anything, Rachel Seymour can deliver."

"Don't underestimate her," Mel advised. "From what I hear, she's very good at what she does." I heard a beep on her phone that indicated an incoming call. "Sorry," she said quickly. "Gotta run."

By then it was truly stop-and-go on what's laughably called a "freeway." In the middle of the afternoon, the trip from I-90 to Belltown Terrace, which used to take ten minutes tops, now took thirty-five. I was out of patience by the time I finally made it into the building and wound my way down to P-4.

My nose had been slightly out of joint over the sincere lack of interest Lucy had exhibited when I was preparing to leave home without her. When I stepped off the elevator, it was gratifying to hear her claws come skittering into the vestibule the moment I put my key in the lock.

"Hey, girl," I said, leaning down to return her ecstatic greeting. "Are you ready to go for a walk?"

"No need," Alan called from the other room. "It's such a sunny day, I wrapped Athena in her sling and we both took Lucy out for a walk just a couple of minutes ago. Any news?"

There was actually a lot of news, and I was delighted to sit in the window seat with the sun on my back while telling him of my day's adventures, including the information about hopefully obtaining DNA profiles from the samples I'd provided. In my rendition of the day's news, I neglected to mention that my own cheek swab was among those DNA samples awaiting profiling. And I was less than forthcoming about Rachel Seymour's hoping to find Naomi at the I-90 encampment and possibly lure her into coming to stay the Pike Street Mission. As the hours went by with no further communications from Rachel, it seemed less and less likely to me that she'd be able to deliver.

"Any news on your end?" I asked Alan once I finished my part of the daily report.

"The pediatrician at Children's said Athena is gaining weight and seems to be thriving. We talked about her needing to have ongoing monitoring and maybe early intervention to overcome what might be deficits due to being both premature as well as addicted."

"As in learning disabilities?"

Alan nodded. "Those and maybe some developmental issues as well. The doctor says I need to bring her in to be evaluated by his PA every other week. She'll need the same kind of attention once we get home to Jasper. He said he'd refer us to someone there. I also spoke to our social worker. She says that if we manage to locate Naomi and if she's willing to surrender her rights, we can set up an appointment for the social worker to come meet with her, bringing the necessary relinquishment paperwork along. She says that if Naomi signs the documents in front of her, the social worker can take them before the judge at a dependency hearing and that's it. That way there'd be no need for Naomi or for us to appear before a judge."

"But if it turns out Petey really is the father, we'll need to find him and get him to sign off as well?"

"I guess," Alan agreed, "but once we make all that happen, Athena and I will be good to go. We'll be out of your hair and headed home."

Saying it like that made the process sound easy as pie. I wondered if it would be.

Time slowed to a crawl. As the afternoon sun waned, so did my hope for a positive outcome from Rachel Seymour. Around four thirty I took Lucy out for one more walk, and then we went back inside so I could feed her.

On Friday evenings when Mel and I arrive in Seattle later than usual, we often go to El Gaucho over on First Avenue for dinner. We could call it our neighborhood dive, except it's anything but. It's a fine-dining establishment, and as far as the neighborhood is concerned, it's only a little more than a block away if we exit our building through the garage-door entrance. We go to El Gaucho often enough to be on a first-name basis with most of the waitstaff and some of the line cooks as well, but tonight I already knew that Mel wasn't coming. Once I finished feeding Lucy, I went looking for Alan, who was in the process of removing the platter containing Marge's leftover lasagna from the fridge.

"How long has it been since you've had a good steak?" I asked.

"Years, probably," he answered.

"You're in luck, then," I told him. "Leave that lasagna where it is. There's a great steakhouse just up the street, and we can be there at five P.M. when the doors open."

"But what about Athena?" he asked.

Detectives must be observant. In the course of a couple of days, I had learned that once Athena was fed, she generally went straight to sleep and stayed that way for the better part of two hours. As it happened, Athena's dinnertime had coincided with Lucy's.

"We'll wrap her up and bring her along. The restaurant is only a little over a block from here. Since we'll be unfashionably early, we'll nestle her into a corner booth and she'll sleep . . . well, like a baby."

We both laughed at that, and it's exactly how things worked out. We walked from the condo to the restaurant, with Alan carrying the infant seat containing a cozily bundled Athena. Roger, the maître d' at El Gaucho, might have been a bit startled to have two women-free older men turn up with a loaded infant seat, but he recovered nicely and took us straight to the corner booth tucked in behind the kitchen, which happens to be Mel's and my favorite spot. Alan deferred to me as far as ordering was concerned, and we ended up with tableside Caesars, filet mignons, an order of mashed potatoes, and a side order of roasted corn. My customary O'Doul's arrived without my having to ask for it. Alan ordered iced tea.

As predicted, Athena slept peacefully throughout the meal without letting out so much as a peep. We had decided against desserts and were in the process of boxing up leftovers when my phone rang—with an unknown 206 number showing in caller ID.

"Mr. Beaumont?" an unfamiliar voice inquired when I answered. "Rachel Seymour here."

My heartbeat quickened as she continued.

"I've located Naomi Dale. Your source was correct, she was at the all-female encampment and agreed to come along to the mission. She's in the process of settling into her room and having a bite of dinner. I told her that a private detective hired on her father's behalf came by looking for her. She's willing to see you, but she's not interested in seeing him. There's evidently some bad blood there."

"Should I stop by tonight?" I asked.

"That's probably the best idea," Rachel said. "She's here, but there's no guarantee about how long she'll stay."

"All right, then," I said. "I'm just finishing up with dinner. I'll be there within the next half hour or so."

The call ended. "Be where?" Alan asked.

"The Pike Street Mission."

"Did they find her?" he asked.

I nodded.

"Amen," he said. "So let's go, then." Jumping up, he grabbed for the infant seat.

"Wait," I told him. "It's not that simple. She's willing to talk to me, but she doesn't want to see you."

Disappointment washed across his face. Alan dropped back into the booth, landing full force, as though someone had just lopped both legs off at the knees. He buried his face in his hands.

"She'll never forgive me," he muttered, "and I guess I don't blame her."

"Forgive you for what?"

"For what I said to her. The last time I ever spoke to Naomi was over the phone. Jasmine was in the hospital dying. I begged Naomi to come home long enough to go to the hospital and say good-bye. She told me to go to hell. That set me off, and the conversation devolved into a screaming match. I told Naomi she was a selfish brat, but that was the least of it. I called her a lot of other things, too—words I should never have used and will regret to my dying day. When the phone call ended, that's when I realized I'd lost my last piece of Jasmine."

It took a moment for me to figure out how to respond to that.

"Look," I said finally. "You were in a terrible spot. Your wife was dying. God only knows what was going on in Naomi's life about then. Maybe you both need a do-over. You hired me to find her, Alan. Let me. I'll do my best to lobby on your behalf and on Athena's behalf, too. Maybe I can talk some sense into Naomi's head."

"Good luck with that," Alan said with a despairing shake of his head. "I'm not sure talking sense to her is even remotely possible."

CHAPTER 19

Pioneer Square may be one of Seattle's trendier neighborhoods, but it's not necessarily a safe one, especially if you're going there alone on a Friday night well after dark. I walked my dinner guests, Alan and Athena, back from El Gaucho to Belltown Terrace, where I traded in the two humans in favor of my guard dog, Lucy. Her original trainer had taught me a set of distinct commands that instantly transform her from an easygoing family dog into a fierce canine security detail. I took her with me, knowing full well that if I needed backup for any reason, Lucy would be there for me. As for the Pike Street Mission? I had no way of knowing whether or not the establishment was, as they say, dog-friendly, but it's always better to beg forgiveness than ask permission.

For the second time that day, I pulled in to the Triangle Parking Lot, and once again Seattle's parking gods smiled on me. That's one of the side benefits about being a cop that I really miss. Back in the day, I could slap an OFFICIAL BUSINESS placard on the dashboard of my unmarked patrol car and park any damn place I wanted. In the private sector, things don't work quite that way.

Earlier in the day, the door to the Pike Street Mission had been open and welcoming. Now that it was dark, the place was locked up tight. A dimly lit intercom with a speaker and button was attached to the wall next to the entrance. A drunk, staggering from one side of the sidewalk to the other, was half a block away and lurching toward us. Lucy kept a wary eye on him while I busied myself with the intercom in hopes of gaining admittance.

"J. P. Beaumont to see Rachel Seymour," I said.

The lock gave an electronically activated thump, and the door swung open. Rachel Seymour stood just inside. She took a wary step backward when she caught sight of Lucy, and no wonder. Rachel and the dog were at almost the same eye level.

"Sit, Lucy," I ordered, and because she was on her best behavior, Lucy sat. "Sorry about bringing a dog along," I apologized, "but Lucy's my backup. When I'm working a case, my wife doesn't want me leaving home without her."

"Is she trustworthy?"

"Very."

"I suppose you can bring her in, then," a resigned Rachel Seymour said. "Come along, both of you. We'll be meeting with Naomi in my office."

"How is she?" I asked, settling on one of the visitor's chairs and putting Lucy into a down stay next to me.

"From what I see, I doubt she's using right now,"

Rachel told me. "In other words, so far so good. The shelter is a drug-free zone. No drugs are allowed inside, but it would be naïve to assume that all of our residents are clean and sober. I think the main reason Naomi agreed to come with me when she did was my offer of a warm shower, a hot meal, and a real bed."

I shook my head. "I don't see how people can live out in the cold and wet like that, day after day, month after month, year in and year out."

"I don't either," Rachel said with a nod. "That's why I agreed to take over running this place after Reverend Beardsley passed away. I didn't want to see it shut down. Still, the homeless problem is so extensive at this point that it's like trying to stop an arterial hemorrhage with a Band-Aid."

The comment made me wonder if perhaps Reverend Seymour had some kind of medical training in her background in addition to her degree in theology. I wondered, yes, but I didn't ask.

"What about Naomi's grocery cart? Did she bring that along, too?"

Rachel shook her head. "I persuaded her to leave it behind. We have a clothes bank here at the shelter for our residents to use as needed. The only thing Naomi brought with her was a paper grocery bag."

The idea that all Naomi's worldly possessions could be stuffed into a single paper bag made my heart hurt. You'd think that after nearly three decades on this planet she'd have more to show for it than the equivalent of a bag of groceries.

Just then there was a knock on the door. "Come

in," Reverend Seymour said, and Naomi Dale stepped inside.

I believe I mentioned before that I've never had much of a poker face. When I saw Naomi in the flesh for the first time, I tried to contain my shock, but I'm not sure it worked. In that moment I knew beyond any doubt that there was no longer any need for a DNA profile. It was as clear as the nose on my face—and the nose on her face as well. Naomi looked so much like my daughter, Kelly, and like me by extension that it took my breath away. Of the two, Naomi was fifteen years younger, but she appeared to be much older. Drug use and years of rough living will do that to you.

"Have a seat," Rachel invited. "This is Mr. Beaumont and his dog, Lucy."

I bumbled to my feet, hand extended. When Naomi's hand met mine, the skin of her palm was dry and rough to the touch. Her fingernails were ragged and grimy, and her limp handshake was halfhearted at best. Her brunette hair, dull and lusterless, had been chopped off in a ragged manner that hinted it was a DIY job, done with a dull scissors and possibly without benefit of a mirror. Her face was chapped and devoid of makeup. She looked haggard, worn, and unhappy, to say nothing of angry. She glowered at me as she took her seat.

At my feet Lucy stirred restlessly. I wondered if her keen sense of smell had somehow made a connection between Naomi's scent and Athena's. If dogs can be used to detect cancer cells these days, it wouldn't surprise me if they could make a mother-and-child connection as well—or even the connection between a father and daughter. Or maybe Naomi's anger was registering on Lucy's threat-detection monitor.

"How come Alan sent a detective out looking for me?" Naomi demanded. "I haven't done anything wrong."

Referring to her father by his first name was a clear indication of disrespect. As for her not having done anything wrong? That wasn't entirely true. From my point of view, abandoning a drug-addicted newborn in a hospital nursery seemed totally beyond the pale. But I wasn't there to address the prickly philosophical differences between right and wrong. I was there to help Alan Dale, Athena, and maybe even my own newly discovered daughter. So I let her declaration of innocence pass without weighing in on it.

"Your father needs your help," I said.

"Why?"

"He wants to take Athena back home to Texas."

"What's stopping him?" Naomi returned. "I left her at the hospital so Grandma could do just that—come get her. These days you're supposed to be able to leave babies at safe places with no questions asked. That's why I gave the hospital Grandma's phone number—so she could come take Athena home."

"I doubt you've been in touch with your grandmother recently," I said. "She's currently dealing with some serious health issues and is no longer able to travel. With her unable to come, your father dropped everything and showed up in her place. He's spent more than a month looking after Athena in the neonatal unit at Children's Hospital here in Seattle. Not only was Athena a preemie, she was also born with a serious addiction to methadone. She had to go through withdrawal before she could be released. That finally happened just this week."

"Oh," Naomi said. There was no acknowledgment that she'd known the baby would be born with an addiction problem and no hint of regret about it either, nor did she ask how Athena was doing now. "Well then," Naomi added with a dismissive shrug. "He should take her back home with him now and be done with it. That's what I wanted to have happen to begin with."

"He can't."

"Why not?"

"Because by abandoning Athena at Harborview, you turned her into a ward of the courts. Your father has been appointed to be her legal guardian, but only on a temporary basis. If it weren't for him, she would already have been placed in foster care somewhere in the Seattle area. In order to take Athena home to Texas, that temporary guardianship needs to be made permanent. That can't happen unless you relinquish your parental rights. That requires a legal document, one you'd have to sign, either in front of Athena's social worker or before a judge."

"Fine," Naomi said. "Bring me the damned paperwork, and I'll sign it right now. Somebody needs to take care of Athena. I sure as hell can't."

She had given a verbal agreement for the signover. Yay! That was a huge step in the right direction. As for her being able to see that she was unfit to care for Athena? I gave her high marks for that as well.

"Are you still using?" I asked.

"What business is that of yours?" she snapped, shooting a withering glance in my direction.

It was far more of my business than she knew, but I stuck to the issue at hand.

"If you do sign off, I don't want you to come back later and say you were under the influence at the time, claiming, as a consequence, that the agreement isn't legally binding."

"I said I'll sign, and I will," Naomi insisted, "and don't worry. I'm not going to change my mind."

"The problem is, your signature will solve only part of Athena's problem," I told her. "Athena's father will have to sign off as well."

"I don't know who the father is," she declared with a dismissive shrug. "I slept around. It could have been any number of guys."

"What if it's Petey Mayfield?" I asked.

I was seated next to her. At the mention of Petey's name, it looked as though a bolt of electricity had shot through her body. A sudden flush spread upward from her neck to her cheeks. There was an involuntary tightening in her jawline, but she said nothing.

"You were living with Petey," I prodded. "It stands to reason that the baby is his."

"Petey isn't Athena's father," Naomi insisted. "He just isn't."

"What if I can prove he is?" I inquired. "What if a DNA profile of Agnes Mayfield reveals a familial connection? In that case, regardless of what you claimed on the birth certificate, once Petey's paternity is legally established, he, too, will be required to sign his own relinquishment."

"That's not fair!" Naomi snapped, suddenly slamming the palm of her hand on Rachel's desk with such ferocity that the blow sent stacks of neatly organized papers skittering in every direction. Her response was so intense that everyone else in the room jumped, Lucy included.

"Petey left us, damn it!" Naomi exclaimed, spitting out the words. "Don't you understand? He abandoned us! He took off, walked out the door, left me there alone, and never looked back! He didn't give a damn about either one of us. Why the hell should he have any say in what happens to Athena? Why should he?"

This was the first time Naomi had exhibited any kind of emotion. Once that initial explosion of fury dissipated, however, it devolved into a series of gut-wrenching sobs. Witnessing Naomi's obvious heartbreak, I was at a loss as to what, if any, my response should be. Reverend Seymour solved the problem for both of us by getting to her feet, coming around the desk, standing on her tiptoes, and wrapping Naomi in a comforting embrace.

"There, there," she crooned softly. "It's all right. You'll be okay."

But now I understood. Petey had deserted them. Suddenly everything that had happened—everything Naomi had done, including abandoning Athena—made more sense.

Eventually Naomi's sobs subsided into ragged shudders. "Take a breath," Rachel advised, stepping away and handing Naomi a handful of tissues from a box on her desk. "I'll go get you a bottle of water."

Naomi nodded. "Thank you," she murmured.

Rachel left the room, leaving the two of us—three counting Lucy—alone.

"How long ago did Petey leave?" I asked.

"How do you know that's his name?"

"I talked to Mrs. Tanner," I answered, "your former neighbor."

"That nosy old lady from across the street?"

"Yes," I said, "that's the one. She saw you walking away with your loaded grocery cart just before Christmas. She was worried about what had happened to you and the baby."

"I managed," Naomi said, regaining a smidgeon of her tough-nut attitude. "We managed," she corrected.

"You still haven't answered my question," I pressed. "When did he leave?"

She shrugged. "Sometime last fall."

"Do you remember the day?"

"Of course I remember!" she replied in sudden exasperation. "It was the day before Halloween. We thought we might have trick-or-treaters show up. Petey went to the store to get some candy in case they did. He came home all excited, brimming over with some weird crap about seeing a sign that meant he and I were going to be rich. Sure, likely story. Grandma Day is one of those people who reads her horoscope without fail and believes in signs and all that other magical nonsense. I've never believed any of it.

"So when Petey told me that, he was so wound up I actually thought he was tripping out and seeing things that weren't there. I even asked him if he was using again. I thought he might have run into one of our old dealers on the street. Anyway, we got into an epic fight. He was furious that I'd accuse him of relapsing. He threw down the bag of candy—spilled caramel corn all over the floor—and then stormed out, telling me he'd by God show me. That was the last thing he said to me: 'You're wrong, and I'm going to prove it.' He left and never came back, ever."

Rachel reentered the room, handing bottles of water to both Naomi and me before resuming her seat behind the desk.

"Where did you and Petey meet?" I asked, continuing the interview but changing directions.

"In treatment," Naomi answered. "Not treatment, really—it's what's called aftercare."

It turns out I had an up-close-and-personal understanding of what the word "aftercare" entails.

"We'd both been through detox before we met at a Narcotics Anonymous meeting. It's called NA," she clarified, although no explanation was necessary.

"We struck up a conversation over coffee," Naomi continued. "Pretty soon one thing led to another, and that was it. A couple of months later, I moved in with him. He was living rent-free in one of his grandmother's old houses, and she let me stay there, too."

"You're saying you met Agnes Mayfield?"

"A couple of times," Naomi replied. "She seemed

kind of strange to me—as though she wasn't quite all there."

"She wasn't," I agreed. "My understanding is that she was having dementia issues back then. That's why her daughter removed her from the home and checked Agnes into some kind of care facility."

"So that's what happened to her," Naomi mused. "We wondered. When she disappeared like that, all of a sudden and with no warning, we had no idea what had become of her or where she'd gone. Let me tell you, it hit Petey really hard. His grandmother raised him, you know."

"Yes," I said, "Hilda Tanner told me that, too, but are you saying that Petey's aunt, Lenora Harrison, packed Agnes off without any explanation to either Petey or you?"

"Not a word," Naomi answered. "We didn't even know his aunt had done it. All we knew was that we hadn't seen Grandma Agnes—that's what Petey called her—around her house for some time, but we had no idea she was gone for good."

"What happened next?"

"Like I said, Petey was upset. I kept telling him she was probably off on a trip, but the longer Grandma Agnes stayed gone, the more he worried. That's one of the reasons I thought he might have had a slip that day when he went to the store. It's why I accused him of buying drugs and getting high. They tell you in treatment that's when addicts are most likely to relapse—when they're upset about something."

"Did he mention why Agnes's absence bothered him so much?"

"He was afraid that without her looking out for us, we'd have to find someplace else to live."

"How long had he been off drugs when all this happened?"

"Six months and a little bit when she disappeared," she said. "We'd both just gotten our six-month chits. Petey had been looking for work, but with his history of drug abuse no one was eager to hire him. He'd been doing odd jobs around the neighborhood, working as a handyman, to keep us afloat. When I found out I was pregnant, I wanted to go to Planned Parenthood to get an abortion, but Petey talked me out of it. He wanted me to have the baby so we could be a real family. He said that since we were both drug-free, it was the right time for us to do it."

"So he wanted the baby?"

"That's what he said," Naomi replied bitterly, "but actions speak louder than words, don't they?"

"You were both off drugs at the time he left?"

"I was for sure. I can't say about him."

"You said he went to the store. How did he get there? Did he drive?"

"Are you kidding? We couldn't afford a car."

"So he was on foot when he left?"

"Yes. I thought he'd cool off and come back home later that night, but he didn't. He didn't come back the next day or the day after that or the next one either. When I ran out of food, I did what I had to in order to survive." Naomi paused for a moment, and then, with a defiant look in my direction, as though daring me to object, she continued. "Some johns pay with money," she explained, leaving me to draw my own conclusions about what she'd done to cover expenses. "Some pay with other stuff."

"Like drugs, you mean?"

She nodded. "There are plenty of those out there on the street, and methadone is easy to come by. Once I had it—without Petey there to talk me down and without going to meetings, it was easy for me to slip back into old habits. But I was careful. I only used methadone, nothing stronger. I didn't think methadone would hurt the baby. I mean, doctors give it out during treatment, don't they?"

Yes, they do, I thought, *but they do so under supervised conditions, and they most likely don't prescribe methadone to addicted patients who happen to be pregnant at the time.*

"So you were left there alone but getting along," I said. "Then what?"

"One morning I got up and discovered that the electricity had been turned off overnight," Naomi reported. "A few days later, the water got turned off, too. It was cold in the house, but at least there was a roof over my head and I wasn't out in the rain. I found an old bucket over by Agnes's garage and used that to collect rainwater so I could flush the toilet. I got drinking water and food from the food bank. I was doing okay. At least I was surviving. Then, two days before Christmas, some asshole from the city turned up. He told me that the house was no longer considered fit for human habitation and that I had to leave. He said the place had been 'red-flagged.' He demanded that I pack my goods and get the hell out—right that minute. He refused to leave until I did."

"That's when you grabbed your grocery cart and took off?"

Naomi nodded.

"How did you end up at an all-woman encampment down by the Mount Baker Tunnel?"

"I asked around on the street," Naomi answered. "Everyone told me if I went there, the women in the encampment would take care of me, and they did. I showed up. Dorothy said I could stay and put me up in a tent. On the night I went into labor, she said it was too soon for the baby to be born and that I had to go to the ER. Some of the women in the camp helped me over the barrier by the freeway so I could flag down someone to help me."

I said nothing about the bus driver and the EMT saying she'd been high at the time. It didn't matter.

"When I left the hospital, I went right back to the encampment. I knew Dorothy and the others would take care of me, but they wouldn't have been able to take care of Athena."

I had already heard at least two other versions of this story, but this was the first time I was hearing it from Naomi's point of view. There was no doubt in my mind that she was telling the truth. The poor girl had been left alone, lost and broken. No wonder she'd gotten hooked again. And when it came to abandoning Athena at the hospital? What she'd done might have been morally wrong, but she'd done it for all the right reasons—so the baby could be properly cared for.

"So Petey really is Athena's father?"

There was no fight left in her. Naomi nodded dejectedly. "He is," she admitted at last.

"And there's been no sign of him since he left your house that day in late October?"

"None," Naomi said. "I've asked about him out on the street, but no one has seen him. I guess he left town."

"As the mother of his child, you'd be within your rights to file a missing-persons report, but the cops might want proof that he's actually Athena's father."

She thought about that for a moment. "I could get proof," she said. "I could give you something with Petey's DNA."

I was dumbfounded. "You could?" I asked.

"I still have his hairbrush," Naomi said. "Would that help?"

The fact that the interview had veered off into an unexpected discussion of DNA really struck me. Our involvement in DNA wasn't just about Petey Mayfield's relationship to Athena. It was also about Naomi Dale's relationship to me. The girl was speaking my language, as though our shared DNA might be pointing her along the same track I had followed. If she got her head on straight, maybe she'd make a decent detective someday.

"You have his hairbrush?" I repeated, still not quite believing my ears.

Naomi nodded. "It was his pride and joy. His grandfather gave it to him for his twelfth birthday. I brought it with me when I left the house, just in case I ever saw him again. I thought he'd like having it back. Do you want me to get it for you?"

The idea that Petey's precious hairbrush was one of the few treasures Naomi had lugged to the mission in her puny paper bag full of possessions raised goose bumps on my legs. She had really loved the guy and still did.

"Please," I said.

"Will I get it back when you're finished with it?"

"For sure!" I promised.

"Okay. It's in my room. I'll go get it."

Naomi left. I glanced over at Rachel Seymour, who was smiling. "I don't think that was quite what you expected, was it?"

Boy howdy, did she ever have me there!

Naomi returned a few minutes later, carrying a man's classic military-style hairbrush with a wooden back. When she handed the brush to me and I examined it, I saw that the black bristles were knotted with strands of light brown hair. If follicles were present, DNA profile here we come!

As soon as I held the brush in my hand, though, I realized that once upon a time I used to have one just like it. My mother had bought it for me, also as a birthday present, at a no-longer-extant Seattle department store called Frederick & Nelson. On our limited budget, buying that brush had counted as a big splurge. My birthday brush traveled with me to Vietnam but never made it back home. I don't know if I simply misplaced it at some point or if someone swiped it. Seeing Petey Mayfield's brush made me miss mine. In that instant it also made me miss my mother.

"I loved him," Naomi murmured sadly. "I really wanted Petey to come back."

"I can tell," I told her.

"If you do find him, will you let me know?"

"Yes," I said definitively. "I certainly will."

When I'd told Hilda Tanner more or less the same thing, I hadn't meant it in quite the same way. This time it was a blood oath.

"What if you find him and he refuses to sign?"

"We'll cross that bridge when we come to it," I told her. "But about that relinquishment of rights, you're positive you won't change your mind after you sign?"

"I won't," she said.

"How can you be sure?"

"I've already demonstrated to myself and to the rest of the world that I don't make good decisions. If I can't be trusted to look after myself on my own, how can I be trusted to look after a baby? My dad and grandma will do a better job of that than I ever would."

"You know that to be true?" I repeated.

"I do."

"Okay, then I'll set it up. We can probably come here for the signing. Is it okay if I give Reverend Seymour a call to sort out the details?"

"That's fine," Naomi said. "I don't exactly own a phone." She stood up. "If it's all right, I want to go now."

"There's one more thing," I added as she headed for the door.

What?" Naomi asked.

"Your dad wanted me to tell you how sorry he is about the things he said to you when your mother was so sick. If he could take back those words, he would."

Naomi looked down at her feet. When she raised her head moments later, her face had softened. "I've been on the streets for a long time, Mr. Beaumont. I've been called lots worse than that more times than I can remember. Tell Dad he's forgiven. And when you set up the time to meet with that social worker, maybe he and Athena could come along. She was so tiny and sick in the delivery room that they took her away from me as soon as she was born. I got to see her, but I never got to touch her."

Suddenly I was beset by a new worry. If Naomi was able to see Athena, what were the chances she might still change her mind about signing? How could she not? That's what I was thinking, but I didn't say a word of it aloud.

"You've got it," I told her. "I expect your dad will be here with bells on."

Lucy and I left then. As we headed home on Fourth Avenue, I knew I was about to have a come-to-Jesus moment with Alan Dale. Yes, I'd done what I'd said I would do. I had found Naomi, and I for sure owed Sam Shelton his five hundred bucks. But I owed Alan something far more valuable than mere money. I owed him the truth.

CHAPTER 20

I REMEMBER READING someplace that 99 percent of what we worry about never happens. It might have been in Norman Vincent Peale's *Power of Positive Thinking*—another long-ago birthday present from my mother. Is there a corollary to that? Maybe that other 1 percent represents the things we really should worry about. For example, after my one-night stand with Jasmine Day, I was never the least bit concerned that she might have gotten pregnant, and yet that's exactly what I should have been worrying about. And now the thing I hadn't given a moment's thought to was right here biting me in the butt.

The phone rang, and Mel's photo appeared on the screen. "Just got back to the house," she said when I pressed the call button to answer. "I'm wearing my robe, sitting by the fireplace, and just finished eating a peanut butter and jelly sandwich. I miss you, by the way," she added. "How are you doing?"

So I told her—the good news and the bad news—that I had found Naomi and she had agreed to relinquish her parental rights. I told her the other part, too, that even without my DNA profile, it was clear to me that Naomi Dale and I were related.

"What are you going to do about it?"

"Fess up," I said. "It's time for me to tell Alan the truth. The DNA is nothing but a formality. Naomi and Kelly could just as well be twins."

"Good luck with that," she said.

"How did your situation sort itself out?"

"All right, I suppose. The bad guys are in jail, the woman injured in the hit-and-run is hospitalized with serious injuries, but she's going to live, and the wreckage has been cleared off all affected roadways. The only thing left to handle is a mountain of paperwork, but that'll have to wait. I deserve a break. As tired as I am, I decided it was too late to head out tonight, but I'll show up there first thing in the morning—probably around nine or so."

"Your usual dressing-room space will be off-limits," I warned her.

"I'm a big girl," she assured me. "We'll manage."

Once I was parked in the garage, I took Lucy out for her final walk of the evening and went looking for Sam. As expected, he was ensconced in his usual digs.

In the old days when I was first on the job, I was lucky if I had fifty bucks of walking-around money in my wallet at any given time. These days I usually have five one-hundred-dollar bills and a few smaller ones tucked into my billfold. It's just my thing. I guess, after growing up poor, it's nice to know I have a bit of spare moola in my pocket—in this case the reward money I owed Sam Shelton.

"Anybody awake down there?" I called into the alcove.

Someone stirred beneath the mound of blankets at the bottom of the stairs. Billy Bob was the first to emerge from under the makeshift shelter.

"That you, Beau?" Sam called.

"It is," I told him. "I came to bring your reward."

"You found her, then?"

"We certainly did, at the all-female homeless encampment you told me about. I'm here to make good on my promise."

Keeping some of the blankets wrapped around him, Sam lumbered up the stairs. "Is she okay?" he asked.

"Yes," I said, "at least I think so. It's hard to tell."

I counted out five bills and handed them over. Sam took one and passed the others back. "I got me Billy Bob, but you know what it's like out here. If I end up getting rolled, I'd rather the thugs get away with only one of these hummers instead of all of 'em. So why don't you put the other ones in an envelope and leave them with that nice doorman, Mr. Bob. When I run low on funds, I can always stop by during one of his shifts and pick up the next one. It'll be sort of like having a savings account. Don't think I've ever had one of those before."

"Envelope it is," I said, putting the four remaining bills back in my pocket. "I'll give these to Bob the next time I see him."

"By the way, I'm still looking for that Petey guy," Sam told me. "I've talked to a couple of people who remember him and his girlfriend, too, but no one has seen him lately, and that's a bad sign. When people disappear off the streets like that all of a sudden, it's usually not good news. You should probably file a missing-persons report on him."

That made me smile—the homeless guy giving the ex-cop law-enforcement advice. "Will do," I told him. "We're working on it."

"Tell Naomi's dad thanks for me," he added, turning and heading back down toward the warmth of his nest. "See you around."

"I will," I said, knowing that in thanking me he already had. "Good night, then," I told him as Lucy and I headed inside.

Upstairs, the moment we entered the unit, Lucy voted with her paws. She turned a hard right and headed straight for the guest room, making it clear where her loyalties lay. I was a bit bemused by her obvious attachment to that little blanket-wrapped creature lying asleep in a crib. Alan Dale, on the other hand, was perched in the window seat, cup of coffee in hand, staring out at Puget Sound, where a couple of ferries were passing each other in the night.

"Well?" he asked.

"Naomi agreed to sign."

"She did? Oh, my God!" he exclaimed. "I can barely believe it. How did you do that? What did she say?"

"That she knows she can't take proper care of Athena and she thinks you and your mother-in-law can. That's what she had in mind when she left Athena at the hospital—that you and/or her grandmother would take Athena back home to Texas. She had no idea that the state would get involved and throw a wrench in the works."

"When do we sign?" Alan asked.

"Whenever you can arrange it," I told him. "but as soon as possible. Naomi is staying at the Pike Street Mission at the moment. Reverend Seymour, the woman who runs the shelter said we can call her to set up a time."

Before the words were out of my mouth, Alan was reaching for his phone. "I'm calling Andrea Hutchins," he explained. "She's Athena's social worker, and she told me to call her anytime, day or night. Nine o'clock's not too late to call, do you think?"

"Not on a Friday," I told him.

"Andrea," he said a moment later. "It's Alan Dale. I've got good news—great news, actually. I'm sitting here with J. P. Beaumont, my detective. He found Naomi, and she's willing to sign. I'm putting you on speaker so he can hear what you're saying. Naomi is staying at a homeless shelter located somewhere here in Seattle. We can meet with her there to get the paperwork signed, but we need to set up a time."

"That is good news," Andrea agreed. "Good work, Mr. Beaumont, glad to meet you."

"Me, too," I told her.

"Here's the thing," Andrea continued. "In my experience the longer we wait around after someone makes this kind of decision, the more likely they are to change their minds and back out. I know it's the weekend, but is there any way we could do this tomorrow?"

"I can see," I said. "What time would be good for you?"

"Eleven, maybe?"

I hauled out my phone, found the number Rachel had called me on earlier, and dialed that.

"Alan Dale is on another line with Athena's social worker just now, and she's wondering if we could stop by tomorrow morning about eleven to sign that paperwork."

"I'm not at the shelter right now," Rachel said. "Let me call the housemother and have her check with Naomi. If that's all right with her, is it okay if I give the housemother your number so she can call you back directly?"

"Of course," I said. "No problem."

It took only another five minutes to nail down all the details. When we called Andrea back to confirm the appointment, once again Alan put the call on speaker. "What was the name of that shelter again?" she asked.

"It's the Pike Street Mission, but it's not on Pike Street anymore."

Andrea laughed aloud at that. "I'm a social worker, Mr. Beaumont. Believe me, I'm up to date on the location of the various homeless shelters in the Seattle area. Rachel Seymour and I go way back."

I didn't hum a few bars of "It's a Small World," but I could have.

With the signing appointment set, Alan was

downright jubilant. I didn't look forward to telling him about my unwitting participation in Naomi's parentage, but I couldn't put it off any longer.

"Look," I said finally, taking a deep breath. "There's something I need to get off my chest. It's time you heard the whole story."

Alan studied me for a moment with a quizzical frown. "About what?" he asked. "About you and Jasmine and that one-night stand?"

You could have knocked me over with a feather—literally. "You knew?" I stammered.

"Not right away," Alan answered, "but we figured it out within a couple of weeks—as soon as we realized she was expecting. Once the doctor told us how far along she was, we were pretty sure you were the guy."

"Why didn't you tell me?" I asked.

"Maybe I'm the one who needs to tell *you* the whole story," Alan said. "I was married once before. I wanted kids. My then-wife absolutely did not want kids. She told me that if I didn't get a vasectomy, she was going to divorce me. I wanted to be married and live up to that whole 'in sickness and in health' thing, so I did what she asked. Guess what? She up and divorced me anyway and ended up having three kids with her second husband. Live and learn, right?"

"Right," I muttered.

"When the show was on the road, there were rumors among the crew that Jasmine was being coerced into playing hostess with some of the high-fliers on the producer's guest list. The talk was she was probably putting out. I already liked her by then. We weren't together yet, but I didn't want to believe the gossip either. I thought it was just a bunch of sour grapes. Then, when the whole drug-dealing thing came to light, of all the cops on the scene, you were the only one who seemed to have Jaz's back—our backs. Later on, when we started getting serious about each other, she told me about what had been going on. She also told me that she doubted you had any idea in advance about the nature of your date. She said that when she hopped into your bed, you'd been pretty much blindsided."

"Blindsided yes," I agreed, "but pretty much blind drunk as well. That was a couple of years before I sobered up."

"Jaz and I were already back in Jasper when she started getting sick. At first we thought it was the flu or else something she'd eaten, but when she went to see a doctor, it turned out to be morning sickness. That's when we counted back and figured out you were probably Naomi's biological father."

"Why didn't you let me know?"

Alan shrugged. "It seemed to me that God was giving me a second chance to finally have a family, and I was afraid to rock the boat. I worried, too, that if you knew Naomi was yours, you might initiate some kind of custody battle. I mean, you were a cop and all, and I'm sure you could have if you'd wanted to."

I wasn't sure he was right, but I let it go.

"So the three of us became a family," Alan continued. "I have to admit that when Naomi hit her teens and turned into such a handful, there were times I thought we might all have been better off if we'd brought you into the picture. We decided early on that when Naomi turned twenty-one, we would tell her the truth, but long before that Naomi took off. A few years later, Jaz was gone, too, and after that last awful phone conversation, I'd lost both of them without ever telling Naomi the truth. With all those DNA companies out there now, I figured there were ways she can find that out on her own without it coming from me. Which reminds me, how did you reach that conclusion?"

"I suspected it when you first showed me Naomi's school photo, the one you keep in your wallet," I answered. "But tonight, the moment Naomi walked into Reverend Seymour's office, there was no denying it. She looks just like my daughter, Kelly . . . my other daughter. But if you knew this all along, why did you come looking to me for help in finding Naomi?"

"Because," Alan Dale said simply, "you were the only person in Seattle I knew I could trust."

"Thank you," I said and I meant it.

Sometimes the bad things you worry about turn out to be the best things, but I went to bed that night and tossed and turned. I thought about my other kids—about Scotty and Kelly. Due to an inheritance from a biological auntie on my father's side, those two kids are both fixed for life, even if I never left them another dime—which I will do eventually anyway. But what about Naomi? What did she have? A cot in a homeless shelter, a paper bag holding all her worldly goods, no education to speak of, an addiction problem, and no hope—no hope at all. Not to mention a broken heart.

And what about Athena? If and when we could locate Petey Mayfield and get him to sign that relinquishment form, Athena would be going off to Jasper, Texas, to live with a loving but impoverished grandfather who would probably be in his late seventies before the child even graduated from high school. Poor Athena. It looked to me as though she, like her mother, was starting life from way behind go.

Reviewing my pantheon of past sins wasn't much fun. Had booze played a part in what happened back then between Jasmine Day and me? The answer to that was easy—of course it had. I finally sobered up and started working my Twelve Steps in AA, but when I got to Step 8, the one where you're supposed to draw up a list of the people you've harmed and then make amends to them, Jasmine's name didn't find its way onto the list. I had put her completely out of my mind.

But what if I'd known about Naomi from the get-go? What would I have done then? Would I have tried to interfere in their lives? Would I have offered to pay child support? When she started getting into hot water as a teenager, would I have tossed my two cents into the mix or tried showing up with a magic-wand checkbook in hand and hoping a bribe would work when discipline and direction hadn't? I doubt that throwing money at the problem back then would have helped. As for any well-thought-out advice I might have offered? We all know that when it comes to kids and discipline, those skills aren't in my wheelhouse.

So I tossed and turned, pounding my pillow and

brimming over with a whole catalog of woulda, coulda, and shoulda interior debates. Finally, sometime around three in the morning, I fought my way through to a possible solution. I hadn't helped with raising Naomi because—God help me—I didn't know she existed. But I knew about her now, and I knew about Athena too, and I needed to make up for lost time. Once Karen and I divorced, hard as it might have been, I never once missed a child-support payment. With Naomi and Athena, I wanted to cover all the back payments I had missed, and with Anne Corley's assistance I would do so— starting that very day.

Once that decision was made, I was finally able to fall asleep.

CHAPTER 21

ON SATURDAY MORNING it wasn't Athena's cries that woke me. And it wasn't the aroma of eggs and bacon either. It was a ding from my cell phone announcing the arrival of an incoming text. When I opened my phone to check, the phone number might have been unfamiliar, but the photo wasn't. I recognized Loretta Hawk's smiling face and squash-blossom necklace right away.

"For ten thousand bucks, I figured I could afford to cough up a little overtime. Your profiles are ready to rumble. Where do you want me to send them?"

I left the message app and called the number on the screen. "What would you say if I said I needed one additional DNA profile?" I asked when Loretta answered.

"You're telling me that three profiles aren't enough?"

"When I brought them to you, it was with the hope of establishing familial DNA connections to a baby who'd been abandoned as a newborn in a local hospital."

"Yes, I remember," Loretta said. "The baby's name is Athena, right?"

"Correct," I replied. "She's cheek-swab letter A."

"Then we've established a complete family grouping," Loretta told me. "Swab B belongs to Athena's maternal grandfather. DNA obtained from the hairbrush comes out as Athena's paternal great-grandmother. So what do you want me to do with these?"

I couldn't answer right that moment because I had my own answer. DNA doesn't lie. Like it or not, I truly was Naomi Day's biological father. And now that I had incontrovertible proof of that, what the hell was I supposed to do with it?

"Hello?" Loretta said into the silence. "Are you still there?"

"I'm here."

"All right, then," she said, "You still haven't told me where you want me to send the results."

"When I know that for sure, I'll let you know. In the meantime hang on to them for me. But here's the deal: I've now found a possible source for DNA material from the guy himself, from Petey, Athena's father. The problem is, he walked out of the house at the end of October and hasn't been seen since, which means . . ."

"If he's homeless, that means he's probably dead," Loretta said, completing my sentence.

"Correct. If an M.E. is involved, having an exact match would probably be better than a familial one."

I sat back and let another silence fill the phone line between us. Yesterday Loretta Hawk had used the story of her mother's long-unsolved homicide to reel me in, thus landing a sizable contribution for the Sholeetsa Project. Today I hoped the reverse was true and the fact that Athena's father was missing and presumed dead might work the same magic for me.

"What kind of source?" Loretta asked.

"Another hairbrush," I replied, "Peter Mayfield's this time. Are you open today?"

"We're not," she said, "but that doesn't mean I won't be here. We also have a secure drop box out front. What time do you think you'll be here?"

"I have an appointment downtown at eleven. I can drop the hairbrush off before that—around ten thirty or so."

"Fair enough," she said. "Have it here by eleven, and I'll ask one of my techs to come in on her day off to process it."

"You'd do that?"

"You're a donor, Mr. Beaumont, one of the project's most recent benefactors, but four profiles is your limit. That's all you get for a mere ten thousand. If you want another . . ."

It was time for me to finish her sentence. "White man will need to show up with another batch of wampum."

"You got it," she said. "For big bucks Sholeetsa will profile."

Now that I had that definitive news, the next step was to share it with Alan.

Soon there was plenty of aromatic evidence in

the air that someone was out in the kitchen making breakfast. It took a couple of minutes for me to make myself presentable. I live in Belltown Terrace's penthouse. The kitchen and living room both face the water, with no intervening buildings to serve as a peeping Tom's base of operations, so I'm accustomed to hopping in and out of the kitchen in my skivvies. With the house full of visitors, that wasn't possible.

"Over easy again?" Alan asked, standing with an egg in hand poised over the top of a buttered and heated frying pan.

"Yes, please."

When I went to get coffee, I noticed that Lucy was already eating. I was clearly the slugabed of the group. Everybody else was already up and at 'em.

"Walked her, too?" I asked, nodding toward Lucy.

"Yup," Alan said. "I did that first thing. She stood in front of the door with the leash in her mouth, whining. It was hard not to get the message."

Athena was strapped into that weird little slanted carrier of hers. She was front and center for all the activity, but she was also sound asleep.

"I spent the whole night worrying about the possibility that Naomi might change her mind," Alan said later as we sat down to breakfast.

I'd been worried about the same thing. In fact, I still was, but there was no sense in both of us freaking out about it at the same time.

"I think she'll be okay," I said. "She seemed to be pretty squared away about it last night."

My words seemed to reassure Alan. They didn't do much for me.

About that time Mel showed up. There was a whole flurry of activity. Lucy was ecstatic to see her. Over Mel's objections Alan hustled around and made breakfast for her, too, while Mel lifted Athena out of her little swingy thing and cooed about how cute and sweet she was. The cops who work for her in Bellingham would have been astonished. So, I suspected, would Mr. Mayor.

As Mel sat down to eat her breakfast, I decided it was time to come clean with both Alan and my wife. "I had a call from Loretta Hawk this morning," I began. "The DNA profiles are back."

"And?" Alan asked.

"Agnes Mayfield is definitely Athena's paternal great-grandmother," I announced to both of them.

Unfortunately for me, Mel can read me like a book. She knew there was more to the story than what I'd said so far.

"And?" she urged. "What else?"

"They also confirm that I'm her maternal grandfather."

The words fell into the room, sucked the air out of it, and left behind a moment of utter silence. Mel, unaware that Alan and I had already covered this ground, shot him a wary glance. She seemed taken aback when his first response was to grin at me.

"Well, sir," he said, "there you have it. Suspicions confirmed. I suppose congratulations are in order, but it's a little too late to be handing out pink cigars.

So who's going to break this earth-shattering news to Naomi—you or I?"

In all the time I've known Mel Soames, this was only the second time I'd ever seen her so utterly gobsmacked that she had nothing to say—nothing at all.

"I should, I think," I answered.

"Fair enough," Alan said.

And that was it, welcome to fatherhood . . . again.

By ten o'clock both Alan and I were dressed in our Sunday-go-to-meeting attire and ready to head downstairs, but leaving took longer than expected. By now Alan was an old hand at traveling with a full panoply of baby gear. Mel had offered to babysit, but for the signing ceremony we wanted Athena along for the ride.

"We'll take you up on the babysitting offer later this afternoon," I told her.

"Why?" Alan wanted to know.

"We need to run a couple of errands."

Mel changed into jogging attire so she and Lucy could go for a run in Myrtle Edwards Park in our absence. In the car I was grateful Alan didn't revisit the DNA conversation. I still wasn't done processing it. At ten thirty on the dot, I stopped the car in front of the Sholeetsa Project. At my direction Alan hopped out and slipped the bag containing the hairbrush into the lockbox.

"Now where?" he asked once he was back inside.

"Now we head for the Pike Street Mission."

It was Saturday morning. I lucked into on-street parking right outside the front door. At that point Alan seemed to be having second thoughts.

"Maybe this isn't such a good idea. Maybe Athena and I should wait in the car."

Just then a tall black woman approached the passenger side of the car and tapped on Alan's window. I buzzed it down.

"Are we going to do this or not?" Andrea Hutchins asked.

"We're doing it," Alan said at once, reaching for the door handle and hustling out of the car. "We're definitely doing it." He grabbed Athena's carrier out of the backseat, and in we went.

Once again Rachel Seymour stood waiting just inside the door to the mission. When I started to make introductions, it turned out that Andrea and Rachel were already acquainted.

"I thought we'd do this in the chapel," Rachel said, pointing us in that direction. "With so many people involved, my office would be a bit cramped."

When we entered the small chapel, Naomi was already waiting there. She sat in the front pew with her head bowed. It looked as though she might be praying. We all paused briefly in the entryway, and Alan was the first one to break ranks. With the infant seat in hand, he loped off down the center aisle.

"Naomi," he called. "Is that you?"

For a seemingly long moment, nothing happened. Then Naomi slowly rose to her feet and turned to look at him. A second later she was racing toward him. They collided in midstride, halfway down the aisle. Alan set the infant seat down on the closest available pew and pulled his sobbing daughter into an all-encompassing embrace.

"I'm sorry, Dad," I heard Naomi murmur softly against his chest. "I'm so sorry for everything."

Alan didn't say a word. He just held on to her for dear life. Believe me, there wasn't a dry eye in the house, but seeing Naomi swallowed up in her father's arms stirred a memory in my soul, a remembrance of that morning years earlier when, after being released from the King County Jail, Jasmine Day had sought shelter in Alan's arms in exactly the same fashion.

When Alan finally let her go, Naomi turned toward the pew where he'd deposited the infant seat. For the better part of a minute, she stood there staring down at her baby, at Athena. Then Naomi turned back to Alan. "She's beautiful," she whispered, with wonder alive in her voice.

"Yes, she is," Alan agreed. "Would you like to hold her?"

Damn. The guy had balls! It seemed to me that letting Naomi hold the baby was a surefire way of having her renege on her agreement. If I'd been in his shoes, I don't think I would have had nerve enough to run that risk. Not Alan Dale. He unbuckled the harness that held Athena in place, picked her up, and handed her over. For the next minute or so, no one said a word. I could see the tears dripping off Naomi's chin as she stared down at her child. Once I saw the tears, that's when I started holding my breath. At last Naomi was the one who broke the silence.

"You'll take good care of her, won't you?" she asked, looking up at Alan.

Unable to speak, he simply nodded.

"Did you bring the paperwork?"

"I didn't bring it, she did," Alan answered, nodding in Andrea's direction. "Ms. Hutchins here is Athena's social worker."

Andrea stepped forward and extended a hand to Naomi. "I'm Andrea Hutchins. I understand you're willing to relinquish your parental rights?"

"I am," Naomi said resolutely. With that she handed Athena back to Alan. "You always were a good dad," she said, "and I know you will be again. Now, where do I sign?"

Rachel Seymour took control of the emotionally overwrought situation. "Perhaps you'd like to use my office for that," she suggested. "That way you'll have some privacy."

Rachel led Andrea and Naomi back down the aisle, leaving Alan and me alone in the chapel with Athena. When I looked at him, I could see he was struggling to contain his own tears.

"That was tough," I said.

He nodded. "Very."

"It might not have seemed like it at the time, but I think you and Jasmine did an excellent job of raising her."

By then Alan was busy buckling Athena back into her carrier. "Naomi still doesn't know the whole truth," he said. "When are you going to tell her?"

"Maybe now would be a good time," I suggested, but before I could do anything about it, Andrea Hutchens came hustling back up the aisle.

"We're done," she said, waving a set of documents in our direction. "Naomi asked me to tell you goodbye. She said she hoped you'd understand."

Alan nodded. "I do," he said. "Thanks."

Knowing that the paperwork was properly signed should have felt like a moment of triumph, but it didn't. Naomi Dale was anything but the monster I'd envisioned her to be to begin with. It had taken incredible courage for her to sign her name and abandon her baby for a second time. My heart ached for both of them—for my new daughter and my new granddaughter.

Not exactly a done deal, I thought. *Next up we need to find Petey Mayfield.*

CHAPTER 22

ALAN WAS SUBDUED as we headed back through downtown Seattle. Knowing the emotional maelstrom he'd just endured, I made no effort to engage him in conversation.

"What errands?" he asked eventually, breaking the silence. "You said earlier that Mel could babysit this afternoon while we run errands."

"We're going car shopping," I told him.

He ran a hand over the shiny layer of wood built into the S550's dash. "This looks like a good enough vehicle to me," he said. "You're really thinking about trading it in?"

"Not car shopping for me," I replied, "car shopping for you."

"For me?" he echoed. "I'm not in the market for a new car. And even if I wanted one, I've got no job and no way to pay for it."

"But you've also got a baby and a whole roomful of baby gear to move around. Once we find Petey, how do you propose to get all that stuff back home to Texas?"

"I guess I hadn't thought that far ahead," he admitted.

"I have," I told him. "You can't fly home with it. The other option would mean driving home in your rented Honda with a U-Haul hooked on behind, but I don't think the rental company will let you do that. Besides, once you get home, what kind of wheels do you have there?"

"A fifteen-year-old Chevy Silverado."

"Not exactly baby-friendly, is it?" I said.

"No," he admitted, "not exactly. You're right, I do need a different vehicle, but I'm not working. The only thing I could afford would be another junker. We'll have to go with what I've got."

"You're not buying the car," I told him. "I am."

"For me? You can't do that."

"Actually, I can and I will. Consider it partial payment of long-overdue child support. If we can find something you like, we'll take it home today and turn your rental in tomorrow."

"But . . ." he began.

"No buts, please, Alan. We're doing this. I'm doing this—for you and for Jaz and for Athena. Okay?"

I could tell I was wearing him down. "Okay, I guess," he agreed reluctantly. "You win."

We stayed at the condo long enough for Alan to change Athena, feed her, and put her down for a nap. It was also long enough for me to bring Mel up to date about what had happened during the course of the morning. When we left Mel on her own to assume babysitting duties, Athena was sound asleep and so was Lucy. In her favorite spot—under Athena's crib.

"So where are we going?" Alan asked once we were back in the car. He still wasn't exactly happy about this, but he was going with the flow.

A couple of weeks earlier, I had attended the annual Golden Beaver Luncheon, sponsored by the Ballard High School Alumni Association and held at the Norwegian Commercial Club. Several of my classmates were in attendance, including Lester Peterson. Lester's dad, Lester Peterson Sr., used to be a mainstay of Seattle's fishing fleet operating out of Fishermen's Terminal on Lake Union. Les worked for his dad during the summers, and his father was the guy who'd given me that ill-fated summer job from which I'd been sent home to Ballard in disgrace with a disabling case of seasickness. Thanks to Les Jr., the story of my ignominious exit from the fishing industry spread throughout the school and made me the butt of countless jokes our senior year.

Oddly enough, once Les Jr. was out of high school, he was more than ready to be out of the fishing business. Rather than heading off to college, he used the money he'd saved from working on his dad's boat to launch his own business, a small used-car lot right there in Ballard. Since then that initial used-car lot had gone upscale and morphed into a full-fledged new-car dealership.

At the luncheon Les had mentioned that the joint Peterson Lincoln/Ford operation had now moved from Ballard to Issaquah. These days he was retired and playing golf while the two dealerships were being run by his daughters, Michelle and Micah. "If you're ever in the market for a car—Ford or Lincoln, either one," Les had told me, "talk to one of the girls and let them know you're an old friend of mine. They'll give you a good deal."

In other words, enough time had passed that my failure at fishing no longer counted against me. That was good to hear. Rather than passing along any of this protracted backstory, I gave Alan's question the short answer. "Issaquah," I told him. "It's on the other side of Lake Washington."

I'd had several hours to consider the situation, and I figured an SUV of some kind with three rows of seats would give Alan room for both seating and cargo, because he was definitely going to need room for cargo.

The two Peterson dealerships sit side by side next to an exit off I-90. I put Alan out to prowl around the Ford dealership and went in search of the manager. It turned out Micah Peterson wasn't in that afternoon, so I moved our search mission over to the Lincoln side of the operation, where, according to a salesman, Michelle was on duty and in her office. I stopped by to introduce myself and have a word. Once I'd established my bona fides with her, I went looking for Alan. He was not happy.

"It's been years since I've gone looking at new cars," he lamented. "I had no idea how much they cost these days. There's no way I'm letting you cough up that kind of money. Let's go check out the used cars."

We finally settled on a two-year-old Lincoln

Navigator, fresh off a twenty-four-month lease. It came with all-wheel drive, a six-speed automatic transmission, all-leather heated seats, Bluetooth connectivity, rear camera, and a power-lift gate—in other words, all the bells and whistles. By the time we got to the part about "What's it going to take to put you in this car today?" Michelle had evidently called her dad to check up on me. Once all was said and done, she didn't just give us a good deal—she gave us a hell of a good deal.

Alan Dale drove his new used car off the lot and headed back to Seattle with a happy smile on his face. There was a smile on my face, too. Go Ballard Beavers!

When we made it back to Belltown Terrace—with Alan using his in-car navigation system—he was ready to turn in his rental right then, and that was fine with me. Mel and I have two assigned parking spots in the building. With four cars currently in residence, we were seriously overstocked as far as vehicles were concerned. Once the rental was returned, we settled in for a quiet afternoon. Alan, Athena, and yes, Lucy, spent most of the time in the guest room. Mel sat at the dining-room table and worked on her paperwork, which follows her everywhere, while I caught up on two days' worth of crossword puzzles. At least that's what I was supposedly doing. Mostly I was thinking about Naomi Dale and Petey Mayfield.

After a couple of springlike days, the weather was suddenly turning again. A blustery windstorm was blowing in off Puget Sound. In the course of an hour, Elliott Bay changed from a serene blue to an ominous green punctuated with whitecaps. By the time rain mixed with hail started pounding against the condo's westward-facing windows, the view of both water and sky had turned slate gray. I was grateful that Naomi was safely inside the Pike Street Mission, and I hoped that Petey, wherever he might be, was also inside and out of the weather. Tonight was going to be a miserable time to be homeless.

Although the social worker had Naomi's signed relinquishment form safely in hand, I was well aware that we were only halfway to where we needed to be. Next up came the job of securing Petey's signature. Knowing now how much he had claimed to want the baby, I worried that once we found him he might be unwilling to sign. The problem was, we couldn't even ask the question without finding him first, and I had no idea where to look. So far Sam Shelton's efforts at nosing around among the homeless folks had come to nothing. So where the hell was Petey?

Thinking back to my initial interview with Naomi, I realized I hadn't recorded it, and now I wished I had. I kept trying to recall the exact details of what had been said, especially what she'd told me regarding that last quarrel between them before Petey had stalked out of the house. According to her, he'd done so on foot.

When law enforcement is looking for someone, they can issue a BOLO—aka, be on the lookout. Information about a missing vehicle, including make, model, and plate number, is passed along to all officers on patrol. In this case we didn't have an army of patrol officers, and we also didn't have a vehicle description. And it wasn't as though Petey had disappeared yesterday or the day before. His departure was now almost five months in the past. Chances of our being able to pick up any kind of trail were slim to nonexistent.

And what was it Naomi had told me about that last fight? Petey had returned from his candy-buying excursion full of some kind of wild story about seeing a sign that meant they were going to be rich. What Petey had called "a sign," Naomi had attributed to "tripping out," as though maybe he'd also paid a visit to a local drug dealer on his way to or from the store. She'd also hinted that the sign might have had something to do with astrology. Had he maybe stopped off at a psychic's office to have his palm or his tarot cards read? In any event Naomi hadn't believed a word of it.

With the rain still pouring down outside, Mel finished her work, came over to the window seat, and cuddled up beside me. "A penny for your thoughts," she said. "You've got your iPad laid out in front of you, but you're staring off into space. What's up?"

"If you and I had a big fight and I stormed off saying I was going to show you who was right and who was wrong, what would you think?"

"First off," she said with a grin, "that would never occur, because I am never wrong. But if you did happen to say those exact words to me, I would assume you intended to do just that—come back straightaway, so you could give me a piece of your mind, prove how wrong I was, and rub my nose in it. Is that what went on between Naomi and her boyfriend? Petey said he'd be back but never showed up?"

"Exactly."

"So the question is, why not? Was it because he didn't want to come back or because he couldn't?"

I thought about that for a few seconds. "Naomi told me that when she turned up pregnant, she had wanted to get an abortion. Petey was the one who talked her out of going to Planned Parenthood. He was the one who insisted he wanted a family. If that was the case, why would he just take off like that?"

"It sounds like you're coming down on the couldn't-come-back side of the story as opposed to wouldn't."

I nodded.

"Did Naomi tell you if Petey had any enemies? If he was into drugs—dealing or using, either one—chances are he made plenty of enemies along the way. Maybe they both did."

"I didn't ask that exact question," I admitted. "If I had, Naomi would have known we were operating on the assumption that Petey might be dead. Until we had that signed document in hand, I didn't want to do anything to rock the boat."

"What about Petey's snooty auntie?" Mel began. "If she did what you think she did and sold her mother's property on the QT in order to cheat him out of his share of the inheritance . . ."

And that's when it hit me like a ton of bricks. The sign—the one that had gotten Petey Mayfield so wound up. It hadn't been an astrological one like the moon being in the seventh house and Jupiter aligning with Mars. And it wasn't a tarot reading or a psychic message from the great beyond either. It was a physical sign made out of wood and paper, and I'd seen it with my own eyes.

"Of course!" I exclaimed. "Petey must have seen the damned billboard!"

"What billboard?" Mel asked.

"About Highline's up-and-coming housing development—Mayfield Glen."

"The one they're planning on building on Agnes's former property?"

I nodded. "I saw it when I first drove up. It talks about this being the site of eight soon-to-be-built houses, starting in the mid–nine hundreds. What about this? What if the day Petey left was also the day the sign was installed? Here's Petey, dirt poor, living hand to mouth, trying to support a pregnant girlfriend. He must have known, or at least hoped, that he was in line to inherit part of his grandparents' residual estate. If he saw the sign for the first time when he was on his way to or from the store to buy that Halloween candy, no wonder he went berserk! Any way you slice it, eight houses selling in the mid–nine hundreds add up to a multimillion-dollar project. Petey and Naomi barely had a pot to piss in. As far as he was concerned, even a small share of that would feel like untold riches."

"Seems to me as though a chat with the auntie is in order," Mel suggested.

"Doesn't it just," I agreed, "but not today. Lenora Harrison lives in Bellevue. I've already driven across Lake Washington once today. I don't want to press my luck."

For dinner that night, we chopped up salad makings and polished off the remainder of Marge's lasagna. Afterward Alan went back to the guest room to watch TV there while Mel and I settled in the family room. AMC was running a Jimmy Stewart retrospective, and we watched *Mr. Smith Goes to Washington*. It was a nostalgic look back at a less toxic time before politics turned into a blood sport. We were almost at the end of the movie when my phone rang. Dr. Roz's photo appeared on the screen as I reached to answer.

"Hey," I said. "How's it going?"

"Not so well, I'm afraid," she said.

"Why? What's wrong?"

"Once Loretta's tech obtained that most recent profile, she called to see if she should send it to me."

"And?"

"Like I told you earlier, the wolves are after me big time, so I asked her to please input the profile into NamUs. She did and got an immediate hit."

My heart fell. "A hit?" I asked. "Does that mean Peter Mayfield is dead?"

"Yup, it does," Dr. Roz answered, "as the proverbial doornail. A few weeks ago, a hiker found skeletal remains as well as some items of clothing scattered along the banks of the Yakima River outside Ellensburg. I just got off the phone with Dr. Hopewell, the Kittitas County medical examiner over there."

I recognized the name. Years before, Mel and I had worked with Dr. Laura Hopewell on another homicide.

"She said there was no ID of any kind," Dr. Roz continued, "but the victim's clothing included a belt with a distinctive buckle that had a mazelike design on it. They entered the victim's DNA as well as the information about the belt buckle into NamUs. Couldn't show any dental information because there were very few teeth left. He had a single bullet hole in the left side of his face that blew out the right side of his head, traveling on a slightly upward trajectory and taking most of his jaw along for the ride."

"So whoever did it was beside him rather than facing him?" I asked.

"Correct," she replied.

Poor Naomi. That was my first thought when I heard the awful words laying out the horrific details of Petey's death. The young woman was already heartbroken and hanging by a thread. How much worse could it get?

"Have you located his wife or girlfriend or whatever she is?" Dr. Roz asked.

"Girlfriend," I answered, "and yes, we have. Her name is Naomi Dale. She's currently staying in the Pike Street Mission down in Pioneer Square."

"Dr. Hopewell asked if my office could handle the next-of-kin notification. I'll be calling Seattle PD to see if they can send someone out to let her know."

"Please," I put in quickly, "let me handle the next of kin. I know I'm not currently a sworn officer, so it's fudging the rules, but at least I'm someone Naomi knows. Better to have me delivering the bad news rather than a complete stranger. Besides, the poor girl's already been through so much today. . . ."

"If you want to handle it, that's fine with me," Dr. Roz said without waiting for me to finish my plea. "Once it's done, give me a call so I can let Dr. Hopewell know it's been taken care of. By the way, do you happen to know if there are there any other relatives who should also be notified?"

"The only one I can think of would be Peter's aunt, Lenora Harrison. She lives over in Bellevue. I've been to see her. I can give you an address, but if you'd like me to, I can notify her as well."

"Sounds good," Dr. Roz said. "I'll leave both notifications to you."

"Would you do me a favor in return?"

"Sure."

"Have Dr. Hopewell text me a photo of that belt buckle. I'd like Naomi to have some solid proof of what happened, rather than just a bunch of empty words spilling out of my mouth."

"Will do."

The call ended. I sat there for a moment, staring at the phone and wondering how long it would take for the text to come in.

"I'll go get dressed," Mel said.

"Why?"

"Because I'm coming with you," she said. "It sounds like Naomi needs all the help she can get, and I need to meet my new stepdaughter."

"She doesn't know about me yet."

"When are you going to tell her?"

"I'm not sure."

"It should probably be soon."

Dr. Hopewell's text arrived. As soon as it did, I pocketed the phone and went to bring Alan up to date. On the face of it, Petey's death should have been good news as far as Alan was concerned. After all, it meant that the relinquishment form with Naomi's signature on it was the only one he would need to establish a permanent legal guardianship. But it turns out Alan Dale is a better man than I think I would have been under similar circumstances.

"That's appalling," he said with a stricken look on his face. "Who's going to tell her?"

"I am."

"Do you want me to come along?"

"No," I said. "Mel and I will do it. You stay here with Athena."

"My poor baby," I heard him murmur as I backed out of the room and closed the door. "My poor, poor baby."

I knew which baby he was talking about, and it wasn't Athena.

CHAPTER 23

As Mel and I headed south on First, I dialed Reverend Seymour's number. It was Saturday night after all, and I wasn't the least bit offended that she didn't sound especially happy to hear from me for the second night in a row.

"Sorry to disturb your weekend again, but something's come up," I told her. "Peter Mayfield's skeletal remains were found by a hiker near the Yakima River a few weeks ago, apparently the victim of a homicide."

"Oh, no," Rachel murmured, "how dreadful! Does Naomi know?"

"Not yet," I told her. "That's why I'm calling. My wife and I are on our way to the mission to let her know."

"Your wife," Rachel repeated. "The police chief from Bellingham?"

"That's the one," I replied. "Mel Soames."

"Hi, Reverend Seymour," Mel said, taking advantage of my being on speaker.

"Good to hear your voice again, Mel," Rachel replied, "but not under these kinds of circumstances."

"I still have the housemother's phone number from our exchanges last night," I said, regaining control of the conversation. "Should I call her directly, or will you?"

"I'll call," Rachel said. "How soon will you be there?"

"Ten minutes, maybe."

"Do you want me to have the housemother tell Naomi what this is all about?"

"No, just say there's something urgent we need to discuss with her."

"Will do." She hung up then.

Mel reached over and patted my thigh. "Almost like old times," she said, "the two of us riding off to do a next of kin."

"You've always been better at those than I have," I told her. "And I want you along when I tell Lenora Harrison, too, because you're also better at reading people than I am."

"We make a good team," Mel said, "but aren't the homicide guys from Kittitas County going to be pissed when they find out we've horned in on their investigation?"

"I doubt it. For one thing, Dr. Hopewell asked us to do this, remember?" I said. "The guys on that side of the mountains may try to investigate Petey's death, but my guess is he died elsewhere and was simply dumped in their jurisdiction."

"You mean elsewhere as in over here rather than over there?"

"Exactly, and by the way and for the record," I

added, "this isn't anything like the old days. In the old days, homicide was an all-male preserve—an old-boys' network. That's not the case anymore. Think about what's going on here. There's you, Dr. Roz, Dr. Hopewell, Loretta Hawk, and Rachel Seymour—an old-girls' network if ever there was one!"

"Quit your bitchin'!" Mel replied with a laugh. "It sounds to me like all those so-called old girls are getting the job done for you."

I had to admit that collection of females was delivering the goods. "They are doing that," I agreed.

I found on-street parking on First, half a block from the mission's entrance. Fortunately, the rain had let up for a time, and we didn't get soaked walking from the car to the mission's entrance. When we got there, I was about to reach for the intercom buzzer when the door opened from inside. Naomi, wearing sweats and a pair of house slippers, stood just beyond the doorway.

"What's happened?" she asked, peering up at me anxiously with a look of dread on her face. "Is something wrong with Athena? Is she okay?"

"This is my wife, Mel Soames," I said. "She's a police officer in Bellingham. Do you mind if we come in?"

Naomi barely glanced at Mel, but she stepped aside enough to allow us to enter. The door to Rachel Seymour's office was closed. The door to the chapel was open. I picked door number two. "We should probably sit down," I suggested.

Naomi sat, but she perched nervously on the

edge of her pew like a bird ready to take flight. "You still haven't told me. What's this about?" she demanded.

"It's about Petey," I said finally, "and I'm afraid I'm about to deliver some very bad news."

Naomi's hand went to her mouth. "No," she whispered. "He's not dead, is he?"

I nodded. "Yes, he is."

"That can't be," she wailed. "How? Where? When?"

In my experience those are questions most killers never bother to ask. They don't need to, because they already know the answers.

I told Naomi what I could, and she listened as though dumbstruck, without uttering another sound. Finally I switched on my phone and opened it to the message app so I could show her the belt-buckle photo that Dr. Hopewell had forwarded to me. Naomi studied it for a long time. Then, closing her eyes, she held the phone with the photo on it close to her breast, as though it were a precious holy relic of some kind. That's when the tears came at last, accompanied by body-wrenching sobs that seemed to come from the depths of her soul. Eventually she quieted.

"Yakima's on the other side of the mountains," she pointed out. "Petey didn't have a car. How did he end up there?"

"He wasn't actually in Yakima," I corrected. "He was found on the banks of the Yakima River, near Ellensburg. But you're right. The body was found on the far side of the Cascades. As to your question? I suspect there's a good possibility that Petey was murdered on this side of the mountains and his body dumped over there in hopes of confusing the issue. What was recovered consisted of skeletal remains only, and no identification was found nearby. Without the DNA samples obtained from the hairbrush you provided, there's a good chance his body never would have been identified."

"But who would want to murder him? And why?"

"That's what I wanted to ask you. Did Petey have any enemies—anyone who would want to harm him?"

Naomi shook her head. "No, not that I know of. He was a good guy. He was big, too—physically big—but he wasn't mean or belligerent. He wasn't one of those guys who goes around picking fights. And he wasn't anything at all like my ex, who used to beat the crap out of me on a regular basis."

For just a moment, I wished I knew who that nameless ex was and where I could find him so I could return the favor by giving him a taste of his own medicine. Tempting as it was to think about, I forced myself back to the issue at hand.

"You said Petey left the day before Halloween."

Naomi nodded.

"What time of day was it?"

"Sometime in the afternoon, I think."

"And he left on foot?"

"How else?"

"Someone might have offered him a ride," I suggested.

Naomi shook her head. "I don't think so. The last I saw, he was walking—walking in the rain."

"It was raining?"

"In buckets."

"You told me earlier that you thought he might have hooked up with one of your old dealers."

"Kenneth," she said. "He hangs around the 7-Eleven where Petey went to get the candy. That's his turf."

"Does Kenneth have a last name?"

"Dawson, I think, but I'm not really sure. Still, he wouldn't do something like that. He's not a killer."

I wasn't so sure about that. Drug dealers tend to carry grudges. They also carry guns.

"Mr. Dawson may not be responsible for what happened to Petey," Mel put in quietly, "but it might be worth talking to him. If he happened to be hanging out around the store that particular day, he might be one of the last people to have seen Petey alive. It's possible he saw or heard something."

Naomi nodded. "Oh," she said.

"When we leave here," Mel continued, "we'll be going to Bellevue to meet up with Petey's Aunt Lenora. Is there anyone else besides her who should be notified of Petey's death?"

"I don't know of anyone else," Naomi answered. She took a deep, shuddering breath. "What happens next?" she asked.

"Don't be surprised if homicide cops from Kittitas County end up coming around asking questions," I warned her, "and maybe detectives from Seattle PD as well."

"Will I have to talk to all of them?"

"Yes, you will," I answered. "I have a feeling this is an investigation that's going to have pieces on both sides of the mountains. And once the next-of-kin notifications are complete, you'll need to look into making funeral arrangements."

"Will those be up to me?" she asked. "How do I go about it? If Petey's body is over in Ellensburg, how do I get him here? And how much will it cost? I don't have any money. And how do I know what's right? I don't have any idea what Petey would have wanted. Where do I start?"

I could see that she was completely overwhelmed by what had happened and by the magnitude of the unknowable tasks that lay ahead of her. And who could blame her? Naomi and Petey had been relatively young. At that stage in their lives—barely starting out and expecting their first baby—the prospect of dying would have been decades in the future. It wasn't a time when they would have sat around discussing each other's preferences as far as funeral arrangements are concerned.

"Funerals are for the living," Mel said quietly, "so think about what you want and about how you would like to say good-bye. It can be as simple and as private as you want it to be. Or you can have a more formal service at a funeral home."

"But I don't even know any funeral homes," Naomi objected.

"Perhaps Petey's Aunt Lenora will be able to suggest someone, maybe whoever handled arrangements for Petey's grandmother. Who knows? She might also be willing to help with the expenses. If all else fails, I'm sure your father will step in and lend a hand."

"My father?" Naomi scoffed. "Why would he? He's probably glad Petey's dead. It's that much less trouble for him—one less signature needed for him to get out of town."

Alan Dale had been Naomi's devoted father all her life. He'd been there for her when I had not, and her instant disregard for all he'd done and been hit me where I lived. He deserved better than that.

"You need to give your dad more credit," I told her reprovingly. "Think about what he's done for the last two months. He quit his job, dropped everything, and came here to look after Athena. He's spent the last six weeks sitting up with her night after night while she suffered through the agonies of withdrawal due to an addiction to methadone. Even so, when he heard about what had happened to Petey, his first concern was for you, not the guardianship. You're all caught up in your own grief right now, but you might want to take a moment and think about what your dad went through when he lost your mother. He loved that woman with all his heart, the same way you loved Petey. He knows what it cost him to lose her, and that means he understands exactly how much you're hurting right now. He's been there and done all of this, Naomi. You've lost the love of your life, and so did he. And whether you believe it or not, he'll do anything in his power to help you."

Naomi bit her lip and said nothing. I thought for a moment she had shut me out and wasn't even listening.

Mel stood up and touched Naomi on the shoulder. "So sorry for your loss," she said, "but we should probably be going."

Much to my surprise, Naomi's next words proved

me wrong. It turned out she had been listening after all. "If I wanted to get in touch with my dad,"
she said quietly, "I wouldn't even know how to
reach him."

I handed her one of my cards. "He and Athena
are staying with Mel and me right now," I told her.
"The number on the bottom is our landline. If it
rings, he'll most likely answer. Feel free to call anytime."

Mel and I headed for the door. "What about
Petey's hairbrush?" Naomi called after us. "You
said I could have it back."

"And you will," I told her. "I had to leave it with
the lab so they could be sure they had a usable DNA
sample. Tomorrow's Sunday. Most likely I won't be
able to retrieve it until Monday, but I'll bring it back
to you. I promise."

"Thank you," she said.

"You were a little hard on her about her dad,"
Mel observed once we were out on the sidewalk.

"I know," I said, "and I probably shouldn't have
been. I just wanted her to understand that Alan is
not the bad guy here."

"But I doubt he's going to be in any position
to help Naomi with body transport or funeral arrangements," Mel said.

"I doubt that, too," I agreed. "He may not be able
to, but we can. Back child support."

It wasn't raining, but the wind was still blowing a
gale by the time we reached the car. From Pioneer
Square the easiest route to the Eastside was the I-90
Bridge. We were in the car and headed in that direction before Mel spoke again.

"You need to be careful," Mel said quietly.

"Careful, why? What do you mean?"

"Naomi's a druggie, Beau," Mel said. "She may or may not be using right now, but she's been a druggie for a long time. Everything that's happening to her right now is incredibly tough, and she might very well fall back into that lifestyle in hopes of dulling the pain. I don't want you getting your heart set on some kind of happy ending that may not happen."

I took those words very much to heart, because in my experience Mel Soames is right far more often than she's wrong.

The bridges across Lake Washington, both the 520 and I-90, are floating bridges. There wasn't much traffic and it wasn't raining, but the eastbound crossing was dicey all the same. Whitecaps, driven by gale-force winds, occasionally crested onto the bridge deck and splashed onto our windshield. One moment you could see just fine, and the next you were driving blind until the automatic wipers woke up and cleared the glass.

When we pulled up to the gated entrance to Lenora Harrison's estate, the contrast between her circumstances and Naomi's couldn't have been clearer. The only thing they both had in common was an intercom-operated entry system.

"Who is it?" someone asked, and I recognized Lenora's voice. The maid who had answered the first time around must have had the evening off.

"J. P. Beaumont," I said. "I was here on Thursday, asking about your nephew, Peter Mayfield."

"I still have no idea where Petey is," Lenora replied. "Why don't you just go on about your business and leave us alone?"

"It turns out I do know where he is," I replied. "His remains are in a drawer in the Kittitas County M.E.'s office over in Ellensburg. Petey's been murdered. That's what I need to talk to you about."

"Who the hell drops by unannounced at this hour of the night?" a man's irate voice rumbled in the background. "Whoever it is, get rid of them."

I had no doubt the lord of the manor was speaking.

The heavy metal gate swung open, and we motored up the drive. When Lenora opened the front door, she was dressed as though she'd just come in from a night on the town. She was wearing a satiny kind of jumpsuit topped by a diamond-solitaire pendant that probably cost more than Alan Dale's new used car. There was alcohol on her breath, and she seemed a little tipsy. A graying man, probably in his late sixties, remained in the background glaring at us. He was dressed in a tux with the bow tie hanging loose around his neck. He held a recently filled rocks glass in his hand, and as he stood there, he swayed lightly on his feet. If it takes one to know one, he was a drunk for sure.

"Who are these people again?" he demanded churlishly. "And what the hell do they want?"

"Isaac," Leonora murmured. "Mind your manners."

So this was Isaac Henderson, the software guru who had funded Leonora's upwardly mobile escape from West Seattle. I wasn't exactly impressed. His being pissed about our visit didn't bother me in the least, nor did his being drunk. From an investigative point of view, interviewing people when they're under the influence can often be very productive. Booze suppresses inhibitions, and when you're a cop working a homicide, it pays to listen closely while possible suspects and persons of interest run off at the mouth. Sometimes they'll end up saying more than they intended.

"It's that detective I told you about the other day, Isaac," Lenora said, trying to smooth things over. "He's the one who was looking for Petey. He says Petey's dead—that he's been murdered."

Mel eased past me into the house, holding up her badge as she did so. She didn't mention that her badge was actually from the Bellingham PD rather than Seattle PD, but that hardly mattered. Neither of the Harrisons bothered glancing at it. For all they cared, her badge could just as well have come from a box of Cracker Jacks.

"In cases of homicide, it's customary to send officers out to do next-of-kin notifications," Mel informed them. "We learned about the case only a few hours ago. Considering the distances involved, Dr. Hopewell, the M.E. over in Kittitas County, asked us to handle the notifications. Once we've done so, she'll be releasing Mr. Mayfield's name to the media."

"So that worthless little creep is dead, huh?" Isaac muttered, giving his wife a scathing look. "If you decide to pony up for his funeral, remember the money will have to come out of your household account. I'm not paying a dime." With that he stalked off into another room, leaving us in the entryway.

Wow! Talk about an arrogant asshole! Clearly sympathy wasn't his long suit. Lenora Mayfield might have married up, as they say, but with a husband that rude, living in a Medina mansion sounded like anything but a bed of roses. As she flushed with embarrassment, I couldn't help feeling sorry for her.

"Let's go into the living room," she suggested.

Lenora led us into a sumptuously appointed room, passing an immense Steinway grand piano along the way. Ornately framed pieces of modern artwork graced the walls. The space was filled with beautifully arranged furniture that was no doubt beyond expensive. Mel and I settled into adjoining wing chairs. Lenora took her place on a spacious white sectional sofa, facing us from the far side of a brass-and-glass coffee table with a goblet of red wine strategically placed in front of her. A mirrored wet bar covered the far wall, and that's where Isaac stood, making himself a refill.

"Would you care for something to drink?" Lenora offered.

"No thanks," Mel said quickly. "We're working."

Beverage in hand, Isaac Harrison came over to where we were sitting. He had probably been handsome in his prime, but he was long past that now. He had aged into a mean-spirited drunk. He stood there for a moment as if considering joining his wife on the sofa before deciding against it.

"I'll leave you to it, then," he said finally, before making his shambling way out of the room. I didn't say "Good riddance" aloud, but that's what I was thinking, and as Lenora watched him leave, she seemed relieved.

"So what happened to Petey?" she asked, picking up her glass and taking a sip of wine.

"He was shot in the side of the head and dumped along the banks of the Yakima River. He went missing several months ago and has been dead for some time. The remains that were located are skeletal in nature and were identified due to a DNA match."

"Oh, my," Lenora said. "How dreadful! Was his death drug-related? I know he was involved in that lifestyle and with those kinds of people."

If Peter Mayfield's auntie was grief-stricken about her nephew's death, she wasn't overplaying her hand. There were no tears, no hysterics. We might just as well have been discussing the untimely demise of a neighbor's pet.

"That's what we're trying to ascertain," Mel said. "Had you been in touch with him recently—at his grandmother's funeral, perhaps?"

"There was no funeral," Lenora replied. "Mother didn't want one, and I abided by her wishes. I had her buried privately in the Mayfield family plot in West Seattle's Pioneer Cemetery along with my father and my brother."

No funeral because of your mother's wishes or your husband's? I wondered.

"Were you aware that Petey was living in one of the existing dwellings on your mother's property?" Mel asked.

"I knew she let Petey stay there from time to time," Lenora answered. "I told her that wasn't a good idea—that she was just enabling bad behavior and probably attracting all kinds of riffraff to the neighborhood. Is that where he was living at the time he disappeared?"

"Yes," I answered, stepping into the conversation. "That's where he'd been staying along with his girlfriend, Naomi Dale. According to her, Petey left in late October after they'd had a row of some kind."

"If Petey had a girlfriend, my mother never mentioned it."

"Or the fact that Naomi was pregnant?"

For the first time in the conversation, Lenora looked startled. "She was?" So much for her being ignorant of Naomi's existence.

"Was," I said, "but isn't now. The baby—a little girl—was born at the end of January."

"Is the baby even Petey's?" Lenora asked. "You said this Naomi was his girlfriend, which means they weren't married. For all I know, she's the same kind of screwup Petey was."

I remembered the tender way Naomi had cradled the phone containing the photo of Petey's belt buckle to her breast. I remembered, too, that when she'd been thrown out into the cold just before Christmas, she had packed Petey's treasured hairbrush into her grocery cart in hopes of returning it. And when she'd come to the mission the other night, she'd brought it with her in that paper bag along with her other paltry belongings. Compared to those three striking images, Isaac and Lenora Harrison didn't have much going for them.

"When did you say your mother died?" Mel asked.

"Not long before Christmas," Lenora said, "on the twentieth of December. She'd been ill for some time with Alzheimer's. She was in a memory-care place in Lake City over in Seattle. It was a blessing all the way around when it was finally over."

"Did you make any attempt to reach out to Petey at the time?" I asked.

"Why would I?" Lenora replied.

"Maybe because he was a beneficiary under your mother's will?"

"I doubt that," Lenora said a little too quickly. "I'm quite sure I'm the only named beneficiary. Well, not really. The will was written years ago when my brother was still alive, so Arthur is probably listed as well, but he's dead now, too."

"And the name of the firm handling your mother's estate would be Stockman and Dodge, located in downtown Seattle?"

Suddenly alarmed, Lenora sat up a little straighter. "How on earth would you know that?" she wanted to know.

"I'm a detective, Mrs. Harrison," I said. "Probated wills are public records. Since Stockman and Dodge handled your father's estate, I assumed they'd likely be handling your mother's affairs as well."

Lenora's initial reaction had already told me what I wanted to know. I was willing to bet that Agnes Mayfield's will had been executed at the same time as her late husband's and that it had remained unchanged from that time until now. When Peter died, he had bequeathed everything to his wife. Only now, with the second death—Agnes's death—

did the full impact of those powerful words "per stirpes" come into play. The remainder of Peter and Agnes's joint estate would then go to each of their children in equal shares. With both Arthur and Petey deceased, Arthur's share of the estate would be passed along to Athena, and I was determined to see to it that she received every last penny. I doubted Lenora was fully aware of any of that, but I sure as hell was.

"Since your mother died several months ago, is there any reason you haven't gotten around to probating the will?"

Lenora shrugged. "It's such a pittance that it's hardly worth going to all the trouble. The estate sale is coming up. I doubt the proceeds will amount to much, and once the lawyer gets paid, there'll be very little left over."

Yes, I thought, *not enough to bother about, especially considering the existence of those very timely quitclaim deeds. Without them there would have been a lot more.*

"Was your mother already suffering from Alzheimer's when she signed the quitclaim deeds over to you?" I asked. "If so, the deeds themselves might be deemed invalid, which might in turn invalidate your later sale of the properties to a third party. If I were you, I wouldn't be surprised if an attorney working on Athena's behalf didn't come around asking questions about all those real-estate transactions."

For the first time in the course of the whole conversation, Lenora Harrison looked truly alarmed, but then she got a grip. "It's late," she said, pushing away her unfinished glass of wine. "I think I'd like you to go now."

"Of course," Mel said, standing up.

I immediately followed suit. "Thank you for your time, Ms. Harrison," I said, "and sorry for your loss."

"You're not the least bit sorry for her loss," Mel observed as we headed back to the car, "and you're grinning like the cat that swallowed the canary. What's up?"

You bet I was grinning. "Because even if we can't invalidate Lenora's sale of those lots to Highline, we might be able to get her to cough up Athena's share of those proceeds."

In my estimation, after decades of police work, when it came to next-of-kin notifications, that possibility made this one count as one of my very best.

CHAPTER 24

WHEN MEL AND I got back to Belltown Terrace, Athena and Lucy were both down for the night. Alan Dale had waited up for us. The first words out of his mouth took my breath away.

"She called," he said. "Naomi actually called. When the phone rang, I never dreamed it would be for me, and I almost didn't answer it. She told me she was sorry—sorry about the way she treated her mother and me, sorry about everything. She asked me if I'd look into finding a suitable funeral home. She says she doesn't want a funeral or a service of any kind. She just wants Petey's ashes."

Something else to push around in an overloaded grocery cart, I thought.

"She wanted to know how long I'd be here. I told her I don't know how soon the judge will sign off on the guardianship, but we'll stay around as long as Naomi needs us—if it's all right with you, that is."

"Not to worry," I said. "You can stay as long as you like."

The problem was, I heard the hopefulness in his voice. Naomi had called him, spoken to him. To his way of thinking, maybe things were going be all right and there would be a real reconciliation between them. In the back of my mind, though, I was remembering Mel's cautioning words to me about not putting too much stock in where Naomi was right now or where she might end up in the future. I wanted to pass that same bit of wisdom along to Alan, but not right then. He was on a high, and I didn't want to burst his bubble.

I pulled out my phone, located the names and numbers of a couple of reputable funeral homes in the area, including the one on Queen Anne Hill that had handled both my grandmother's funeral and my stepgrandfather's as well.

"Check these guys out," I told Alan after texting him the information. "Once you choose one, have them be in touch with Dr. Hopewell over in Ellensburg."

"Should I try calling tonight?"

"My guess is they'll have someone on duty to handle calls. And remember, I'll take care of whatever expenses are involved."

"Beau," Alan objected. "You can't do that."

"I can and I will."

At that point the conversation veered into our telling Alan about the trip to Bellevue. Enthralled, he listened to every word. "It's possible Athena might be in line to receive some of her great-grandmother's estate?" he asked in disbelief.

"It is," I replied. "Over the weekend we'll need to see if we can find representation for someone to look out for Athena's interests. Next week we'll have them contact Agnes Mayfield's attorney's office to inquire after the stipulations in her will."

Alan was already shaking his head. "Hiring attorneys will cost even more," he objected.

"Yes, it will," I told him, "and it will be money well spent."

"Do you really think Petey's aunt may have forged her own mother's signature in order to gain ownership of those lots so she could sell them?"

"I do."

"But it sounds like she's got plenty of money of her own, so why would she cheat her own mother?"

"That's most likely the problem," Mel told him. "There may be plenty of money, but it's not Lenora Harrison's. It belongs to her husband, and I'll bet he keeps a tight hold on the purse strings. She probably has to account for every nickel she spends."

I nodded my agreement. "I have a feeling Isaac Harrison has zero knowledge about his wife's real-estate transactions. Lenora wanted her mother's money to be her money."

"It's a familiar pattern," Mel told us. "When I was a kid, in sixth grade or so, we were living in the officers' quarters at Fort Meade. Our next-door neighbors were the Blackmans. Their daughter, Silvia, and I were good friends. Her dad and mine were both captains in the army and made almost the same amount of money. Unlike my father, Mr. Blackman made sure that everyone knew he wore the pants in their family. He was also in charge of the checkbook. Mrs. Blackman had a budget for groceries and everything else. If she overspent, everyone in the neighborhood heard about it. She finally managed to get a job as a teacher's aide at a local preschool. When she came home with her first paycheck, he demanded that she hand it over. She didn't. There was a hell of a row. The next day she loaded the kids in the car and left."

"For good?"

"Yes, for good," Mel replied. "The last my mom heard from her, Mrs. Blackman had remarried and was living happily ever after somewhere in Georgia."

"After what we saw tonight," I observed, "I have to say Isaac Harrison is clearly an overbearing asshole and a tightwad besides. What's keeping Lenora from pulling a Mrs. Blackman and taking off?"

"Because she's spent years letting him handle the finances while she's been living in the manner to which she's become accustomed," Mel replied. "According to what Hilda Tanner told you, Isaac was already well off before Lenora married him. I'm betting there's an airtight prenup lurking in some attorney's file drawer that takes a deep bite financially if she divorces him."

"I didn't make you sign a prenup," I said.

"Ditto for me and Jasmine," Alan put in.

Mel smiled at both of us. "That's because the two of you are both nice guys," she told us, "something Isaac Harrison definitely is not."

At that point Athena let out a tentative cry. Alan excused himself and went to their room to tend to her and go night-night while Mel and I stayed up talking.

"On our way to Bellevue, you were thinking Lenora was going to end up as a suspect in Petey's death, didn't you?" she asked.

"She still might be," I responded. "I need to check on that Mayfield Glen billboard and see when it went up. If that really is the sign Petey mentioned to Naomi, he might have gone to Bellevue on his own to read Lenora the riot act about what was going on. Depending on what Agnes told him, maybe he suspected that Lenora's dealings with her mother were underhanded if not downright fraudulent. If he threatened her with exposure, no telling what she might have done."

"I think you're wrong," Mel countered. "It seemed to me she regarded Petey as more of a nonentity rather than a serious threat. When you brought up the will situation, Lenora was downright slack-jawed. I don't think she'd had a clue about that before you mentioned it. By the way," she added, "did you happen to lay hands on copies of those quitclaim deeds?"

I had brought the file folder up from the car with me, but the day had been so busy that I had yet to examine them. "They're in the bedroom," I said, getting up. "I'll be right back."

Returning to the family room, I slipped one of the documents out of the folder and handed it to Mel for her examination. Donning my reading glasses, I sat down to study another. I shuffled through to the back page and concentrated on the signature line. Agnes Matilda Mayfield's notarized signature was scrawled in a shaky and almost illegible fashion.

"When did Lenora move her mother into the nursing home?" Mel asked.

"Sometime last summer. Hilda Tanner wasn't sure of the date."

"In that case this looks like elder abuse to me," Mel said. "If Agnes was already exhibiting symptoms of dementia or Alzheimer's before she left West Seattle, would she have been in any condition to sign a legally binding document?"

The deed in my hand was dated August 1. But then as my eye fell on the notary's stamp and signature at the bottom, a pulse of recognition shot through my body. "Holy Crap!"

"What?" Mel demanded. "What's the matter?"

"Look at the last name," I said handing it over.

Mel studied the document. "I think the first name's Danielle," she concluded at last. "I can't quite make out the handwriting."

"I can. It is Danielle," I told her, "but it's the last name that counts."

"Why?" Mel asked.

"It's Nishikawa."

"The same last name as whoever bought the quit-claimed lots from Lenora?"

"Exactly, and this strikes me as a little too cozy."

"Are you thinking there's something irregular about Agnes's notarized signature?"

"I certainly am," I declared.

"Fraud or forgery?" Mel asked.

"Maybe a little of both," I said, "with a dash of collusion thrown in on the side."

"What now?"

"I think it's time for us to do a deep dive into the life and times of Suzanne Nishikawa," I answered. "I've seen the collection of bragging-rights photos she keeps on the wall. I've read what the Highline Web site has to say about her. What I need now is all the information that isn't readily available to the general public."

"So you're calling for reinforcements from everyone's favorite hacker?" Mel asked.

That was a reference to a guy named Todd Hatcher. Mel and I had first encountered Todd when we worked for SHIT and Ross Connors had brought him in as a consultant. He's a forensic economist who absolutely doesn't look the part. Raised on a ranch in southern Arizona, he's a cowboy at heart and dresses that way, complete with worn jeans and dusty boots. Where other people go for baseball caps as fashion statements, Todd prefers Stetsons. When SHIT shut down, he traded his dusty boots for muddy ones. He and his wife, Julie, moved to a ranch near Olympia, where they're busy raising quarter horses along with their now-toddler daughter, Sabrina.

Bowlegged, lean and lanky, Todd can easily be written off as a country bumpkin at first glance. That's a mistake, however. Todd is a geek's geek, one who has access to countless databases that can track down supposedly confidential information on anyone and everyone.

"He'll be able to tell us everything there is to know about Suzanne and Lenora, too, for that matter. Whether any of that helps us uncover what happened to Petey remains to be seen."

"Fortunately," Mel told me, "what happened to Petey is not your problem."

I glanced at my watch. It was almost midnight.

Todd and Julie live in the country. They are definitely early-to-bed-and-early-to-rise individuals. In my experience, dragging someone like that out of bed in the middle of the night in order to ask a favor is not a good idea. Nor was putting my request into an e-mail. I didn't necessarily want to leave behind a cyber trail considering what I was asking Todd to do.

"I'll call him in the morning," I said.

"Good thinking," Mel told me. "Let's hit the hay."

I had cleared off the counter in my bathroom so Mel could unpack her daunting collection of makeup, lotions, and potions. We have dueling bathroom counters at both ends of the road for good reason. With Mel's usual dressing room currently functioning as guest quarters for Alan and Athena, there was a bit of grumbling on both our parts before we finally managed to get undressed and into bed.

It turns out, however, that Mel was one hundred percent wrong about Petey Mayfield's homicide not being our problem. That changed early the next morning when my cell phone, sitting on its bedside charger, jarred me awake at 7:00 A.M. Mel opened one eye. Since it was my phone ringing instead of hers, she rolled over, plastered a pillow over her ear, and tried to go back to sleep.

"Hey, Beau," a cheery woman's voice said into the phone when I answered, "Detective Lucinda Caldwell here. How's it going? Long time no see."

That would be Detective Lucinda Caldwell of the Kittitas County Sheriff's Department. As far as I knew, no one ever called Lucinda Caldwell "Lucy," and that was a good thing. Having a second Lucy in my life at that point would have been too much of a complication.

I had been working for SHIT when I'd encountered Lucinda Caldwell as part of an investigation involving human trafficking that stretched from southern Arizona to the Pacific Northwest. She'd been a relatively new detective at the time, and our initial interactions had been problematic at best. By the time the case was resolved, I had figured out that she was a smart and very capable investigator, working and surviving in a department where she was partnered with a male chauvinist pig who still thought a woman's place was in the home, where she was expected to occupy herself perusing cookbooks rather than murder books.

"I'm guessing you're working a case of skeletal remains found along the Yakima River."

"Yup," she said, "you've got that right. I'm lead, by the way."

"Really?" I asked. "Whatever happened to that obnoxious partner of yours?"

She laughed. "Gary Fields, you mean? He got his walking papers after three different women in the department filed sexual-harassment claims against him."

"Which you could have done but didn't, right?" I asked.

"Correct," she replied, "but how did you know that?"

"Because I saw you outwit the poor guy five ways to Sunday. You walked all over him, and he didn't even realize he'd been had."

Lucinda Caldwell laughed aloud. "When you're stuck with a jerk like that for a partner, manipulation is the name of the game and the only way to survive."

I could only wish someone had bothered to point that reality out to me back when I was stuck at Seattle PD with Paul Kramer as my partner.

"Anyway," Lucinda continued, "about that case. Skeletal remains again, but at least these weren't burned to a crisp. Dr. Hopewell tells me that you're the one who both ID'd the victim and did the next-of-kin notifications. That surprised me. I thought the new AG shut down SHIT."

"He did," I said. "I'm a private investigator now, and I stumbled across Petey Mayfield as part of a missing-persons case I've been working. Dr. Roz—that's short for Rosemary Mellon—is the M.E. here in King County. Once Laura Hopewell contacted her and since I know some of the individuals involved, Dr. Roz asked me to do the notifications."

"You were investigating Peter Mayfield's disappearance?" Lucinda asked.

"No," I answered, "it was a related case. I was actually looking for Petey's girlfriend, who was also among the missing. It wasn't until after I located her that I realized he was missing, as well."

"You're saying the girlfriend is still alive?" Lucinda asked.

"Yes, she is."

"Is she a suspect, then?"

"No," I answered. "I don't believe she's responsible."

"In other words, you know way more about this

case than I do," Lucinda concluded. "We're operating on the assumption that our victim was murdered elsewhere and dumped here. In order to sort that out, I'll be leaving Ellensburg shortly to head over the pass to your part of the state. How about if I give you a call once I get there so we can have a sit-down and you can bring me up to speed."

For any number of reasons, I didn't want to carry on any kind of detailed discussion of what was now an active and ongoing homicide investigation at home in front of Alan Dale.

"Tell you what," I said, "depending on when you get here and what you're in the mood for, we can have breakfast or lunch—your choice, my treat."

"Deal," she said. "See you then."

CHAPTER 25

THE COFFEE MACHINE came to life in the kitchen. That meant Alan Dale was up and at 'em in the other room. Leaving Mel to the unusual luxury of sleeping in, I eased out of bed, showered, dressed, and then ventured out to face the day. I collected the leash and Lucy so we could do our first walk. Sam and Billy Bob had already departed by the time we got downstairs, but seeing their empty alcove made me realize I needed to replenish the supply of cash in my pocket. Sam had helped me find Naomi, and that in turn had led to finding Petey as well. Petey might have been deceased, but he'd been found, and that meant that promised reward went to Sam as well.

On the way back upstairs, I stopped off in the lobby. On the doorman rotation, Sunday was Bob's day off, but I left word that I needed to talk to him the next time he was in.

"Breakfast?" Alan asked, standing at the stove, spatula in hand.

"Not today, thanks," I told him as I walked over to the coffee machine and punched the button. "Mel's still sleeping, and I've got an appointment later on for either breakfast or lunch, depending on traffic."

"I got in touch with that funeral home on Queen Anne," Alan said as he slid eggs out of the frying pan and onto a plate.

"And?" I asked.

"They told me not to worry—that they'll handle it, starting with arranging transport. I've got an appointment early this afternoon to stop by and choose a suitable urn."

"When you're there, have them call me so I can give them my credit-card number."

He started to voice another objection, but after a look from me he gave it up as a lost cause.

Walking into the family room, coffee in hand, I checked my watch. It was just past seven. Ellensburg is right around a hundred miles from downtown Seattle. On a good day in good traffic, it's an easy two-hour trip. On a Sunday in Snoqualmie Pass, heavy traffic is always a possibility, and that increases the chances that a wreck of some kind will be added to the mix. I'd expect Detective Caldwell if and when I saw her, and not a moment earlier. Rather than turning to my crossword puzzles, I got out my phone and dialed Todd Hatcher's number.

"How are things down on the farm?" I asked when he answered.

"It's a ranch, not a farm," Todd corrected. "We raise horses."

"And fresh vegetables," I put in. "I've seen Julie's garden. She definitely raises vegetables."

"Okay, you've got me there," he said. "What's up?"

"I need some help."

"Data mining, I presume," he replied. "Who do you want me to look into?"

"Three people," I said. "Agnes Mayfield, currently deceased but formerly of West Seattle. Lenora Harrison, Agnes's daughter, who's married to a guy named Isaac Harrison. They reside in Bellevue. And finally Suzanne Nishikawa, who's the CEO of a company called Highline Development."

For the next several minutes, I gave him an overview of the case—all of it, including the fact that both Naomi and Athena happened to be blood relations of mine, something I'd been leaving out of my previous briefings on the situation.

"So your primary concern isn't the homicide so much as it is making sure that Athena isn't being cheated out of what's rightfully hers?" Todd asked when I finished. "You're not working the homicide?"

"No," I said. "Detective Lucinda Caldwell from Kittitas is running that show."

"Okay, then," Todd said. "I'll see what I can do."

"There's one more thing," I added. "Do you happen to have a handwriting expert in your bag of tricks?"

"Maybe, why?"

I explained my concern about the validity of those quitclaim signatures.

"I've got someone in mind," Todd told me. "His name is Joseph Stallings. If Joe's available, I'll have him give you a call."

Todd was as good as his word. Sunday or not,

Joseph Stallings called me back a mere ten minutes later.

"Mr. Beaumont?" he asked. "Joe Stallings here. I understand you have some concerns about possibly forged documents?"

"Call me Beau," I said. "And yes, I do."

I scanned the three documents I'd obtained from Linda Collins and texted them to him, and then I returned to my crossword puzzles. I had finished one and moved on to the next when Joe called back.

"My initial look-see suggests that all three of these were signed by the same person, but there are some hesitations and an absence of fluidity that make me think you might be right and the signatures could be forgeries. Do you have any other samples of Mrs. Mayfield's handwriting?"

I thought about Hilda Tanner, still in possession of a key to Agnes Mayfield's abandoned house. "I don't have any at this moment," I said, "but I have an idea where I can lay hands on some."

"Good," he said. "If you're able to do so, send them along. You already have my number."

I thought about calling Hilda Tanner but decided against it. Just because I was up at this ungodly hour didn't mean everyone else was. Instead I went to the kitchen for a second cup of coffee. When Alan showed up with Athena snuggled in the crook of his arm, I made a cup for him, too, and then we all headed into the family room. I think Alan was ready for a little adult companionship. Lucy came along as well, sinking to the floor near Alan's feet. Since Mel had not yet appeared, I figured now was as good a time as any to have "the talk."

"You've never had a substance-abuse issue, have you?" I said.

"Who, me?" Alan asked with a laugh. "Nope, not me, not ever."

"I have," I told him, "and one thing I can tell you for sure, drunks and druggies are all alike, and they lie like crazy. They dish out all kinds of commitments and promises and don't keep any of them. They'll say whatever they have to in order to get back into your good graces, and once they are? You're screwed."

"What are you saying?"

"When Mel and I came home last night, you were on cloud nine because Naomi had called you and actually apologized. Good for her, but please don't believe everything you hear coming out of her mouth right now, and don't put too much store in it either. For your sake and for Athena's, too," I urged, "don't get suckered into believing there's going to be some kind of magic reconciliation between you and Naomi or an instant cure for her substance-abuse issues. If Naomi wants back into your life or Athena's, she's going to have to earn it."

"How will she do that?"

"These days there are plenty of inpatient treatment options. They generally last for six weeks or so at a minimum. If Naomi is ready to make some serious changes in her life and agrees to go into treatment, I'll help her get admitted and pay the fare, but she's the one who'll have to do the work."

Alan shook his head. "Naomi sounded so sincere last night, and I was hoping—"

"I know you were," I told him. "That's why we're

having this chat. Believe me, it's every bit as much for me as it is for you. You have a lot more time and effort invested in Naomi than I do, but she's mine now, too, and I want to help."

"Okay," Alan agreed finally. "I'll keep that in mind." That's what he said, but he didn't sound completely convinced.

Mel appeared in the doorway of the family room. She was fully dressed and made up and looking like a million bucks. She was also carrying a cup of coffee. "Good morning, everybody," she said cheerfully, "how's it going? Or should I say good afternoon?"

Together Alan and I updated Mel on everything that had happened so far, with one minor exception. He didn't mention our little talk, and neither did I. Detective Caldwell called about then. She was stuck in the pass behind a jackknifed semi and probably wouldn't be out of the resulting backup for another hour at least.

"Tell you what," I said to her. "Since the last place Petey Mayfield was seen was West Seattle, why don't we meet up there. I'll spring for Sunday brunch at Salty's on Alki Beach, and then I can show you exactly where all this played out."

"Wait," Mel said, "if you're going to Salty's, I'm tagging along."

The phone wasn't on speaker, but Lucinda Caldwell heard her voice. "Hi, Mel," she said, "and good-o. See you both when I get there. I'm setting the GPS right now."

We were in the car and winding our way up through the garage levels when Mel aimed her icy blue-eyed inquisitor's stare in my direction. "Okay," she said, "tell me. What are you really up to?"

"We're going to go pay a visit to Hilda Tanner."

"Your source of information for all things Agnes?" she asked.

"That's right. Todd's handwriting expert needs some more samples of Agnes's handwriting. If they exist, Hilda is the one person who can get them for us."

"Fun," Mel said. "Exactly what I want to do on my day off—work one of your cases."

The strange thing is, I knew she was telling the truth. Mel's a cop after all, and there's nothing she likes better than solving cases, day off or not. That's why when I knocked on Hilda Tanner's door half an hour later, Mel was at my side.

"Who's there?" Hilda demanded from inside the house.

"J. P. Beaumont," I told her. "I brought my wife along. Her name is Mel Soames."

"What do you want?"

"I need to ask a favor."

"Oh, all right."

I heard her collection of locks being unlatched. When Hilda opened the door, she was once again wearing the apron I'd seen her in before—the old-fashioned one with the same telltale bulge in the pocket.

"What kind of favor?" Hilda asked, but her customary pugnacity was missing. She seemed strangely subdued.

"Did you hear that they found Petey?" I asked.

Hilda nodded as her face twisted into a somber

grimace. "It's terrible. One of the neighbors saw it on the news first thing this morning and called to tell me. She said his case is being treated as a homicide. I can barely believe it. It almost makes me grateful Agnes is gone. Knowing that Petey had been murdered would have broken her heart."

With that, Hilda stepped away from the door. "Come on in," she said.

As Mel and I entered the room, a whole herd of cats made a mad scramble for parts unknown, with the notable exception of Rocky, who maintained his regal pose in the middle of the dining-room table, regarding us with disdain and objecting to our unwelcome presence by lashing his long tail back and forth.

"First off," I said taking a seat, "I need to say thank you."

"For what?"

"Because you supplied Agnes's hairbrush, we've been able to confirm that she was Athena's paternal great-grandmother."

At that point Hilda Tanner burst into tears. Eventually she dredged a used Kleenex out of the same apron pocket that held her .22. She mopped her damp eyes with that and blew her nose as well.

"Oh, my," she said finally. "Agnes would have been over the moon about that. She really wanted a great-grandbaby, you know. Hang on just a minute. Let me get something."

Hilda used the walker to lever herself erect, then clumped off into another room. When she returned, there was a small tissue-wrapped package resting in the basket between the handles on her walker.

"They're the wrong color, I know," she said, handing me the package. "I made them last fall when that poor girl was there all alone. I planned on giving them to her once the baby came. I had no idea the city was going to run her off the way they did."

I opened the package and found myself staring down at a pair of tiny blue booties. I was incredibly touched, and it took a moment for me to make my voice work.

"How very kind of you," I managed at last. "Thank you. I'll be sure Athena gets them."

"You're welcome," Hilda said, grabbing her walker and stomping back to her chair. "Now, what about that favor you wanted?"

"My client is Athena's maternal grandfather, so I'm working on his behalf and also on hers. It has come to my attention that there may be some irregularities in the paperwork that transferred Agnes's property over to her daughter. In order to determine that, I need a sample of Agnes's handwriting."

Hilda Tanner was nobody's fool. "The lots, you mean?"

I nodded.

"That witch Lenora was trying to cheat Petey out of his share, wasn't she!" she declared, and it wasn't a question.

"That's one possibility," I admitted.

"All right, then," Hilda said, grabbing her walker and prying herself erect again. "Let me get the key to her house. I can give you a whole bunch of samples."

"You can?"

"You bet. Agnes didn't believe in all this newfangled online-banking nonsense, and neither do I for that matter. Like me, Agnes preferred writing out the checks herself. And again, just like me, she kept her bank statements with copies of her canceled checks for the whole seven years, the way the IRS says you're supposed to."

"Do you know where she kept them?"

"Of course I do," Hilda snapped at me. "Our houses are exactly alike. Agnes kept her statements in the same place I keep mine—in the coat closet by the front door. Come along, you two."

And come along we did. Hilda set off at a determined pace. Mel and I followed her down her wheelchair ramp and across the street. When we got to Agnes's front steps, I handed the walker off to Mel while I helped Hilda up and onto the porch. Just inside the front door, Hilda dove into the coat closet and pulled out a precarious stack of seven shoe boxes. All of them were neatly labeled with numbers from one to seven. Hilda extracted the box marked with the number one and passed it to me. Once I opened it, I discovered it contained exactly six bank statements.

"If Agnes was having dementia issues, who helped her with all this filing?" I asked.

"That would be me," Hilda admitted. "She kept worrying about running out of money, even though I kept telling her she wouldn't, but for the last year or so I helped Agnes pay her bills. I also balanced her checkbook."

"You wrote the checks?" I asked.

"She couldn't fill in the information the last few

months, so I did that for her, too, but she's the one who signed them."

"And June is when the last of these statements came in?"

Hilda nodded. "Lenora swooped in and took her away just a couple of days later. After that she must have changed the address. I kept checking her mailbox for a while after that, but it was always empty."

Without electricity, the light inside the house was too dim for the job, so I went outside and sat on the top steps while I sorted through the contents of the envelopes one at a time. There were two automatic deposits made each month—Agnes's Social Security check and another, smaller one that was evidently a survivorship benefit from her late husband's pension. Taken together they didn't add up to much, but obviously they'd been enough, because there was always a slightly larger balance remaining. The days of banks sending back actual canceled checks have gone the way of the buggy whip, but the scanned copies showed a total of a dozen or so transactions each month. They always amounted to less than the amounts deposited. What was jaw-dropping was the six-figure balance remaining in the account each month—close to two hundred thousand dollars according to the June statement.

Mel and Hilda had followed me outside.

"Did you know that Agnes had this much money in the bank?" I asked Hilda, pointing to that six-figure balance.

"Of course I did," she said. "I told her she shouldn't just leave it sitting in a checking account like that—that she should start a savings account or buy a CD or do something with it, but she wouldn't hear of it."

Considering the value of the four lots as well as the balance in the checking account back in June, Agnes Mayfield's estate would have totaled close to a million dollars. Maybe Lenora Harrison could refer to an estate that size as "a pittance," but most people wouldn't, especially Alan Dale.

I took the time to scan each page of copied checks into my phone, sending them along to Joseph Stallings as I did so. The thing is, you didn't need to be a handwriting expert to see how far Agnes's signature had deteriorated between the statement sent for January and the one for June. In January the words were still fairly readable. By June all that remained was an illegible scrawl that bore no resemblance whatsoever to the signature on the notarized quitclaim that had been dated August 1. Someone had signed that document in front of a notary public, but it sure as hell hadn't been Agnes Mayfield.

And that led to only one conclusion: Whatever Lenora Harrison had been up to, the folks at Highline Development had been in on it, too. If Petey had threatened either of them with exposure, he had most likely signed his own death warrant. That meant that it was high time for me to pay their CEO, Ms. Suzanne Nishikawa, another visit ASAP, and I fully intended to bring an active-duty homicide cop along for the ride!

CHAPTER 26

BRUNCH AT SALTY'S on a Sunday can be your basic mob scene, and that was certainly the case on that particularly sunny March morning. After leaving Agnes's house, Mel and I drove there, put our names on the list, and waited in line for a good forty-five minutes before we were summoned. But the wait was worth it. The hostess led us to a table with a breathtaking view of downtown Seattle. Our waiter had just delivered cups of coffee when Detective Caldwell showed up. She and Mel had met before in the course of that previous SHIT investigation, so there was no need for introductions. They greeted each other warmly before Lucinda sank gratefully onto the booth's bench seat.

"I absolutely hate I-90," Detective Caldwell muttered as she settled in, "and I hate Snoqualmie Pass even more."

I wasn't especially sympathetic. "If you live in Bellingham like we do, you're stuck with I-5, and if you're going to live in Ellensburg, you're stuck with I-90. You pays your money and makes your choice."

"Gee, thanks," she said.

When our waiter walked past with a coffeepot in hand, she signaled him over. "Let's eat and then get started," she said. "For budgetary reasons known only to the sheriff himself, I'm not authorized to spend the night. That means I'll be crossing back over the pass later this evening when we finish up. Just so you know, I'm here and making the effort, but since this case was five months old before we even identified the victim, I'm not holding out hope for much progress."

"Don't be so sure," I told her. "Mel and I may have uncovered a suspect or two, along with a million dollars' worth of motive."

"That's good news. Tell all, but before you do, let's go tackle that buffet. It looks amazing."

And amazing it was, but that morning gourmet dining took a backseat to full disclosure. This was no longer my missing-persons case. It was now a homicide investigation, and Detective Lucinda Caldwell needed to be briefed completely, including the background on how I had come to be involved in a search first for Naomi Dale and later for Petey Mayfield. With Mel sitting there nodding encouragement, it was a painful recitation of "all my sins remembered," but I told the story of my biological connection to Naomi and her baby without pulling any punches. Lucinda Caldwell, for her part, took careful notes without casting any aspersions.

"So you had no idea that Naomi even existed until late last week when Alan Dale showed up on your doorstep in Bellingham?"

"None whatsoever," I said.

"You said earlier that you might have uncovered some suspects. What about Naomi?" Lucinda asked for the second time. "Is she on the list?"

That was only to be expected. When it comes to homicide cases, the spouse or lover is always first choice as a person of interest.

"I don't think so," I said. "She said that after he left, she stayed on at the house, hoping he'd come back."

"But she didn't report him missing?"

"No," I answered. "Both Naomi and Petey both spent years living on the streets and doing drugs. That kind of history isn't conducive for developing a warm and fuzzy attitude toward the cops."

"Will she be willing to talk to me now?" Lucinda asked.

"I believe so. I already warned her that with Petey dead, detectives would need to speak to her."

"Where is she?"

I read off the name and location of the Pike Street Mission. For completion's sake, I threw in Rachel Seymour's contact information as well.

"What about her father?" Lucinda asked, and then paused, looking uncertain, as though she had blundered and said the wrong thing. Considering what she'd just been told about my connection to the family, Lucinda's momentary confusion was understandable.

"You mean do I think Alan Dale was involved?" I asked.

Lucinda nodded.

"Look," I said, "Alan Dale has been Naomi's father since long before she was born. I'm a latecomer to the situation and qualify as sperm donor only, but the answer to your question is no. I don't think Naomi's father was involved. For one thing, at the time Petey disappeared, Alan was working a bus-and-truck show somewhere back east. I'm sure his employer's records will confirm that. Besides, Naomi had been out of touch with him for years. Since he didn't know where she was, how would he know about Petey? Until Harborview Medical Center called Naomi's grandmother and told her about Athena, he didn't have any idea she was even in Seattle."

"I'll still need the name of that bus-and-truck show," Lucinda said.

She was being thorough, and I couldn't fault her for that. "Right," I said. "I'll get the information from Alan and send it along."

"Okay, then," she said, as though switching gears, "my department is operating on the assumption that the place where the remains were found is a dump site only, rather than the scene of a homicide."

"Did you turn up any forensic evidence?" Mel asked.

"Some, but not a lot," Lucinda answered. "A few items of clothing—shirt, shoes, jeans—that I'll be asking Naomi to identify if she can. There's also that very distinctive belt and buckle."

"Which she did recognize," I interjected.

"The belt buckle?"

I nodded, and Lucinda made a note to that effect.

"In addition," she continued, "we found an acrylic nail at the scene, a nail covered with polish—Big Apple Red, I'm told—which may or may not be connected to our homicide. There are lots of river rafters on the Yakima these days, and water is notoriously tough on manicures, acrylic or otherwise. So it could have come from our killer, or it could have been dropped off by a passing rafter."

"What about shell casings?" Mel pressed. "Did you find any of those?"

"Nothing like that, and no slug either. Whoever shot Petey Mayfield fired the murder weapon into the side of his lower jaw and blew out most of his teeth. Trying to identify him through dental records would have been impossible. That's why Dr. Hopewell went to the trouble and expense of creating and posting his DNA profile. The crime scene, wherever it was, would have been an appalling mess."

"Makes sense," Mel said.

"Without a specific crime scene, are we all on the same page in thinking that he was most likely murdered on this side of the mountains and transported there?" Lucinda asked.

Mel and I both nodded.

"So who do you have in mind as a possible suspect?" Lucinda asked.

"Lenora Harrison, Petey's aunt, for starters," I said without hesitation. "I doubt she'd do the job herself, but she'd certainly have the means to hire someone else to do her dirty work. She also has the motive. I'm pretty sure she's been doing her damnedest to ace Petey out of his share of his grandmother's estate. Bank records show that early last summer Agnes Mayfield had nearly two hundred thousand dollars lying around in her checking account. I saw bank statements up to and including the one for June, but I'll bet that cash is long gone. I can text those statements to you if you'd like."

"No thanks," Lucinda said. "This is a homicide investigation. On the off chance the money ends up being connected to the murder, I'm not touching anything that might turn into evidence without a properly drawn search warrant in hand, but I admit to being curious. How is it you happen to have access to Agnes's bank statements?"

"Her former neighbor, Hilda Tanner, had a key to Agnes's residence. She's the one who let me in so I could retrieve a hairbrush for DNA-profiling purposes. According to Hilda, Agnes was suffering from some kind of worsening mental condition— dementia or Alzheimer's. When Agnes could no longer handle her own financial affairs, Hilda stepped in and did the bill paying."

"She's the one who gave you access to the statements?"

I nodded.

Lucinda shot me a disparaging look. "That's what I hate about private eyes," she grumbled. "They don't have to screw around with minor details like having probable cause or obtaining warrants. So it sounds as though I'll need to speak to Naomi, Lenora, and Hilda. Anyone else?"

"Suzanne Nishikawa," I answered. "She's the CEO of Highline Development, the company that purchased the Mayfield properties from Lenora

Harrison. We're looking into some irregularities in the way the properties were transferred from Agnes to her daughter. Someone from Highline may be involved with that."

"How so?"

"We're looking into the possibility that Agnes's supposedly notarized signatures might have been forged."

"Interesting," Lucinda said, adding that tidbit to her copious notes. Each time I gave her a name, I provided her with all the necessary contact information. "Who's next?" she asked once she'd finished her notation on Suzanne Nishikawa.

"The only other possibility is a drug dealer named Kenneth Dawson, who was evidently one of Petey and Naomi's former suppliers," I continued. "According to Naomi, Kenny hangs out around a 7-Eleven just up the street from where Petey and Naomi were living at the time. When Petey came home from a trip to the store babbling about their being rich, Naomi thought he'd paid a visit to Kenny and was tripping out. I've driven past the place a couple of times. I think he's a long shot as far as being the shooter is concerned, but if he was on the scene that day when Petey went to buy candy, the dealer may be one of the last people to see our victim alive. We can show you where the 7-Eleven is located when we drive over to the neighborhood. I'm assuming you want to stop by there."

"Absolutely," Lucinda Caldwell said with a nod, "but not until after I take a crack at that dessert table."

Mel and Lucinda took off. I was going to follow suit, but my phone rang just then, with Todd Hatcher's name in the caller ID.

"Got any news for me?" I asked, dropping back into the booth.

"Would I be calling this soon if I didn't?" Todd replied. "Of course I have news!"

"What?"

"Suzanne Nishikawa has frequent-flier status at any number of casinos within driving distance of the Seattle metropolitan area. She generally sticks to high-stakes poker games. Last summer she ran into a string of bad luck and reportedly lost a bundle."

"She has a gambling problem, then?"

"Evidently, and she might have been using company funds to keep herself afloat. Highline may hold the titles to the properties once owned by Agnes Mayfield, but that Mayfield Glen development project of hers is on hold and going nowhere fast. Last summer the company was operating on a nearly depleted line of credit and hadn't been able to put together enough funds to complete the building-permit process. With no permits there's no building. January of this year saw a big infusion of cash that paid off the line of credit. The permit process is once again under way, and Suzanne is back doing her weekly casino crawls."

"Interesting," I said.

"But that's only part of it," Todd said. "Suzanne Nishikawa's current favorite is Cascade Crest east of Issaquah. She spends time there on weekends. As one of their high rollers, she usually has her hotel room comped, but here's the real kicker," Todd added. "Didn't you tell me that Petey Mayfield disappeared on the afternoon of October thirtieth, 2016?"

"Yes, he did."

"That was a Sunday. You'll never guess who reported her vehicle, a 2015 Lexus, missing from the parking lot at Cascade Crest Casino early Monday morning, October thirty-first. She claimed it had been stolen out of the parking lot overnight."

"Stolen and never recovered?"

"Never recovered, and my suspicion is it most likely never will be," Todd agreed, "especially if the tribal police exhibit the same kind of casual disregard toward property crime that everybody else does."

Analyzing crime statistics was Todd Hatcher's major claim to fame.

"Having her car stolen that very night is quite a coincidence," I said.

"That's what I thought," Todd concurred.

"And the casino would be on the way back to Seattle from Ellensburg, where Petey's remains were found."

"Yup," Todd replied.

I thought about how the events had played out. Suzanne's office was well within walking distance from where Petey and Naomi had been living. It made perfect sense that after seeing the Mayfield Glen billboard, Petey might go there in an effort to find out what was going on. And then I thought about Suzanne's shiny little red Boxster S parked just outside the door to Highline's office. It had looked brand-new to me. Maybe she'd used insurance proceeds from the stolen Lexus to purchase the Boxster as a replacement.

As for the Lexus itself? That's when I remembered what Dr. Roz had said about the trajectory of the bullet that had taken Petey's life. The shooter had been to his left rather than facing him, and the bullet had traveled at a slightly upward angle. Petey had stood six foot two. Suzanne was five-one if that. Had they been standing, the angle would have been sharply upward rather than slightly. But if victim and perpetrator had been seated side by side in a vehicle? That would have evened the playing field. So had Suzanne's Lexus really been stolen, or had she needed to unload it because the interior was spattered with broken teeth, blood, and brain matter? I happen to know that there are plenty of chop shops out there, operated by lowlifes who'll turn a blind eye to almost anything in order to make a profit.

"I'll check all this out, Todd, and thanks a bunch," I told him, "but I've gotta go. I have a hunch you may have located both our shooter and our missing crime scene."

Across the room I could see Mel and Lucinda laughing and chatting as they headed back toward our table carrying plates laden with desserts.

"Wait, don't hang up," Todd said urgently before I could end the call. "There's something else you need to know."

"What's that?"

"Suzanne Nishikawa happens to have a concealed-carry permit, and she owns a Ruger semiautomatic pistol—an LCP."

There you have it, what guys in homicide call the

basic recipe for murder—motive, opportunity, and means, MOM for short.

"In other words, we should consider her armed and dangerous."

"Exactly," he said. "When it comes time to talk to her, don't do anything rash, and don't let anyone else screw up either."

"I'll do my best."

Mel must have been watching me as she and Lucinda approached our booth. "Who was that on the phone?" she asked, carrying a plate that contained at least five different kinds of chocolate delectables. Have I mentioned that Mel loves chocolate?

"Your hair isn't exactly standing on end," she observed, "but it's close, so what's going on?"

Mel set her plate down on the table, and that's when I noticed her bright red nails. Nail polish is so much a part of who Mel is that I seldom pay any attention to it. This time I did, and that's when I remembered Suzanne Nishikawa's perfectly manicured red nails. Big Apple Red, maybe?

"That was Todd Hatcher on the phone," I said. "I think he might have broken our case wide open."

CHAPTER 27

Chocolate be damned, once Lucinda Caldwell heard Todd's news, she set her dessert plate aside, hauled out her phone, and tracked down a number for the Snoqualmie Tribal Police. On a Sunday afternoon, the chief himself wasn't in, but she managed to get put through to someone in Records who was able to confirm that Suzanne Nishikawa had called in at 7:45 A.M. on October 31 to report that her vehicle had been stolen.

With the phone turned on to speaker, Mel and I listened in on the conversation between Lucinda and the nameless records clerk who reported that a patrol unit had been dispatched to the scene. A subsequent investigation had revealed that casino security cameras showed that Ms. Nishikawa had parked her vehicle in the casino's parking lot at 12:54 A.M. A little over an hour later, at 2:07 A.M., a man wearing a hoodie approached the vehicle, opened the driver's-side door, climbed in, and drove out of the garage. He exited the property onto Casino Drive, heading in a northbound direction that would have taken him back toward I-90.

"Would it be possible to speak to the investigators assigned to the case?" Lucinda asked. "Did they check to see if the stolen car showed up on any of the traffic cameras along I-90?"

A long pause followed. "This is a property crime," the clerk replied. "The information was forwarded to the Washington State Patrol, of course, and to the victim's insurance company as well."

"In other words," Lucinda said, "you're telling me there was no investigation."

"We're a small department," the woman said huffily, "and we operate on very limited resources."

"I'm sure you do," Lucinda replied. "Thank you for your help." Putting down the phone, she turned to Mel and me. "That was a waste," she muttered.

"Maybe not," I replied. "We're all agreed that Suzanne is at the very least a person of interest in Petey's homicide, right?"

Lucinda and Mel both nodded.

"Naomi told us that Petey walked out on her the day before Halloween, which would have been Sunday afternoon. Todd says Suzanne Nishikawa often stays at casinos on weekends, but if you were planning a weekend casino getaway, wouldn't you check in on a Friday instead of in the early hours of Monday morning?"

Lucinda nodded. "I see what you mean. You're thinking Petey walked over to Suzanne's office and confronted her, and something bad went down after that?"

"He probably got into the car with her at the

wheel," I suggested. "Todd tells me Suzanne has a concealed-carry permit for a Ruger LCP. Somewhere between here and Ellensburg, she might have hauled off and shot the guy before dumping his body along the riverbank. Think about it. That would explain why no one heard the sound of shots fired. If you're speeding along an interstate, no one would hear a thing. That scenario is also consistent with what Dr. Roz told me about the bullet's trajectory."

Detective Caldwell was now on full alert. I could see that my theory was making sense to her. "If she transported a gunshot victim in her Lexus, you can bet it was teeming with forensic evidence. She didn't go to the casino to spend the night. She went there to facilitate ditching that vehicle."

"So what's next?" Mel asked.

Lucinda stood up, leaving her dessert plate untouched. "Let's go have a heart-to-heart with Ms. Nishikawa. I think it will be interesting to see her initial reaction once she learns Petey's remains have been located and identified."

"She may already know that," I cautioned. "Hilda told me that the story was reported on a local news channel earlier today."

"It's Sunday," Lucinda said brightly. "Maybe we'll get lucky and she doesn't watch the news on the weekends. I know I don't. We'll stop by the office first and see if she's there. If not, we'll track her down at her residence."

"You're saying 'we,'" Mel said. "Does that mean you want us to come along?"

"Why not?" Lucinda asked. "In this instance I

don't think three's a crowd, and so far we're making a good team."

I paid, and we headed out. We left Salty's in a two-vehicle caravan and traveled from the north end of West Seattle to the south, with me leading the way and with Lucinda Caldwell trailing behind in her unmarked patrol car. During the drive I told Mel what I'd remembered about Suzanne Nishikawa's nail polish. When we got to the strip mall, there was no red Boxster S in the parking lot, but the lights were on inside Highline Development's office, and an Open sign hung inside the front door. Someone was seated at the reception desk. Unfortunately, that someone wasn't Suzanne Nishikawa. She was an older woman with short gray hair.

Lucinda and I ventured inside while Mel stayed in the car. "Is Suzanne in?" I asked.

"Not at the moment," was the answer. "She's out of town for the weekend. Can I help you with something? If you're interested in one of her properties, you can leave a name and number, and I'll have her be in touch with you as soon as she returns."

I had no intention of leaving my name and number. "No thanks," I said. "Not necessary, I'll catch up with her later."

Lucinda and I exited the Highline office only to discover that Mel was no longer in the car. While Lucinda was on the phone to her records department obtaining Suzanne's home address, I was looking around for Mel, who had seemingly disappeared into thin air. I was about to call her phone when Mel exited the nail salon that was one of Highline

Development's strip-mall neighbors. She was grinning from ear to ear and giving me a thumbs-up.

"What?" I demanded.

"Big Apple Red is Suzanne Nishikawa's color of choice."

Lucinda, finished with her phone call, looked stunned. "How on earth did you figure that out?"

"When someone has a broken or wrecked nail and needs it fixed in a hurry, proximity is everything," Mel said. "I went inside and told them that Suzanne is a good friend of mine who keeps bragging about the nail salon she uses. I asked if they were it, and it turns out they are. Guess what they call her? 'The Big Apple Red lady.' They asked if I wanted an appointment. I told them not today, but that I'll be making one soon."

Edmond Locard, a noted early twentieth-century French detective, is credited with what's called Locard's Principle of Exchange, which forms the basis for all of modern forensic science—from fingerprints right on up to DNA and beyond. He concluded that every human interaction leaves behind some trace, and that is just as true now as it was a hundred years ago. That bit of trace evidence in this case—an acrylic nail found at Petey Mayfield's dump site—had just upgraded Suzanne Nishikawa from the "person of interest" category to "prime suspect" status.

Lucinda immediately busied herself with taking down the name and number for the salon. "It'll be interesting to see if she happened to come in later that week to have a missing nail replaced, but I'll check on that later. First let's find her."

The residential address supplied by the records clerk took us to a low-rise condo development known as Alki Pointe. The building was located only a few blocks from Salty's. Feeling a bit like traveling yo-yos, we motored the length of West Seattle again, this time south to north. Units in the building with unobstructed water views would have been both costly and desirable. A buzzer panel was posted beside the front door, with each buzzer accompanied by a resident's name. When Lucinda Caldwell pushed the one marked Penthouse, followed by the name S. Nishikawa, there was zero response.

"What now?" Lucinda asked.

"I say we head for Cascade Crest," Mel suggested. "Suzanne is a legitimate suspect in Petey's homicide. We know from the tribal police that she arrived at the casino in the early hours of the morning on the day after he disappeared. In my experience casinos have security cameras everywhere. Let's go there and see if we can find out exactly what she was up to."

"Good thinking!" Lucinda told us.

A moment later she was on the phone to the security department at Cascade Crest Casino. After identifying herself as a Kittitas County detective who was investigating a recent homicide, she told him that we needed to view any overnight security footage for October 30 and 31, especially ones that might include images of one of the casino's regular customers, an individual named Suzanne Nishikawa. Lucinda told whoever answered that she and her "associates" were on their way to review the material.

Associates? I wondered. Lucinda was a cop. Mel was a cop. At that point I was definitely not a cop, but I think Lucinda had decided that if it came to sitting on butts in front of video monitors and scouring through hours and hours of security footage, the more the merrier.

Between Mel and me, she's a far more assertive driver. She also has a badge. In order to get from West Seattle to Cascade Crest Casino in the most expeditious fashion possible, I turned the keys over to her and settled into the passenger seat. Not unexpectedly, there was traffic. Those quaint words "never on Sunday" don't apply to Sunday-afternoon traffic anywhere in the Seattle area.

"Do we need to let someone at Seattle PD know that there's a possible homicide on their patch?" Mel asked as she negotiated the exit off I-5 and onto eastbound I-90.

"With Paul Kramer at the helm?" I replied. "Not on your life. We're not calling them in until we absolutely have to."

Dreading how long our search of the footage would take, I called Alan to let him know I had no idea of when we'd be home. When we got to the casino, Detective Caldwell was already waiting outside. Her badge was sufficient to have us escorted through the lobby and whisked into a dimly lit back-of-the-house room where the walls were lined with row upon row of monitors. Once I saw the magnitude of the problem, I thought we were most likely in for an all-nighter and started worrying about getting Mel back home to Belltown

Terrace in time for her to make it to work in Bellingham the next morning.

On that score I couldn't have been more wrong. Casinos are big business. Big business attracts big money, and big money can afford high-tech with all kinds of bells and whistles. Inside the room a burly man in a suit introduced himself as Philip Rhodes, the casino's head of security. It turned out that during our drive from West Seattle someone had informed him about our request for assistance, and by the time we got there, Mr. Rhodes was locked and loaded.

"I believe I've isolated the segments of footage you need," he said after Lucinda showed him her badge. "I've had all of them merged into a single file and sent to my office. If you'll come this way, please." The idea that the man had just spared us hours of staring at black-and-white security footage came as welcome news indeed.

Philip Rhodes's office was far different from the dimly lit, monitor-lined dungeon where a dozen tech people had been hard at work observing the various screens. No, Mr. Rhodes's office looked like the kind of place where a highly paid CPA might hang out. He invited us to be seated. Once we were ensconced in modern and surprisingly comfortable chairs, he used a remote to turn on an immense monitor that covered most of one wall. When the screen came to life, it showed a driver exiting a vehicle at the far edge of a seemingly vast and mostly empty but well-lit parking lot. The time stamp in the corner showed 10/31/2016 1:01:10 A.M. Try as

I might, I couldn't make out any features or even determine if the individual on the screen was male or female. As he or she moved out of one camera's view, the footage switched over to the next camera.

"Are you saying this person is Suzanne Nishikawa?" I asked.

Philip Rhodes nodded.

"I can't make out any details," I said. "How can you be sure it's her?"

"We use the latest in military-grade facial-recognition software," he replied with a grin, "and our facial rec is never wrong. Everyone who applies for casino membership is issued photo ID. We keep those on file. We also maintain a collection of photos of known undesirables so they can be removed from the property before they cause trouble."

"Cheaters, you mean?" Lucinda asked.

Rhodes nodded. "Card counters and the like. When my assistant told me you were interested in Ms. Nishikawa, I used facial rec to scan through our security footage for October thirtieth and thirty-first. This is the first place I found her."

"What's the deal?" Lucinda asked. "If the parking lot is almost empty, why did she park so far from the building?"

"I was wondering that, too," Mel agreed.

Eventually a new camera took over. This one showed a more detailed figure, now recognizable as a female, approaching the front entrance of the building from the outside. The one after that showed her entering the lobby itself and turning at once toward the right, where the hotel registration desk was located.

The casino's facial-recognition software might have known who the woman was, but the person I saw walking across the lobby bore almost no resemblance to the well-put-together CEO I'd encountered days earlier in the offices of Highline Development. Version 2.0 of Suzanne Nishikawa, date-stamped at 10/31/2016 1:03:53 A.M., looked like your basic street person. She appeared strikingly similar to how Naomi must have looked as she pushed her loaded grocery cart down the sidewalk after being evicted.

Suzanne's once perfectly coiffed hair was in tangled disarray. It looked like it had been dunked in a bucket of water and dried without benefit of either comb or brush. Instead of a coat or jacket, she wore a man's sweatshirt that was so big on her that it fell past her knees. Her hands were completely invisible inside the oversize sleeves. On her feet were a pair of floppy tennis shoes at least two sizes too large. She carried a purse but no visible luggage.

"She's traveling pretty light," Mel observed.

"I'll say," I agreed, "very light indeed."

The next camera must have been located directly over the front desk. It showed her signing the registration form. From that angle her fingernails were on full display. The footage was in black and white, but nine fingers had polish showing. One, the index finger on her right hand, was distinctly polish-free.

"Bingo!" Lucinda said under her breath. "We've got her."

"Would you like to speak to Ms. Nishikawa?" Philip Rhodes asked.

That grabbed our attention. It's safe to say that

three separate sets of eyes bugged out of our heads. "Wait," Lucinda said, "she's here right now?"

Rhodes nodded. "Since she's here so often on weekends, I checked earlier and discovered that not only is she here, she's doing remarkably well."

"Where is she?" Lucinda wanted to know.

"In the Tahoma Room," he replied. "It's our high-stakes area. It's set apart from the rest of the casino and has its own entrance."

According to some local tribes, Tahoma is the indigenous name for Mount Rainier, the largest mountain in the Cascade Range, and since Cascade Crest is a tribal casino, the name made perfect sense.

"Can you take us there?" Lucinda asked.

Rhodes sighed. "You said on the phone that you were investigating a homicide, but you didn't indicate that Ms. Nishikawa was the suspect."

"She is now."

"And you intend to arrest her?"

"I don't have an arrest warrant in hand," Lucinda replied. "Even if I did, the casino is considered to be tribal lands, and a county-issued warrant wouldn't be valid. I have no jurisdiction here. At the moment all I have in mind is interviewing her."

Someone tapped lightly on the office door. "Come in," Rhodes said.

The door opened, and a uniformed cop entered the room. He might have been a few years older than Philip Rhodes, but otherwise he was a carbon copy. The nameplate pinned to his chest said CHIEF ALTON RHODES.

"This is my brother Alton," Philip explained. "I asked him to stop by."

Philip began making a round of introductions. When he got as far as Mel, the two chiefs of police smiled at each other, nodding in mutual recognition.

"I believe we've met before," Alton said.

"Yes, at that conference over in Spokane," Mel agreed. "I seem to remember that you do double duty. You serve as both chief of police and tribal chairman."

He grinned back at her. "Yes," he said, "you could say I'm chief in every sense of the word."

It occurred to me then that there might be the tiniest bit of nepotism involved in the fact that the tribal chairman's brother had hired on as head of security for the tribal casino, but it wasn't my place to point that out, so I didn't.

"Aren't you a long way out of your jurisdiction, Chief Soames?" Alton asked.

"I am," she agreed. "Consider me your basic ride-along. My husband, Beau, is a private investigator." I stood up. Alton and I shook hands before Mel continued. "Beau has been working a missing-persons case that we believe is connected to a homicide that Detective Caldwell here has been investigating in Kittitas County."

Lucinda, too, stood to shake hands. With introductions complete, we all took our seats, including Chief Rhodes.

"According to my records clerk," he began, "this may be connected to the alleged theft of a late-model automobile that disappeared from the casino's parking lot late last October?"

Chief Rhodes framed his statement as a question, causing all of us—Mel, Lucinda, and I—to nod in turn. But it was the words "alleged theft" that caught my attention.

"Maybe you'd all be so kind as to fill me in on this situation," Chief Rhodes suggested.

Rank hath its privileges. With no discussion needed, Lucinda and I zipped our lips and let Mel do the talking. When she finished, Chief Rhodes looked at his brother. "Did you locate that other security footage?"

Philip nodded. "I certainly did."

Chief Rhodes turned back to us. "I regret to say that it appears that my department's investigation into this particular matter was . . . well, let's just say inadequate," he continued. "I was surprised and disappointed to learn that although my investigators knew about the casino's video footage, they never bothered reviewing any of it. I asked Phil here to retrieve it for me. He sent me the file earlier, so I've already seen it. If you wouldn't mind playing it for these folks . . ."

Phil was already reaching for the remote. When the screen lit up, the only thing showing was a parked vehicle, Suzanne Nishikawa's Lexus, lit by the glow of an overhead lamp. As the time stamp showed 02:10:15 A.M., OCTOBER 31, 2016, a hooded figured appeared in the frame, materializing out of the darkness beyond the vehicle and approaching the Lexus from the front. He walked directly to the driver's side, opened the door, got in, and drove off—just like that, without a moment's hesitation. I know for a fact that even the most efficient car thieves take longer than that to break into a vehicle, spoof the alarm/lock system, and make their getaway.

"I'm guessing the car door was unlocked and the keys were left inside," Chief Rhodes remarked. "From what you've told me, I think there's a good chance that whatever happened to Mr. Peter Mayfield may have occurred inside that vehicle."

"That's our suspicion as well," Mel agreed.

Chief Rhodes glanced over at his brother. "Is she still at the table?" he asked.

Philip worked his remote. A moment later a felt-topped poker table appeared on the screen—a poker table surrounded by six players, one of whom was a readily recognizable Suzanne Nishikawa. Seated behind several stacks of what I later learned were hundred-dollar chips, she was engrossed in studying the hand of cards she'd just been dealt.

"Yes, she is."

"Very well," Chief Rhodes said. "I don't have enough evidence to actually charge her, but based on what we've seen, I suspect she was somehow responsible for the theft of her own vehicle, perhaps in relation to some kind of insurance fraud. I'm prepared to take her into custody on suspicion of making a false police report. It's a minor violation, but enough for me to bring her back to the department, book her, and place her in a holding cell. There'll be less of a ruckus if you watch the action from here rather than the Tahoma Room, but once we book her, you're welcome to stop by for a visit. While she's sitting around cooling her heels, maybe you'll be able to obtain that arrest warrant."

The last was addressed toward Lucinda. "Will do," she said, "an arrest warrant and a search warrant for her phone records. With any luck those will tell us what really became of that Lexus."

The two brothers stood at once, as if prepared to head out to confront Suzanne together. I felt that a word of caution was in order. "You do remember Mel saying that Ms. Nishikawa has a concealed-carry permit."

Philip grinned at me. "That won't be a problem," he said. "Here at Cascade Crest, we don't like to infringe on people's Second Amendment rights. We're not so concerned about the areas open to the general public, but occasionally tempers flare up in the high-stakes rooms. For that reason we have declared the Tahoma wing to be a gun-free zone. Everyone entering that area has to pass through a metal detector. We've provided locker space for people who need it. Alton here will be armed. Ms. Nishikawa most definitely will not."

They went out then, closing the door behind them and leaving us alone with Philip Rhodes's monitor, still showing the ongoing scene at Suzanne's poker table. Mel was the one who broke the silence.

"Whoa," she said. "I never saw that coming."

"Me either," I agreed, "never in a hundred years."

CHAPTER 28

When Mel and I left Belltown Terrace earlier that morning, I don't think either one of us anticipated our being involved in a takedown operation, but here we were—sort of—and it turned out to be one of the most elegant arrest situations any of the three of us had ever seen. Philip Rhodes walked up to the table, leaned over, and whispered something in Suzanne's ear. She nodded. As soon as that hand played out, she collected her chips, stood up, and followed him from the room. Philip had seen to it that the whole thing happened without any disturbance to Suzanne's fellow gamblers. When she went to collect her Ruger from the storage locker, I had no doubt that Chief Rhodes would be waiting.

We decided that it was best for us to stay where we were, remaining tucked away and out of sight until Suzanne had been removed from the premises. Lucinda used the wait time to call into her department and detail the situation to her superiors, ultimately speaking to the sheriff himself.

"He seems to want more probable cause before we go for a warrant," Lucinda said when the conversation ended. "He wants me to call him back after the interview. Let's hope she doesn't decide to lawyer up on us."

Philip reentered the room. "Okay, folks," he said. "It's a done deal. Ms. Nishikawa is on her way to the tribal police headquarters in the back of Alton's car. Do you know how to get there?"

"I do," Lucinda said. "I've been there before. Mel and Beau can follow me."

We caravanned there, this time with Lucinda in the lead. Once at headquarters we waited in the public lobby while Suzanne's booking process played out.

"Be sure to ask her who Danielle Nishikawa is," I told Lucinda. "I still want to know who notarized Agnes Mayfield's signatures on those quitclaim deeds."

"Maybe I'll start there," Lucinda said after a moment. "If I come at her from way out in left field, she's less likely to lawyer up."

When Chief Rhodes escorted Lucinda into the interview room, Mel and I were on the far side of the glass, observing from outside rather than participating directly. Suzanne had been required to change into an orange jumpsuit. Sitting there alone and waiting for someone to show up, she looked angry, impatient, and out of sorts.

"I'm Detective Lucinda Caldwell, a homicide detective with the Kittitas County Sheriff's Department."

Maintaining her poker face, Suzanne made absolutely no response to Lucinda's self-introduction. As far as I was concerned, that was telling. I believe I might have mentioned earlier that killers seldom ask many questions. Why should they? They already know.

"Who's Danielle Nishikawa?" Lucinda asked.

That unexpected question, however, did provoke a reaction. Suzanne seemed puzzled. "She's my mother. Why?"

"Would it be possible for me to speak to her?"

"I'm afraid not," Suzanne said. "She developed dementia issues. Last summer I had to put her into a nursing home in Lake City. Unfortunately, she came down with a serious case of the flu and died last October."

"When in October?"

"The tenth," Suzanne replied, "As she had previously requested, my mother was cremated. Her memorial service was held the following Saturday."

"Had she been ill long?" Lucinda asked.

"She'd been going downhill for several years, but last spring it started getting much worse. That's when I finally had to break down and place her in a home."

Suzanne's answer might not have bolstered Lucinda's case, but it certainly made my day. All along I'd wondered about the connection between Suzanne Nishikawa and Lenora Harrison, and now I had a possible answer. If Danielle's symptoms had been serious enough for her to be admitted to a nursing-care facility sometime over the summer, how could she possibly still have been notarizing signatures early in August? Was it possible

that two frail old women, Danielle Nishikawa and
Agnes Mayfield, had been confined to the same facility by a pair of double-dealing daughters and had
died within weeks of each other? That struck me as
too much of a coincidence. As for Lake City? It's a
neighborhood located in the far northeast quadrant
of Seattle—about as far from West Seattle as you
can get. In terms of avoiding visits from inconvenient friends or relations, maybe that was the whole
point.

"So what can you tell me about Petey Mayfield?"
Lucinda was asking, suddenly veering the interview
away from Danielle and taking it in a very different
direction.

"Who?" Suzanne asked.

"Peter Mayfield was his name, but he went by
Petey. He was murdered in October of last year. His
remains were located along the bank of the Yakima
River and have only just now been identified. I was
wondering what, if anything, you might be able to
tell me about that."

"I believe I want to speak to an attorney."

Without batting an eyelash, Lucinda smiled back
at her. "I'm sure you do," she said, rising to her feet,
"and believe me, you're going to need one."

"How'd I do?" Lucinda asked when she joined
Mel and me in the observation room.

"Take a look," I said.

Back inside the interview room, Suzanne was on
her feet and pacing back and forth. She hadn't been
especially worried earlier, but she was now.

"Chief Rhodes told me he's going to leave her

there for a while and let her stew in her own juices. I'm assuming she'll be hiring a private attorney rather than casting her lot with a public defender."

"You can count on it," I said, looking back and forth between Mel and Lucinda. "How much do you want to bet that neither Agnes Mayfield nor Danielle Nishikawa died of natural causes?"

"I'd put the odds at ninety percent," Mel said.

Lucinda nodded. "Me, too," she said. "How many memory-care facilities are there in Lake City?"

Mel was already doing a Google search. "One only," she said. "It's called Lake City Memory Manor."

By then I had my phone in hand and was dialing Alan Dale's number. "Hey," I said, "can you do me a favor?"

"Sure, what do you need?"

"I left a file folder on the side table in the family room. There are several papers inside, and one of them is a copy of Agnes Mayfield's death certificate. Could you get it for me?"

"Sure," he said. "Hang on."

As he made his way from one room to the next, I could hear Athena crying in the background. Next I heard the sound of shuffling papers. "Okay," he said. "Here it is. What do you need?"

"Look at the bottom where the signature is."

"The one that says attending physician?"

"Right."

"The signature is hard to read. It looks like Dr. something-or-other Blaine."

"Does it say where he's from?"

"Sure, he printed that so it's more readable," Alan replied. "It's a place called Lake City Memory Manor."

It was your basic eureka moment. I felt chills on my legs. "Thanks, Alan. You've been a great help."

I ended the call and turned to Mel and Lucinda, who were watching me expectantly. "Well?" Mel asked.

"I believe we may have just uncovered a possible double homicide. Petey Mayfield might not have died in Seattle, but his grandmother did, and so did Danielle Nishikawa, both of them at Lake City Memory Manor."

"And since they were both under a doctor's care when they died," Lucinda said, "no autopsies were required."

"Right."

"So somebody could have overdosed them on sleep meds or any number of other things, and no one would have been the wiser."

Mel was giving me her look. "Isn't it about time you called Captain Kramer?"

"Who's that?" Lucinda asked sharply.

"He's the guy who's currently in charge of the homicide unit at Seattle PD," Mel explained.

"He's also a former partner of mine who would have given your pal Gary Fields a run for his money."

"That says a lot," Lucinda observed.

"It does," I agreed. "He never wanted to do any of the work, but he sure made sure he got all the credit. He's a guy I'm not eager to have a chat with now or ever."

"Sounds like there's a lot of history there."

"And none of it good," I added.

"So in terms of opening a joint investigation," Lucinda said, "maybe it would be best if I were the one who gives Captain Kramer a call?"

It was all I could do to keep from reaching out and hugging the woman, but I don't think Mel would have approved.

CHAPTER 29

ON OUR WAY back to Seattle, Mel and I stopped off at Issaquah's Triple XXX Rootbeer Drive-in and split a burger and fries. Once we got back to the condo, even though it was almost nine, Mel decided to pack up and head north right then, choosing to spend the night at home in Bellingham rather than fight Monday-morning traffic.

So when I woke up the next day, I was alone in bed. I could hear voices in the other room, which most likely meant that Marge Herndon had already shown up and was on the job. I certainly wasn't ready to face her, so I didn't exactly bound out of bed. Instead I lay there feeling sorry for myself.

The previous day I'd given a big boost to solving one homicide and had been instrumental in uncovering two additional deaths that were likely homicides, but now I was out of the action—sidelined with nothing to do. I was a private investigator, not a homicide cop. The ball was currently in Lucinda Caldwell's hands. It would be up to her to bring Seattle PD and the King County Attorney on board as far as investigating and prosecuting Lenora Harrison and Suzanne Nishikawa for their possible involvement in the murders of their respective mothers, but from my point of view that morning a successful outcome on that score seemed unlikely.

Without benefit of contemporaneous autopsies, it would be difficult to prove foul play. Sexist though this may be, female killers tend to use poisons as weapons of choice, and some poisons linger in the bodies long after death, but obtaining that kind of physical evidence in this case would involve at least one exhumation. Those are expensive, time-consuming propositions, and I doubted that King County's penny-pinching county attorney would be willing to foot the bill.

That meant any conviction would have to be based on circumstantial evidence alone, and maybe, just maybe, that's where I could help, not by focusing on the homicides but by doing what I'd been hired to do—protecting Athena's interests. I needed to come up with solid evidence—proof that would stand up in court—that Lenora and Suzanne had acted as co-conspirators in a plot to cheat first Petey and, as a consequence, Athena of their rightful inheritance. That realization was what finally got me out of bed and into the shower.

Whatever I came up with needed to have legal standing, and my best source for all things legal has always been Ralph Ames. When my second wife, Anne Corley, died, not only had I inherited her fortune, she had also bequeathed me the services of her trusted attorney. Over the years he and I became good friends, enough so that when I was in deep trouble in the booze department, Ralph was the one who made the case for my going into treatment. He's mostly retired now. He and his wife, Mary, winter in Surprise, Arizona, where I understand he plays golf almost every day. While I was standing in the shower, I realized that in all the hubbub of the last week, I hadn't called him to discuss the long-term ramifications of my changes in family status due to my newly discovered case of fatherhood.

Any discussion of that wasn't something to carry on with Marge Herndon bustling in and out of a room and hanging on my every word, so I went to the kitchen, collected a cup of coffee, and returned to the privacy of my bedroom to make the call. Fortunately Ralph wasn't out on the golf course just yet.

"Hey, Beau," he said, "are you ready to come down to enjoy some Arizona sunshine?"

"I'm not looking for sunshine at the moment," I said. "What I need is help."

By now I was sick and tired of telling the story of my one-night hookup with Jasmine Day and the resulting complications, but tell it I did. Ralph knew me when I was at my worst. To his credit, he heard me through without comment. When I finished, he asked the kind of question only a good friend can ask: "Have you told Scotty and Kelly?"

I sighed. "Not yet, but I will soon. In the meantime I need to know what I should do about protecting Athena's inheritance on her father's side. We'll sort out my side of that equation eventually. I also need to find a way to postpone the estate sale Lenora Harrison is planning for this coming weekend. I made copies of Agnes's bank statements, but in order for us to prove conspiracy and fraud, the statements themselves need to be collected under the protection of a search warrant."

"I take it you and Mr. Dale are on good terms?" Ralph asked.

"Yes."

"And he's been appointed to be the child's temporary guardian?"

"Correct. Naomi has relinquished her parental rights, but there has to be a court hearing to make the guardianship permanent."

"Even on a temporary basis, Mr. Dale can ask the court to appoint an attorney ad litem to act on Athena's behalf in protecting her financial interests. Her social worker should be able to help with that. Considering the circumstances, I believe they'll be able to make a case that the appointment should be done on an emergency basis. Once the guardian ad litem is in place, he or she can request a court order delaying the estate sale on the grounds that information contained in the residence may support Athena's claim to her great-grandmother's estate. They can also request an audit of any transactions made on Agnes's behalf within the last six months prior to Agnes's death, which should in turn enable them to require Petey's aunt to hand over Athena's rightful share of those funds. But here's the real question: Do you know for sure that she really is beneficiary under the will?"

"I believe so," I answered, "but I'll make it my

business to check that out today. I know the name of the law firm involved."

"If they're unwilling to give you the information," Ralph said, "the attorney ad litem will be able to demand it."

"Okay," I said. "Sounds like I have my marching orders."

"Maybe where Athena is concerned," Ralph countered, "but what about Naomi? Does she know the truth about you?"

"I haven't told her yet either."

"Is she still using?"

"I can't say for sure one way or the other."

"Do you think she'd agree to go into treatment?"

"I don't know," I said. "But if she's willing, I'm good for it."

"Okay," Ralph said. "I'll make some calls. Going to treatment certainly helped you. With any kind of luck, it'll be good for your daughter, too."

"I hope so," I told him, feeling that tricky lump in my throat again. "Thanks a lot."

I had ended the call and was on my way out of the bedroom when my phone rang again. The day before, while we'd been twiddling our thumbs waiting for Suzanne to be booked, I'd had brains enough to add Lucinda's name and numbers to my contact list, and hers was the name showing in caller ID.

"Good news," she said. "I obtained a search warrant for Suzanne's cell phone. Tracking down cell towers is above my pay grade, so someone else is handling those. What I'm looking at are the billing records for October thirtieth and thirty-first. There are three calls between her number and a cell phone I've identified as belonging to Lenora Harrison."

"If they were calling back and forth, are you suggesting that Lenora might have known what was going on with Petey?"

"I'd be surprised if she didn't. The first call was placed at eight P.M."

"Most likely when Petey was already dead," I suggested.

"That would be my guess, too," Lucinda agreed. "After that there's a long pause between calls. The next one comes in at eleven fifteen. The one after that was placed at one thirty."

"After Suzanne checked in to the casino."

"Right. Between the eight P.M. call and the one at eleven fifteen, there are several other calls, one of which happens to be to an individual known to law enforcement for . . . wait for it . . . car theft. Obviously Suzanne was looking for help in a big hurry, or she wouldn't have left a phone trail behind."

I was impressed. "Great work! If Lenora knew what was going on, at the very least she's an accomplice after the fact."

"And with any kind of luck," Lucinda added, "Lenora may be willing to roll on Suzanne if she can cut a plea deal."

"Anything else?"

"I'm actually on my way back to Seattle right now—just coming up on the pass. If the phone was in the front seat of the Lexus when the fatal shot was fired, some of that high-velocity blood spatter, including Petey's DNA, might have been propelled into the inner workings of the phone. I've been told that phones are notorious sources of DNA evidence. Just because someone cleans the outside surface doesn't mean there isn't usable evidence lingering inside. I know the odds are low, but the sheriff is letting me bring the phone over to the Washington State Crime Lab to be dismantled and examined. I also have a search warrant for Suzanne Nishikawa's condo, along with Agnes Mayfield's house. I want to be sure to have those bank statements in hand before they disappear."

"Good idea," I said.

"I also spoke to your friend Captain Kramer," she added. "You're right about him. He's a real jackass, but he finally agreed to send along a detective to help me execute the two warrants with regard to Petey's case. So far, however, he's not much interested in what happened to either Agnes or Danielle. If we can prove that both Lenora and Suzanne were involved in Petey's murder, maybe we can bring Kramer around to believing they worked together on the other two cases as well. And while I'm in town, I plan on tracking down the attending physician for Lake City Memory Manor. I'll let you know what he has to say."

"What detective?" I asked. "Which one did Kramer send?"

"A guy by the name of Greg Stevenson? Ever heard of him?"

"He was new to the job when I was leaving, but he's a good guy. Tell him I said hello."

"Will do," Lucinda said.

Her call made me feel like we were making progress, and on that note I left my bedroom to see what else was going on. In the kitchen Marge was cleaning with a vengeance. I dodged out of her way, brewed a cup of coffee, and headed for the living room. Athena was fast asleep in her bouncy chair, which had been placed on the far end of the window seat. Lucy is far too big to be encouraged to lounge on the furniture, and I had never before seen her on the window seat. But in this case she had somehow scrambled up onto the loose cushions and lay there with her nose touching the foot of Athena's seat. She thumped her tail when I came into the room, but she didn't bother to raise her head.

"Obviously you've been fed and walked," I told her.

"Yes," Alan supplied, entering the room on my heels. "I took her out early, right after I got up."

I clued him in on the conversation I'd just had with Ralph Ames. He immediately got in touch with Athena's social worker and brought her up to speed, repeating what I'd just told him almost verbatim. When he finished, he listened for some time before he spoke again.

"I already have a copy of Petey's death certificate," he said, obviously in answer to a question from Andrea. "The funeral home gave me a copy of that, but I'm not sure about the other." He held the phone away from his ear and turned to me. "Andrea wants to know if we can provide any proof that Petey Mayfield was Athena's biological father."

Loretta Hawk hadn't yet supplied me with written reports detailing the DNA-profiling results, but I was sure they could be produced in short order.

"I don't have the profile results on me," I said.

"But I can probably pick them up later today when I stop by the Sholeetsa Project to retrieve Petey's hairbrush."

Alan went back to his phone call while I sat there realizing that when I delivered the brush to Naomi, I'd have to tell her the rest of the story—both hers and mine—and I wasn't looking forward to it. Maybe Petey's hairbrush would serve as a peace offering.

It was still too early to head off to see the legal eagles at Stockman and Dodge, so I looked through my notes, found Hilda Tanner's phone number, and called her.

"J. P. Beaumont here," I said. "I need your help."

"Again?"

"Yes, again," I told her. "You know that sign about Mayfield Glen that's just down the street?"

"That eyesore?" she asked. "The whole neighborhood is up in arms about it. Why?"

"Could you maybe see if the name of the sign company is on it? It's usually there just under the sign content itself."

"I suppose," she said, "but don't expect me to call you right back. It's a long walk from here to there, and I'm not as young as I used to be."

Next on my list was Loretta Hawk, and I gave her a call. "Thank you for your help," I told her when she came on the line. "Thanks to you and the Sholeetsa Project, Petey Mayfield is found."

"Is he okay?" Loretta asked.

"Unfortunately not," I said. "He's deceased, but with your help there's now a good chance that we'll catch his killer. And since you've also established that Petey Mayfield was Athena's father, she may be in line to benefit from her great-grandmother's estate."

"A good thing, then?" Loretta asked.

"Yes, definitely a good thing," I replied. "Several of them, in fact."

"I'm a little curious about that third swab you brought in along with the ones for Agnes," Loretta said. "That one wasn't labeled, but the profile obviously belongs to Athena's maternal grandfather."

It took a moment before I could actually spit out the words to this woman who was little more than a virtual stranger. Still, she was involved in all this, and I owed her. "That profile would be mine," I said huskily. "Naomi's mother and I had a one-night stand decades ago. Until last week I had no idea Naomi existed, to say nothing of Athena."

There was a moment of stunned silence on the other end of the line. "Oh," Loretta said.

I was instantly sorry that I'd involved her in this complex family drama, but I suspect it wasn't the first time her company had unearthed unsettling and inconvenient results.

"Is there anything else I can do to help?" she asked a moment later.

"Actually, there is," I said. "Is it possible to get paper copies of the reports linking Athena to Petey Mayfield?"

"Of course," Loretta said. "They usually go out by mail, but as it happens, you were a walk-in."

"I'll need several printouts," I said. "One for Athena's social worker so it can be presented at the legal guardianship proceedings, one for the attorneys probating Agnes Mayfield's will, one for Athena's attorney ad litem, and one for Naomi herself. In addition, I'd like two copies of my own profile. I need to be able to show that to Naomi, too."

"She doesn't know?" Loretta asked.

"Not yet," I said. "I'm coming by in a little while to pick up Petey's hairbrush. I'd like to pick up the printouts at the same time."

"No problem," Loretta said. "Whenever you get here, they'll be ready."

CHAPTER 30

I LEFT BELLTOWN Terrace a little later with another full-blown to-do list and not a whole lot of heart for the job. I was dreading the coming conversation with Naomi more than I can say.

My first stop was the offices of Stockman and Dodge at Third and Marion. It took some assertive behavior on my part before I was finally granted admittance to the private office of one Richard Stockman, Esquire. He was an older gentleman, maybe ten years my senior.

"What seems to be the problem?" he demanded. "I understand you've been making quite a fuss with the girls in the outside office. I've been told that this concerns one of my clients—a deceased client. Surely you understand that due to client-attorney privilege, we're unable to divulge any information."

Let me just say that none of the so-called girls in the outer office was under the age of fifty.

"I'm here asking about two of your clients rather than just one, a husband and wife, and both of them are deceased," I explained, handing over one of my cards. "I'm working on behalf of the legally appointed guardian for an underage minor named Athena Dale. Athena happens to be Peter and Agnes Mayfield's great-granddaughter. Her father, also named Peter but generally referred to as Petey, is also deceased. It has come to my attention that Petey's aunt, Lenora Harrison, may have hatched a scheme to drain away most of Agnes's remaining assets prior to her mother's death in order to cheat Petey out of the portion of his grandparents' estate that might have been due him. With Petey now deceased as well, it's my belief that his share should rightfully pass on to his daughter."

"You're raising some serious allegations, Mr. Beaumont," Stockman said after a moment. "Do you have any proof, or is this all pure speculation on your part?"

"I'm working on it," I said. "I've been to the courthouse and gone through the stipulations of Mr. Mayfield's will. I noticed that his assets went first to his wife. In the event of her subsequent death, the remainder of their joint estate was to be divided equally between his two children, a daughter named Lenora and a son named Arthur, with the further specification that if either of them were deceased, their portions were to pass automatically to their offspring in equal shares, per stirpes."

Stockman took a long breath. "Of course the terms of probated wills are open to the public, but since the one for Agnes is still a private matter, and I can't divulge—"

I cut him off. "Shortly before her passing, Agnes's

neighbors say that her mental capacities were diminished, enough so that she required assisted living. Lenora had Agnes admitted to a memory-care facility sometime last summer, and she remained there until her subsequent death, but I have a problem with that. I've located some quitclaim deeds dated August first of last year in which Agnes signed several real-estate properties—valuable real-estate properties—over to Lenora, who subsequently sold the whole collection of lots to a developer. I have a forensic handwriting expert who tells me that Agnes's signatures on those documents appear to be forged."

For the first time, Stockman looked uncomfortable. "Do you really believe you can prove that?" he asked.

"I do," I replied

"Even so," he said, "I'm still not at liberty to discuss the contents of Agnes Mayfield's will."

"What about the date?" I asked.

"The date? What about it?"

"When was Agnes's will written?"

"That's easy," he said. "It was written decades ago. I was new to the firm when Mr. and Mrs. Mayfield came in to have their wills drafted, and I handled the matter myself. A month or so ago, when Mrs. Harrison came in to discuss probating her mother's will, I remember looking at the document and realizing that she must have been little more than a child when the will was drawn up."

I stood to leave. "Thank you," I said. "That's all I need."

Stockman seemed taken aback. "It is?"

"If Peter and Agnes Mayfield drew up their wills at the same time, I'm guessing they were very similar. Since the term 'per stirpes' was in Peter's will, I'm betting it will appear in Agnes's as well. Alan Dale, Athena's legal guardian, is in the process of obtaining an attorney ad litem to act on her behalf. I don't know who that person will be, but when he or she comes calling, you'll know I sent them. In the meantime, if Lenora Harrison comes around trying to hurry the probate process along, I'd suggest you do what you lawyers always seem to do best."

"What's that?" Stockman asked.

"Stall," I told him. With that I showed myself out.

On the way to the elevator, I did a few quick steps and heaved an imaginary ball down the long corridor, pretending I'd just bowled a strike. A passing secretary looked at me as though I were nuts, but I didn't care. So far today I was picking them up and knocking them down, and my next stop would be at Loretta Hawk's front door.

I had just pulled in to the Sholeetsa Project's parking lot when my phone rang. Thanks to having added Hilda Tanner's name to my contacts list, I knew who was on the phone.

"King Kong," Hilda said without preamble. "The company who put up the sign is called King Kong Billboards. It's based in Renton."

"Okay," I said. "Thanks so much. I really appreciate it."

"Is this going to help you find whoever killed Petey?"

"I believe so."

"I'm happy to help, then." She paused. "Did you give Naomi the booties?"

I had found Hilda's hand-knitted booties in my pocket and had stuffed them into the glove compartment of my Mercedes shortly after she gave them to me. I'd meant to show them to Alan. The truth is, until now I'd forgotten about them completely.

"Not yet," I said guiltily. "I'm on my way to see Naomi in a little while. I'll give them to her then."

"Be sure you do."

Inside the lobby at the Sholeetsa Project, the receptionist nodded me in the direction of Loretta Hawk's office, the door to which stood wide open. "She's expecting you."

And Loretta *was* expecting me. On her desk was a manila envelope with my name on it, along with the reloaded plastic bag Alan and I had used to deliver Petey's hairbrush on Saturday morning.

"The printed reports are in here," Loretta said, pushing the envelope across her desk so it was within my reach. "If there are any legal proceedings that require expert testimony, you can rely on us."

"Thank you," I said. "You've been a huge help."

"I'm sure having a previously unknown child pop up at this juncture in your life is challenging to say the least," Loretta offered, "but it happens a lot in this business—far more often than you'd expect. Some people find it a blessing. Others? Not so much."

"I'm not sure what's going to happen," I admitted. "I have yet to tell her. That's my next stop.

Naomi's had a tough time. She's been homeless for years, and she's just learned that the father of her baby has been murdered."

"Were they into drugs?" Loretta asked. "There's a lot of murder and mayhem in the drug world."

I nodded. "I'd like to help her beat the drug habit if I can, but . . ."

"But she may not be willing?"

"Yes."

"Give it to her straight," Loretta advised. "For a white guy, I think you're pretty squared away, and if your newly found daughter has any brains, she'll listen."

Bolstered by that unexpected show of moral support, I took my leave. Before starting the car and heading back north into downtown, I located the number for King Kong Billboards and placed the call as I drove.

"I'm calling about your sign in West Seattle," I told the woman who answered the phone, "the one for Mayfield Glen."

"Seems like half the people in the neighborhood want that sign to come down. Are you one of those?"

"No, I'm not," I said. "I'm looking for information."

"What kind of information, exactly?" she asked, suddenly sounding distant. "We're in the sign business, not the information business. We do signs. That's all we do."

"I'm wondering when it went up?"

"When the sign went up?"

"Yes."

I expected to be told to go to hell, but I wasn't. "That's the Highline Development sign, isn't it?" the woman asked.

"Yes, ma'am."

My mother always told me that a little bit of politeness can go a long way, and it worked like a charm this time around.

"The work order was signed off as completed at two thirty P.M. on October thirtieth, 2016. We've had to require documented work-order sign-offs because some customers have tried to claim that their signs weren't up when we knew good and well they were. These days the crews take time-dated photos and send them in when the job is done. We attach the photo to the file as proof positive."

"You have crews working on Sundays?" I asked.

"This is a family business. We're generally a six-day-a-week operation," she told me, "but we work Sundays, too, if we get behind, as we were back then. Two guys quit in late October, and it took until close to Thanksgiving before we got squared away again."

And there I had it for sure—Petey's sign. The billboard probably hadn't been there when he'd left the house to go buy that Halloween candy, but it had been when he came back. No wonder he'd been so wound up about it.

"Thank you," I told the lady on the phone. "I appreciate your help."

It seemed like I was saying thank you a lot that day.

Ten minutes later I was looking for a parking spot in Pioneer Square. The closest one I could find was three blocks away, and I didn't mind a bit. The longer I could put off the inevitable, the better, because I still hadn't decided on what I was going to say. When it was time to get out of the car, on an impulse I opened the glove box, grabbed Hilda's booties, and stuck them in the clear plastic bag along with Petey's hairbrush.

Inside the mission Rachel Seymour peeked around from behind her computer screen and waved me into her office. "Naomi's busy right now," she said. "She's taking a practice GED test."

"A practice one?" I asked.

"It's more for assessment purposes than anything else. Many of our residents are unemployed because not having educational credentials seriously limits the kinds of jobs for which they can apply. For someone without a high-school diploma, a GED can be a first step out of the homeless/jobless cycle. Occasionally one of our residents is able to pass the test without any additional tutoring. What the practice tests tell us is where and how much remedial instruction is necessary."

"You offer that as needed?"

"Yes, we have a set of volunteers, mostly retired teachers, who serve as tutors."

"What about AA and NA?" I asked.

"We encourage participation in those where necessary," Rachel said, "but attendance isn't mandatory. We try to be helpful without being judgmental."

That's a tightrope all right, and my only question was whether or not I'd be able to walk it, too. Sitting there, I was well aware that I'd neglected to tell Reverend Seymour the whole truth, just as I'd neglected to tell a lot of people the whole truth. Maybe it was time I started.

"Is there a place where I could speak to Naomi in private?" I asked.

Rachel frowned. "Is this something to do with the baby?"

"No," I said. "It's something to do with me. My DNA profile has just confirmed that I'm actually Naomi Dale's biological father. I didn't know about her until last week, and now—"

"Does she know?" Rachel asked.

"No," I said. "That's why I'm here—to tell her."

Rachel picked up her phone and typed a text. When she finished, she turned to me. "I've asked that Naomi come to my office when she finishes the test. I'll leave the two of you here alone for as long as you need."

Rachel disappeared behind her monitor. Sitting there listening to her fingers flying on the keyboard, I cooled my heels and waited. A few minutes later, a text came in from Ralph Ames.

Does our girl need detox? If not, I've found a place in Moses Lake called The Haven. They could admit Naomi as early as next Monday. They'll hold a spot for us for the next twenty-four hours but no longer. Will she go or not?

Can't say for sure. I'm waiting to talk to her about it now.

Are you going to tell her?

That's the plan.

Good luck, then. May the Force be with you.

That's what I need, all right, I thought, *a good healthy dose of the Force.*

A few minutes later, although it seemed much longer, there was a tap on the door. Rachel's head popped out from behind the intervening monitor. "Come in, Naomi," she said cordially. "How was the test?"

When Naomi entered, I was surprised to see a smile on her face. In our previous interactions I'd never seen an actual smile.

"Mrs. Murray said that I did well and that I should sign up to take the real test as soon as possible."

"That's wonderful news," Rachel said. "I'm delighted to hear it, but in the meantime Mr. Beaumont just showed up and would like to have a moment with you in private."

Naomi's smile disappeared, and a look of alarm spread across her face. "Is something wrong with Athena?" she asked. "Or is there something wrong with the paperwork?"

I removed Petey's hairbrush from the bag and held it up. "I came to return this."

When Naomi stepped forward, reaching for it, Rachel stood up and discreetly exited the room, closing the door behind her.

Naomi sank down on a chair next to me. "Thank you," she said, holding the brush close. "Thank you for keeping your word."

"There's something else."

I pulled out the booties and handed them over. Naomi held them up and stared at them, frowning. "Where did these come from?" she asked.

"Hilda Tanner knitted them for you," I said. "She was going to give them to you before you had the baby, but you were evicted before she had a chance. She wanted me to tell you that she's sorry they're the wrong color."

For a moment Naomi said nothing. I could see she was struggling to find words. "Will you tell her thank you for me?" she said at last.

"I'll be glad to," I answered.

"But you should probably give these to my dad," she added. "He's the one who's going to need them, not me."

"Before you return them to me, let me ask you something. Have you thought about going back through treatment?"

In a split second, Naomi's anger reappeared, in spades. "Did he send you here to ask me that?"

"No," I said. "I'm asking on my own behalf, because I want to know."

"It's none of your business."

"I'm afraid it is my business," I told her.

She stood up then, as if intent on storming out.

"I knew your mother once," I added quietly. "We were together."

Naomi sat back down. "What do you mean 'together'?" she repeated.

"Not together for the long haul," I said. "It was a one-night stand."

"So it was like that," she sneered. "All the time my mother was complaining about what I was doing, she was doing the same thing?"

"Had done," I admitted, "and you were the result."

"You know that how?" Naomi demanded.

"I suspected it the moment I saw the school photo of you that your dad carries around in his wallet. You look just the way my daughter, Kelly, looked at that age. But now I have proof."

"Proof?"

Before coming into the mission, I had removed the printed copies of Athena's and my profiles and slipped them into my inside pocket. Now I pulled them out and handed them over to Naomi.

"What's this?" she asked.

"They're reports containing Athena's DNA profile and mine," I told her. "You can read them for yourself, or we can cut to the chase. You'll find that they show me to be Athena's maternal grandfather."

I had been prepared for a storm of hysterics, with Naomi railing at me and claiming it wasn't possible. Instead, without bothering to unfold the papers, she dropped them into her lap and simply stared at me.

"Does my dad know?" she asked finally.

The manner in which she asked the question gave me goose bumps, because from the way she said the words, I knew exactly what she meant. She was worried that if Alan Dale found out the truth about her and me, it would break his heart. And in that moment I had my first clear inkling that Naomi was someone worth saving.

"He knew almost from the beginning," I told her. "The two of us—you and I—were the only ones left in the dark. Your folks became an item shortly after your mother and I . . ." I didn't finish that sentence. There was no way on earth I could finish that sentence.

"They went back home to Texas," I continued after a pause. "When your mother discovered she was pregnant and how far along she was, it was no problem for her to figure out who the father had to be. Your dad had always wanted to have kids but couldn't. He took you to raise as his own because he loved you, Naomi, and he still does."

For a long time after that, we just sat there, with neither of us saying a word. That's one of the things I learned in my youth, back when I was selling Fuller Brush door-to-door and while conducting interviews. You don't oversell. You don't make like a pushy car salesman and try to force the issue. Nope, you zip your lip and let the other guy think things through, and the longer the silence lasts, the better your chances for a good outcome.

"I know he does," she admitted at last, "but what's the use of my going back to rehab? I did that once and I screwed it up."

"I've been in AA for more than twenty years," I said. "I sobered up a couple of years after you were born. I've had one serious slip since then, and I've been tempted more than once, but when that happens, I go to meetings, I talk with my sponsor, I get help. But about your slip, Naomi? Don't blame yourself too much for what happened. When you thought Petey had abandoned you, you were left with less than nothing to hold on to. Under those circumstances most people would have fallen into the same trap you did and relapsed into old behaviors. But the point is, you're smart enough to have taken responsibility."

"I have?"

"You recognized you weren't in the right place to care for your child. You signed Athena over to your dad. If the state had been forced to take charge and revoke your parental rights, Athena would have been lost in the system and you'd never have a chance to see her again. With your father in charge as Athena's legal guardian, decisions about whether or not you can see your child again will be up to him. How those decisions turn out will be up to you, because the only way he's going to allow you in Athena's life is if you clean up your act for good. Are you using right now?"

Naomi ducked her head and shook it. "I'm clean," she said in a strangled whisper. "Some women at the encampment were helping me."

"As long as you don't require detox, I have a spot in a rehab program over in Moses Lake on hold for you for the next twenty-four hours. If you decide to go, check-in will be on Monday. But here's the thing, and I can't say this strongly enough: You have to go to rehab because you want to go for you. You can't do it because I want it or because your dad wants it. If you do it for anyone else but you, it won't work."

"Do I have to make up my mind right now?"

"No, I want you to think about it—really think about it, but while you're making up your mind, try thinking about how smart you are. Your tutor just said you could probably ace the GED test right this minute without any problem. You're still young, Naomi. With a GED in hand, you can go back to school to become whatever it is you want to be. And when it comes to schooling, rest assured I have the resources and am fully prepared to help you with that as well, but my offer of help is contingent on your willingness to help yourself. The only way I'll help you is if you're prepared to buckle down and do the work—both in rehab and in school."

Another period of silence ensued. "You said you had a daughter?" Naomi asked finally.

"Yes," I said, "I have both a daughter and a son. My son's name is Scotty. He works in the Tactical Electronics Unit at the Seattle Police Department. He and his wife, Cherisse, are expecting their first child, a boy, a couple of months from now. My daughter, Kelly, lives in southern Oregon. She was a lot like you when she was younger. She got pregnant, dropped out of high school, and ran off with a kid named Jeremy, who wanted to become a musician."

"Are they still together?" Naomi asked.

"They are. Jeremy is a high-school band teacher now. Kelly went back to school, got two degrees, and now runs a chain of preschools. They have two kids, a boy and a girl. Kelly and Scott's kids are Athena's cousins," I said. "I never had the benefit of having cousins to hang around with. I'd like that for Athena."

"Do Scott and Kelly know about me?"

"Not yet," I said. "But they will, and if you'd like to meet them, I can make that happen."

"You would?"

"Naomi," I said, "you have to understand, you might have been an accident, but you are not a mistake. Alan Dale is your dad and will always be your dad, but now that I'm in the picture, I'd like to stay that way. Still, it's up to you, if you want to have these connections and maintain them, you'll have to earn them. No free ride, got it?"

She nodded.

I stood up. "I'm going now," I said. "Do you still have my number?"

She nodded again.

"When you make your decision, call and let me know, but bear in mind—that twenty-four-hour holding period started to count down about an hour ago."

With that I walked out of the room. When I closed the office door behind me, Naomi was still sitting there holding Petey's hairbrush in one hand and Athena's baby-blue booties in the other. If anyone was going to give Hilda Tanner's booties to Alan Dale, it would have to be Naomi herself.

Rachel Seymour caught up with me before I made it to the outside entrance. "How'd it go?" she asked.

"Beats me," I said. "The jury's still out."

CHAPTER 31

I WALKED AWAY from the mission with no way of knowing if I'd closed the deal or not. Had I said enough? Had I said too much? Would what I'd said make any difference one way or another? My phone had buzzed at me silently a couple of times while I was at the mission, but I'd had ignored it. Once I got back to the car, I saw a whole series of notifications, all of them from Lucinda. Four were missed calls. The last was a terse text.

I've got something. Why the hell aren't you picking up? Call me!

I called.

"Where the hell have you been?" Lucinda wanted to know.

"I was at the mission, talking to Naomi. Why? What's up?"

"Detective Stevenson and I are just about to leave

Memory Manor. We've been talking to Dr. William Blaine, the facility's attending physician."

I'd understood that Kramer had sent Stevenson along to execute the warrants, but I was surprised to hear that he'd accompanied Lucinda to Memory Manor.

"Both of you?" I asked.

Lucinda laughed. "Dropping your name broke the ice. When it came time to go to Memory Manor and talk to Dr. Blaine, I didn't even have to hold a gun on Detective Stevenson. He was all in."

"What did Dr. Blaine say?"

"He remembers those two cases vividly—Danielle Nishikawa's and Agnes Mayfield's. He says the two women were already frail when they came down with severe flulike symptoms several weeks apart. Neither of them responded to treatment, and eventually both died. Danielle was stricken in early October and passed away within days of becoming ill. Agnes became ill two months later. When she, too, died, Dr. Blaine was suspicious and went so far as to suggest having an autopsy performed. Lenora said absolutely not—she didn't want an autopsy."

"I'll just bet she didn't!" I said.

"According to Dr. Blaine, wishes from the next of kin carry a lot more weight around Memory Manor than do those of the attending physician."

"Did he have a theory?"

"Actually, he does. He told me he did some research after the fact and wonders if both women weren't possibly victims of ethylene glycol poisoning."

"Antifreeze?" I asked.

"Antifreeze," Lucinda confirmed.

"If the doctor figured out that much, or at least suspected it, what did he do about it—report it?"

"Evidently Dr. Blaine has had some issues with the state medical board in the past and is no longer allowed to maintain a private practice. Instead he serves as the attending physician for several nursing-home and rehab facilities. When he spoke to the director of Memory Manor about referring Danielle's and Agnes's deaths to the authorities, the director warned him that if he did so, he would be out of a job at Memory Manor and that she personally would see to it that he was let go from those other facilities as well."

"Yes, I suppose publicity about two suspected homicides at Memory Manor would've been bad for business. And that having been threatened with firing, Dr. Blaine kept his mouth shut."

"Until today," Lucinda said. "But he told Greg and me something neither of us knew before now."

"What's that?"

"Once ingested, ethylene glycol forms into crystals inside the human body, crystals that are readily identifiable long after the fact."

"So an exhumation might well be called for?" I asked.

"Greg is on the phone checking to see if he can get a court order for that."

"What about the search warrants?"

"Executed as requested, and Agnes's bank statements are now firmly in hand. If the money that was there in June has mysteriously gone missing, that certainly speaks to motive."

"Anything else turn up?"

"Not at Agnes's house," Lucinda said, "but at Suzanne Nishikawa's condo it would appear we hit the jackpot, not that we realized it at the time."

"What do you mean?"

"We found an urn containing Danielle's ashes on a shelf in Suzanne's garage, but you'll never guess what else."

"What?"

"A gallon jug of antifreeze with a little over half of it missing. Suzanne Nishikawa doesn't strike me as a DIY mechanic. How about you?"

"Not in a million years," I replied. "She really did do it—she killed her own mother!"

"That's how it looks. Since we didn't need a new warrant to go back and collect the antifreeze, we're doing that now."

"What's next?" I asked.

"Obviously Suzanne Nishikawa is a hard-ass. Greg's and my next stop will be a visit to Petey's Aunt Lenora. If she's involved in all this or even knows about it, I'm thinking she might be the weaker link. Are you interested in tagging along?"

I could not believe my ears. "Are you kidding? Of course I'm interested. I can hardly wait. When?"

"Right now."

"Fair enough," I told her. "I'll meet you there."

CHAPTER 32

I HAD CROSSED Lake Washington so many times in the past few days that I was beginning to feel like a regular commuter. But this time I had plenty to think about. The phone calls back and forth between Suzanne and Lenora on the night of Petey's death, along with the similarities in their two mothers' deaths, certainly made it appear as if the two women might be partners in crime. When it came down to interrogations, which of them would crack first?

Suzanne was a poker player capable of bluffing with complete aplomb. On the night of Petey's death, she had possessed both the presence of mind and the necessary contacts to finagle unloading what we suspected to be a gore-filled Lexus. In other words, she was a cool customer who was unlikely to buckle under pressure. Lenora, accustomed to a cosseted Eastside life, would be far more susceptible to accepting a plea deal.

I arrived in Medina first. Driving in, I realized

that it wasn't a good strategic move for us to show up at the house in a whole herd of vehicles. I found a nearby church and called Caldwell and Stevenson with the address, suggesting that we meet up in the parking lot there so we could arrive in one vehicle rather than three. Even though it was my bright idea, when it came time for us to clamber into Detective Stevenson's unmarked, I was the one who ended up in the backseat. Locked in behind closed doors with no interior handles, I couldn't help but feel as though I'd been kicked to the back of the bus. And even though I was the one who'd supplied Lenora's address originally, when we drove up to the Harrisons' rusty corten gate, Detective Stevenson was the one who pressed the buzzer on the intercom.

"Who is it and what do you want?" Once again the brusque voice speaking over the intercom belonged to Lenora herself.

"I'm Detective Greg Stevenson with Seattle PD. I'm here investigating the disappearance and subsequent murder of your nephew, Petey Mayfield. A representative from the Kittitas County Sheriff's Department, Detective Lucinda Caldwell, is along for the ride, as is my former colleague at Seattle PD, a gentleman by the name of J. P. Beaumont. I believe you might already have met him."

Without a verbal response, the gate swung open. If Lenora Harrison had suspected for a second that she herself was under investigation, I doubt she would have granted us admittance. As it was, she not only opened the gate, she once again ventured out onto the front porch to greet us. With the ceremonial display of Greg's and Lucinda's respective badges concluded, Lenora invited us into the house. As we followed her inside, I noticed that Lenora was dressed for an occasion of some kind—as though she expected to go somewhere as soon as she could get rid of us.

In the living room, she pointed Lucinda and me toward the chairs Mel and I had occupied on our previous visit. Then, assuming Greg was in charge, she seated him next to her on the sectional and focused her full attention on him.

"Whatever this is, you'll need to be quick about it," she told him. "I have a luncheon engagement, and I don't want to be late. Now, what's all this about Petey? I had no idea he'd disappeared, to say nothing of his having been murdered, until Mr. Beaumont here turned up over the weekend and told me what had happened. In other words, there's not much I can tell you."

"Still," Greg said, "given that you're Petey's nearest blood relative, we really do need to hear what you have to say. To that end I'd like to ask you to come to our headquarters in downtown Seattle for an official interview."

Lenora's reaction to that was as understandable as it was immediate. "Go all the way into downtown Seattle in order to carry on a simple conversation over nothing?" she demanded. "Certainly not, it's out of the question. There must be some other way to do this."

Greg frowned and stared off into space for a moment, as if puzzling over how to deal with this seemingly insoluble problem.

"Well," he said, at last, "I suppose if you didn't mind our recording the conversation here—"

"By all means," Lenora interrupted impatiently. "I'm totally in favor of that. Let's get this over with, the sooner the better."

Lucinda reached into her purse—a briefcase-size bag that Mel would have loved—and produced an iPad complete with an easel-backed cover that allowed the device to stand on its own.

"Is there a place where we could set this up?" she asked.

"You mean, like a table or something?"

"Exactly," Lucinda said. "A table would be perfect."

With that, Lenora rose to her feet and led us into an ornate dining room, complete with a massive and highly polished cherrywood table. Lucinda placed the iPad in the middle of that, closer to the near end. After turning it on, she directed Lenora to sit at the end of the table facing the iPad with Lucinda and Greg situated on one side of the table and me on the other. Once Lucinda had adjusted our positions so all our faces showed on the screen, she turned the device to record.

"You're on, Detective Stevenson," Lucinda said, "over to you," leaving it to Detective Stevenson to be our master of ceremonies.

"I am Homicide Detective Greg Stevenson of the Seattle Police Department. This is an official interview with Lenora Harrison into the apparent homicide of her nephew Peter 'Petey' Mayfield. At Ms. Harrison's request and convenience, we're conducting and recording this interview on an electronic device at her residence in Bellevue, Washington, rather than in a formal interview room at Seattle PD. Present for the interview, in addition to myself and Ms. Harrison, are Homicide Detective Lucinda Caldwell of the Kittitas County Sheriff's Department and Private Investigator, J. P. Beaumont, a civilian with some knowledge of the Mayfield case. Ms. Harrison, would you be kind enough to state your name for the record and to acknowledge that you are a willing participant in an interview conducted under these circumstances?"

Fixing a steely-eyed gaze on Stevenson alone, Lenora gave her name and delivered a clipped, "I do." Obviously yours truly wasn't worthy of even so much as a withering glance. Neither was Detective Caldwell.

"In addition to the four of us, are there any other people present in the residence at this time?" Stevenson asked.

"I'm here by myself. It's spring. My husband's out playing his first round of golf and the maid has the day off."

"Were you close to your nephew?" Greg began.

"Not at all," Lenora answered. "My brother, Arthur, was a bum—a complete loser. I'm sorry to say that Petey took after his father in that regard. He got into trouble and into drugs early on. He spent time in juvie as a teenager and in jail as an adult. The less I had to do with either Arthur or his son, the better I liked it."

"You mentioned earlier that you had no idea until just recently that Petey had gone missing."

"That is correct. Mr. Beaumont here stopped by

to give me news about his disappearance sometime last week. Then, over the weekend, Mr. Beaumont and his wife came to inform my husband and me that Petey had in fact been murdered."

"Did you know that Petey was staying on property formerly owned by your mother at the time of his disappearance?"

"I suppose I did know that," Lenora conceded. "I'm sure she must have mentioned it, but he came and went so often I'm afraid I stopped paying attention. As I said, the less I had to do with Petey and his sort, the better I liked it."

"His sort?" Greg repeated.

"As I mentioned earlier, Petey was a drug user—a drug abuser," she corrected. "Is it any wonder that I didn't want to have anything to do with him?"

"Is it true that your mother quitclaimed her various real-estate properties over to you sometime in the course of last summer?"

"That's true," Lenora agreed at once. "She was getting on in years and required help looking after herself as well as her financial affairs. She transferred her properties to me so I could handle the property taxes and make sure the utilities were paid on a regular basis."

"Had she not signed the properties over to you, would Petey have been entitled to inherit a portion of their value?"

For the first time, Lenora's veneer of being fully in charge showed the smallest hint of cracking.

"Wait," she said, "are you trying to imply that I may have had something to do with Petey's death?"

"Did you?" Greg asked.

"Certainly not!" Lenora replied indignantly. "I can't imagine what would lead you to believe anything so outrageous!"

"Were you aware that at the time of his death Petey and his girlfriend were expecting a child?"

"I was not at the time, but because of Mr. Beaumont here I know about that now."

Greg did an abrupt change of course. "Tell me about your dealings with Suzanne Nishikawa of Highline Development," he said evenly.

"What about them?"

"Do you have a client relationship with her and her firm?"

"Yes, of course I do," Lenora answered indignantly. "I learned through a mutual friend that her company was looking for property in West Seattle that would be suitable for development. My mother's contiguous lots filled that bill perfectly."

I spoke up for the first time. "If those lots were so perfect for development, it's surprising that you sold them at prices well below the going rate."

She glared at me and then turned back to Greg. "Does he have to be here? Since he's obviously here only to advocate for Petey's child, I don't believe he has any right—"

"Did you sell the lots at below-market value?" Greg asked.

Lenora seemed momentarily flustered. "Well, yes, I suppose I did," she admitted finally, "but the original sales price was only part of it. Suzanne and I have a side agreement, you see. Once the houses in Mayfield Glen are built, one of them will be coming to me."

"To you alone or to you and your husband?" I asked.

"That is none of your business," she replied.

"So you and Ms. Nishikawa have a side agreement which would give you title to one of the completed residences in that development?" Greg's follow-up question told me that Lucinda had done an outstanding job of laying out the situation.

"Yes," Lenora said, "but it's not for me. It's for my son—for Mark and his partner, Jess. Mark is gay, you see. My husband, Isaac, is a bit old-school. Once Mark came out as gay, Isaac cut off all contact with him and cut him out of his will as well. Mark and Jess are getting married next year, and I wanted to be able to give them the house as a wedding present—something that was from me alone."

That was a biggie for me. I hadn't realized that the Harrisons even had a son—a son who was Petey's cousin and who would also have been in line to inherit from Agnes and Peter Mayfield's estate. By reducing Petey's potential share of his grandparents' estate, Lenora had automatically guaranteed that her own son's share would be larger.

"Are you saying your husband is unaware of these various real-estate transactions?" Greg asked.

"I suppose," Lenora conceded.

She kept her voice even, but two angry red spots were clearly visible through the layer of makeup covering her cheeks.

"So on the day that Petey disappeared," Greg continued, "the calls that went back and forth between your phone and Ms. Nishikawa's phone were strictly related to those aforementioned real-estate transactions?"

Lenora hesitated for a heartbeat. "I'm sure they were," she said finally.

"And your business relationship is close enough that she would call you several times over the course of that weekend, even into the early hours of Monday morning?" Lucinda continued.

"I suppose," Lenora said.

"It wouldn't have anything to do with her telling you that Petey had come to her, threatening to expose what was going on—that you and Suzanne were trying to cheat him out of his rightful inheritance?"

"This is utterly unacceptable!" Lenora exclaimed. "I won't sit here in my own home and have complete strangers accusing me of being involved in my nephew's murder. I want all of you out of here."

She was angry now, but not smart enough to shut up or ask for an attorney. In interview situations that always gives the cops a home-field advantage.

"What can you tell us about Danielle Nishikawa?" Greg asked.

"What about her?" Lenora exclaimed.

"Did you know her?"

"Yes, she and my mother were in the same nursing home for a while. In fact, Suzanne was the one who recommended that particular facility to me. So yes, I knew her."

"And was Danielle already a patient there at the time you placed your mother there?" Lucinda continued.

"I suppose she was," Lenora said, "but I'm not sure."

"Did you ever meet her prior to your becoming acquainted at Memory Manor?" I asked.

"Of course not," she said. "Why would I?"

"I believe she was the one who notarized your mother's signatures on those quitclaim deeds."

"I wasn't there when those were signed," Lenora responded, "so how would I know if she was there or not? I'm telling you, I never met Danielle Nishikawa until Suzanne introduced me to her at Memory Manor."

"Is there a chance your mother's signatures were forged on those documents?"

"Forged? Absolutely not!"

"Good," Greg said, shutting down the interview. "I believe we have everything we need. Thank you so much for your cooperation, Ms. Harrison. We'll be glad to show ourselves out."

I gave Detective Stevenson points for having ended the interview before Lenora got around to asking for an attorney. The next time they met up in an interview room, she probably would have done so, but in the meantime we had plenty of damning circumstantial evidence on our iPad video. And if Lenora Harrison was under the impression that Suzanne Nishikawa was our sole target, she was dead wrong!

As we walked out to Greg's unmarked, it was all I could do to contain my excitement. The investigation had reached critical mass. The pieces to the puzzle were laid out in front of us. Now we just needed to put them together. As we drove out through the Harrisons' massive rolling gate, Greg and Lucinda were already strategizing on their next steps for doing exactly that and theorizing about which of these two bad girls, Suzanne and Lenora, would be the first to turn on the other.

The problem is, once we got back to the church parking lot, I found myself summarily thrown under the bus and tossed off the team as well. At this point in the investigation, Greg and Lucinda were the actual cops. I was an unsworn outsider—a helpful but nonessential one. They would bring in their own handwriting expert to evaluate the forged signatures. They'd have their own cyber folks examine Suzanne's cell-phone trail and triangulate whether or not she'd been anywhere near where Petey's body had been dumped on the night of his murder. And they were the ones who would determine whether Agnes Mayfield's body would be exhumed in order to learn if there were ethylene glycol crystals lingering in her remains.

I was both fuming and dejected about that as I headed onto the 520 Bridge, but somewhere midspan I came to my senses. I really wasn't a cop anymore. Alan Dale had come to me asking that I find our mutual daughter and to protect the interests of our mutual granddaughter. I had done just that. If the signatures on the quitclaims had been forged, the transactions selling those lots to Highline could most likely be invalidated. And if Lenora was found to have been involved in her mother's death, she would automatically be disinherited. Beneficiaries are not allowed to profit from their own misdeeds. I wondered if, in a per stirpes situation, did that same disqualification pass through to their children?

By the time I hit the perpetually snarled I-5 exit known as the Mercer Mess, I was in better spirits. Alan Dale's request for help had been asked and answered. So yes, when it came time to cuff Suzanne and Lenora, I wouldn't be on hand to see them loaded into squad cars, but I had the satisfaction of knowing that I was the one who'd blown the whistle on them and laid the foundation. I had gotten the ball rolling by discovering that crimes had been committed in the first place, thus putting sworn officers on the trail, so good for me.

"Not bad for an old guy," I told myself aloud, "not bad at all."

CHAPTER 33

WHEN I STEPPED off the elevator at Belltown Terrace and heard the sound of voices coming from inside the unit, I wondered who the company was. Lucy came to the front door to greet me, and so did Alan Dale.

"Andrea Hutchins is here," he told me, "and so is Jane McCall."

The way he spoke that latter name implied it was one I should recognize, but I drew a blank. "Who's she?" I asked.

"Athena's guardian ad litem," Alan answered.

I was suitably impressed. "You got that taken care of today?" I asked.

"We got everything done today!" he announced jubilantly, engulfing me in an unexpected bear hug. "There was a cancellation on the judge's docket, and Andrea was able to get us squeezed in. The permanent legal guardianship is a done deal. Jane will be in charge of looking after Athena's financial interests here in Washington, and as of now Athena and I are free to pack up and go home."

Okay, so I'll admit I was more than a little tired of having company underfoot, but the idea of having Alan and Athena out of my house and life put a sudden clutch in my gut. They couldn't leave so soon. I wasn't ready.

"How did that all come about?" I asked.

Alan and I had been walking into the living room as we talked. Athena was in her infant carrier on the floor in front of the window seat. Lucy was stretched out beside her. Andrea Hutchins, the social worker, was seated on the window seat itself along with a stranger, a silver-haired woman of a certain age. I heard the two of them chatting as Alan and I entered the room. The conversation broke off abruptly as the woman I didn't know rose from her perch and came forward to greet me, hand extended.

"You must be Beau," she said. "I'm Jane McCall. Ralph Ames happens to be an old friend of mine. Once he brought me into the picture about what's been going on in this little tyke's life, I was able to work with Andrea here to expedite a few things. After being stuck here for coming up on two months, I believe Mr. Dale is eager to head home."

"I am," Alan agreed with a nod. "My plan is to pack up tomorrow and hit the road first thing Wednesday morning."

The words that went through my head were, *Not so soon.* What I asked aloud was, "Driving by yourself?"

"Not exactly," Alan answered. "Believe it or not,

Marge has offered to ride along with us. She'll catch a plane home once we get home to Jasper. She's already made arrangements for someone to look after Stubs while she's gone."

It was shocking to hear Alan call Harry "Stubs," but it was hardly surprising. That's what Marge called her husband. I doubt Alan had a clue that Harry I. Ball was a double amputee.

"Marge will be taking care of Athena while I do the driving," Alan added.

"How long will it take?" I asked.

"If we can make four hundred miles or so a day, we should arrive in about five days, maybe a little longer. I'll need to spend some time mapping out hotels where we can stay along the way."

The idea of spending that many hours and days in a car with Marge Herndon would have made me want to slit my throat. Obviously Alan was made of sterner stuff. In actual fact I'd been worried about that long drive home and had even considered offering to go along myself. Now the problem was solved without my involvement. I wasn't sure how I felt about that. Relieved, maybe, but also a little disappointed.

Everyone else resumed their seats while I found one of my own. "Sounds like we've had a very busy day," I said, "me included. I talked to Naomi," I added for Alan's benefit. "She knows about me now."

"What about you?" Jane asked with a frown.

Ralph might have brought her in on the case, but he clearly hadn't told her everything, so I clued her in. Then I went on to tell everyone involved what all had transpired on my end. When I began explaining about what had come to light concerning Lenora and Suzanne's underhanded machinations to cut Petey out of his inheritance, Jane produced a tablet and began to take notes. I sent her the contact information for Joe Stallings, Todd Hatcher's handwriting expert, and for Agnes Mayfield's attorney, Richard Stockman, as well so she could be in touch with all of them on her own. I also gave her contact information for both Detective Stevenson and Detective Caldwell, although I doubted either of them would be able to discuss their current ongoing investigations. That was the one good thing about my being a civilian. They couldn't talk about active investigations. I could and did.

Something I didn't mention in the course of all this was my offer to help Naomi into substance-abuse treatment. Knowing that the twenty-four-hour deadline was gradually ticking down, I'd been keeping an eye on my phone and hoping for a call. So far it was no dice, and I was beginning to lose heart.

An hour or so later, when Jane got up to leave, I walked her to the door. "Thank you for telling me the whole story, Beau. I can see why Ralph wanted me to be appointed as Athena's guardian ad litem. He was looking for someone with my particular skill set."

"What skill set is that?" I asked.

"I was a cop once, too, back in the early eighties. I wanted to be one of those female pioneers in law enforcement. My partner and I went on a domestic-violence call. By the time we got there, the woman and her two kids were already dead. We took out the perp, but in the process my partner was shot in the back and permanently disabled. After that I couldn't do it anymore. I turned in my badge and gun, went back to college, and got a law degree. I'm fierce when it comes to fighting for women and children, most especially children. I'll be in touch with Mr. Stockman first thing tomorrow morning. If Agnes's will does indeed specify per stirpes, you can bet that estate sale will be canceled within minutes, and I'll be looking into that handwriting situation as well. If those real-estate transactions were accomplished by fraudulent means, I should be able to untie that knot."

"Thank you," I said. "I'm sure Athena's interests are in good hands."

Andrea Hutchins departed shortly after Jane did. Once we realized we'd been left on our own for dinner that night, Alan whipped up some grilled cheese sandwiches. When it was time for Mel's and my commute-time phone call, I went into the bedroom to talk to her. In order for me to bring her up to date on the day's activities, our usual half-hour call turned into an hour or more.

"So," she said when I finished, "it sounds like you've told almost everyone about the situation with Naomi and Athena, with the notable exception of the two people who really need to know, Kelly and Scott."

"You've got me there," I admitted. "That's next on my list."

"Get to it, then," Mel urged, "and let me know how it went when you finish."

By the time I got off the call with Mel, my ear

was burning and the battery in my phone was down to less than 10 percent. I plugged it in and walked away, ostensibly to give it a chance to charge. Halfway across the room, I realized that was all a ruse—a delaying tactic to avoid doing what needed to be done. I went back to the phone, picked it up, and, with the charger still attached, dialed the first number.

My mother always said that the best way to get something done was to tackle the hardest part first. That's why I called Kelly. I figured she was the one most likely to give me grief about all this.

"Hey," I said when she answered. "What are you doing?"

"I'm getting our tax package ready to go to the accountant. Jeremy took the kids uptown for some ice cream to get them out of my hair."

Having this challenging conversation without Jeremy and the kids around was exactly what I wanted. "Do you have a minute to talk?"

"Sure, Dad," she said, "but this sounds serious. Is something wrong?"

One of the things I've learned in AA is that it's important to take responsibility for what you've done—to own it. I had hoped to inject a little good news/bad news–style humor into the situation, but I dropped that idea and told the story straight out—warts and all. Even though Karen and I had been divorced for years before the incident with Jasmine Day occurred, it was nevertheless painful to have to tell my daughter about my hooking up for an irresponsible and drunken one-night stand with someone I barely knew and that as a result I had fathered a child, a daughter, who'd grown up without my ever knowing of her existence. I figured it was better for me to deliver the news now rather than having Kelly's kids find out the truth years down the line from coming across a previously unknown relative's profile posted on a public DNA forum.

I'm sure it sometimes comes as a big surprise when kids finally realize that their parents are human after all. Kelly knew enough about my past that she didn't voice any real shock. Still, she said not a thing while I was telling her the story. In fact, she was so quiet that for a brief moment I thought maybe she'd hung up on me. I had to check my screen to make sure the call was still connected.

"So Alan and Athena are leaving for Texas on Wednesday morning?" Kelly asked when I finished.

"That's the plan."

"What about Naomi? Is she going to stay on in Seattle?"

"I don't know."

"Could I meet her?" Kelly asked.

"That would be up to the two of you," I said. "I can give her your contact information. That way if she wants to be in touch, she can. Is that okay?"

"That's fair," Kelly said. "Leaving the decision up to her is probably the best idea." There was a pause after that, before she added, "That could have been me, you know. I could easily have ended up like Naomi. When I ran away from Mom and Dave's place down in California, if Jeremy had been some other kind of guy, I could have found myself out on the streets and homeless with a baby on the way."

"Jeremy's a good guy," I said, "and I think maybe Petey Mayfield was trying to be a good guy, too."

"Well," Kelly finished, "let Naomi know that if she's interested in being in touch, I'm available."

"I will," I said.

In the background I heard the hubbub of Jeremy and the kids coming back into the house. We had finished just in time.

"But, Dad, are you all right?" Kelly asked.

It warmed my heart that my daughter was concerned about me. "It's been a bit of a shock," I admitted, "but I'm coping. Thanks for asking."

"And Mel?" Kelly asked. "How is she with all this?"

Mel and Kelly had formed a closer bond than I ever would have expected.

"She's okay with it, too," I told Kelly. "I'm lucky to have two very understanding women in my life—my daughter and my wife."

"You do know that I'm going to have to tell Jeremy and the kids about this."

"Of course," I said. "Trying to keep something like this a secret will end up exploding in all our faces later on. Tell them however much you need to, the sooner the better."

"Will do, Dad," she said. "I've gotta go. Love you."

"Thank you—" I began, but she was already gone.

Relieved beyond words that the first conversation was done and wanting to give my overheated ear some time to cool off, I went out into the other room, collected Lucy's leash, and took her down-stairs for a walk. Sam's grocery cart was parked at the top of the stairway leading down to the fire escape. He and Billy Bob were most likely already tucked in for the night, and I saw no reason to disturb them.

When Lucy and I came back upstairs, Alan and Athena were in the guest room with the TV set humming away. While Lucy went to join them, I collected my partially charged phone, went into the family room, and did the evening's next-hardest thing—telling my son about his previously unknown half sister.

The truth is, I had thought all along that Scotty would be cool about this that we could have a man-to-man conversation and both be fine on the other side of it. That didn't happen. We were most assuredly not fine.

"So you're telling me that the name you had me run the other day—Naomi Dale, the missing runaway who turns out to be both a druggie and a small-time crook—is actually my sister?" he demanded when I finished.

"Your half sister," I corrected.

"Surely you can't expect Cherisse and me to welcome her into the family with open arms and treat her fatherless baby like she's our baby's cousin!"

"Athena is your baby's cousin," I pointed out, "and the only reason she's fatherless is due to the fact that Petey Mayfield was murdered. I feel responsible for this child, Scotty—responsible for her and for her mother. I'd like you to be welcoming to them, but I can't force that issue. What you do or don't do on that score will be entirely up to you."

"Good," Scotty muttered, "let's keep it that way."

He hung up on me then, leaving me sitting there holding on to a silent phone and a jagged piece of broken heart.

CHAPTER 34

As I HEADED for my bedroom that night, the door to the guest room was ajar and the lights were on. When I peeked inside, everyone was sound asleep. Athena was in her portable crib, Lucy curled up in her bed under the crib, and Alan sat dozing away in the borrowed rocking chair. I guess his weeks of doing nighttime nursery duty had made him capable of sleeping almost anywhere.

He had told me over dinner that Helen, his mother-in-law, was in the process of arranging for a slightly used fourteen-by-seventy-foot mobile home to be delivered and installed on the back of her five-acre property outside Jasper. He and Athena would be able to stay in that once they came home to Texas. Living in a secondhand mobile home wouldn't have been my first choice of living arrangements, but it was a reasonable solution to several problems. It meant that Alan and Athena would have a rent-free place to live and someone who, if push came to shove, might be able to help out with child care.

When I climbed into bed, I couldn't sleep. You would have thought I'd be thinking about that difficult phone call with Scott, but I wasn't. His reaction was a done deal, and there was nothing I could do to fix it. Instead I thought about the wilds of Texas and what kinds of dangers might lurk out there in the wide-open spaces for a little kid venturing outside on her own—rattlesnakes certainly, coyotes perhaps, and maybe even the occasional boar. By the time I finally fell asleep, I had made up my mind and knew what I was going to do.

The next morning as the coffee machine rumbled to life in the kitchen, I got up, dressed, and then went pawing through my dresser drawer in search of a single piece of paper. When Lucy first came to live with us, I had encountered her original trainer, Colleen McDaniel of the Academy of Canine Behavior in Bothell, Washington. In explaining Lucy's Irish wolfhound origins, Colleen had pointed me in the direction of a poem by William Robert Spencer called "Beth Gelert." According to the story, a hunter returns home from the hunt only to discover his baby missing from a blood-soaked nursery. Assuming that his hound, Gelert, has killed the child, the angry father puts the dog to death. Later, when the baby is found safe, the father discovers the bloodied body of a dead wolf lurking inside the house. The dog, rather than killing the child, had been protecting him, but by then it was too late because the faithful dog was already dead.

I had read the poem online at the time. After Lucy saved Mel's life, I'd printed out a copy, intending to have it framed and hung on the wall. Somehow I never quite got around to the framing part. Dressed and with the poem in hand, I went in search of Alan Dale. He was in the family room, holding a sleeping Athena in his arms and staring out at the water. Naturally, Lucy was there, too.

"Here's something I'd like you to read," I told him, handing over the poem. Leaving him to it, I went to fetch my own coffee. When I came back, the paper was on the side table next to his chair and Alan was mopping his eyes.

"Sad story," he said.

"Irish wolfhound," I replied. "That's what Lucy is, and that's exactly what she'll be to Athena if you take her home to Texas with you. She'll be Athena's protector."

"Wait, take her home?" Alan echoed. "Are you serious?"

"Dead serious," I told him. "From the moment you brought Athena into the house in Bellingham, Lucy has been totally focused on that baby. In fact, she's barely had time to give me the time of day."

"But you love her," Alan objected. "Why would you give her up?"

"I do love her," I agreed, "but the original agreement was for Mel and me to foster Lucy until the right forever home came along. I happen to believe her forever home is in Jasper, Texas, with you and with Athena."

"You're sure?"

"I'm sure," I answered. "Once you leave here, I won't be able to help look after Athena, but I'll have the comfort of knowing I sent along someone else who will—if there's enough room in the car, that is."

"If there isn't enough room, I'll make room," Alan declared.

"Marge won't be happy about this, you know."

"Marge will cope," Alan told me with a grin. "She sounds fierce, but the other day, when she didn't know I was looking, I caught her slipping Lucy treats."

"No."

"I kid you not. We'll be fine, Beau. Growing up in central Oregon, I always had dogs around, and now Athena will, too."

And just like that, it was a done deal. Then, as if to put a punctuation mark on it, my phone rang with Rachel Seymour's name showing in caller ID. It turned out my caller wasn't Rachel—it was Naomi.

"Okay," she said after a moment's hesitation. "I'm in. What time do you want to pick me up on Monday?"

A layer of goose bumps swept up and down my legs. "How about ten or so?" I asked after I got my bearings. "The worst of the commuter traffic should be over by then, and we can stop off for lunch somewhere along the way."

"Okay," she said. "Sounds good."

"The permanent guardianship went through yesterday," I told her.

"I know. Andrea Hutchins stopped by to tell me in person. I thought that was nice of her."

So did I.

"That means your dad and Athena will head out for Texas tomorrow morning. Would you like to stop by and say good-bye? I could come pick you up this evening and bring you by here for a little while."

"No, thank you . . ." she began, and then paused uncertainly. "I know who you are, but what am I supposed to call you?"

"Call me Beau, Naomi," I said. "Beau will be just fine."

"Okay, Beau. Thanks for the offer, but it's better if I don't come by. It'll only make it harder for everyone, but if you don't mind, I do want to keep the booties."

"Good call," I said, "and if you change your mind about any of this, you have my number."

I turned to Alan and gave him a thumbs-up. "Naomi's agreed to go to treatment."

Alan was utterly agog. "Really?"

"That's what she says."

Then a bit of disappointment set in. "So even though she told me she was sorry the other night," Alan said, "she still doesn't want to come by to see us?"

"She said it'll only make it harder for everyone, and I have a feeling she's right."

And when it came time for me to say good-bye to Lucy, I was pretty sure I was going to feel the same way.

CHAPTER 35

A GLANCE AT my watch told me we were well within the twenty-four-hour time limit on the Moses Lake admission hold, so I called Ralph Ames back immediately and asked him to confirm it. Within fifteen minutes an e-mailed pre-admission form showed up, asking for all kinds of information on Naomi Dale. Much of it Alan was able to provide, while I would have been completely stumped. We filled out the paperwork together, except for the financial-responsibility end of it. That was mine to handle, and I did.

As long as we were dealing with financial matters, I called the funeral home to give them my credit card to pay for Petey's transport, cremation, and urn. I was told the cremation was done and the urn was ready to go. All I had to do was stop by and pick it up. That was a sticky topic, however. When Naomi left the Pike Street Mission on Monday morning to head for rehab in Moses Lake, she couldn't exactly drag a funeral urn along with her.

And it didn't seem appropriate for me to ask Alan to take it home to Texas either.

Alan and I spent the rest of the morning mapping out logistics for their trip back home to Jasper. The plan was for Marge and Athena to be in the back middle seat with Lucy riding shotgun up front with her bed and a duffel bag of dog necessities packed into the passenger footwell. With the Navigator's third seat folded down, there was still a good deal of room in the luggage area for them to take along everything else that needed transport.

While Alan set about packing and organizing, I went to work on the Internet searching for hotel accommodations, allowing for 450 to 500 miles between each stop. I soon discovered that budget-friendly hotels discriminate against large dogs. If Lucy had been under twenty-five pounds, she could have stayed almost anywhere. Clocking in at ninety-plus pounds meant she could stay at only the very best, so that's where I booked them in, going through the pain of sending along the paperwork for third-party payment of all expenses for Alan's room and for Marge's. It was not an inexpensive arrangement. If Alan had had any idea about the costs involved, he would have pitched a fit. The truth is, I probably could have flown them home on a private jet for about the same amount of money, but a jet wouldn't have been able to accommodate all the necessary baby gear, and it wouldn't have gotten the Navigator home to Texas either.

By late afternoon Alan and I had everything that wasn't needed overnight loaded into the vehicle, leaving just enough room in the back for the crib along with Alan's and Marge's day-to-day luggage. I gave Alan a folder containing printouts of all the hotel accommodations so he'd be able to feed addresses into his GPS as they went along. For dinner that night, we celebrated a job well done with a pizza delivery.

When I talked to Mel that evening and told her I was giving up Lucy, she was surprised and a bit sad to hear it. "I guess I should have seen that coming," she said.

"Are you sure you don't mind?" I asked.

"It was meant to be a fostering arrangement from the start, but it's entirely up to you," Mel said. "Lucy's been your dog far more than she's been mine."

"It's really up to Lucy," I replied. "The dog has worshipped Athena from the moment she laid eyes on that little kid, and Alan jumped at the idea of taking her home."

When I told her about Kelly's and Scott's two very different reactions to learning about Naomi, Mel was surprised and a bit sad to hear that as well. "I'd have thought it would have been the other way around," she said, "that Kelly would be upset and Scotty would be okay with it."

"That was my thinking, too," I said.

"So are you going to come back up to Bellingham after they leave tomorrow, or are you going to stay in Seattle?"

"There are still a few loose ends to tie up down here," I said, "but if you want me to come home . . ."

"No, you stay put," she said. "I'll come back down on Friday night. Our season tickets for the 5th Avenue are this weekend, remember? It's *Mamma Mia!*"

As a couple we'd had season tickets for the 5th Avenue for a number of years. Right this minute, however, that was one of the last places on earth that I wanted to revisit, but I knew I would. As Lady Macbeth would say, I'd "screw my courage to the sticking place" and go see frigging *Mamma Mia!*

We were still on the phone when call waiting buzzed. "It's Lucinda," I told Mel after checking the screen. "I'll take this and call you back."

"We have a bingo!" Lucinda announced when I switched over to the other line. "We've got a jail-house snitch whose cellmate in the Yakima County Jail was bragging about how much money he'd collected for getting rid of a blood-spattered Lexus he just happened to steal from the parking lot of the Cascade Crest Casino in the early morning hours of October thirty-first. How do you like them apples?"

Petey Mayfield's homicide had gone from dead cold to white hot in a matter of hours rather than months or years.

"Amazing!" I said. "Will the car thief testify to that effect?"

"Maybe," she said. "I believe the county attorney is going to offer him a plea deal—suspended sentence on the automobile-theft charge and accomplice after the fact to the homicide on the condition that he testify against Suzanne in court. In the meantime Suzanne has been transferred from the tribal jail to our county lockup on suspicion of homicide. If the snitch accepts his plea deal, she'll be arraigned on homicide charges in the morning."

"Let's hear it for plea deals, then," I said, and believe me I meant it.

"And I have even more good news."

"What's that?"

"Dr. Blaine spoke to the King County M.E. and explained that it had come to his attention that perhaps his designation of natural causes in regard to Agnes Mayfield's death had been in error. He has officially changed the manner of death to 'undetermined.' That means Dr. Roz can request a court order authorizing the exhumation of Agnes's remains to allow her to perform an autopsy."

"Thank God for small blessings," I breathed.

"Yes indeed!" Lucinda agreed.

"Sounds like you've put in a good day's work."

"And I'm not done yet," she told me.

I could tell that Lucinda's adrenaline rush had kicked in, and I knew the feeling well. If you're a homicide cop, once a case starts coming together, hours on the clock don't matter. The clock doesn't matter. Sleep doesn't matter. Food doesn't matter. Family doesn't matter. It's one of the reasons they say that homicide is a young man's game—or in this case a young woman's.

"Where to next?" I asked.

"The jail in Ellensburg," Lucinda answered. "I'm going to stick Suzanne Nishikawa in an interview room and see if I can bluff a bluffer."

"What do you mean?"

"Greg returned to her house with that warrant and removed the funeral urn. According to the label on the bottom, it contains Danielle Nishikawa's cremated remains. I'm going to ask Suzanne if she can explain why ethylene glycol crystals were found scattered in among her mother's ashes."

"Is that even possible?" I asked.

"Probably not," Lucinda said with a laugh, "but I'm betting she doesn't know that. Talk to you tomorrow."

Lucinda had signed off in such a hurry that I hadn't had a chance to tell her any of my news, but that was fine. My news could wait. Nailing Suzanne's feet to the ground was a much bigger deal and far more important.

I called Mel and passed along what Lucinda had told me. When I got off the phone with Mel, I was feeling great—absolutely great. For the first time in a long, long time, I felt like having a drink, a celebratory drink—only one, of course. That's the problem with drunks—they drink when they're happy, they drink when they're sad, they drink when they're neither, and the end result is always the same. Thankfully, I understood the inherent dangers in that siren's call only too well and was smart enough to do something about it. I pulled on a jacket and stopped by the guest room long enough to tell Alan I was going out.

"Are you taking Lucy for a walk?" he asked.

"Nope," I said. "I'll do that later, when I get back."

I went down to P-1, let myself out through the garage entrance, and made my way across Clay. This time around I avoided the church's dog-walking area and went inside. A few minutes later, I was downstairs in the social hall seated in a circle of folding chairs. I had arrived in time so I was there when the meeting started.

"Hello," I said, when it came my turn to speak. "My name is Beau. I'm an alcoholic."

CHAPTER 36

THE MEETING WORKED. I didn't have that celebratory drink of booze that would quite naturally have led to many more. I went home and went to bed, having made it through yet another day, one day at a time, but it had been a very close call. There'd been so much going on in my life the past week that I had very nearly slipped.

I might not have had any booze that evening, but I did have coffee—way too much coffee. When I went to bed that night, I was wide awake and still on as much of a high as Lucinda had been earlier. Somewhere in the wee hours of that mostly sleepless night, I had a brainstorm. If Dr. Roz was going to exhume Agnes Mayfield's body, that meant that the poor woman's grave site would have to be dug up in order to remove the coffin. Wouldn't it be a good idea for Petey's remains to share the sacred ground where the woman who'd raised him was also buried? Wouldn't he be better off in the Mayfield family plot in West Seattle's Pioneer Cemetery, rather than being rolled around the streets in a tarp-covered grocery cart?

By seven the next morning, far earlier than I was ready, the coffee machine came online in the kitchen. I started to grab a robe, but when I heard Marge's voice coming from the other room, I went to the trouble of getting dressed before venturing out of my room. Alan was at the stove frying eggs. Marge was buttering toast.

"Over easy?" Alan asked.

"Please."

"We want to be on our way by around eight," he said. "The first stop is at the Ashland Springs Hotel, and that's a long way down I-5."

After breakfast, while Marge was cleaning up, Alan filled Athena's crib with what would be their nightly in-and-out luggage and rolled the crib out the door on its way to P-4. Once the crib disappeared, Lucy, seeming to sense that something was up, began pacing anxiously back and forth in the kitchen.

"Come on, girl," I told her at last, grabbing for her leash. "Let's you and I take one last walk before you go."

We rode all the way down to P-4, where I told Alan what was up. "I'll bring her back here as soon as we finish."

"Sounds good," he told me.

Lucy and I went out. Despite Alan's plan to the contrary, it was now after eight. Sam Shelton and Billy Bob were already up and out, and that was just as well. I didn't much like the idea of someone seeing me walking my dog, talking to her a blue streak and crying like a baby.

"You're going to love Texas," I explained to her when her business was done. "You'll have the run of five acres instead of having to be walked on sidewalks on a leash. I'm sending along some of your Frisbees, and I've told Alan how much you like to chase them. I need you to look out for Athena, Lucy—for Athena and Alan and Helen Gibbons, too. You got that, Lucy girl?"

She looked up at me then, thumping her long tail against my leg, probably because she had heard her name and knew I was talking to her. I hoped she understood how much I cared about her and how much I was going to miss her. Leaning down, I buried my face in the long, silky hair of her ears and used that to dry my tears.

"Let's go, girl," I said, straightening up. "Off you go to your new life."

We went inside. Down on the P-4 level, Alan handed over the pocketful of keys and clickers he had used to get in and out of the garage and our condo. Before Marge climbed inside and fastened her seat belt, I gave her a hug and told her to give me a call as soon as she was ready to book her flight home.

"Don't forget to return Mrs. Bailey's rocking chair," she admonished me.

"Thanks for the reminder," I said. "I won't forget."

I went around to the far side of the car and leaned in to give Athena Dale a kiss, my very first one, and for all I knew, maybe my last—a grandfather's kiss meant to say both hello and good-bye. Only then did I turn my attention to Lucy. She was sitting proudly upright on the passenger seat as though she'd finally found her perfect place and that was where she'd always been meant to ride. I couldn't cry about that. In fact, I laughed aloud. "You doofus," I said.

When it came time to say good-bye to Alan Dale, we hugged. "Thank you," he whispered in my ear. "Thank you for everything."

"And thank you," I said, "for giving me the rest of my family."

I followed them up to P-1 and watched as they drove out of the entrance and turned right onto Clay. I'm glad I didn't run into anyone either on P-1 or in the elevator, because it turns out that once again I was mopping away tears.

Back upstairs in a unit that was suddenly far too quiet and far too empty, I made another cup of coffee and called Dr. Roz. "Do you have the court order on Agnes Mayfield's exhumation?" I asked.

"It's a formality at this point," she said. "Getting one won't be a problem. Why?"

"Do you know when you'll do the autopsy?"

"As soon as possible, I would imagine. Today if we can get it to work, or tomorrow at the latest."

"Her grandson's remains have been cremated," I told her. "I'm wondering if his urn could go into the grave with her when you rebury Agnes's coffin."

"It's no skin off my nose," Dr. Roz said. "I suppose you'll need to speak to the next of kin about that. I've notified the daughter about the exhumation, and I can tell you she's none too happy about it."

"In this case I don't think it's any of Lenora Harrison's business. I'm going to check with Petey's girlfriend and the mother of his child."

I left Belltown Terrace and drove straight to Pioneer Square. At the Pike Street Mission, Rachel Seymour's office door was closed with a Do Not Disturb sign firmly in place on the outside. One of Rachel's assistants came to ask what I needed. When I told her I was looking for Naomi Dale, the assistant directed me to wait in the chapel while she went to fetch Naomi.

"Are they gone?" Naomi asked first thing when she appeared in the chapel a few minutes later.

I nodded. "They headed out a little over an hour ago. Lucy went with them."

"Your dog?"

"I thought she was my dog," I said, "and she was, right up until she met Athena, but then something magic happened and Lucy transformed herself into Athena's dog. I believe it was love at first sight."

Naomi put her hand over her mouth. "Thank you," she whispered.

"I'm here about something else. I was just speaking to the King County medical examiner. It turns out Agnes Mayfield might have been murdered. They'll be exhuming her remains to perform an autopsy. I've had a call from the funeral home. Petey's urn is ready to be picked up. I know you're not interested in having any kind of a funeral service, but when Agnes's remains are reburied, would you like Petey's urn to be placed in the same grave?"

"I'd like that," Naomi Dale said after a brief pause. "I'd like that a lot, and I think Petey would, too."

While I was waiting in the chapel, I'd found a scrap of paper and written Kelly's contact information on it. "Here," I said, placing it in her hand.

"What's this?" she asked.

"My daughter's info," I said. "If you're interested in speaking to Kelly, you're welcome to give her a call."

"So you told her?" she asked.

"I told both Kelly and my son."

"I take it Scotty's not eager to be in touch?"

"Not so much," I admitted.

"Okay," she said pocketing the paper. "Thanks."

I went outside into bright, early-spring sunshine. There was a BofA branch on the corner, so I stopped in long enough to get an envelope of cash to leave with Bob for Sam to collect his reward piecemeal and as needed. Then, not wanting to return to the empty condo, I made instead for West Seattle. I had told Hilda Tanner that I would keep her in the loop. Considering how much of a help she'd been, I figured I owed her. Not surprisingly, I found her outside taking a walk, clumping along after her walker.

"Where's your dog?" she asked when I stopped the car alongside her and got out.

"Lucy's on her way to Texas with her new owners," I answered.

"You just gave her away?"

"My wife and I were temporarily fostering her," I explained. "Now she's headed to her forever home, with Alan Dale and Athena. The dog really loves that kid."

Hilda gave me a disparaging look and shook her head. "Doesn't matter," she insisted. "I could never give away a single one of my kitties."

She invited me into the house. We went inside, where I told her what had happened and what was still happening, including the possibility that her friend's body was being exhumed to determine whether Agnes Mayfield was the victim of a homicide. She shed a tear over that.

"At least now her friends will know where she is," Hilda said. "We can go there and pay our respects."

I explained how her help had led to Petey's remains and how finding those had led to his alleged killer, Suzanne Nishikawa, who was now under arrest on suspicion of homicide.

"The woman from Highline Development?" Hilda asked.

"One and the same."

"And was Lenora in on all this? Was she responsible for both Petey's death and Agnes's?"

"It's too soon to tell," I told her. "The investigation is ongoing."

"I see," she said.

"There's one more thing I need to tell you," I said. "I gave the booties to Naomi. She wanted me to tell you thank you."

"She's most welcome," Hilda said. "I hope she and Athena get a lot of use out of them."

I didn't disabuse her of that notion. There was no need.

CHAPTER 37

It was a little past noon when I stopped by the funeral home on Queen Anne, paid the bill, and collected Petey Mayfield's cremains. Alan Dale had picked out a brass urn, which, when I lifted it, was surprisingly heavy. It made me glad that Naomi had agreed to the idea of placing Petey's urn in the same grave with his grandmother. If I'd done nothing else, at least I had divested Naomi of the necessity of carrying that sad burden along with her wherever she went. Outside, I opened the trunk of the S550 and secured the urn with the netting designed to keep groceries from spilling. I didn't want Petey's ashes to end up scattered all over my trunk, even though the lid on the urn seemed to be properly attached.

As I left the funeral home, I was still at loose ends, but there was one more stop I needed to make. Instead of heading back downtown to Belltown Terrace, I turned north on Highway 99 and headed for Phinney Ridge. The GPS told me that Holman

House was located on Sycamore Avenue Northwest, just off NW 65th Street. It was a pleasant enough single-story brick building surrounded by trees that were just now sprouting leaves.

At the registration desk, thanks to Corky's granddaughter, Linda Collins, I was able to ask for the man by his real name, Conrad, rather than by his Seattle PD handle. I was directed down the hallway to Room 118, where a gaunt old man I barely recognized was sitting up on a raised hospital bed while an elderly woman, seated next to his bed, patiently fed him by hand. Since she wasn't wearing a uniform, I assumed this had to be Corky's wife rather than a nurse. I knew I'd met his wife at the retirement party, but for the life of me I couldn't remember her name.

As soon as I appeared in the doorway, Corky's expression brightened. "Spencer!" he exclaimed delightedly. "It's so good to see you. Are you here to go to the game?"

I knew for sure that I wasn't Spencer, and I had no idea what game he was talking about. Turning in her chair, the woman sat with a loaded spoon in her hand. "Spencer was his younger brother," she explained. "He's been dead for forty years. I'm Melinda, Conrad's wife, but today he thinks I'm his mother. Who are you?"

"J. P. Beaumont," I said. "Corky and I used to work together at Seattle PD." There was no sign of recognition from Corky, but Melinda smiled and nodded.

"Of course you did," she said. "Nobody but the guys at the cop shop ever called him Corky."

When she turned back to her husband, he swatted the loaded spoon away with enough force that the food flew off in every direction.

"No more food," he objected, in a sudden state of agitation. "We need to leave right now, or we'll be late for the first inning."

"Don't worry, Conrad," she told him soothingly. "We'll be sure to get you and Spencer to the game in plenty of time. You should rest for a little while. You won't be late. I promise."

He seemed to take her at her word. She adjusted the controls until the bed was flattened and then she fluffed his pillow. Within seconds Corky was seemingly fast asleep, leaving Melinda to pluck scattered particles of food off his bedding. I wanted to ask a dozen questions. How long had he been like this? How long would it go on?

Melinda seemed to understand my unasked questions. "He has a DNR," she said, pointing to the bright red DO NOT RESUSCITATE sign posted over to Corky's bed. "When he stops eating, it'll be over. For now he's comfortable and relatively stable."

"I'm so sorry," I said. "I only just heard about him last week, from Linda. I'm a private investigator now. Your granddaughter was helping me collect some paperwork I needed for one of my cases, and she recognized my name."

"I'm not surprised," Melinda said. "Conrad used to talk about you often. Seems like the two of you spent a lot of time hanging around the Doghouse."

"Guilty as charged," I admitted.

"Linda's a great girl," Melinda said. "She usually stops by of an evening to sit with him after I go home. It's too bad her father, my son, can't see beyond the pink hair, the studs, and the tattoos."

Knowing I wasn't the only person in the room dealing with generational challenges should have made me feel better. It didn't.

"Linda tells me that you're here every day."

Melinda nodded. "I come over each morning in time to feed him his lunch. I usually stay until suppertime or until it gets dark, whichever comes first."

"Every day?" I asked.

She nodded again. "Every day."

"Even though he doesn't know who you are?"

Melinda smiled. "I know who I am," she said, "and that's what counts."

There are all kinds of kick-ass women on TV these days, young hotshot women who duke it out with the best of them, jujitsuing their way through countless hulking bad guys and mowing them down, seemingly with the greatest of ease. In that moment in Corky Collins's room at Holman House, I realized that in meeting Melinda Collins I had come into the presence of something far greater. It was a humbling experience.

"How do you do it?" I asked.

"Patience," Melinda said, with a weary smile, "patience and acceptance."

Those were exactly the words I needed to hear right then—patience and acceptance. And that was exactly what I needed to be—patient and accepting. There was no point in going back to the condo and sitting around there fretting about what would or wouldn't happen. My role in the Naomi Dale/Petey Mayfield missing-persons case was over. What I really need to do was drive home to Bellingham and spend some time with my wife, with Mel. When I came out of Holman House half an hour later, I turned left on 65th, heading for northbound I-5 and home.

It was good to be out of the city. Driving along, there was still a hurt in my heart over the way things had ended with Scotty, but there was nothing to be done about that right now. All I had to go on were Melinda Collins's powerful words of wisdom.

Mel was both surprised and glad to have me home. We missed Lucy's boisterous presence in the house, but it was time for us to adjust to a new normal. We were having our customary dinner— peanut butter and jelly sandwiches—when Alan called to say that they were safely arrived in Ashland. They had checked in to the hotel. Alan was downstairs ordering dinner while Marge looked after Athena and Lucy upstairs.

"You pulled off a whole set of miracles," Mel observed once the call ended. "Petey's homicide is solved, Athena is in the best possible hands, and Naomi's on her way to rehab."

"No guarantee that she'll make it," I said. "Treatment doesn't necessarily take for everybody."

"I have a good feeling about this," Mel said. "I think she and Petey were both getting better when she lost him. In a way you've given him back to her. And by working things out between her and Alan, you may have ended up giving her a path back to Athena as well."

"I hope so," I said, but all the while I was wondering if I'd be able to find my own way back to my son.

I spent the next two days monitoring Alan and Marge's slow progress across the country and rearranging some financial details. That included setting up an appointment with my estate-planning adviser, Ralph Ames's designated successor. I directed him to draw up the same kind of trust for Athena that I'd established for the other grandkids, knowing as I did so that I would repeat the same process again as soon as Jonas Pierre Beaumont appeared on the scene.

Lucinda called me on Thursday afternoon. The guy who had disappeared Suzanne's Lexus, one Roberto Joaquin Perez, had accepted the plea deal and agreed to testify against Suzanne, who was being held without bond on a charge of first-degree homicide in the death of Petey Mayfield.

"Any progress on the other two cases?" I asked.

"Not so far."

Dr. Roz phoned about one thirty on Friday afternoon. "You called it," she said. "Autopsy is done, and ethylene glycol crystals were definitely present," she said. "Agnes Mayfield was murdered. I believe Detective Stevenson is bringing Lenora Mayfield in for questioning as we speak."

"When will you rebury the body?" I asked.

"We'll be transporting Agnes's remains back to the cemetery later this afternoon. According to the guy I talked to, they're overbooked for tomorrow, and the earliest Agnes's coffin can go back in the ground will be tomorrow afternoon."

"Thank you," I said. "I'll check with Naomi and see if she wants to be there."

I called the cemetery myself and got the guy

pinned down to a 1:00 P.M. time slot. Then I called the Pike Street Mission and spoke to Naomi.

"Yes," she told me. "I'd like to be there."

"Okay," I said. "I'll pick you up at twelve fifteen."

Mel and I drove into town in two vehicles that evening, so we'd be able to go our separate ways come Sunday and Monday. I left early enough so I had a chance to do a few housekeeping chores before she got there. I started some laundry, put away the bed in the guest room, and cleared the decks in Mel's bathroom so she'd be able to access the countertops. By keeping busy enough, I almost, but not quite, forgot about missing Lucy.

When Mel showed up that evening, we walked over to El Gaucho for a late dinner. It was a quiet meal, just the two of us.

"Would you like me to go with you and Naomi to the cemetery tomorrow?" Mel asked.

"Yes," I said at once. "I'd like to have the backup."

A little after noon on a cold and drizzly Saturday, Mel and I walked Naomi Dale across the grass at West Seattle's Pioneer Cemetery. Mel held on to Naomi's arm, offering her support while I lugged Petey's increasingly heavy urn. I had asked for directions to the grave site, but I didn't really need one. The front-end loader was already parked in one corner of the cemetery. It was poised on the edge of the grave, with the operator waiting for us.

"Coffin's already in the ground," he said.

He waved us over. "Understand you've got something you want to add?"

I was happy to turn my burden over to him. Doffing his cap, he placed the urn inside the bucket tool on the loader. "Anyone want to say a few words?" he asked.

Tears were running down Naomi's cheeks, but she nodded. "I want to say good-bye," she said.

Walking over to the graveside, she reached into her pocket, pulled out Hilda's booties, and tossed them into the bucket next to the urn. "Good-bye, Petey," she said. "I love you, and I know now that you didn't mean to leave us."

The operator lowered the bucket, then waited long enough for us to walk away before he began moving the dirt from the pile next to the grave back into it.

I for one was glad it was raining. I had shed more tears in the last couple of days than I'd done in a lifetime, and I was glad to have some rain to give me cover.

When curtain time came at the 5th Avenue that evening, I had managed to talk myself down out of my tree. The ghost of Jasmine Day had finally been put to rest, and when the audience started singing along with all those ABBA songs, so did I. Not only that, I enjoyed it.

CHAPTER 38

DETECTIVE STEVENSON CALLED late on Sunday afternoon. "Lenora crumpled like a house of cards," he told me. "Even with Medicare and Social Security, she had realized that keeping Agnes in Memory Manor was taking too big a bite out of her inheritance. Suzanne had convinced her that it would be easy to fix that, with no questions asked. Then she pitched in and helped Lenora do the job."

"Whoa!" I said. "What about Danielle, then? Did Suzanne's mother die the same way?"

"Good question, but with no autopsy it can't be proved, but here's a new wrinkle. Several years ago, Suzanne's father died shortly after being hospitalized for a heart attack. He died while under a doctor's care, so . . ."

"So there was no autopsy," I finished.

"You got it," Stevenson agreed. "A death with no autopsy followed by almost immediate cremation."

"So it's possible Suzanne was responsible for the deaths of both of her parents?" I asked.

"Possible though not provable, but Lenora has agreed to testify against Suzanne in Agnes's death."

"What about Petey?" I asked. "Were they both involved in what happened to him? There were all those calls from Suzanne to Lenora the night Petey died."

"According to what Suzanne told Lenora, Petey showed up at Highline Development that afternoon, raising hell and saying that Agnes never would have sold the lots without letting him know. Threatened with exposure, Suzanne took care of the situation, but she was evidently under the mistaken impression that Lenora was the one who'd told Petey about what was going on. So we've got Lenora on tap for one count of murder and Suzanne for two. Lenora will plead guilty to second-degree. Suzanne will likely plead not guilty and go on trial for first-degree murder."

"Let's hope she doesn't get away with it," I said. "Does Lucinda know?"

"Hell yes, she drove over and sat in on the interview."

Yes, I thought. *Homicide is definitely a young people's game.*

"Good work, Greg," I said. "The two of you make a great team."

CHAPTER 39

I PICKED NAOMI up at ten on the dot on Monday morning. She was standing outside waiting for me when I drove up to the mission. Next to her feet was a duffel bag packed with whatever clothing the clothes bank had been able to provide. The duffel itself was a big improvement over her paper grocery bag, and I had no doubt that Petey's hairbrush was nestled safely inside.

"Are you ready for this?" I asked, rolling down the window.

"I hope so," she said.

For a long part of the trip, we didn't say much. Then, about the time we started up Snoqualmie Pass, the silence was broken. "You know all about where I came from," she said. "What about you?"

So I told her. I probably said way more than she wanted to know. I talked about growing up in Seattle in the aftermath of World War II as the son of an unmarried woman who, despite her parents' disapproval, had refused to give up her out-of-wedlock baby after her fiancé died in a motorcycle accident. I told her how my last name, Beaumont, had come from the Texas town where my father had grown up rather than from his last name.

"I guess girls being in trouble is a long-standing family tradition," Naomi observed.

I laughed about that. "It's true," I admitted, wondering if knowing those stories would make Naomi more or less interested in being a part of her own daughter's life.

I told Naomi about how my drinking had caused Karen's and my divorce and how a trip to Ironwood Ranch had finally gotten me to sober up. I also told her that getting sober wasn't a one-and-done proposition and that I'd come close to having a slip myself that very week.

"Because of me?" she asked. "Were you upset because you found out about me?"

"No," I said, "I was happy—giddy, almost—because we'd succeeded in nailing Petey's killer. People don't fall off the wagon just because bad things happen. Sometimes they go off the rails when good things happen."

That comment elicited no response.

About that time we pulled in to the parking lot of the Red Horse Diner in Ellensburg, dodging all their vintage automotive kitsch as we did so. Much to my surprise, there was a new-to-me cannabis shop right next to where I'd parked. I was pretty sure that hadn't been there the last time I stopped by. I noticed it and wondered if Naomi had.

"Don't worry," she told me as we hurried toward

the diner's entrance. "Marijuana has never been my thing. I always go for the harder stuff."

Great, I thought.

Inside, we ordered burgers, ate same, and got back on the road. By the time we arrived at the front gate of the Haven in Moses Lake, I was completely talked out, but I felt I owed her that much—as complete a history of my side of the family as I could provide. When I pulled up in the drop-off zone in front of the building, she hesitated before opening the door.

"Do you want me to walk you inside?" I asked.

"No," she said. "I need to do this myself. Thank you for driving me all this way, and for telling me who you are, Beau. It's what I needed to hear today." She sounded hopeful and scared. So was I.

I watched her heave her duffel bag out of the backseat, heft it, and head inside.

"Go with God," I heard myself saying under my breath.

I filled up the gas tank in Ellensburg and then continued west. I felt completely wrung out, as though I'd been through some grueling, mind-numbing test. I was coming up on the far side of Snoqualmie Pass when my phone rang with Scotty's photo visible on the caller ID's screen on my dashboard.

"Hello, Dad," he said. "How's it going?"

He'd called me "Dad" rather than his customary "Pop." So what was I supposed to tell him? Was it time for more BS or time to be real? I went for the latter. "I'm on my way back from Moses Lake," I said. "I just dropped Naomi off at a rehab place called the Haven."

"Is she going to be all right?" he asked.

That was unexpected. "I don't know," I said. "Sometimes rehab takes, sometimes it doesn't."

There was a long pause in the conversation. I was tempted to fill it but didn't.

"I'm calling to apologize," Scotty said. "I never should have gone off on you the way I did. Cherisse has been all over me about it—told me I was acting like a complete jerk."

"You'd just been given a whole lot of news you didn't expect. I think you get a pass—at least you get one from me."

"Good-o, Pop," he said. "Love you. I've got to get back to work."

When the phone call ended, I realized that my sins as a father had all been forgiven. I spent the rest of the trip, all the way home to Bellingham, thinking about Melinda Collins and her watchwords—patience and acceptance.

She was right about those—absolutely right!

Next up for J. A. Jance fans . . .

Turn the page for a sneak peek at Joanna Brady's latest riveting investigation, which involves her college-age daughter, who is caught up in a missing person case—forcing Joanna to be both mother and sheriff in a race against time.

Sheriff Joanna Brady's daughter, Jennifer—a sophomore at Northern Arizona University—is cast into the role of big sister for a new roommate, Beth Rankin, a brilliant but inexperienced freshman who was homeschooled and who is now getting her first taste of both freedom and unfettered internet access. When Jenny brings Beth home for a school holiday, her mother's life is already in turmoil due to fallout from an officer-involved shooting that has placed the lives of two young children in jeopardy, leaving Joanna ill prepared to deal with a fragile young houseguest who has suddenly gone . . .

MISSING AND ENDANGERED

Coming soon in hardcover
From William Morrow

PROLOGUE

LATE ON MONDAY afternoon, the first week in December, Sheriff Joanna Brady sat at her desk, mired in paperwork. She was laying out the details of a request for a budget increase for the next fiscal year, something that had to be in the hands of the county supervisors the day before Friday morning's weekly meeting. At this point, Joanna's department was grossly understaffed, and only an increase in the bottom line would allow her to hire more sworn officers. To her anguish, right this minute, Joanna's heart wasn't in it.

When her cell phone rang with her daughter's photo showing on the screen, Joanna welcomed the interruption. "Hey," Joanna said, more cheerily than she would have thought possible. "How's it going?"

"It's snowing," Jenny said, not sounding happy about it. She was in her second year at Northern Arizona University in Flagstaff where she had quickly run out of patience with Flag's winter barrages of snowfall. That had happened during the second blizzard of her freshman year, and now the *Farmer's Almanac* was claiming that this would be a record-breaking year in terms of snowfall. "We'll probably have a foot here by morning," she added gloomily.

Joanna had to bite her tongue to keep from mentioning that Jenny could have chosen to go to school in Tucson where it was much warmer, but the offer of a scholarship and a spot on NAU's rodeo team had carried the day as far as Jenny was concerned.

"How are things with you?" Jenny asked.

"Fine," Joanna replied, but that was an outright lie, because things definitely weren't fine, not even close. As Jenny rattled on about her day and about the latest rivalries on the rodeo team, her mother's mind wandered back to a conversation with Ernie Carpenter earlier that afternoon.

Ernie, who had been Joanna's lead investigator for as long as she'd been sheriff, had let himself into her office unannounced and then closed the door behind him before dropping into one of her visitor's chairs.

"It's back," he said.

Joanna struggled for several long moments, trying to come to terms with exactly what "it" was, but then, observing his somber demeanor, she got his drift.

"The cancer?" she asked.

He nodded.

Years before, Ernie had been treated for prostate cancer, choosing to go the radiation seeds route. Since then he'd been in remission long enough that Joanna had almost forgotten about it, but now she realized he had lost some weight recently and was looking a bit worn.

"It's metastasized," he added. "It's in my lymph nodes and my liver."

"I'm so sorry," Joanna murmured, "so very sorry. Does anyone else know?"

"Only Rose," he said. "I'm not ready for the guys around here to start treating me like the cancer guy with one foot in the grave, even if it's true."

Joanna couldn't help half smiling at that. When it came to gallows humor, Ernie Carpenter had always been at the top of the class.

"So here's the deal," Ernie continued. "I'm letting you know that I'm pulling the plug as of January 1. Rosie and I have talked it over. The seeds gave me a pretty good run, but it looks like that's come to an end. I'm not going to put myself though some kind of god-awful treatment that would maybe give me a few more months at best. That's not fair to me, and it's sure as hell not fair to Rose. I'm going to take my retirement, and the two of us will hit the road. We'll travel while I can travel, and when I can't do that anymore, we'll come home."

He left off there. The recurrence was bad enough news, but the idea that Ernie planned to forego any additional treatment was stunning. Joanna's first instinct was to ask, "Are you sure?" But the set of Ernie's jaw made her stifle. Yes, he was sure. He and Rose were sure. They had obviously reached this conclusion together, and it was nobody else's business.

"How can I help?" Joanna asked quickly. "What can I do?"

"Keep this under your hat for one thing," he replied. "You find sympathy in the dictionary between shit and syphilis, and I'm not interested in sympathy. I wanted to give you a heads up in advance so you can start getting your ducks in a row, but I don't want a lot of hoopla about this. I'll tell Jaime, of course. He's my partner, and I owe it to him, but that's it. I'm not telling anyone else."

Joanna thought about that before speaking up. "I'll give you a week," she said.

Ernie seemed taken aback. "I beg your pardon?"

"You have until a week from today to tell Jaime whatever you decide to tell him about why you're retiring. You can let him know about the cancer or not, that's entirely up to you, but after Monday all bets are off. If you don't want to be labeled cancer boy on your way out the door, you'd better put on your big boy underwear and announce your upcoming retirement because there's no way in hell I'm letting you leave this department without a retirement party, and that will need to be scheduled ASAP. Got it?"

Sitting there at her desk, she met Ernie's gaze and held it. He was the one who blinked first.

"Yes, ma'am," he said finally. "I hear you loud and clear." Ernie had stood up to leave, but then he had paused in the doorway and added, "By the way, I'll be using up some of my vacation time and taking tomorrow off. Rose and I are going to Phoenix to pick up the RV, and we'll be spending the night."

"Good-o," Joanna said with a wave. "Travel safe."

When the door closed behind him, Joanna was left alone with the word "RV" echoing in her heart.

When her mother and stepfather—Eleanor and George Winfield— had hit retirement age, they too had dived into the RV life, expecting to spend their "golden years" cruising the USofA. Unfortunately, that plan had been cut short. A hail of bullets fired by a disgruntled teenager from a highway overpass had forever ended George and Eleanor's travels together. Joanna dreaded the idea that Rosie and Ernie's traveling days, too, would end in a different but equally tragic way. When she had turned back to her report, it's no wonder she hadn't been up to the task.

"Well, Mom?" Jenny's exasperated voice broke into Joanna's reverie. "Have you heard a word I said?"

"Sorry," Joanna replied. "Something's going on, and I was distracted. What did you say?"

"I was asking if you and Dad would mind if I brought someone home for Christmas vacation."

The fact that Jenny routinely called her stepfather, Butch Dixon, Dad was something that never failed to gladden Joanna's heart. But Jenny was planning on bringing someone home for Christmas? Who? A boyfriend maybe? Jenny had friends who were boys— most notably Nick Saunders, the kid from St. George, Utah, who was also on the NAU rodeo team. He and Jenny boarded their horses at the same place in Flag, and sometimes looked after one another's mounts when one or the other of them was out of town. Joanna knew the two were good friends, but as far as there being any romantic links between them? There had been zero mention of that. So if this was someone else, who was he and what were his intentions?

"Who is he?" Joanna asked.

Jenny laughed aloud. "It's not a he, Mom," she said. "It's a she—Beth, my roommate. That's her name, remember—Beth Rankin."

Jenny's reply sent Joanna spinning down yet another mental rabbit hole. Halfway through her sophomore year, this was the first time Jenny had suggested bringing one of her college friends home for a visit. But having someone stay over for several days might be problematic. Family members were all used to the inconveniences of having a one-year-old in the house. A college student might not be up for that. And then there was the challenge of sleeping arrangements.

"With the guest room changed into a nursery . . ." Joanna began.

"Don't worry, Mom," Jenny put in quickly. "I'll bunk on the sofa in the living room. Beth had a huge blow up with her folks over Thanksgiving, and she isn't planning on going home. The idea of having her stuck on campus all during our winter break is just . . ."

"Of course she can come," Joanna said quickly. "Didn't you tell me she's an only child?"

"Definitely," Jenny returned, "with an over-the-top helicopter mom."

"You might want to warn her in advance that a household with a one-year-old and a seven-year-old may be a little more than she bargained for."

"I'll pass that along," Jenny said. "But maybe being around Sage will do the same thing for Beth that it did for me."

"What's that?"

"Being around a baby made it blazingly clear that I'm nowhere near ready to have a baby," Jenny answered. "Sort of like making the case for birth control without anyone having to say a word."

It was Joanna's turn to laugh. "In other words, birth control by remote control."

"You've got it."

"Well, she's more than welcome," Joanna added. "And thank you."

"Thank you for what?"

"For being the kind of daughter you are," Joanna said, "and for reminding me of what the season for giving is all about."

"You're welcome," Jenny said, "but now that I've asked you, I'm going to call Dad and make sure my bringing home company is okay with him, too."

"Good idea," Joanna said. "No, make that an excellent idea, but I can't imagine he'll say no."

"I doubt it, too, but I'll call him anyway. I don't want him to think we're ganging up on him."

"Okay," Joanna said, "bye."

When the call ended, Joanna felt as though she'd just been run through an emotional spin cycle. Glancing at her watch, she was surprised to see that it was already after five. That meant that her secretary, Kristin Gregovich, had most likely already bailed. Just to be sure, Joanna walked over to the door Ernie had closed when he left. Sure enough, the chair behind Kristin's desk was empty, as was the dog bed next to it where Spike, the department's recently medically retired K-9, spent his days.

Kristin happened to be married to Terry, Joanna's K-9 officer. During a shoot-out nearly a year earlier, Spike had taken a bullet that had been intended for Joanna and very nearly died as a result. Spike's extensive injuries had made his returning to active duty impossible. When his replacement, a newly trained pit bull named Mojo, appeared on the scene, Spike had been disconsolate each morning to see Mojo ride off in Terry's patrol vehicle each morning when it was time to go to work. Kristin had taken pity on the grieving dog. Rather than leaving him at home alone, she had asked Joanna if she could bring Spike along with her. These days, Spike spent his time dozing on a dog bed beside Kristin's desk while Mojo went out on patrol.

With the outer office completely deserted, Joanna didn't linger. "Okay," she said to the empty room. "Since everyone else has called it quits for the day, I guess I'll do the same."

She went back into the office long enough to gather up her laptop and stuff it into her briefcase. Then, with her phone in one hand and the strap of her purse slung over her shoulder, she headed home, leaving through the private door that led directly to her reserved parking place just outside.

Joanna had a short commute—eight minutes door-to-door—from the Cochise County Justice Center to her home on High Lonesome Ranch. She sometimes wished it were longer to give her a larger buffer between her life as an Arizona sheriff and her life as a wife and mother; between dealing with bad guys and dealing with kids; between fighting bureaucracy and handling dirty diapers. The bureaucracy battle would be never ending, but with

Joanna's daughter Sage was now more than a year old. With any kind of luck, the end of the diaper era might be only a matter of months away.

At the moment, Joanna's husband, Butch Dixon, was off on the second stint of a book tour for his latest novel, book number five, *A Step Too Far*. His light-hearted, genre-jumping stories might have been cozies but for the fact that his main protagonist, Kimberly Charles, was a law enforcement officer. Her books were set in a small and non-existent town in southern Arizona. The strong resemblance between Sheriff Brady and Butch's fictional Sheriff Charles was hardly coincidental.

Butch's editor referred to him as a solid "midlist" author, and for authors in that category, going on tour was mandatory. In this instance, conflicting scheduling issues had required breaking the tour into two separate parts. The half before Thanksgiving had focused on out-of-state appearances. The second half featured drivable events in Arizona and New Mexico. For the earlier part of the tour—the national one—Butch had used media escorts. Now, for the more local venues—the ones in and around Tucson and Phoenix—he was driving himself.

With Butch out of town, Joanna checked his schedule daily. Today she knew he had a three-hour dinner break between the end of his afternoon event in Mesa and the start of an evening one at White Tank Library in Waddell, Arizona. Joanna had never heard of Waddell until she googled it and learned it was a Phoenix suburb located at the base of a mountain range on the far western side of the

Valley of the Sun. In terms of the Phoenix metropolitan area, Waddell was about as far from Mesa as
humanly possible.

Once in the car, Joanna plugged in her phone
and dialed Butch's number. "How's your day going?" she asked when he picked up.

"Pretty well," he said. "I'm grabbing a burger
at a Denny's in Avondale right now so I don't have
to fight rush hour traffic all the way from central
Phoenix to White Tank. Since I'm on my own, I
can't use express lanes, and that's a pain."

"How was attendance this afternoon?" Joanna
asked.

"Red Mountain in Mesa was a full house," he
replied, "but people are still surprised when Gayle
Dixon turns out to be male instead of female. And
as far as the bookstores are concerned, I get the
feeling that they aren't exactly thrilled to have an
author out on the road this late in the season. With
Christmas on the way, it's as though I'm more of an
annoyance to them than a help."

"Speaking of Christmas," Joanna said, "I just had
a call from Jenny. She was asking if it was okay for
her to bring someone home for Christmas vacation."

"I know," Butch said. "She called me about that,
too. I was afraid it was going to be a boy, and they
were coming home to announce an engagement. I
told her sure, the more the merrier."

Joanna was incredibly grateful for the relationship that had blossomed between Butch and Jenny,
between her husband and his stepdaughter.

"I met Beth last fall when I drove up to Flag to

help get Jenny and Maggie settled in before school started," Butch continued.

Maggie was Jenny's quarter horse—the equine half of a prizewinning barrel racing team.

"She seemed like a mousey little thing," Butch added, "smart enough but very shy. Jenny's so outgoing, I wondered if they'd get along."

"Based on the Christmas invite, I'd say they're doing fine," Joanna assured him. "School lets out on Friday, the fifteenth. That's when finals are over. I'm guessing they'll show up late on Friday evening or else sometime during the day."

"That's what she told me, too," Butch said. "When I get home this weekend, I'll have to get my rear in gear if I want to have Christmas decorating and holiday baking in hand before they show up."

"Why not leave most of that for the girls to do when they get here?" Joanna suggested. "Jenny's always loved decorating, and Denny is big enough to be a help this year. Ditto for making Christmas goodies. Put all three of them to work in the kitchen. It'll give them something to do."

"Besides staring at their cell phone screens you mean?"

"Exactly," Joanna agreed with a laugh.

"Based on what Jenny had to say about the weather up in Flag, I'm really glad New York left the northern end of the state off the tour schedule this time around. Phoenix traffic is a pain, but it's better than driving in snow and ice." Then, after a brief pause, he added, "So what are your plans for tonight?"

"I'll be up to my neck in Christmas cards," Jo-

anna told him with a sigh. "Eva Lou said she would
stop by this afternoon to help address envelopes. I
left her a copy of the lists, but I'm the one who has
to do all the signing and stuffing."

Eva Lou Brady had been Joanna's first mother-
in-law. After Andy Brady's untimely death, she and
her husband, Jim Bob, had stayed close to their
daughter-in-law and granddaughter, and that relationship hadn't diminished once Butch appeared on
the scene. They had welcomed him with open arms
as though he were their own son-in-law, and they
had greeted the births of both Sage and Dennis
with the same kind of loving enthusiasm.

Joanna's folks—her father and mother as well as a
beloved stepfather—were all gone now, and Butch's
parents, his father, Don, and an incredibly toxic
mother, Maggie, were full-time RVers who, to the
relief of all concerned, preferred to spend most of
their time east of the Mississippi. In other words,
as far as grandparents were concerned, Jim Bob and
Eva Lou Brady were the only ones left standing.

"Eva Lou's a doll," Butch said, "and I'm glad
she's helping out, but I should have worked on the
Christmas card issue before I left on tour."

"You did," Joanna reminded him. "For one thing,
you wrote, laid out, and printed the Christmas
newsletter, but if I remember correctly, at about the
same time, you had a horrendous batch of copyedit-
ing to do."

"Right," Butch muttered, "with a brand new co-
pyeditor who was very challenging to deal with."

"So get off your cross as far as the Christmas
cards are concerned," she told him, as she pressed

the remote and opened the garage door.

"Sounds like you're home."

"I am," she said. "I'll let you go. Give me a call once the event is over and you get back to the hotel."

"Will do," he said. "Love you."

"I love you, too," Joanna murmured. "I love you a lot."

CHAPTER 1

WHEN JOANNA OPENED the car door, the irresistible aroma of cooking food—most likely a beef stew—filled the garage, and she uttered a small prayer of thanks for the presence of Carol Sunderson in their lives.

Carol was Joanna and Butch's not-quite-live-in nanny/housekeeper. Years earlier, Carol and her physically disabled husband, Leonard, had been living in a rented and extremely decrepit mobile home while caring for two preteen boys, grandchildren who had been abandoned by their daughter. Leonard had perished in a house fire caused by a faulty electrical circuit that their landlord could and should have corrected.

The fire had left Carol and the two boys, Danny and Rick, homeless. All this had come about several months after Joanna and Butch had moved from the High Lonesome's original ranch house into the new one they'd had built a little farther up the road. For a time they'd had renters in the old house, but when the renters decamped within days of the Sunderson mobile home fire, Joanna had suggested letting Carol and her grandsons live there.

Carol Sunderson may have been poor but she was also proud. Disinclined to accept charity, she had offered to help out in the Brady/Dixon household in lieu of paying rent. Joanna had encouraged Carol to take her former landlord to court where he had been held liable for damages in Leonard Sunderson's death. A court-awarded settlement had improved Carol's financial situation immeasurably, but her living arrangement with Joanna and Butch remained in place. She and the boys continued to live rent free in their old house while Carol helped out as needed in their new one.

Her grandsons, Rick and Danny, were both in high school now. Rick was a senior with a driver's license, an old clunker of a car, and a part-time job delivering pizza. Danny, a sophomore, was making a name for himself on Bisbee High School's varsity basketball team. With the boys able to come and go relatively independently, Carol was a daily calming presence in Butch and Joanna's busy home. Joanna's position as sheriff called for long hours at times, and without Carol's logistical assistance in terms of household management, Butch wouldn't have been able to write books, much less go on book tours.

Joanna entered the house via the laundry room, pausing there long enough to put her weapons away in the gun safe. Once that was done, she closed the metal shutters that covered the exterior windows and doors. High Lonesome Ranch was located at the base of the Mule Mountains on the far western edge of the Sulphur Springs Valley. As the crow flies, the two houses were less than ten miles from the international border with Mexico. As cartel-related smuggling had become more and more prevalent in the area, living there had become risky. As a precautionary measure, Butch and Joanna had installed rolling shutter systems on both houses. Joanna had always loved sleeping with the windows open, so sleeping in what amounted to a locked vault wasn't her first choice, but better to be safe than sorry.

Entering the warm kitchen, Joanna found herself in a kind of controlled bedlam. Sage, squealing with delight, rocketed around the room in her walker, leaving behind a trail of Cheerios. Lucky, a deaf black lab Jenny had rescued years earlier, followed dutifully in Sage's tracks, sniffing out and scarfing up abandoned Cheerios as he went. Carol stood at the counter, dishing stew out of their relatively new programmable pressure cooker into a serving bowl while a frowning Denny worked on setting the table. He stood at Joanna's end of the kitchen nook with a table knife in his right hand and with that hand over his left heart. That way he could be sure the knife would be placed on the correct side of his mother's plate.

"Soup's almost on," Carol announced. "You might want to get Sage out of the cart, change her, and strap her into the high chair."

"Will do," Joanna said, giving the housekeeper a mock salute before capturing the child, lifting her out of the walker, and heading for the nursery. A few minutes later, as Joanna strapped Sage into her high chair, she noticed that the table was set for only four. On nights like this, Carol usually cooked enough for everybody, and Carol's crew ate here in the kitchen right along with everyone else.

"The boys aren't coming?" Joanna asked.

"Rick's working, and Danny has a basketball game in Douglas. I'll take some stew home for them to eat later on."

"Are you going to the game?" Joanna asked.

"I don't know," Carol said. "The varsity game starts at seven. Danny wanted me to come, but I wasn't sure if you'd be home in time."

Showing up at home on time was often a sore subject with Butch and occasionally with Carol, too.

"Well," Joanna said, "since I'm home now, you'll be able to go. I'm perfectly capable of cleaning up and getting the kids to bed."

While Joanna supervised Denny and Sage, Carol bolted down some dinner of her own. Then, after loading stew into plastic containers for each of her boys, she headed out. It was after eight-thirty before Joanna had the kids bathed and in bed and the kitchen cleaned up as well. Only then did she sit down at the dining room table—the space deemed Christmas Card Central—to deal with the task at hand.

When Joanna had first decided to run for the office of sheriff, it hadn't occurred to her that she would end up having to become a politician as well. Her first husband, Andy, had been a deputy sheriff running for office against the then-sheriff when he'd been gunned down by a drug cartel hit man out on High Lonesome Road. It had been after Andy's funeral when someone had first broached the idea of Joanna running for office in his stead. She had done so, more or less in the heat of the moment, not because she expected to win and certainly not because she had expected a career in law enforcement. But now, almost a year into her third term in office, both of those things had come true. Not only had she had won the election, it turned out that serving as sheriff was now her chosen life's work, that of being a professional law enforcement officer—a LEO. Unfortunately, in order to keep that job, she'd been forced to become a politician, and that was what had brought her up against the Christmas card problem.

In ordinary times—meaning prior to her becoming sheriff—a single box of twenty-five cards would probably have been enough to do the trick. As far as her personal list was concerned, that still held true—at twenty-five or so. Those were longtime friends and relations—the ones who got the family holiday newsletter with the year-in-review updates: the photo of Denny's missing front teeth; Jenny in a cowboy hat sitting astride Maggie, both of them celebrating their latest barrel-racing win; Sage and Denny posing with a mall Santa in a photo Butch had managed to have taken the day after Thanksgiving. Denny had been grinning from ear to ear while Sage screamed her head off. Santa photos were like that, Joanna supposed, you win some; you lose some.

Joanna wasn't at all surprised to see that Eva Lou, approaching the problem in a logical fashion, had succeeded in addressing all the envelopes in her flawless, old-school penmanship. The resulting stacks were divided into two distinct groupings.

In the personal one, cards along with a pre-folded newsletter were slipped under the flap of each accompanying envelope. Since that grouping included a much smaller number of envelopes, Joanna tackled that one first—signing both the cards and newsletters and adding personal notes as needed.

She was done with that one and starting on the larger stack when her phone rang with Butch on the line.

"How'd it go?" she asked.

"Well enough, I guess," he answered with a singular lack of enthusiasm. "I'm getting pretty tired of giving the same old talk and answering the same old questions, but I love telling stories, so I should shut up and enjoy it, right?"

"Right," she replied.

"What are you doing?" he asked.

"Christmas cards," she answered. "Eva Lou got all the envelopes addressed. I'm doing the personal list first."

"And saving the best for last?" he quipped.

"Not exactly," she answered.

"What's going on at work?" And that's when Joanna realized she hadn't told Butch about Ernie Carpenter's bad news. Ernie may have sworn Joanna to secrecy as far as the department was concerned, but that didn't mean she couldn't tell Butch. More accustomed to using a keyboard than writing by hand, Joanna leaned back in her chair to rest her aching shoulder as she told Butch what had happened.

"That's going to leave you pretty shorthanded as far as detectives are concerned, won't it?" Butch observed when she finished.

"Very," Joanna agreed with a sigh. "I'll be down to only two detectives, Jaime and Deb."

Jaime was Jaime Carbajal, Ernie's longtime partner and the other half of what had always been known as "the Double Cs." Deb was Deb Howell, who had been promoted from deputy to detective due to Ernie's careful mentoring.

Joanna had expected Deputy Jeremy Stock to be next up in the detective ranks. He had passed the exam, and she had been waiting to bring him on board when his hidden life as a fatally abusive husband and father had come to light. Not only had he murdered his remaining family members before taking his own life, he had come dangerously close to taking Joanna's as well. And Joanna's next candidate for promotion, Deputy Daniel Hernandez, had left her department in order to take a job with Tucson PD at substantially higher wages.

"Didn't you tell me Garth Raymond passed the test?" Butch asked.

Joanna nodded. "Yes, he did and with flying colors. The problem is he's my youngest deputy. He took the test on a dare because some of the other guys were hassling him about his being a 'college boy.' He outscored all of them, so yes, Garth is a 'college boy,' and smart as a whip, as well, but he's also been with the department less than two years. If I end up fast-tracking him to detective, I'm worried there'll be some blowback."

"Young and smart sounds like a good combination," Butch observed. "After what Garth did to save that girl out in Skeleton Canyon last year, it seems to me as though he's also an altogether good human being. In other words, if I were you, I'd discount young and go for smart."

"I'll bear that in mind," Joanna said.

"And you should probably give Myron a call," Butch added. "If you're going to give Ernie an appropriate send off, the clubhouse at Rob Roy Links is the place to do it right, but with the holidays in full swing, his banquet facilities may already be totally booked."

Myron Thomas had managed to establish and maintain one of the best golf courses in southeastern Arizona, creating a resort-worthy facility out of what had once been open farm land along the San Pedro River.

"A big party there will cost money," Joanna said. "The board of supervisors will never approve of having the department pay for it."

"Then we'll pay for it," Butch declared, "as in you and me, babe. Fortunately I just turned in a manuscript, and that delivery and acceptance check is burning a hole in my pocket."

Butch's career as a mystery writer had grown into something neither of them had ever anticipated, and having chunks of discretionary cash show up occasionally for them to use as needed was a real blessing.

"Thank you," Joanna said. "I'll give him a call first thing tomorrow."

"Okay," he said, "I'm doing an early morning TV interview, so I'd best hit the sack. What about you?"

"I'm going to keep plugging away on the cards a while longer," she told him. "Have a good night. I miss you."

It was nearly eleven when she finished the last of the personal cards, then she sat for a moment, contemplating the daunting task ahead. Here there were no newsletters. She could easily have opted for using cards with her signature supplied by the printer, but these messages were going out to many of her supporters as well as her loyal volunteers. Joanna felt that, at the very least, each of these folks deserved the courtesy of a personal signature on their holiday greeting. And that was why the cards had to be done entirely at home. Marliss Shackleford, a local newspaper reporter and Joanna's personal nemesis, was always on the lookout for the slightest misstep on Joanna's part. If there had been any hint of Joanna doing politicking while on the job, Marliss would have made sure it was headline news in the *Bisbee Bee*.

She would do them, Joanna decided, and she would do them at home, but not tonight. "Tomorrow's another day," she said aloud. "Come on dogs, it's time to go get busy."

Lady, Joanna's Australian shepherd, got to her feet and headed for the back door. Lucky, deaf as a post and sound asleep, didn't move a muscle. Joanna reached down, touched him awake, and then delivered the same command in sign language.

Joanna opened the rolling shutter on the back porch and then stood there waiting for the dogs to finish doing their duty. The night was clear and bitingly cold, with the dark sky overhead alive with glimmering stars. Living in the shadow of the Mule Mountains, the lights from Bisbee didn't detract from the nighttime sky, nor did the lights from Douglas and Agua Prieta, twenty-five miles away.

Standing there, enjoying both the chill and the stars, Joanna focused on one star that clearly outshone all the rest. She wasn't sure what star it was, Venus, most likely, but it reminded her of that other star, and the one that shone over Bethlehem. After all, wasn't it a time for peace on earth and good will to men? As a sense of peace settled over her, she spoke to the dogs.

"Come on, guys," she said. "Let's go to bed."

The dogs came at once, and they all went inside, but as far as peace on earth was concerned, Joanna Brady couldn't have been more wrong.

HARPER LARGE PRINT